The waiter left and Chatterjee turned back to me. I told him about the viral meningitis, and Vector Biology's inability to culture it, then switched directions on him. "Years ago," I said, "I read that the EVM and Great Flu viruses might have been engineered. Is that technically feasible?"

He answered as quietly as I'd asked. "With the requisite facilities, yes. But deadly pandemics have occurred throughout history. Nature is quite able to produce them unassisted."

"A pandemic isn't what I'm concerned about, Doctor. I'm wondering about a virus tailored to kill a single individual—and no one else. Is that feasible?"

He thought for a minute. "Mr. Seppanan," he said, "I'm sure you're familiar with killer bees."

I wondered what killer bees had to do with it. "As familiar as most people," I told him. "I've read a little, and saw a TV special on them once. They're the same as our domestic bees, except for a set of genes passed along by the drones, which are haploid. Genes for aggressiveness and rapid population growth."

He nodded, then went on. "Earlier this year, Dr. Kareem Bennett, at Stanford, succeeded in tailoring a disease that should eliminate all bees in the Americas that carry the genes for killer bee aggressiveness. The working details will be published later this week in the *Journal of Genetic Engineering*. And guiding on his procedures, any properly equipped laboratory could produce the sort of thing you spoke of."

That's it, I thought, counting mentally on my fingers. *Incentive, opportunity, and now modus operandi.*

BAEN BOOKS by JOHN DALMAS

The Puppet Master

Soldiers

The Regiment
The Regiment's War
The Three-Cornered War

The Lion of Farside
The Bavarian Gate
The Lion Returns

The Lizard War

THE
PUPPET MASTER

JOHN
DALMAS

THE PUPPET MASTER

Copyright © 2001 by John Dalmas. "A Most Singular Murder" was first published in *Analog*, Vol. CXI, No. 5, April 1991.

A Baen Books Original

Baen Publishing Enterprises
P.O. Box 1403
Riverdale, NY 10471
www.baen.com

ISBN: 0-671-31842-X

Cover art by Gary Ruddell

First printing, October 2001

Distributed by Simon & Schuster
1230 Avenue of the Americas
New York, NY 10020

Production by Windhaven Press, Auburn, NH
Printed in the United States of America

CONTENTS

This book is dedicated to Herbert D. Clough, 30 years with the FBI who, with the collaboration of the originator, Leslie Charteris, resurrected the fabled SAINT magazine. Distribution problems shot her down, but for three wonderful months in 1984, she flew. A lovely project.

FOREWORD

These stories are set in a time line that branched from yours and mine sometime after the close of World War Two. Much in it remains familiar; some things are very similar. But major differences have developed. The geogravitic power converter has energized economies while greatly easing energy, water, and pollution problems.

But the blessing is mixed. The GPC has brought more than cheap, clean, abundant energy and the new physics: The resulting flood of scientific and technological innovations is accelerating changes in society, with outgrowths positive and negative, attractive and ugly, exciting and fearsome.

Homo sapiens has major adjustments to make.

A MOST SINGULAR MURDER

A NOVELLA

1

My name is Martti Seppanen, and I work for Prudential Investigations and Security, Inc. Things had been slow, and I'd had nothing much to do for a day and a half—since I'd finished rounding up the collusion evidence against Funsch, Carillo, and Wallace. So I stood there in my two-by-four office—ten by ten feet, actually—looking westward across the L.A. basin toward the higher rises of Lower Wilshire. While drilling Spanish.

I don't mind days like that. But there was the nagging worry that if business didn't pick up, Joe might have to lay people off. Me for example. Times like that you can wonder whether it had been a good idea when Joe leased the whole ninth floor of this high-rent high rise. Of course, the old building got sold out from under him and knocked down. The old buildings are disappearing.

Besides, when I don't have a case, I get the munchies worse than usual, and I gain weight too easily.

I kept drilling, using a question and answer program on intermediate spoken Spanish. The computer would voice a question in fairly simple Spanish, and I'd answer it. Or it would tell me to discuss some simple thing. Then it would critique my diction, grammar, and pronunciation, and we'd repeat it till the program was satisfied with my performance.

¿«*Donde guardan los documentos financiales*»? the computer asked me. ("Where do you keep your financial records?") The program is part of the department's advanced language training.

«*Debajo de la bañadera*, I answered, *donde nadie los buscaria*». ("Under the bathtub, where no one would ever look for them.") You do enough of those drills, you learn what the program will accept.

That's where things stood when Carlos looked in on me. "Come in my office," he said. "We've got something for you."

"We" meant himself and Joe Keneely. Joe's the founder, principal shareholder, and CEO of Prudential. Carlos is the senior investigator, and I was his protégé, top of the list of junior investigators. And the something would be an assignment.

I followed Carlos down the hall. His office was big enough for a small conference without people sitting in each other's laps. He sat down behind his desk, and I took the chair across from him. Fingering his computer, he turned on the wall screen. A picture formed and stopped. It showed Joe Keneely's office, with Joe and Carlos, and some guy I'd never seen before.

"The client is Donald C. Pasco," Carlos said. "All the way down from Sacramento. Joe just signed a contract with him." He said it as if it tasted bad. I'd heard of Pasco. He was director of the Anti-Fraud Division of the California Department of Commerce, and had a reputation as an aye-aitch.

The picture came to life, and I watched their conference. Actually I watched Pasco bitch and snarl. About three weeks earlier, an astronomer named Arthur Ashkenazi had read a paper to the California Section of the Astronomical Society of America, at the section's annual meeting. The paper was what had gotten Pasco upset. Pasco didn't have much presence, but he had rank and venom. After playing back the meeting with Pasco, Carlos ran Ashkenazi's

talk for me. I'd been aware of it before, just barely. It had
been written up in the papers, but I hadn't read it. I read
fast, but the *L.A. Times* is thick, and the talk hadn't had
any significance for me.

Now, watching him deliver it, it turned out to be pretty
interesting. It didn't offend me at all, but it had offended
Ashkenazi's audience. He'd hardly gotten well underway
when people started to leave. "Stalked out" is the best
description.

About halfway through his talk and three-quarters of the
way through his audience, one of them got up and shouted
that Ashkenazi should be thrown out. That what he was
spieling was astrology, not astronomy. And another guy
stood up then, apparently an officer of the meeting, and
told the guy yelling that he'd either have to sit down and
be quiet, or leave. The guy left, madder than hell, most
of the remaining audience following him out in a bunch.
Ashkenazi finished to a dozen listeners, probably mostly
reporters, and didn't seem upset at the exodus. I suppose
he wasn't surprised.

Basically what Ashkenazi was reporting was, he'd run
correlations of events of one sort and another against the
positions of stars and planets. Which did amount to astrology, as far as I could see. And while I'm no statistical
analyst, I do know that the kind of correlation coefficients
he was claiming aren't the sort of thing you get by chance.
Not in the real world.

He'd done it the hard way, too, or that's how it looked.
He hadn't picked a scattering of historical events that
fitted his purpose. Over a period of almost thirty years
he'd predicted events, supposedly from the positions of
stars and planets, and published them in various newsletters put out by different astrology groups, New Age
groups, and groups into psychic phenomena. And a lot
of his predictions came out as forecast, his scores getting better as he improved his system. Predictions like
droughts, major political shifts, uprisings, big stock market swings, major deaths . . . If the publications were real.
In 1994 he'd even predicted that a then-unknown source

of electrical power would be released in 1997 that would change the world. Which of course was Haugen's geo-gravitic power converter! That was uncanny.

I could see why astronomers might get spooky about stuff like that. But why was Pasco so upset? Even if Ashkenazi made it all up, it wasn't illegal and it wasn't commerce. Which was what the Anti-Fraud Division was supposed to be concerned with—criminal fraud in commerce. This was something the astronomers could take care of themselves if they wanted to, by kicking Ashkenazi out of their society. Which in fact they had, for misrepresenting his talk to the program committee.

From the recording of the meeting with Pasco, I could see that Joe felt uncomfortable with the job, the same as I did. Because what Pasco wanted was a fishing expedition at taxpayers' expense. We were supposed to investigate every damned thing about Arthur Ashkenazi. Everything but his finances; the California Commerce Department's Audit Division would cover that. To quote Pasco: "Find something discreditable about this Ashkenazi, preferably something criminal."

I asked Carlos why Joe had accepted the contract. I guess I knew, but Joe spelled it out for me: "A fair amount of our business comes from Commerce. We're their number one contractor in southern California, and we can't afford their turning to another investigation firm."

2

I could have turned the assignment down. Joe's used to my being a hardhead, and I'd earned enough points with him and Carlos that they wouldn't have been too mad at me. But somehow I took it.

Back in my office, I sat down at my computer, accessed the L.A. library and called up what the media—print, Webworks, and TV—had said about Ashkenazi's talk. The professional media had had people there of course—probably stringers and junior staff. And since the news had been dull for a while, they'd played up the Ashkenazi flap pretty big. Mostly tongue in cheek, but pretty much without ridiculing it. The syndicates had gotten hold of it then, pontificating. Then *Time* magazine did a feature on it, treating it straight, and Ashkenazi made the talk show circuit.

All of which had burned Pasco up, and he was using his position, and us, to try to punish Ashkenazi at pubic expense.

Usually you start a case with evidence of a crime, and that gives you something to orient on. This one was different.

Since it was almost five o'clock, I killed a few minutes, then left the office promptly at quitting time. It wasn't a workout day, and I had a date that evening, so I went straight home, showered, re-shaved, dressed semi-dressy, and picked up Tuuli. We took my car—hers is nicer, but she's considerate about things like that—and drove to Mr. Ethel's on North La Cienega. They specialize in health foods, especially low-fat foods, but the quality is excellent and the prices affordable. The waiters are a little strange, but they're at least as courteous as their customers.

Tuuli doesn't worry about fat. That's my problem. She's the same age as me, thirty, but only five feet tall and fine-boned. She probably doesn't weigh more than 85 or 90 pounds, which is 40 percent of what I weigh. About a third of what I weigh, sometimes. She's the only Lapp immigrant I know; actually half-Lapp. Her father's a Finn, same as mine was. Born in the little mining town of Tuollivaara in Swedish Lapland, she grew up partly there, and partly on a backwoods farm near Koivujoki, in Finnish Lapland. Came to America when she turned eighteen. Her story is, she decided to emigrate when someone told her that in California women could be shamans, and all the shamans were rich.

She's been psychic, she says, since she was a little kid. From what I've seen, it's easy to believe. Her great-great-grandfather had been one of the last active Lapp shamans; the state church pretty much shut shamanism down in Sweden a hundred and fifty years ago. The basic lore got passed down to Tuuli through her mother, even though they were females. How I got to know her is, she sometimes consults for police agencies and private investigation firms in greater Los Angeles. The police don't like to acknowledge it—bad for their image—and she doesn't publicize it. She just deposits their credit transfers in her bank account.

But she built her reputation through the rich and famous. There's a lot of rich people around L.A., and most of her income is from them. It doesn't hurt that Tuuli Waanila's an interesting looking woman, either. Not just tiny. She has elfin features, sandy hair, and slanty hazel eyes. It especially helps with entertainment people. Looks mean a lot to them. Also she sounds good. She's got a light accent that sounds pretty much Finnish. She's well-named, too. Her full name is Tuulikki, which in Finnish means graceful. Her dad named her that when she was born, and it turned out to fit.

Anyway, at Mr. Ethel's we got a booth in a corner, and while we waited, we drank coffee and talked. "What do you think of astrology?" I asked.

Her eyes were direct, as usual. "Astrology? I'm not very informed about it. I don't practice it. But I usually look up my horoscope in the paper, in the morning."

"Really?"

"Sure. It's good to have a source of outside information. Psychics usually see better for others than for ourselves."

I didn't leave it at that. I had to pump her a little. It goes with the profession. "But astrology!" I said. "I mean, I can imagine people getting information through the omega matrix maybe, but from the positions of the planets?"

She shrugged. "You read the papers."

"Not the horoscopes, I don't."

"Did you read about the astronomer, Ashkenazi?"

"Do you believe him?"

"Nobody seemed anxious to try proving him wrong." She paused, looking pointedly at me. "Why don't you tell me why you brought this up?"

So I did. "And now Ashkenazi's my job. Thanks to Mr. Paska. Oops, Pasco."

She tried to grin and wrinkle her nose at the same time. The nose won out. "*Paska* is a good name for him."

"You know Pasco?"

"In my business, he has a reputation. He hates people like me. He's California's main agitator for laws to stop us from practicing our profession." Her eyes looked thoughtfully at me. "You've heard the saying, 'In the land of the blind, the one-eyed man is king.'"

"Yeah?"

"The person who said it was mistaken. In the land of the blind, the one-eyed man is apt to be considered a liar and a fraud." She paused again. This time her eyes seemed

to focus somewhere above and beyond my right shoulder.
"You're likelier to find something criminal about Pasco than
about Ashkenazi."

"Are you serious?"

"Yes I'm serious."

"What should I look for?"

Tuuli shrugged. "I don't know. If you're interested in
Ashkenazi, look way back. To when he was young." She
paused. "Ashkenazi's not his real name, his original name."

"How do you know?" I assumed she'd read it somewhere. "What is his real name?"

"I don't know. You should be able to find out. And it's
something you really should look into. And find out about
his twin. His twin brother. I'm pretty sure it's a brother."

I didn't know how to take that—whether she'd read
something, or if she was being psychic. "And you say I can
find something criminal about Pasco if I try?"

"I'm not sure. The feeling I get is a little confusing. It
may be something he hasn't done yet."

"Huh! I'll keep that in mind," I told her. "But tomorrow I start checking on Ashkenazi."

3

An investigation contract with a public agency gets you direct access to the confidential State Data Center through your computer. You call and enter your case ID. Their computer checks the ID and your face and thumbprint against their records, then you insert the contract card so they know what it's all about. After that you tell them what you want, with a brief oral justification. If it sounds reasonable to them, and if everything checks out, the information downloads into your computer for your temporary use.

As for "temporary use," you're supposed to erase stuff within three business days of contract termination. Actually they give you a two-day grace period. The information is flagged in their computer when you get it, and they check contractor computers from Sacramento, to be sure the stuff has been erased. Obviously it's possible to hold out on them; make hard copies for example. But if you're caught, it can cost your license, as well as a fine and possible criminal charges.

Joe's grace period is less than Sacramento's. On the morning of the third day, the company checks. Your first violation brings a reprimand. The second time you're fired, or if you're lucky as hell, put on probation. That's part of the orientation pack you get when he hires you. Plus Joe tells you himself, with his bushy black Irish-Cornish eyebrows drawn up in a knot to make sure you take him seriously. He fires your ass, and the reason will be on your employment references.

So anyway, I called up all the information on Ashkenazi in the state's files, with the exception of tax and census data. Tax records are accessible only if your contract is with the California Franchise Tax Board. Census data isn't available under any contract, and I'm told if you even ask, the state investigates you.

I learned a lot about Ashkenazi: His current address, past addresses with dates . . . all kinds of stuff. But the most interesting item was that Arthur Aaron Ashkenazi was an assumed name. Just like Tuuli said. He'd been born Aldon Arthur Ashley, and had legally changed it in 1973, seven years before I was born. There was no hint of why.

There was nothing there to focus an investigation on except the name change, and offhand that didn't look very promising. So I decided to interview him. I'd present myself as a freelance writer doing an article on spec for the pop-science magazine *Cutting Edge*.

I had his unlisted number from the state, but using it might bring questions I wouldn't care to answer, so I dialed his answering service, which was listed. The woman who answered had a face like a bulldog. I decided right away he didn't want calls from strangers.

"I'd like to speak with Mr. Ashkenazi, please."

"What may I tell him the call is about?"

"It's confidential."

"Mr. Ashkenazi doesn't accept confidential calls at this number."

I'd only waste my time trying to cajole her. "Tell Mr. Ashkenazi I want to interview him. If I can't, I'll have to interview his twin. Tell him that. If you cut me off, he's going to be madder than hell at you."

Her look almost melted my set. I wished I'd looked up his twin's name, if he actually had a twin. I shouldn't have

overlooked that. Using a name would have been more
convincing. After glaring for a couple of seconds, she put
me on hold. A minute later, Ashkenazi's face appeared on
my screen. He looked mildly annoyed, nothing worse.

"What's this about?" he said.

"I've read and screened your address to the Astronomical Society, and some of the things written about you.
I'm preparing an article for *Cutting Edge,* and I'd like
to interview you."

"I don't give interviews."

"I appreciate that, Mr. Ashkenazi, and I respect your
feelings on it. But I still plan to write the article. The
direction it takes, and what I feature in it, depends on the
information I have."

For a moment he just sat looking at me via our connection. "An interview," he said. Sounding resigned. "All
right. Where are you calling from?"

"L.A."

He grunted. "This evening then. I'll give you thirty minutes, beginning at seven. Do you know how to find me?"

"You're at 4231 East Encino Road. I assume that rental
cars in Santa Barbara have the Montecito grid in their
computers."

"They may, but I'm three miles outside Montecito, in
the Rhubarb Canyon development. I don't know if they've
extended the grid this far out yet. If you have any trouble,
call. I'll tell Mrs. Bowser to put you through to me. My
place is fenced, with a remote control gate. The call box
will get the house, and someone will let you in. That's this
evening at seven."

"Thank you, Mr. Ashkenazi," I told him. *Mrs. Bowser!*
I could hardly believe it.

Then I got Sacramento again. I needed to get all the
available information on his family, something I should have
already done.

4

Since geogravitic power, air transport has gotten cheaper and a lot more convenient, with virtually no risk of crash, short of collision. Floaters are AG, stable in flight, easy to operate, quiet, and don't pollute. From the office, if I want to fly somewhere, I drive a mile and a half to the Larchmont Station, where shuttles fly to LAX, Long Beach, Hollywood-Burbank, Ventura, or Santa Barbara at half-hour intervals.

I caught the 5:15 airbus to Santa Barbara and got there at 5:40. The air was clear as polished crystal. With the mountains behind her, L.A. looked beautiful, the Pacific magnificent, and the Sierra Madre rugged and wild. At the Santa Barbara Station I caught a turkey salad sandwich and at 6:23 was in a rental car headed for Montecito. The Montecito grid did cover the Rhubarb Canyon development, so all I had to do to find Ashkenazi's place was follow the route on the computer. It took me 16 minutes: I was 20 minutes early. Instead of using the call box, I voiced his number on the phone in the rental car and told him I was there already—that if he wanted I could drive around awhile. He said to come on up to the house, and a few seconds later the security gate opened.

His place was on two or three acres of land. You couldn't see the house from the gate because of the tall hedge along the road. Behind it was a concrete wall a yard high, eight feet of chain link with the waxy luster of new HardSteel above that, and razor wire on top.

Pretty mild, actually, for a development like Rhubarb Canyon in these days of trashers. Nothing at all like Ojibwa County, Michigan, where I grew up. His driveway started in through a stand of scrub live oak, but the house itself was surrounded by lawn, shaded thin by big encina oaks. The house was fairly large, partly one story and partly two, with big windows and glass doors. There were five paved parking places, one occupied by what had to be his car, another by a middle-aged pickup that probably belonged to household staff. Apparently Ashkenazi wasn't big on entertaining. I pulled into one of the other spaces, stepped up onto the porch and knocked. A man answered, wearing a sort of semi-uniform. He let me into an entryway and pressed a button.

Half a minute later, Ashkenazi was there, shaking my hand, cordial as you could hope for. Making the best of a regrettable situation, probably. He looked heavier than on the video, but healthy. I suppose he exercised. We went into a room lit by the yellow rays of a setting sun, and sat down. He looked at a wall clock. "Six-forty," he said. "We might as well start. Let me ask the first question: How did you know about Eldon?"

Eldon was his twin brother. Their parents' names were in the data on Ashkenazi, and I'd called up information on them that afternoon. There wasn't much of it, of course. But their children's names and birth dates were there. "Mr. Ashkenazi," I answered, "a writer learns research techniques, just as an astronomer does. I haven't taken the trouble to learn much about your family though. I haven't decided just what form the article will take, so I don't know what's relevant to it. I am, of course, interested in your research and yourself."

"You've read my paper."

"And watched you read it to the Astronomy Society."

"Then you saw how it was received by my professional brethren."

"Right. I also saw interviews with a few of them. They said what you talked about was astrology, not astronomy."

Ashkenazi smiled. "Astrology without astrological terminology. I followed basic astrological principles but abandoned the traditional framework and analyzed large volumes of data." The smile became a grin. "I call it 'predictive astronomy,' to irritate the astronomical fraternity."

"But apparently you don't know why it works. If you could have described the mechanism, you would have. Wouldn't you? You must have some kind of theory."

He shook his head. "If Ali Hasad's *Limited Theory of Generated Reality* is valid, it provides a partial explanation."

One of the advantages of reading 800 to 1200 words per minute is, you can read a lot of books and magazines. So I knew a little of what he was talking about. "Isn't Ali Hasad's theory rejected by scientists?"

"By most of them. Not all. If you polled the physics community, maybe six of ten would reject it out of hand, two would withhold judgement but express strong skepticism, and two would say something like, it's heuristically interesting and might lead to new understanding.

"But science isn't supposed to be democratic, in the sense of a vote making a theory viable or valid. Most of those who reject Ali Hasad's theory haven't read it, except perhaps the summary of his first paper on it. And aren't likely to.

"Its chief problem is, it supports and thus revives an old contention of Fred Hoyle's, based on the values of basic physical parameters of the universe."

I knew what he was talking about, and kept my mouth shut, letting him continue.

"The basic parameters are those fundamental forces on which the universe depends for its characteristics. And if those parameters were even moderately different than they are, we wouldn't simply have elements and planets and life somewhat different than they are. We wouldn't have them at all. And considering probabilities, Hoyle couldn't accept that those parameters are what they are simply by accident. He contended that it must have been designed. That this universe is an artifact programmed by some superintelligence operating outside our universe.

"An intelligence that some people identified with God, which is a word with a lot of unfortunate Bronze Age superstitions attached to it."

He cocked an eyebrow. "Have I thoroughly confused you?"

"I'm familiar with Hoyle's view," I said. "I never read anything by him, but I read an article about it years ago. It sounded reasonable enough, and when I read a description of Ali Hasad's theory, it did remind me of Hoyle. But I'm in no position to evaluate either one scientifically."

Ashkenazi chuckled. "Neither are the physicists who refuse to look. It's interesting how much of advanced physics is nonexperimental. Which in the traditional sense means nonscientific. That's not to knock it. Given the problems, they do what they can. For decades, the frontiers of physics have lain largely in the realm of mathematics. The subject demands theories that commonly *can't* be tested physically. They test them by seeing how consistent the math is, particularly with other, already-accepted math that describes physical phenomona.

"That's a simplification, I'll admit, but basically it's accurate. And Ali Hasad's math *is* compatible with the Meissner-Ikeda Lattice. And accommodates the math, such as it is, of the omega matrix."

My half hour was melting, but I let him go on. I had a notion he might let it stretch to as long as it took.

"You don't look old enough," Ashkenazi went on, "to remember when legislative know-nothings had the Tarzan books banned from school libraries in Tennessee. They said Tarzan and Jane weren't married, were living in sin, and the books were a danger to the morals of young people.

"Actually they were married. In Book Two. Jane's father was a professor, and they were married in the jungle at Tarzan's family's cabin, if I remember correctly. The damned know-nothings had never read the sonofabitch. Typical.

"Well, Ali-Hasad's critics haven't examined his math. There are know-nothings in science, too.

"Considering the track records of all the earlier mathematical super-theories, Ali-Hasad's will probably turn out to have serious holes and loose ends, but . . ."

He stopped and grinned, shaking his head ruefully. "You punched my buttons," he said. "And I suppose you're recording this."

I was, and admitted it. My audio recorder was in my shoulder bag, beside my chair. "But you'll have a chance to critique the manuscript," I told him.

"Hmh! That's something, anyway. As for my work, it has no theory. It's totally empirical."

He turned serious again. "I'm not worried about explanations. Arne Haugen had only a rough notion of the basis for the geogravitic power converter, but that didn't keep him from inventing it. I've established a certain predictive and planning value in a revised and sharpened form of astrology I developed empirically. It's no big deal to me if the astronomical community doesn't accept it. I'd have given odds of a hundred to one against it, and taken all the bets I could cover.

"My career doesn't depend on anyone's approval. My degrees are in astronomy, but I've never been employed in it. I made my initial money in computer software and consulting, back in the days before the personal computer. My real wealth I made through investments. Guided, I might add, by every predictive tool, including astrology, that I could program. Also I have clients, as many as I care to deal with, who don't give a damn about explanations, and even less about compatibility with current theory. They're interested in results, and that's what I give them."

With that, he seemed to have run down. I nodded. "And what does Eldon think of all this?"

His eyebrows raised. "You *don't* know much about Eldon, do you. He probably doesn't think about it at all. He's an invalid. Been brain-damaged since 1973. From an auto accident."

"Ah. Then I probably shouldn't bother him."

"I'm quite sure Veronica would prefer that."

What I said next was a shot in the dark, totally unpremeditated. "Do you, uh, contribute to his support, Mr. Ashkenazi?"

He frowned. "Really, Mr. Seppanen, I don't care to . . ." He paused, lips pursing. "I will answer that question. A number of years ago I set up a trust fund. Not that it's necessary. Veronica is a capable provider. She's the trust fund's payee of course, not Eldon.

"And she's a COGS," he added drily. "COGS put a lot of emphasis on being financially honorable and intellectually shabby."

A COGS! She wouldn't like at all what Ashkenazi was into. The Church of God in Science—COGS—is an attempt to meld fundamentalist Christian views with classical science. It's become a fairly major church since the plagues of 1999 and 2000. It's how some people are trying to come to terms with the accelerating changes in the world. The way that COGS feel about anything like astrology or psychic phenomena pretty much ranges between contempt and hatred.

And suddenly I got the idea that if I checked on Donald C. Pasco, I'd find he was a COGS, too. It would fit him like pantyhose.

"Thank you, Mr. Ashley—excuse me; Mr. Ashkenazi," I said getting up. "You've been very helpful. I'll phone you again when the article begins to take form. To fill holes."

Calling him Ashley hadn't been a slip. I wanted to see if he'd react. He had, with a look of annoyance. It rekindled my curiosity about the name change. "Maybe I'll start checking my horoscope in the morning paper," I added. "It might prove helpful."

Driving back to Santa Barbara, I examined what I'd learned. I couldn't see it leading anywhere, but I realized I liked Arthur Ashkenazi. He seemed like what the Jews call a "mensch," which I've had explained as someone who is able, responsible, decent, and feeling. I hoped I *didn't* learn something discreditable about him.

5

Meanwhile it was my job to look. So the next morning I hired a statistically sophisticated CPA intern to check the entries—the dates and contents of the actual publications—and the computations in Ashkenazi's research. It was a lot different than anything she'd done before, but she had the right attitude—she was a skeptic who liked a challenge. And it seemed to me she had the tools.

Then, independent of that, I went to Pasadena and hired a Ph.D. candidate in astronomy at Cal Tech, to check the same stuff from the viewpoint of an astronomer. I'd met him at Carlos' place that summer, at supper. He was a friend of Carlos' son, Keith. It seemed to me he'd be reasonably open-minded. He was an ex-member of the "New Gnus"—the Church of the New Gnosis—and you had to be damned flexible to even consider that one.

I also visited the Santa Monica High School library and looked through the 1968 and '69 yearbooks. I got a list of students who might have been personal friends of Aldon Ashley, kids who'd been in the same student activities. Then I did essentially the same things with the UCLA yearbook for 1973. After that it was back to the State Data Center for locations and phone numbers—the drudge work of investigation. Nearly half the people I was interested in had died in the plagues of '99 and 2000, but phone calls still got some information.

The most productive was a friend of both his high school and college days, who still exchanged Christmas/Hanukkah letters with him. They'd see each other every five or ten years. The guy lives in Minneapolis, so I didn't talk to him eyeball to eyeball, but a telephone call was useful.

For one thing, I learned why Aldon Ashley had changed his name, and there was nothing discreditable about it. The same weekend he'd graduated from UCLA, he'd gotten in some kind of fuss with his sister-in-law, whom this guy characterized as a real bitch. Eldon, Ashkenazi's twin, got upset listening to it, and left to drive around. And smoke dope, something Eldon was into. He ended up losing an argument with an overpass abutment, which is how he became a brain-damaged cripple.

The sister-in-law told their father that the reason Eldon had done this was, Aldon had insulted him. And for whatever reason, the father believed this, and raised hell with Aldon. Told him it was his fault his brother's life was ruined. Apparently overlooking the daughter-in-law, the dope, and Eldon's decision to drive recklessly.

So Aldon left home, and that summer changed his name. Something his father wouldn't learn about for years, the break was that complete. When Aldon's grandfather was young, he'd resigned from being Jewish, and changed his name to Ashley. Aldon, as a sort of resignation from being his father's son, had switched back to something about as Jewish as he could find. He even learned to speak some Yiddish. It was his Methodist mother, though, who secretly helped him through grad school at Arizona. She'd inherited money of her own.

All of which was interesting, but didn't seem to lead anywhere. It occurred to me that maybe I *should* write that article about Ashkenazi, or a whole damned biography. Make a truthful man of myself.

Something else Ashkenazi's buddy gave me was the name of a woman Ashkenazi had gone with for years, in their middle age. Again the Data Center gave me a location and phone number. After setting up an appointment, I took a short airbus hop down the coast to Oceanside, rented a car, and interviewed her in person.

They'd dated for several years, she said, and she'd liked him a lot. But she liked to travel and entertain, and had money of her own. While Aldon liked to stay home, read, walk, and play with his computer. "Arthur's idea of a night out," she told me, "was to take his portable telescope and we'd drive up to Pine Mountain Summit, in the Sierra Madre above Ojai. To look at stars. Our most typical dates were pleasant drives along the coast, stopping to walk on the beach. Then have a nice meal at some expensive restaurant, followed by a movie."

Which she'd enjoyed, she said, but they weren't enough. She'd ended up marrying a widower who also liked to travel and entertain.

She also told me about Ashkenazi setting up a trust fund for his brother, with his hostile sister-in-law as payee. Something I'd already verified through the Data Center. Ashkenazi might or might not hold grudges, but apparently he could set them aside when it seemed right to him. A *mensch* all right. I was getting to like him better all the time, and Pasco less.

I also talked to a guy who'd known him pretty well in grad school at the University of Arizona. The scene there was a set of grad students with a lot of attention on the problems of getting jobs once they graduated. People who spent so much time on their studies and assistantship duties, they'd hardly had any left for social life.

Aldon never did get a job in astronomy. But in the process of getting his degrees, he'd gotten well trained in math, statistical analysis, and computers. So he took a job with a Santa Monica firm called Spectronics. Within two years he was an independent software consultant and troubleshooter, and built a successful business. Meanwhile investing. Successfully. Another interview with the Minneapolis buddy got me the information that those were the years Aldon had begun "playing with astrology."

A couple of Aldon's software clients during those years said his prices had always been reasonable and his service good. And he'd always been pleasant and easy to communicate with.

By '92 he'd dropped out of the software business, apparently living on his investments. I learned little about his investment activities during those years. The broker he'd dealt through had suicided in the Great Crash of '96, and the broker's secretary had died, along with more than a billion other people, of epidemic viral meningitis in 2000.

6

None of that was going to make Pasco happy. I woke up one morning with the decision to lay it all out for Carlos and recommend we tell Pasco that was it. I was composing the recommendation in my mind when I walked into Morey's Deli on Beverly Boulevard, a block from the office. I generally eat breakfast there. When I eat at home, I keep going back for refills. At Morey's the only refills are coffee.

When I walked in, a guy waved to me, a guy called Indian. He wears a big feather in his sweatband; calf-length, moccasin-style boots with a fringe on their turned-down tops; and a beaded leather vest. I went over and sat down with him. Indian's got hair about the color of mine—halfway between brown and blond—a red, Viking-looking mustache, and a ruddy complexion. Pretty un-Indian looking, except for facial structure. He insists he's a quarter Chippewa, and that his mother grew up on the Bad River Reservation in Wisconsin.

Whatever, he's an Angeleno, born and raised. A tallish, strong-looking guy who works for Yitzhak's Transit as a casual. Some days Yitzhak has work for him, some days he doesn't. When he doesn't, Indian comes in to Morey's, about two blocks from Yitzhak's, for coffee and a fat, glazed doughnut. I see him quite a lot.

Yitzhak's a New Gnu, and almost all the people who work for him are New Gnus, but not Indian. Indian's a Loonie, belongs to a cult of moon worshipers. They don't actually worship the moon, but they meditate on it. And it occurred to me a Loonie might know something about astrology. So after I gave Morey's daughter my order, I asked Indian about it.

"Don't know much," he said. "But Moonbeam does. She checks the horoscopes in the paper each day and tells me if there's something I need to watch out for. Moonbeam's pretty spiritual, you know? She's part Indian too, and an Aquarius, so she's got a better feel for that stuff than me. That's why she's our house mother." He stopped and examined me a moment. "You got a girlfriend? You never talk about one."

"Yeah, I've got one. Her name is Tuuli."

"Tooley? That's a neat name! What does she do? For a living I mean?"

"She's a professional psychic."

"Hey! Wow! That's a coincidence! We got a fortune-teller in our house!" Indian's life is full of coincidences. "Her name is Becky. She's from Sacramento. You know they made a law against telling fortunes in Sacramento County?"

I did. But to keep him going, I said no, I didn't.

"Yeah. Ain't that crazy? What kind of country is this, they can make a law against telling fortunes? Becky didn't have no job, so she told a guy his fortune, and he's an undercover cop. She couldn't pay the fine, so they put her in jail. And when she got out, she still didn't have no job. A friend of hers, a hooker, give her the money to come down here."

Indian grinned. "The hooker said she'd get even for her, with the guy that got the law passed. She didn't say how. Maybe he's a customer or something."

Sometimes I just half listen to Indian. He rambles. This time he had my attention. "What's the guy's name?" I asked.

"I don't know. She said, but I don't remember."

"Wellington?" I threw that out to test him.

"Nah, nothing like that."

"Miller? Pasco?"

"Pasco! That's it! You know about him?"

"I've heard of him. He doesn't like psychics."

Indian looked suddenly wary. "It's not against the law in L.A., is it? Nah, couldn't be. Besides, your girlfriend is a psychic."

"Is Becky pretty good at fortunes?" I asked.

"I don't know. I guess. You want yours told?"

"Maybe. Tuuli won't tell me mine. Can I get in touch with this Becky?"

"There's a house on Franklin, on one of those little streets east of Bronson. It's got a little sign in the front yard—*House of the Moon*. They rent rooms to fortune-tellers to tell fortunes in. It's close enough, Becky don't need no car, or to take the bus or anything. She just walks there from the house about a mile. The hill climbing's good for her."

He told me Becky didn't leave for work till after nine, and gave me the phone number where he lives. So when I got to my office, I called her. A reading, she told me, cost ten dollars, and she'd be at the House of the Moon by ten o'clock.

I was too. She called herself Madame Rebecca, wore a head kerchief, a black satin shawl with white stars and moons, and a dress to her ankles. The face beneath the kerchief was small and pointy, vulnerable looking. I suspect going to jail in Sacramento wasn't her first visit from hard luck.

The fortune she told me was interesting. I'd entered a time of challenge and uncertainty, she said. And if I passed through it safely, I'd overcome the challenge. There was a special person in my life, someone with whom I shared a special communication, who would disappoint me. But if I persisted, I'd win there too. All this with appropriate silences and frowns, and passes at her crystal ball.

The whole thing was general enough to give me a choice of things it could allude to. I could interpret the uncertainty and challenge as the Ashkenazi case, though I couldn't imagine any danger there. The special person in my life I could take to mean Tuuli. We even shared a special communication—Finnish—though hers is a lot better than mine. I learned some of it from my dad, and after he died, I lived with my older brother Sulo and his wife, who talked it to me.

When Madame Rebecca had finished and I'd paid her, I got down to the questions I was really interested in. "Indian tells me you're from Sacramento," I said.

She admitted she was.

"I'm going up there on business next week. A couple of days. Can you recommend a lady I could look up? Someone reasonably nice looking, who's healthy and likes a good time?"

She gave me a name—Marilyn Vanderpol—and an approximate address. She didn't remember the phone number. I gave her another Hamilton and left.

ings it could allude to. I could interpret the

7

Back in the office I checked with the Data Center again and learned that Marilyn Vanderpol had died of a drug-induced heart attack five weeks earlier. Probably not that unusual for a hooker, I told myself. On a hunch I also got the name and number of the investigating officer. I called him, identified myself, and gave him my contract number. Then I asked him about the death of Marilyn Vanderpol.

Sergeant Luciano is the kind of cop that doesn't have to refer to the files. He gave me the information off the top of his head, and I had no doubt he knew what he was talking about. The evidence, he said, would remain on file for at least two months from the time of death, because it appeared to be crime related. In this case drug related. Then the evidence, including the body, would be disposed of.

"You said *appeared* to be drug related. What did you mean by appeared?"

"It *was* drug related, but there was no evidence of previous drug use, or even an alcohol problem. But she'd apparently been servicing a john when it happened, and the drug in her bloodstream was HS, Harem Smoke. It doesn't do anything for the woman, but it enables repeated male orgasm and intensifies male climax, so it was probably his. And it's been known to trigger heart attacks." He paused and shrugged. "In males in climax. A coroner's decision is hard to argue with. He's the expert, and . . ." He shrugged again.

"And she was a hooker."

He nodded. And she was dead of a heart attack. Why complicate things? "Look," I said, "I'll fly up tomorrow morning. Can you show me the evidence?"

"Tomorrow's Saturday."

"I know." I could hardly justify the trip as a job expense. I'd have to go on my own time and money.

"I'm on duty till noon," he told me.

"I'll be there by ten."

8

I was there at 9:32, according to Luciano's wall clock. He showed me his brief written report, plus the evidence in a plastic bag. The report included photographs and a diagram. Vanderpol had been sprawled on the floor naked. In the plastic bag was a small fumer with Harem Smoke ash. Dope! I remembered my dad and mom dead in our living room, and feeling my mouth start to twist, took several deep quiet breaths. The opening step in a mental drill my therapist had taught me.

Other items included a Franklin—a hundred-dollar bill that had been lying on an end table; a small, clear plastic pillbox that looked empty; and a plastic needle cap with a flattened tip and ornamental grooves. "What's in the vial?" I asked.

"Semen. Found on Vanderpol."

I didn't get any subconscious twitches from that, but I did from the needle cap. "You know what this is," I said, pointing at it.

"Sure. A needle cap. It was lying on the shag carpet.

"One of the outpoints in the scene was, Vanderpol's arms showed no sign of needle useage, and there wasn't any needle lying around. And Harem Smoke was the only drug in her system. The needle could have belonged to the john, of course, and he could have taken it with him. Odd though."

"It's not that kind of needle cap," I told him. "Unless I'm mistaken, this is off a cork popper. Look at the size of the hole where the needle fitted. Druggies don't use needles that big. Or that long."

He looked puzzled. "Cork popper?"

"Instead of using a corkscrew, you push a long needle through the cork and release a little jolt of compressed air. Pops the cork right out."

Luciano nodded thoughtfully. "Was there a wine bottle there?" I asked.

"Yeah. Two-thirds full, on her kitchen table. But it was Gallo port. They've got a screw cap."

"Hmh!" Something was niggling my mind, just below the surface. "Look. Can you do something for me?"

"Maybe."

"I'd like this stuff sequestered."

Luciano frowned. "Sure. I can do that. What's going on?"

"I'm not sure. I'll let you know as soon as I do. Did you get any prints?"

"Off the bill, the wine bottle, and the screw cap. Didn't do anything with them though. The coroner's report, you know."

I did know. And she was a hooker who died of a heart attack. But the thing about the needle was surfacing in my mind. With Luciano beside me, I borrowed his office phone and used my code card to dial a friend of mine— an assistant L.A. county coroner, at his home. With the phone on speaker. "Elisio," I said, "what would be the effect of injecting a person with a jet of compressed air? With a cork popper."

"Depends on where. In the brain or spinal column or heart, or a major artery, it would kill them."

"Would the injection into one of those give the appearance of a heart attack?"

"An injection into the heart would *cause* a heart attack."

"If a woman was injected in the heart, what evidence would there be? Assuming she died at once."

"Huh. To start with, there might be a spot of blood at the point of injection. The perforation would be visible anyway, if you looked closely enough. And minor damage to the capillaries in the skin and intercostal muscle, and in the heart. If the needle didn't penetrate into one of the chambers, and the compressed air was released into the myocardium itself, there'd be conspicuous local tissue damage."

"And that would be deadly?"

"Definitely. It would cause severe myocardial trauma."

It helped to have had Introduction to Forensic Medicine back at Northern Michigan.

Luciano looked impressed and pleased. "I'll write this up," he said, "and check those prints against the files."

"Shave Vanderpol's head, too," I told him. "She wouldn't have held still for someone stabbing her with a needle like that one, unless she was unconscious. She may have been blackjacked. If she was, there ought to be discoloration. Maybe swelling; I'm not sure. And look under her left breast. That's a logical place to have injected her; it wouldn't show there. And if she was, check the breast for prints."

9

I left Sacramento with something further to do. Prints in the FBI archives are from police files. Access to print files of the military, government employees, and so forth are only accessible with a subpoena. And you need substantive evidence to get one. But Donald Pasco would have left prints on the video cubes he'd brought with him. They'd have other prints on them too, but with today's technology you can get useful images of prints overlain by prints, along with how many layers down any given print is. If prints on, say the bill and the needle cap, matched any of those on the cube, that would be evidence enough for the subpoena.

And enough to get a hair sample for a DNA analysis, to compare with one of the semen. Assuming there was clear evidence she'd been killed by an injection.

There were prints on both the cubes. I eliminated some of them as Joe's and Dalili's, his secretary. The rest, with a note, I sent from our computer to the police computer in Sacramento, attention Sergeant Luciano. Then I went home, stopping for a six-pack on the way, stripped down to cutoffs, and spent the rest of the day on my recliner watching baseball play-offs. Getting up mainly to put a frozen Mexican pizza in the oven. I felt like I'd earned it, calories and all, even if I hadn't made much progress on the Ashkenazi job.

10

On Monday I told Carlos about the Sacramento connection, which might or might not have anything to do with Pasco. I also ran down for him what I'd learned and hadn't learned about Ashkenazi, and recommended we call it a done.

He thought about that a minute. "No," he said, "stay with it for now. If we get lucky, and they arrest Pasco, then you can pull together what you've learned about Ashkenazi, and we'll go over it with whoever replaces Pasco as director there."

That meant waiting, not my favorite inactivity. So I took some compensatory time off and went to the club, where I stretched and did Choi Li Fut forms till I'd worked up a good sweat, then put in an hour on the exercise machines, twenty minutes on the bike, and an hour dozing on the grass in Plummer Park. After that I ate lunch and went to a matinee of *A Man for His Time* at Mann's Chinese Theater, where I ate a tub of popcorn. Finally I went back to the office. Vanderpol had been sapped and murdered, just as I'd figured. The prints on the needle cap and the bill were Pasco's. So were prints on Vanderpol's left breast. Pasco was being held without bond, for Murder One, and

DNA prints were being made from the semen and hair. I played it for Carlos, and he congratulated me.

"Write up your report on the Ashkenazi investigation tomorrow, and we'll see what Anti-Fraud says when they see the bill. They won't be happy, but we've got a signed contract."

I went out to the parking lot, started my car, and turned on the radio to KFWB News Radio. I don't often listen to news while driving. It's a distraction. But this time I did, just in time to hear about the murder of Arthur Ashkenazi! The body had been discovered that morning and none of us had heard about it. He'd been shot in bed, through the head. I was back in the elevator in about fifteen seconds, up to the ninth floor, and caught Carlos just getting ready to leave. I told him what I'd heard.

"Ashkenazi's place is outside Montecito," I said, "so it'll be in the sheriff's jurisdiction. We ought to get the contract for it. We can tell them we've been investigating Ashkenazi for the state, which gives us a head start on the case."

He got on it right away. Carlos has the authority when Joe is out. The sheriff went for it, and Carlos told him I'd fly up that evening. I caught supper at Morey's, then headed for the Larchmont Station, and a flight to Santa Barbara.

At the Santa Barbara sheriff's headquarters I learned something about the case that hadn't been released. Ashkenazi had been critically ill when shot. Possibly even dead, according to Sheriff Montoya. He'd been shot through the brain, a shot that wouldn't have caused much bleeding alive or dead. The reason for keeping this quiet was, the coroner said the disease symptoms were of viral meningitis. And he didn't want to start a panic. People would remember EVM, the epidemic viral meningitis that had killed more than a billion people, planetwide, in the winter of early 2000.

Tissue samples had been sent to the California Department of Health Services, attention the Chief of Vector Biology and Control. She and Sheriff Montoya were the only persons the coroner had informed. He hadn't told his secretary, hadn't entered it on his autopsy report, hadn't even informed the county health department. The sheriff didn't tell me until I'd signed an injunction in advance, forbidding me to tell anyone without his approval. Even his undersheriff didn't know.

Viral meningitis! I wasn't very enthusiastic about going out to Ashkenazi's place, but I didn't have much choice.

A deputy drove me. It was dark when we arrived. There was another deputy at the house, and Ashkenazi's servants were still there.

The bedding was just as it had been when the body had been taken away, but not as it had been when he was found. Ashkenazi had been somewhat wound up in the sheet, and they'd had to cut it to disentangle him. There was little blood. More sweat stain than anything else, from the meningitis. The pistol must have had a silencer; the shot hadn't wakened the servants. There'd been faint powder burns; the shot had been fired from about three feet, from the side toward the window. The gunman must have stood almost against the queen-size bed. The 9mm slug had been dug out of the floor for ballistic tests. There was no cartridge case. Probably the action had been hand operated to give more effective silencing.

The house doors had all been locked—that was done by a single switch—and there'd been no forced entry. But a reasonably agile gunman would have had no trouble getting in through the window, which had been open. A moment's discomfort—the insect screen had been electronic—but no actual difficulty. Climb the encina oak in the side yard, walk out on a massive limb, then step off on the first-floor roof and walk to Ashkenazi's bedroom window.

I talked to the servants, a middle-aged Hispanic couple whose English was more fluent than my Spanish. At about 5:20, Mr. Ashkenazi had told Mrs. Ruiz he was going to eat supper out, something he did occasionally, but almost never without giving her a lot longer notice. He'd seemed quite cheerful. "Mr. Ashkenazi was a very nice man," she added. Then her face crumpled, and I waited till she'd had a brief cry. He'd left the house about 5:30 and returned at 7:28; she'd looked at the clock when she heard him come in.

"Did you notice if he seemed well?"

"Well? I don' know. I didn' actually see him. But I heard him talkin' to his *periquito*—his bird—when he walked through the livin' room. He sounded like he always sound; very frien'ly." Her voice broke, and she started to cry again.

I made two working assumptions. One, that the supper date had somehow been connected with Ashkenazi's death. And two, that the date had been arranged very shortly before he told Mrs. Ruiz.

When she calmed down again, I asked: "Did he have any company today?"

It was Mr. Ruiz who answered this time. "No sir. He didn' have no visitors since you the other day."

That made the supper date doubly suspicious. He must have eaten somewhere fairly near, though, to have left at 5:30 and gotten back at 7:28. But there are a lot of restaurants between, say, Santa Barbara and Ventura.

After a few more questions, we left. As we drove back to Santa Barbara, I found my attention going to two people: Veronica Ashley and Donald Pasco, two unlikely suspects. Presumably Veronica was more or less Ashkenazi's age, and I couldn't imagine a woman of, say 55 or 60 years climbing that encina. As far as that was concerned, I couldn't picture Pasco doing it either, and anyway he'd been in jail by then. Following that line of reasoning, the gunman must have been a hired professional, and it occurred to me the supper date might have been to get the gunman onto the property.

But that really didn't make sense, and anyway it *felt* wrong. Also it seemed to require the cooperation of the servants, who then would hardly have told me about the supper date.

I decided I'd better sleep on it.

11

I woke up the next morning knowing what I had to do. Not *why*, but what.

Meanwhile there was the matter of breakfast. The night before, when I'd arrived back at the Larchmont Station, I'd stopped at a Nielsen's, bought a half gallon of butter brickle, went home and binged out. So to partly make up for it, I had fat-free cottage cheese for breakfast, with Rye Krisp, carrot sticks, and black coffee. My low-fat, high-protein penance. Then, having halfway atoned for the binge, I went to the office and accessed the state's data on Veronica Ashley.

It started with her current address and phone number, then got into more personal stuff. She'd been born Veronica Sue Pipolli, on 10 November 1950, in Culver City. An Angelena all the way. Married Eldon Robert Ashley on 21 March 1972, received her BS in biology *magna cum laude* from UCLA on 2 June '73, and her MS in molecular biology two years later. After five years as a lab technician in the med school there, she'd moved to the genetics research lab in the biology department, as a senior research assistant. It was a level she'd stay at for twenty years, the cost of not having a doctorate.

In April of 2000, she'd been jumped to research associate. Like everything else, the research staff and supply of new Ph.D.s had been decimated by the Great Flu and EVM, and they needed to fill vacancies, Ph.D. or not.

Her father had died in an auto accident in October '75, her mother in the Great Flu in December '99.

She had memberships in Phi Kappa Phi, which given her scholastic record was no surprise. And the Church of God in Science, which Ashkenazi had already told me.

And Veronica Ashley had a criminal record! Not much of a record—a misdemeanor: disturbing the peace. Specifically, blocking the entrance of a church and interfering with worship during a demonstration outside a Church of the New Gnosis in West L.A., in June 2006. The New Gnus were supposedly into psychic practices. In August '09 she'd been detained, then released without charge, after allegedly throwing rotten eggs at windows and doors of the Hollywood Hilton, and at security officers, during a demonstration against an International Conference of Parapsychologists.

So Veronica was not only a COGS. She was an activist member. Whatever malice she may have felt for her brother-in-law earlier, his new astrology must have pushed her buttons pretty hard.

I figured to go talk to her, and to Eldon if he seemed mentally functional. But just now she'd be at work, so it was time to follow up on the only real lead I had, thin though it seemed. Data Center got me the record of the previous day's phone traffic to and from Ashkenazi's residence. There almost wasn't any: Two calls received through his answering service, and one on the direct line. That one was made from a Dairy Delite in Ventura, at 5:14 P.M. The timing fitted perfectly, though Dairy Delites weren't the kind of place at which I pictured Ashkenazi eating.

I keyed directory assistance, and a page came onto my screen. There was only one Dairy Delite in Ventura, the cursor flashing beside it. The number didn't match the one on the list of phones, but that was no surprise. The call to Ashkenazi would have been from their pay phone.

I memorized the address without trying, a matter of simply intending to remember. It's a knack I have that's a lot handier than writing everything down. Next, accessing the Data Center again, I got color copies of the photos from Veronica's and Ashkenazi's driver's licenses. Finally I called the Ventura Dairy Delite number, which got me an order girl, as I'd expected. I asked her who worked the cash register weekdays at suppertime. The manager did, she told me. He came in at noon and usually stayed till 9 or 10.

Carlos had looked in while I was on the line to Ventura, so I went to see what he wanted. He'd had a call from an Inspector Zebriski in Sacramento, Sergeant Luciano's big boss. The DNA print from the semen was Pasco's. The district attorney said they had an ironclad case. The inspector was very happy with Prudential, which of course could mean future business for us, and reflected back on me. I could have that. I didn't plan to be a junior investigator all my life.

12

After lunch I drove to Ventura and found the Dairy Delite. I'd never been in one before. It turned out to be more than just an ice-cream place. They had burgers, chicken, a salad bar . . . the whole list. It was a little past two. The guy at the cash register wore a tag that said FRANK, and beneath it, MANAGER. I showed him my ID and contract cards, and asked to talk to him privately. He led me into his office. The plaque on the door said MR. PIPER.

I showed him the pictures of Ashkenazi and Veronica Ashley, and asked if he'd ever seen either of them before. Not so far as he knew, he said. "What'd they do? Rob a bank?"

"One of them died," I told him. "The other one didn't." Then, for no reason I can think of, I added, "The poisoner and the poisonee."

"Huh! If you know that, why snoop around any further?"

"You go to court with as much evidence as you can muster."

I had a fishburger then and left. It felt as if I'd just wasted a couple of hours on a false lead, but in my profession you get used to that. The names of the game are patience and thoroughness. Two of the names.

❖   ❖   ❖

My next stop would be Veronica Ashley's place, but I didn't want to get there too early. A little before she got home from work would be about right. Maybe 5:15. So it being a nice sunny day, I drove to a nearby beach, took off my shoes, and had a nice, hour-long hike along the surf line, enjoying the feel and smell of the sea breeze and getting my feet wet now and then. After letting Fidela know, back at the office. When I got back to the car, I rolled down my windows, let the seat back, and took a short nap. My car computer woke me up at 3:30, and I headed for Westwood, and Veronica Ashley's address. It was an older house, probably from before World War Two, because the glass doors had a lot of little diamond-shaped panes instead of being single panes of safety glass. It was two-story, pseudo-Moorish pink stucco, and had a small balcony upstairs with a little wrought-iron railing. Tall Washingtonia palms stood along the curb, and the walk to the front door had a big date palm on each side. There were glossy-leaved shrubs in front, with big pink blossoms, a kind you see a lot of in L.A. but I never heard a name for.

It occurred to me I was resisting going to the door, so I took myself by the scruff and started walking. Then there was nothing for it but to ring the doorbell. A big, strong-looking black lady answered, wearing a light green uniform like a nurse's. I introduced myself, showing my ID, and told her I'd come to talk to Mr. and Mrs. Ashley. I figured Veronica wouldn't be there yet, and I was right. The nurse? housekeeper? also told me that Mr. Ashley didn't see anyone.

"He's looking at me right now," I answered. Dimly I could see him through a doorway behind her, in a poorly lit inner room. My eyes hadn't adjusted from the late sunlight outdoors, and he looked vaguely like an ape on all fours. "If Mrs. Ashley isn't in, I'll speak with Mr. Ashley."

I sort of pushed past her, she giving way to one side, and I walked through the vestibule into a comfortable living room. Sky light came through a tall south window, thinned by trees and drapes. It jarred me to see Eldon Ashley, and to realize he was Aldon's twin. Both legs had been amputated, leaving stubs maybe eight inches long. And instead of prosthetics, he moved on his knuckles. No, on thick blunt fingers! His torso was small, but below the sleeves of a body shirt, his arms were corded with muscle. His eyes were wary, and did not seem unintelligent. Brain-damaged he might be, but he looked aware and alert.

"Mr. Ashley," I said, "my name is Martti Seppanen." I didn't offer my hand; he was standing on his. I'm one of the stronger people I know, but I doubt I could hold my own in a grip-down with Eldon Ashley. "I'm an investigator for the police," I went on. "I'm here because your brother Aldon was shot in his bed, night before last."

"Night . . . before . . . last?"

Not "Shot?"; just, "Night before last?" As if the time meant something to him.

"I've been assigned to investigate," I went on, then paused, trying to read his eyes. In that light they could have been marbles. "Do you have any idea who'd do such a thing?"

There was a long response lag, which in his case could have been physiological instead of psychological. There was no sign of grief, but his face seemed to have shrunk. When he answered, it was quietly. "No."

"Have you talked with your brother lately?"

He stared blankly, saying nothing. The nurse came into the room then. She showed no sign of hostility, only concern, presumably for Eldon. "I've called Mrs. Ashley," she said. "She'll be here in a few minutes."

"Right. Did you know that Mr. Ashley's twin brother was shot, night before last?"

Instead of looking shocked, she looked puzzled.

"Didn't you know he had a brother?"

"No sir, I didn't."

"How long have you worked here?"

"Five years last May."

"Do you live on the premises?"

"I have a room upstairs."

"Um. His brother's name was Arthur Ashkenazi, but it had been Aldon Ashley." I was addressing myself to the nurse, but my eyes were on Eldon. I had no idea why I was saying these things. "He changed his name after a big row with their father," I went on. "After Veronica, Mrs. Ashley, had told their father that Aldon had said terrible things to Eldon. She said Aldon was to blame for Eldon's auto wreck, the wreck that left him—" I groped. "Without his legs."

Eldon's eyes had opened wide. His mouth opened too, not to speak, but in shock. *He never knew!* I thought. *Eldon Ashley never knew!* Then a terrible thought hit me. Maybe it hadn't happened that way. I'd had the story from Ashkenazi's old college buddy, who'd had it from Ashkenazi, but how accurate was it? If it wasn't true, I'd done a very bad thing to Eldon, and to his wife.

The nurse brought me out of it. "Uh, sir, can I bring you some tea?"

I told her yes, and when she left, I asked Eldon if I could sit down. It took him a few seconds to answer, but he said yes, so I sat. Then, using his stubs as the third point of a mobile tripod, he went to another chair and got into it with a remarkable movement, a one-armed vault, torso twisting, free hand grasping the far arm of the sturdy overstuffed chair. And this man was 61 years old! I curbed my gawking and made a little small talk, an awkward, one-sided monolog.

The nurse came in with a tray, holding a teapot, two cups and saucers, a cream pitcher, and a sugar bowl with tongs. And oatmeal cookies. There was a little side table by each large chair; she served and left. I sipped, and tried to think of something to say that wouldn't sound inane. "Are you and Aldon identical twins?" I asked, then realized the question was insensitive on two counts. But after the typical long pause, he answered.

"Yes. Identical. But...we...were...always...different."

He may be brain-damaged, I told myself, *but he's not stupid. Not across-the-board stupid.* I found myself saying, "Different but close, I suppose."

"Yes," Eldon said. "Close. Stood . . . up . . . for . . . each . . . other. Always."

It hurt to hear it. But he seemed okay now. Not cheerful, but resigned. Accepting.

Then I heard the front door open, and got to my feet. A minute later Veronica Ashley strode into the room. Her eyes moved to me like a laser. She was not pleased. "I'm Veronica Ashley," she said. Making it a challenge. "Mr. Ashley's wife."

She wasn't a tall woman, but she had presence. Her build was sturdy. I got the impression of someone who worked out, probably at the faculty women's health club. But the strongest impression was of will, perhaps mixed with unforgivingness. Maybe she *could* have climbed the encina with a gun and shot Ashkenazi.

"You're also Arthur Ashkenazi's sister-in-law," I said. "My name is Martti Seppanen. I presume you've heard about his death."

"I was informed by his attorney."

"He was shot in the head," I added. "Once, right through the brain, with a 9mm pistol."

She was definitely startled by that. "He didn't tell me that," she said. "I'd assumed—assumed he'd died of natural causes."

Something felt wrong here, but I had no notion what. "I'm investigating the death on a contract with the Santa Barbara County Sheriff's Department. Do you have any idea why someone would shoot your brother-in-law?"

"None at all." Veronica Ashley was fully in control of herself now.

"Have you had any contact with him recently?"

"We haven't seen Aldon since their mother's funeral, ten years ago. And barely then."

"Not even in connection with the trust fund he set up for you? To help take care of Eldon?"

She grimaced, her face darkening with blood. "No. His attorney handled it."

I glanced at Eldon. He was watching intently, his mouth slightly open. His eyes were unreadable, but it seemed to me he was comprehending it all. And that it was new to him.

"You're the payee of the fund. What do you suppose your brother-in-law was worth?"

Her answer was stiff. "I have no idea."

"I don't either, Mrs. Ashley, but apparently quite a few million." I changed direction on her then. "Perhaps you have some idea who might have killed him. Think back. These things can grow out of old grudges."

Her lips had compressed. Now they opened. "Am I a suspect, Mr.—?"

"Seppanen. Detective Seppanen. Family is often suspect in these matters, Mrs. Ashley. That's a general rule."

"Well I'm afraid I can't help you. And you can believe this or not, but I hope you catch the gunman. If for no other reason than to remove any suspicion from me."

The way she said it, it felt like the truth.

13

I drove home trying to make sense of it, and getting nowhere. Back in my apartment, I phoned Tuuli. It was late to ask for a date that evening, so knowing her taste for space opera, I suggested the *Star Wars* festival showing at the New Hollywood Palladium. The first three movies in one marathon night! In honor of the ninetieth anniversary of George Mather, who'd produced the special effects for the first one.

When I finished my pitch, she answered me in Finnish. "Martti," she said, "that was nice of you. But what you're really looking for is distraction from whatever is on your mind. And I don't feel like being a distraction tonight." She may have picked up that I felt abused by her answer, because after a moment she added: "But I'd enjoy visiting on the phone awhile. Tell me about your day."

So I did: the day and the night before. When I'd told her about getting the data on Veronica, Tuuli interrupted. "When was she born?" When I said November 10, 1950, she laughed.

"A Scorpio! It fits like a glove. Sometimes they don't. Just a minute." I waited. After a minute she was back. "I just looked up her horoscope in this morning's *Times*. It

49

says Scorpios should avoid strangers today, that they could cause serious danger." She laughed again. When I'd run the rest of it by her, she said I was getting close, that it would start coming together soon. Starting tomorrow.

"What do you mean?"

"It's not explicit. But a lot of things are going to simplify for you." She paused. "You might want to call Carlos this evening."

So I let her go and phoned him. His machine told me he and Penny had gone to the New Hollywood Palladium, to the *Star Wars* festival. It struck me as uniquely twenty-first-century American: Carlos, grandson of Japanese peasant immigrants, who grew up on a hardscrabble farm in Colorado, and Penny, who'd been a child on a paddy farm in wartime Viet Nam, driving downtown in a car powered basically by gravity, to sit in the New Palladium watching a laserized renovation of a space opera classic about a war "a long time ago, in a galaxy far far away."

14

So what happened when I got to work in the morning? I had two messages waiting. One was from Carlos, telling me to see him first thing. He wasn't in yet. Then I played the other message, from Sacramento, and shared it with him when he did get in.

The evening before, a patrol car had been chasing a guy for driving erratically. Finally he stopped on a bridge and threw something in the Sacramento River before they grabbed him. In his luggage they found a silencer for a 9mm pistol, and a box of 9mm cartridges. A magnetic sounder team then recovered a 9mm pistol from the river, and his prints were on it. Ballistics test-fired it, and computer checked the slug against the national files. It matched the slug dug out of the floor of Ashkenazi's bedroom.

The guy's driver's license address was obsolete, but his auto registration address had been current. A search of his apartment turned up several Franklins—hundred-dollar bills. They'd checked for prints and found Pasco's.

Pasco's! It's one thing to be uptight, maybe even a little crazy, about someone "promoting" astrology. But to have him assassinated?

What struck Carlos most about it was that the Sacramento

police had accomplished it all in one night. The result of technology, including computerization of damn near everything. And budgets that allowed a full night shift. Twenty years earlier, he pointed out, it would have taken days, a week, and they might not have found the pistol at all.

Not only was Pasco discredited and in jail, but the shooting of Arthur Ashkenazi was solved. Which should close the contracts with the Anti-Fraud Divison and Santa Barbara County, and the company could collect its fee. My problem was, I felt uncomfortable with it, and said so to Carlos.

"Tell me about it," he said.

"Well, Montoya said Ashkenazi might have been dead when he was shot. And if that's true, then Ashkenazi died of natural causes. And Pasco's hit man was guilty of illegal entry, illegal discharge of a firearm, mutilation of a corpse, and attempted murder, but not murder."

Carlos frowned. "So I'll phone Sacramento and let them know what Montoya told you. Is that all?"

"No. I'm hung up on what the 'natural cause' was, of Ashkenazi's death. I was told what it was, but I'm under an injunction not to tell anyone. It's really bad. Dangerous. But keep the Santa Barbara contract open till noon. To authorize some calls, and maybe some data access."

Carlos gave me a long look. Then he nodded and left without asking anything more. I got on the line with Sacramento again, this time to the Chief of Vector Biology and Control. No, she said, there hadn't been another reported case of viral meningitis except for Ashkenazi's. Not anywhere in the world, so far as she knew, for ten years. And "remarkably," as she put it, they hadn't succeeded in establishing a colony of Ashkenazi's virus on human tissue cultures. Considering its swift development in Ashkenazi, and its apparent identity with the EVM virus, that was hard to accept. Especially after they repeated their attempts, this time being extraordinarily careful to do everything just right.

"How do you explain something like that?"

Her image shrugged on the screen. "I don't. I'm calling it a noninfectious virus, and describing its infection of

Mr. Ashkenazi as an unexplained anomaly. But we're taking no chances with it."

I thanked her and hung up, then told Carlos about it. Talking around it, never saying the words *viral meningitis*. "I think," I told him, "that I just may find the explanation. Can you come up with a contract that'll pay for it?"

He leaned back in his tilt-seat swivel chair. "Martti," he said, "I've got a lot of confidence in you. I did before, and I've got a lot more since you nailed Pasco. That was brilliant. And I'd really like to accommodate you. And if I did, Joe would probably go along with it. But with no more to go on than you just gave me, there's no way."

He sat back up. "However, if you want to do it on your own time, I'll give you unpaid adminstrative leave. Keep track of your time and expenses, and if you come up with something that will justify pitching a contract to—who? Vector Biology?"

I nodded.

"If you can do that, we'll pitch it to them. And if we get a contract, we'll charge them retroactively for your time and expenses. There's plenty of legal precedent, and right now your stock is high."

15

I called Vector Biology, and asked the director if they
planned to keep the virus. She said absolutely. They had
it on file in a freezer. Something as weird as it was, they'd
definitely not discard. I told her I was involved with the
Ashkenazi case, and had a data trail that might lead to an
explanation. Admittedly I exaggerated, but it would set her
up in case we hit her later with a contract request.

Then I called Santa Barbara and asked Montoya for his
approval to mention the case of viral meningitis. Recording the call, of course. I said it was vital to following up
a lead on the case. He told me the injunction was still
legally binding, but considering the time elapsed, Vector
Biology's inability to culture it . . . If it was really necessary, and *if* nothing bad came of it, he wouldn't pursue the
matter.

I didn't tell him I'd have done it anyway. We were both
on record on the matter, our asses half covered.

Next I phoned the Westwood Station of the LAPD and
got the name of a restaurant—Peri's Cafe—favored by their
people for private one-on-one meetings. According to
Lieutenant McNab, the food wasn't great, but the booths
gave maximum privacy.

Finally, I called the genetics lab at UCLA and asked to talk to the director. The receptionist asked what I wanted to talk to him about, and when I said it was confidential, she told me Dr. Chatterjee didn't accept calls on that basis. But when I told her it was a legal matter, she put me through. Suspecting she might listen in, I told Chatterjee I was an investigator for the state, and we needed his expertise.

I'd appealed to his sense of professional pride, so he gave me a one o'clock lunch appointment, suggesting a faculty dining room. Still suspecting a snoopy receptionist, I told him I'd meet him there, and how he could recognize me. I was pretty sure I'd recognize him, with a high-caste Hindu name like his.

I parked in a restricted faculty parking lot and met him as agreed. Showed him my ID and told him that actually I needed to talk somewhere more private. He went for it, intrigued by the sense of secrecy, I suppose. At Peri's, after we'd gotten menus and a pot of tea, I said in a low voice: "Doctor, what I'm going to tell you is strictly confidential. I'm working on a case that's highly sensitive and secret." Then I told him about the viral meningitis, and Vector Biology's inability to culture it.

"First, though— Years ago I read that the viruses that caused the Great Flu and EVM, maybe even the AIDS virus, might have been engineered. In your opinion, is that technically feasible?"

He answered as quietly as I'd asked. "Many things are feasible today. Thirty years ago, when AIDS first appeared, genetic engineering was quite primitive. But today, yes. Something like those could definitely be engineered. If one had the requisite facilities. It's not something one could do on a carpentry bench in one's garage.

"On the other hand, there's no need to blame genetic engineering for devastating plagues. Deadly pandemics have occurred throughout history without humans engineering them."

I said nothing to that for a minute, just looked at him, setting him up. "Dr. Chatterjee, I'm not interested in a virus that could infect millions. Can a virus be engineered that could infect only one person? One genotype?"

It took him a minute to answer. "You are familiar with killer bees?" he said.

"Not directly. I've read about them. Saw a TV special on them once."

"Then you are aware that what people today call killer bees are not the same insects imported into South America half a century ago. The killer bees we have here are the result of hybridization and introgression. They are an introgressed form of our domestic, mild-mannered *Apis mellifera*—but as dangerous as the original African bees.

"However, earlier this year a geneticist at Stanford, Kareem Bennett, succeeded in tailor-making a disease that should eliminate the killer bee genes from the Americas. He started with an old endemic viral disease of the domestic bee, one that's been around for as long as anyone knows. And created a genetic component in the virus that makes it far more virulent than the normal virus." He paused, shaking a finger for emphasis. *"But only for bees with the genes connected with killer bee aggressiveness.* In a few years it will probably have killed all the bees south of Nebraska. Then the normal, gentle *Apis mellifera* from farther north can be reintroduced."

I was starting to feel excited, instead of merely hopeful. "How difficult is it to do something like that?"

"Now that it's been done once, it should not be so difficult. Assuming you have a properly equipped laboratory and the necessary skills. First Bennett engineered a viral genome that was totally nonvirulent. That was the most time-consuming step. Then he tailored a selected low-grade virulence for genomes that included what we can call the 'killer' genes. With that accomplished, he altered *that* virus for an extreme virulence which worked slowly enough that infected bees will be able to spread the virus before succumbing to it. It will be released extensively into colonies next spring."

"And other geneticists can adapt his procedures to their problems?" I asked.

"That is correct. Bennett's completed work has just been published in scientific journals. And, of course, a fully detailed description is available through the virological, medical, and entomological networks. As a referee for the AIBS journal, I received a draft of Bennett's manuscript, and with his permission circulated copies in our laboratory. I considered his work that interesting."

"Umm. And a virus could be tailor-made for a single specific human being and no other?"

"A specific human genotype, almost certainly. One person, and any twins and other clones that might exist of him or her. But to make it specific, it would probably be simplest, certainly safest, to key the virus to that person's total genome. Which would seem to require working with diploid material from that particular person or his clone."

"What sort of diploid material?"

"Hair would suffice."

It was looking more and more as if this was the right track. "If," I said, "a meningitis virus was designed to kill Arthur Ashkenazi and only Arthur Ashkenazi, I suppose they'd have started with the EVM virus. Correct?"

For just a moment, Chatterjee's eyes widened. Up till then we'd been talking bees and hypothetical humans. Now we were down to cases. "Probably not," he answered. "There is something available that would make the work much quicker and easier. Assuming the designer had diploid material from Mr. Ashkenazi.

"The EVM epidemic simply ran itself out, you know. Epidemics do that. And may renew themselves later with genetic variants. The great flus of history, for example, and the Black Death. Meanwhile, researchers all over the world had worked desperately to develop a vaccine, and finally succeeded. If EVM should now recur in some genetic variant or other, there exists a noninfectious, nonvirulent form with which people may safely be inoculated. Unless they happen to have an allergic reaction. A form which will give them immunity without even a mild fever. It can even be taken orally.

"Thus if someone wished to tailor a virulent form, one

would best start with the vaccine. A major part of the work has already been accomplished."

Something else occurred to me. "How long would it take to do it?"

"It is difficult to say. Three months perhaps. Or possibly as little as two weeks, considering that one would be designing it for a complete genome. Also, one would not need to go through the steps of designing a low-level virulence and then modifying it for a greater. So let us say ten to thirty days."

"And how long would it take after inoculation to make the victim sick?"

"It's difficult to state in advance with any certainty. It might be quite quick."

"Hours?"

"Quite possibly."

"Who'd have access to the vaccine?"

"Many persons. Many principal hospitals must have it on hand. I'd be exceedingly surprised if we didn't have a supply here at the medical center. They'll have an abundance of it at the Office of Vector Biology and Control in Sacramento."

"Who'd have access to the supply here in the med center?"

He looked thoughtfully at the question. "Assuming they have it, probably many persons. Numerous materials must be stored in their freezers, and presumably quite a number of persons go in and out. How many know where, in the freezer, to find it is another matter."

"Right. Dr. Chatterjee, thank you very much. You've given me serious food for thought. And remember, sir, it's important—vital—that you don't mention our talk to anyone. Not your friends, your wife, or anyone on your staff."

For a moment I'd thought of telling him who, specifically, I was interested in—Veronica Ashley. That she was Ashkenazi's sister-in-law. It would make the importance of silence more real, and reduce the chance of a leak. But it wouldn't be fair to her. I felt reasonably sure she was guilty, but I'd been wrong before.

After driving Chatterjee back to his office, I called the
UCLA med center, got connected to Medical Supplies, and
talked to the guy in charge. That night at nine he let me
into the freezer room where the EVM vaccine was kept,
and I took print masters off the drawer and flasks that held
the vaccine. The next day our lab sorted out the prints,
but none matched Veronica Ashley's in the national print
archives. She could, of course, have worn gloves, but I
wouldn't have expected her to.

16

After driving Chatterjee back to his office, I called the
UCLA med center, got connected to Medical Supplies, and
talked to the guy in charge. That night at nine he let me
into the freezer room where the EVM vaccine was kept,
and I took print masters off the drawer and flasks that held
the vaccine. The next day our lab sorted out the prints,
but none matched Veronica Ashley's in the national print
archives. She could, of course, have worn gloves, but I
wouldn't have expected her to.

So all I had was an ingenious theory and some circumstantial evidence. Nothing a prosecutor could make work
in court. I went to Carlos' office and ran it all by him, hoping he'd see something I'd missed. He didn't. He asked
if I wanted to continue on administrative leave, or if he
should line me up with a new assignment. I said I'd keep
plugging, then went to my own office wondering if I was
just being stubborn.

I called Tuuli and told her answering machine I wanted
to take her out for Mexican food that evening. I'd call her
again before five. Then I went to Gold's and worked out
for the first time since Monday, extra hard to make up for
the calories I intended to take on that evening. After that
I went home for a nap.

About the only satisfaction I had that day was listening to KFWB on my car radio. Arthur Ashkenazi's will had left the bulk of his estate to the Hypernumbers Institute, a psychically oriented group. For research into the multidimensional nature of reality. Veronica Ashley would be fit to kill.

17

It was getting dark when Tuuli and I got to her building from Casa de Herreras. I felt stuffed. There was a parking place made to order, and I grabbed it. Then, instead of getting out of the car, we sat for a few minutes in a weird, silent mood.

"I don't think you'd better come up tonight," she said at last.

I got out, went around and opened the off-side door for her. She looked worried. "I mean it," she said.

"What's wrong?"

"I'm not sure, but . . . Something doesn't feel right."

I reached to help her out. "I'll just walk you to your door and leave," I told her. We walked up the sidewalk between her building and the thick, eight-foot hedge bordering the property. There was night jasmine around somewhere, smelling a bit like Michigan in lilac time. Night jasmine's one of the things I like best about L.A. Tuuli's apartment was on the second floor, front corner. Like a lot of places in L.A., the stairs were outside, leading to an outside second-floor walkway. I opened the screen, intending to hold it for her while she unlocked her door.

I heard a *chuff*, and a bullet clunged like a hammer against an ornamental wrought-iron upright from the walkway railing to the overhang. A fragment bit my cheek. I threw Tuuli to the deck, then vaulted over the railing, hearing another *chuff* as I did so. The sound of a silenced pistol. I landed on the hedge, half scrambling, half falling off it onto the sidewalk. A third shot *chuffed*, and I heard the slug spending its energy clipping hedge stems as I ran crouching for the street and my car. I got there panting more from excitement than exertion, fumbled the key into the lock, and snatched my car gun out of the door pocket.

The shots had come from the building next door, and I couldn't make up my mind whether to go there, or back up to Tuuli's. While I crouched there trying to decide, her front window opened. "Martti!" she called softly. "Stay there! I'm all right. I'll call 911."

I didn't take her advice. Instead I went back to the stairs, and crouched listening in the cover of the hedge in case whoever it was came over. Although I was pretty sure he wouldn't. It was me he was after, and having lost his surprise, he'd taken off. Maybe to set another ambush at my place.

Things were still as midnight. We hadn't made enough noise to draw attention. I had no idea who the gunman might be. In my business you offend people who might take a notion to exercise their grudge that way. Something I'd learned the hard way. And while most of them end up domiciled with the state for extended periods, there are always some running around loose.

Two or three minutes later the police pulled up, and after I'd identified myself, we went next door together. There was a sign out front:

APTS FOR RENT
1 & 2 BEDROOMS
SEE MGR
9 AM–7 PM

We went up the stairs two at a time, and along the

second-floor walkway on the side facing Tuuli's. The drapes were open wide in one apartment, the window was open, there was a hole in the screen, and it was dark inside. One of the officers went and got the manager.

All we found inside were three empty cartridge cases: .40 caliber. I was damn lucky he hadn't hit me. By that time another patrol car had arrived, this one with a senior sergeant. After talking with him, I got in my car, and the first officers followed me home. Staying close on the chance the gunman might try for me again.

My apartment's in a security building on Lanewood, with a basement garage. They waited in the patrol car while I stopped on the ramp to insert my key card. Lanewood has a row of big shaggy Mexican pines on each side of the street, and it was darker than hell, but it seemed to me someone was crouched in the tall shrubs ten feet from the ramp. While the door opened, I spoke into my shortwave mike. "Car 1094," I said, "I think our man's in the shrubs just to the left of the ramp."

Then I rolled in, got out of my car, and with pistol in one hand reopened the garage door from the inside. The officers had already moved in on the suspect. He had his hands in the air.

A little peering around with a flashlight found his gun where he'd dropped it. Then they took both of us to the Hollywood Station on Wilcox, where they questioned us. I answered everything they asked. The gunman told them only his name. Said he'd gone into the shrubbery to take a leak. They booked him for creating a public nuisance, and carrying a gun illegally. He had a record.

His name was Harley Suk O'Connell. Part Afro, part oriental—Korean, judging by his middle name. He was reputedly a freelance hit man who did occasional jobs for the black mafia. So far as I knew, I told them, I'd made no particular enemies there.

When they were done with me, I talked in the hall with the sergeant on the case. Someone must have paid O'Connell to try for me, I said. If they checked out his pad, they might find some cash in large-denomination

bills. Which might have useful prints. He agreed it could
be worthwhile.

Then they took me home, and I phoned Tuuli to tell
her what happened. She'd been waiting for my call, and
worrying because I hadn't. She told me to come over.

I was back at her place in five minutes. She'd been
watching for me, and met me at the stairs, wearing her
jacket. In her purse, I was willing to bet, was the little .25
caliber Lady Colt I'd given her. It's just a few blocks from
her place to Laurel Canyon. Laurel Canyon Boulevard
crosses the Santa Monica Mountains, a range of high, rugged hills that divides the L.A. Basin to the south from the
San Fernando Valley to the north. From Laurel Canyon,
narrow residential streets zigzag their way up among the
slopes and draws.

I drove up one of them without either of us saying
anything. Finally I parked at a place we like, in a tiny park,
on a crest overlooking the basin. It's not the safest place
in the world, but I had a gun under my left arm, and my
car gun in the door pocket.

Since the internal combustion engine had been
banished by the geogravitic power converter and the
stringent air protection laws that followed, you can see
forever from up there: a vast sea of city lights. To the
south is a big unlighted area that I suppose is a golf
course. And more miles and billions of lights farther, the
hills of the Palo Verdes Peninsula, sparkling in white, red,
green, and blue. Amazing that you can see individual lights
so far away! And over all, scattered tall clouds side-lit by
the city. It's one of the most beautiful sights in the world,
another reason I love L.A.

I reached over, took Tuuli's hand, and for maybe the
dozenth time asked her to marry me. She leaned against
me and said she loved me, but no, she wasn't ready to
commit herself. Might never be. "If I change my mind,
Martti," she said in Finnish, "you'll be the first one I tell."

How could I argue with that? After a little bit I drove
her home, and she invited me up.

18

The next day I slept till ten. Then I called the Hollywood Station to see what they'd learned from O'Connell's apartment. They'd found bundles of Franklins in a dresser, with prints they'd already identified as Veronica Ashley's. They planned to question her.

I asked them if they'd hold off on that for twenty-four hours. Otherwise it might queer a case I was working on. They agreed. There was no hurry. They had all they needed to put O'Connell away for a while.

Why, I wondered, would Veronica get a contract on me? I'd offended her all right, but what had I said and done that might have scared her? I called up the data on her from my files. And stared. Veronica Ashley, nee Pipolli.

Pipolli. Piper. Could be. I called the Data Center again, using the Santa Barbara County contract, and accessed Dairy Delite in Ventura. The franchise holder was Francis Gustavo Pipolli, DBA Frank Piper. His records gave his father's name, and his father's records showed *his* father's, and his showed a daughter, Veronica. Veronica Ashley was Piper's paternal aunt.

Something else struck me, too, something I'd overlooked before and shouldn't have. GTE's computer records show when a call was made from a pay phone. I checked again. The call to Ashkenazi hadn't been. She had to have called from her nephew's office, so he might very well know what she was up to. And I'd said something to him about "poisoner and poisonee." He'd almost certainly called and warned Veronica.

I laid it all out for Carlos, and his eyes lit up. He'd take it up with Vector Biology right away, and if he couldn't get a contract on it from the state, the firm would cover the cost. And use the case for publicity

Assuming it worked out.

Carlos didn't ask me what I was going to do next, and I didn't volunteer. I spent most of the day catching up on odds and ends, and working on my Spanish. Then with my pocket recorder and my gun inside my jacket, I headed for Westwood to confront Veronica Pipolli. I'd start dumping my evidence on her now—it might even be enough for a prosecutor to take her to court with—and maybe she'd start saying things.

If she was home.

She was, and unfriendly. When the nurse-housekeeper announced me, Veronica came into the living room like a drill sergeant. Eldon came swinging in too, on his fingers and stumps, looking somehow more formidable than most guys with legs. I started by telling her that Harvey O'Connell botched his contract, and the LAPD had him locked up. Sarcastically she said that was nice, and who was Harvey O'Connor?

I matched her tone. Sarcasm can get people to say things they otherwise wouldn't. "O'Connell," I said, "not O'Connor. I thought you knew him. Or do you give bundles of hundred-dollar bills to people you don't know? Or maybe there's something new in the world: two people with the same fingerprints. O'Connell had three shots at me, incidentally, and all I got was a fragment in the cheek."

I touched my face as I said it, my eyes on hers. She showed no fear. What I was looking at was supressed rage.

"The fingerprints weren't your only mistake," I went on.

"That was stupid, using your nephew's phone to set up the date with Arthur. Aldon, that is. Why didn't you use the pay phone?"

With that her face went white, but she didn't look faint at all. The muscles in her jaw lumped like walnuts. "Was that when you hired O'Connell to kill me?" I asked. "After I talked with Frank? The timing's about right. It would have taken O'Connell awhile to learn where I lived. And maybe follow me around until he saw a good opportunity."

She still wasn't saying anything, so I tried another shot. "They've decided Aldon was dead before he was shot," I lied. "I'd never have figured out how you killed him, if I hadn't heard about the killer bee research. Do you keep some of your tricked up meningitis virus around the house? Maybe you plan to use it on your husband next. He's Aldon's twin, after all."

That broke it. "*Get out!*" she shouted suddenly. "*Get out of this house! Now!*"

I shook my head. "Not without the rest of the virus."

"*All right!*" she shouted, "*I'll give it to you!*"

And stomped out of the room. For the first time that day I turned my attention to Eldon. He was in a state of shock. In ten seconds Veronica was back. But what she had in her hand was not a flask or vial or petri plate, it was a snub-nosed .32, looking bigger because it was pointed at me. All that saved me getting shot was, she was too damned mad to simply kill me. She was going to blast me with venom first, with words.

Before she got any of them out though, Eldon was between us, facing her. I wished he was taller. "You . . . killed . . . Aldon," he said. "And . . . you . . . lied . . . about . . . him . . . to . . . father. How . . . could . . . you . . . do . . . that? You . . . said . . . you . . . loved . . . me!"

The steel and the fire went out of Veronica Ashley as if they'd never been. "I do love you, Eldon," she said, and watching her, I knew she meant it. "I love you very much. I've always loved you."

"No," he said, and moved toward her on splayed and calloused fingers. "You . . . can't . . . love . . . me. You . . .

killed . . . Aldon!" Then he launched himself at her, I'm not sure just how, tackling her, scrambling all over her. I ducked out of the room and drew my own gun. She screamed, and hers went off, once, and after a couple of seconds a second time. Crouched and ready, I looked back in.

Veronica sat on the floor against a heavy chair, weeping quietly, her hands on her belly. Her face was already gray. Eldon lay sprawled on the floor, his head a ruin, far worse than Aldon's had been. One way or another she'd been gut-shot, then he'd put the barrel in his mouth and pulled the trigger. Her eyes moved to me when I stepped back into the room, the hatred gone from them, replaced by shock and something else. Grief.

"Jesus," I said to her. "Jesus, Veronica, I'm sorry. I'm really really sorry." And I meant it.

19

It was all recorded, of course. At the hospital next day, Veronica Ashley told everything, and naturally the papers picked it up. And played hell out of it. They gave Prudential a lot of good publicity and made me sound like Sherlock Holmes. So of course I got promoted. I don't wear *junior* in front of *investigator* anymore.

As a matter of policy, I'd phoned Carlos from the Ashleys' right after I'd called the police. When I told him what happened, he said come to the office as soon as I possibly could. He knew what was coming. When I got there, he was waiting with Joe. In my profession it's best not to have your face on the six o'clock news. So Joe gave me a paid vacation as a bonus, and sent me to his place to hide till I could leave town. I phoned Tuuli from there, and she surprised me: She agreed to go with me!

I left Joe's at 4:30 the next morning, picked her up, and we flew to Hemlock Harbor, back in Ojibwa County, Michigan. Where she met my sister Elvi, and my half brother Sulo. Sulo's more than old enough to be my father. Both of them loved Tuuli right away. Now she and I are roughing it in dad's old fishing shack, his *hytti*, back in the bush on Balsam Lake, where I'm taping this. Elvi said I owe it to my nieces and nephews, and whatever children Tuuli and I might have.

Yep, Tuuli and I got the license the second day there, and got married in Hemlock Harbor's Trinity Lutheran parsonage. She says I'll have to improve my Finnish now, speak it as well as Elvi, or better yet, Sulo. Next week we'll go back to L.A. and find a security building in a good location. One where she can rent an efficiency apartment in the same building we live in, for her consulting office.

And that's all there is to the story, so I'll go split some wood for the stove. I'm not missing L.A. too much yet.

THE PUPPET MASTER

―――――

A NOVEL

PART ONE:
CHURCH OF THE NEW GNOSIS

PROLOG

Actually it was a bedroom in a private home, but it looked like a large, private hospital room in baby blue, with vases of varied, freshly cut flowers adding indigo and white, violet and butter yellow against the delicate green of ferns. The bed was a hospital bed, and a private nurse sat beside it in a chair. Next to her stood a cart, an instrumented, stainless-steel life-support system on wheels, with LEDs displaying the patient's critical biofunctions. A telescoping rod extended upward from it, topped by a pivoting arm that dangled wires and a tube to disappear beneath the bed cover.

The nurse was reading a paperback novel—one of the New Age novels that were popular then. Just enough daylight filtered through the thick drapes to show it was morning.

The figure in the bed was male and elderly. He appeared to have a glandular disorder; his face was like raised bread dough, puffy and pale. It was also drawn down on one side by stroke, leaving the wide mouth twisted. Just now the muscles were slack and the eyes closed, their lids thick.

Given the puffy face, one might have expected a great swollen body. Actually, its bulk beneath the soft cotton *sheet was not particularly large, but it seemed to spread, as if its bones were cartilage, not rigid enough to support it.*

The eyes opened. Their blue was faded, their whites yellowish. They shifted to the nurse, not in an invalid's drugged or helpless or apathetic gaze, but coldly. As if feeling the touch, she set the book aside.

"Ten twenty-six, sir," she said as if answering a question, and stood up. She pressed two keys on a small control box at the foot of the bed, and slowly the bed took a shape suited to reading.

Nothing more was said. She didn't ask if he was hungry or wanted an alcohol rub or to relieve himself. Instead she took the eyeglasses from the bedside table, made sure again that they were clean, and carefully set them on the puffy face. Laser surgery could have corrected his astigmatism, but he'd declined it. He intended to correct it himself one day, along with much else.

Next she swung a hospital reading screen on its arm and positioned it, looked questioningly at him, then sat down at a small table and keyed in instructions on a small console. The masthead for the L.A. Times wire edition lit the screen for a moment. The date was 2008 August 13, and the edition, 1000 hours. A menu screened. One of the selections was scan, and touching, she activated it, controlling the speed with a knurled knob. Page one scrolled up too rapidly for all but the swiftest readers.

From where she sat, to watch the screen would have been awkward, and she didn't try. Her eyes stayed mostly on the old man. Now and then she slowed the image for a moment or for several, as if sensing his wishes and his reading rate. As one of the items brought a change of expression to his face, she slowed the scrolling nearly to a stop. It read:

Ex-OSS Official's Daughter Weds Gnostie
Gloria DeSmet of Pacific Grove, 21-year-old daughter of retired OSS Deputy Director Alex DeSmet, has married Fred L. Hamilton, a counselor for the Church

of the New Gnosis in Los Angeles, according to a friend of the DeSmet family.

A student at Stanford University, Gloria DeSmet was employed for the summer at Holy Redeemer Hospital in Monterey. Hamilton, who'd concealed his affiliation with the Gnostic cult, had also been employed there, as a psychiatric assistant. (Supp A). Hamilton and DeSmet had been dating.

Hamilton's use of Gnostic counseling procedures on patients at Holy Redeemer was discovered, and he was discharged. Last Friday, after telling her parents that she would spend the weekend near Grass Valley with friends, Gloria DeSmet followed Hamilton to Los Angeles. She was not missed until she failed to show up for work on Monday. She and Hamilton were married in Los Angeles on Tuesday. She then notified her family.

The old man began to chuckle.

1
DEBRIEF

2012, July 5

It was a UCLA project. Its purpose was to record "the anatomy of selected investigations."

Martti Seppanen watched the young woman adjust her camcorder and other gear, skeptical that anything useful would come of it. To him it smelled like academic/ bureaucratic barn waste. The case was already thoroughly documented in his taped debriefs, and in case and court records.

Also it would end up in UCLA's security archives, because Martti would be freeflowing, and some or much of what he said would be about persons not guilty of any crime, persons whose privacy had to be protected. It would be seen only with hard-to-get approvals, mainly by candidates for advanced degrees in law enforcement.

Joe Keneely didn't think much of the project either, because confidentiality prevented using it as promotion. He could have refused, of course, but the California Department of Justice had pushed, and the state was a major client of Prudential Investigations and Security, Inc. Within the limits of ethics and the law, it was desirable to humor them.

Why video? Martti wondered. All it would show was him sitting with his eyes closed or unfocused, talking. Maybe it had something to do with the aura analyzer she'd set up beside the camcorder. Presumably it would be monitoring his frame of mind while he talked.[1]

The aura analyzer was more than just a lie detector. According to articles in the *Journal of Law Enforcement Technology*, they were more reliable than polygraphs, and gave broader information.

They're not going to believe everything I say anyway, Martti told himself, *regardless of what my aura shows.*

It occurred to him that some of what he might say could surprise him, too. He'd read that with a Veritas injection, you remembered a lot you otherwise wouldn't, and in detail. Supposedly even stuff you'd psychologically suppressed after it happened. And while you could hold back under Veritas, you'd rarely feel an impulse to. Normally you just freeflowed. Probably the aura analyzer would show if you were withholding.

He decided he'd view it himself when they were done. There might be insights for him.

The woman removed a syringe from a small, flat, velvet-lined box. "All right, Mr. Seppanen," she said cheerily, "I believe I'm ready. How about you?"

He'd eaten a pizza half an hour earlier, so hunger wouldn't distract him, had avoided caffeine with its diuretic effects, and had just been to the restroom. He took a deep breath and let it out. "Yeah, I'm ready."

"Good," she said, and stepped over to his chair. "You don't need to speak loudly. Just murmur. It's easier on the

---

[1] In 2009, President Douglas Ishimatsu declassified a number of mood- and mind-altering devices previously withheld under the International Traffic in Arms Regulations, or by the FDA, while legalizing private research and the publication of results. Why most of the devices had been withheld in the first place is difficult to imagine, beyond the bureaucratic dictum: "Cover your rear." Legalization has brought a flurry of new research on the mind and neuro-electrical fields.

throat, and my corder will get it. Now if you'll just give me your hand . . ."

He laid a thick hand on the corner of his desk. She took it, held the syringe against the back of it, and pressed the trigger. The hiss reminded him of the adjustment valves on the exercise machines at Gold's. "It'll take a minute or so," she said, and sat down across from him, her laptop open in front of her on the folding laptop table she'd brought. Bit by bit he felt his mind relaxing. The room blurred, and though he found he could bring it back in focus, it didn't seem worthwhile to. It was easier just to close his eyes. His lips opened, and he started to speak.

2
GNOSTIES

In a way, I got involved with the Christman case in May of 2010, a year and a half before Christman disappeared. I was an investigative assistant here, with an MS in Law Enforcement from Northern Michigan University and four years of experience on the Marquette, Michigan, police force. I'd just spent five months apprenticing under Carlos—that's Carlos Katagawa, Supervisory Senior Investigator here at Prudential. He'd told Joe—Joe Keneely is president and majority shareholder—that I was ready for a case of my own, and Joe said go ahead. So when I came in that day, Carlos called me down the hall to his office and played a cube for me.

They'd recorded it late the day before. It showed a handsome, well-dressed woman in her forties, telling Carlos and Joe what it was she wanted, and answering their questions. Her name was Angela DeSmet. Twenty-one months earlier, her twenty-some-year-old daughter, Gloria, had "run away" to L.A. and married a guy who worked for the Church of the New Gnosis. The mother had tried to get in touch with her, but the church is—*impenetrable*, the papers have called it.

So Angela DeSmet had hired an investigator from Monterey—the DeSmets lived in nearby Pacific Grove—

but the guy couldn't even learn where the daughter was, let alone get to her. He said the church might have sent her to any one of its locations in or out of the country.

Angela had wanted to hire a serious investigation then, but her husband, Alex DeSmet, wouldn't go for it. Gloria was a grown woman, he'd said. She had the right to live her own life, and if she got unhappy with the church, she could always walk out. And come home if she wanted to.

Then DeSmet had gotten a consulting job with the Republic of India, and a few weeks after their daughter left, he and his wife had gone to New Delhi to live. He was a retired technical specialist with the State Department, she said. After a couple of years, India started having severe civil disturbances, the ones that led to it splitting off from ECOTEB, the Eastern Co-Prosperity Technical and Economic Bloc. Splitting off and starting SACU, the Southeast Asian Co-Prosperity Union. Anyway, Alex DeSmet had sent his wife back to the States, and she'd decided it was time to find her daughter. Carlos and Joe had decided I was the one to do it.

My own case! I had nervous stomach. The first thing I did was sit down at my terminal and call up the accessible information on DeSmet. Which was not a lot, because the case didn't get us access to the State Data Center. It takes a contract from the city or county or state for that. The DeSmet family, I learned, was big in shipping. It also had a family history of public service dating back to Gerhard DeSmet, a New York banker who'd helped finance the colonial army during the Revolution. Every generation of the DeSmet family had had a career officer in either the State Department or the armed forces or both. Alex DeSmet hadn't been in the State Department though, regardless of what his wife claimed. He'd been in the CIA until '96 or '97, when President Haugen took its Office of Special Projects and recreated the old OSS out of it. DeSmet ended up being deputy director there, after the Great Flu killed the guy who'd been holding the job.

I suppose Gloria had grown up mainly with her mother. Odds were that Alex had been away a lot.

Then I keyed up the L.A. City Library and selected a summary article on the Church of the New Gnosis. It was interesting but not particularly helpful. Some of it I'd read before, here and there. Before I'd finish that case and the Christman case, I'd know a lot about the church that the writer hadn't. Meanwhile, the only lead I had on Gloria DeSmet was her married name, Gloria Hamilton.

California has the world's largest concentration of cults, and there are more every year, but the Church of the New Gnosis has got to be the biggest, even bigger then the Institute of Noetic Technology when it was going strong. Its world headquarters—what it calls its "World Episcopate"—is here in L.A., on what used to be the campus of Pacific Southern University.

I signed out a car and drove over there. I'd never really paid any attention to the place before. It still looked pretty much like a mid-city college, built after real estate got so expensive. After the GPC boomed the economy, and Congress passed the Education Rights Bill. Including its parking lots, the campus covers what originally had been four large city blocks, containing several large buildings. Unfortunately it failed—went bankrupt when the Great Flu and Epidemic Viral Meningitis cut populations, enrollments, and faculty too drastically.

The surrounding neighborhood is mostly post-plague apartment houses, built around security courtyards with swimming pools. The streets are lined with tall Washingtonia palms, and the campus grounds have well-tended lawns, flowerbeds, and night jasmine, with ornamental-orange hedges.

One of the buildings has a sign in front that reads NEOPHYTE BUILDING. That sounded about right for me, so I went in to ask questions. Careful questions. Sneaky questions. The church has a reputation for secrecy, and I was there to get answers, not thrown out. I had no trouble recognizing staff. They wore one-piece, sky blue space-cadet uniforms, with tapered legs tucked into light weight white boots that had to be a nuisance to keep clean. Also, staff members tend to walk fast or even jog, as if they're in a hurry.

It turned out that the staff who deal with new people are trained to control the conversation. Mostly they seem friendly, but all you learn is what they want you to know. I went along with their pitch, figuring that if I became part of the scene, I'd learn things. I ended up registering for a free introductory lecture that evening. That introductory lecture's about the only thing they don't charge for, and even then they practically insisted that I buy *A Beginner's Book on the New Gnosis,* written by their guru, Raymond Arthur Christman, whom they call "Ray."

By the time I'd gotten registered, it was noon. It turned out they have a staff dining room, but some staff members who can afford to, eat out. So I followed a couple of them across the street to a place called the Saints' Deli, carrying my book to mark me as a would-be new member. I figured to get into a conversation, or maybe eavesdrop.

The Saints' Deli is a Gnostie hangout run by Gnosties. It's a strange kind of place for L.A.; it felt as if everyone there, including the waitresses, belonged to a family. And I was an outsider. They had a big menu board on the wall, chalk on green, and I ordered "Saint's Delight." It turned out to be cream cheese and ripe olives on sourdough bread, with kosher dills on the side. It was a day for new experiences. Then I got my coffee and number tag, and looked for a place to sit.

Almost everyone was sitting with friends and talking, a lot of them animatedly, most of them wearing civvies. But at a table for two, a skinny guy in his late thirties or so, wearing a staff uniform, sat alone by an empty chili bowl, sipping coffee and reading a paperback. I went over. He drank his coffee black, and from what I could see of the cover, the book was science fiction. His uniform was threadbare and too big for him, but clean except for ring around the collar.

"Mind if I sit here?" I asked.

He looked at me, then at my beginner's book. "If you insist," he said, "but please don't open a conversation with me. I deal with neophytes eight hours a day, seven days a week, and three further hours a day I attend class. On my free time I like to sit alone and relax with some light reading."

"Class?" I said.

"Staff are required to be on some approved course or other at all times. I'm studying to be a Gnostic counselor. Now if you please . . ."

He withdrew his attention as if I wasn't there. I sipped my coffee and people-watched. Some would stop by a notice board and browse the stuff posted there. After a few minutes a waitress came with my sandwich, dill pickle spears, and some damned good potato salad.

To me a diet is something to fall off of, and I'd been holding to mine fairly well—I'd weighed 226 pounds that morning—so when I finished, I ordered a milkshake, which turned out to be a jumbo. When I'd finished that, I went to see what sort of stuff got posted on the notice board. Some of it was advertisements, which from the jargon seemed to be by small Gnostie businesses. A few were hand-scrawled notes from one person to another, or "to anyone traveling to the such-and-such area."

Most, though, bore the official logo of the church, some of them notices of special-price offers for what appeared to be services that the church sold its members—counseling and classes. Several were headed DECLARATION OF EXPULSION, or even DECLARATION OF APOSTASY AND EXPULSION. Each of these began with a stock statement: *Further unauthorized contact with the below named is an act of treason*. Below that, in bold black capitals, would be one or more names. From one of them, the name jumped out at me: **FREDERICK L. HAMILTON.** It was dated nearly three months earlier. Below it was a short list of what appeared to be statute numbers, presumably of church laws he'd broken. It seemed to me I had my lead.

As I stood looking at it, a hand touched my shoulder.

"Don't let the declarations disturb you." It was the guy I'd sat with. "Staff members are an elite, and when one of us refuses correction, he has to be pruned away. To refuse correction is to hold to one's weaknesses and evil impulses, and that is a further act of evil. Most people who get expelled will eventually desire correction, and return to be saved. But if their intentions are evil enough to threaten the Church, something invariably happens to them, something unpleasant. I could give you examples. The Church doesn't do it—don't take me wrong. The *universe* punishes them."

Then he turned and left, leaving me staring after him, my scalp crawling. *Evil,* he'd said. I wondered if the evil wasn't inside the church instead of out.

Back at the office I called up the directory listings under EMERGENCY AID > CULT WITHDRAWAL, and found one that called itself Gnostic Withdrawal Assistance, at 1764 Hillhurst. I dialed their number and learned they had someone on the desk twenty-four hours a day. They did not discuss business over the phone.

So I drove over there. The guy on duty was black, about six-five and maybe 280 pounds; could have played defensive end for the Steelers. His eyes were calm, and as direct as any I'd ever seen. His face had multiple scars, and his nose had been flattened badly enough that it looked like the business end of a double-barreled shotgun, yet he didn't look mean or even hard, just someone who was in charge of himself. The church had a reputation for intimidating people it considered its enemies, but I couldn't picture anyone intimidating that guy. I told him I wanted to get in touch with someone named Fred Hamilton, who'd gotten kicked out about three months earlier. Did he know him?

"Yeah, I know Fred," he told me. "I've known him for years. When they kicked him out, they hadn't paid staff their weekly ten dollars for four weeks. As punishment because church income was down. He came in here in grief, without a dime. I let him use my phone to call his parents, so he could ask them for skybus fare. They weren't home, so he stayed with me overnight."

"Could you give me his address?"

"We don't give out addresses. For all I know, you could be one of Lonnie's goons—Lonnie Thomas'—looking to harass him."

Lon Thomas. I remembered the name from the summary article. The author called him the administrative chief of the Gnosties, the guy in charge of day-to-day operations. The goals, the directions, and the central policies, on the other hand, supposedly came from Ray Christman.

I took out my wallet and showed the guy my Prudential ID plate. He couldn't have looked less impressed. "Look," I told him, "I don't care one way or another about whether Hamilton is in or out of the church. He has a wife, and her mother wants to know how she is. And where."

He appraised me with dark, reddish brown eyes. "Our standard offer for something like that is, you give me twenty-five George in cash, and I'll call and give him your phone number. And tell him what you want. If he wants to, he'll get in touch with you. If not . . ." He shrugged.

I took one of my business cards and two bills out of my wallet, gave them to him and asked for a receipt. "One more question," I added. "You told me you've known Fred Hamilton for years. How'd you get to know him?"

"We were on staff together at the Campus. Shared a room, along with ten other guys. They kicked me out a year and a half ago, for thinking for myself—asking questions and being critical." He shrugged again. "You live in the church like that a while, it takes some adjusting to live in the real world again. For some people it's pretty bad, so I started this place."

"Got it," I said. "Where'd you get the money?"

"To start this? Same way I got money before I joined. In the ring." He grinned. "I wasn't much for finesse, but people liked to watch me. Now I run this place on money from people I help, after they get their feet on the ground. People like Fred. Or from their families." He held up the bills. "And now and then someone like you, who wants a line to one of them."

Then he gave me a receipt and I left, hoping he was making it all right. Providing a service that depended on gratitude for pay sounded pretty uncertain to me.

Back at the office I read the book by Christman. It was kind of fascinating, actually. I could see how it might hook people. My main problem with it was, I kept dozing off, interest notwithstanding. Then I checked out early and went to the health club for an hour before going home.

That evening at 7:57, my phone rang. It was Hamilton. He looked older than I'd expected, probably in his thirties, intelligent and well groomed. I asked him if I could record our conversation and he said, "Sure, go ahead."

The guy at Withdrawal Assistance had told him what I was after, but Hamilton waited for me to ask. "Gloria lives right there at the Campus," he answered. "When she first joined church staff, on the same day we got married, the church sent her to Australia for a while, to put distance between her and her parents. She had money—she'd emptied out her checking account at Pacific Grove—so while she was in Australia, she bought 'soul salvage' and 'spiritual enlightenment,' a couple of counseling levels. When she got back to L.A., she was broke." He grinned ruefully. "And a dedicated Gnostie, like her husband."

"They kick her out too, did they?"

He chuckled. "She was on the Board of Review that kicked me out! She'd decided her husband was an evil person who was trying to drag mankind the rest of the way into ruin by harming the church. Right after that she filed for divorce. I tried to get custody of our baby girl, but no luck. She already had a would-be stepfather lined up for her. Gloria is Gloria Hebner now."

Angela DeSmet was not going to be thrilled. "What's your daughter's name?" I asked him.

"Spirit," he said. "Nice, eh?"

"How do you raise a kid on ten dollars a week?"

He grunted, and smiled a small wry smile. "You don't.

In L.A. the staff lives in, and the church raises their kids.
More or less. Unmarried staff members sleep in double-
and triple-deck bunks in dorm rooms. Married staff couples
get a small room to themselves in an old dorm wing, and
share a coed community bathroom with about twenty
others. Fun. Especially when the plumbing screws up, or
someone uses newspaper for toilet paper, and a commode
floods. That happens quite a bit, because you have to
provide your own toilet paper, and sometimes you're broke.
Lots of weeks we didn't get that ten. Five maybe, or
nothing.

"The children live in another building, on a floor
called the Child Nurture Center. You get to see them
during 'parents' hour'—that's actually for half an hour
after supper—unless your supervisor decides there's something more important you should be doing."

He was rambling. I let him.

"The Child Nurture Center is really bad. Complain-
ing about it got me in trouble more than once. It's dirty,
for one thing. A goddamn roach nest. And most of the
time the kids have head lice. Twice a year, before the
semiannual inspection by the County, the church assigns
a bunch of parents to clean the place thoroughly and
delouse the kids. The rest of the time, the church gives
it bottom priority, because time and money spent on it
don't produce income."

"Why do the parents put up with it?"

He grimaced. "They believe the church is out to save
the world from an evil conspiracy. Sacrifices are necessary."

There was that word: *evil*. I told him the thought that
had come to me in the Saints' Deli. He grinned lopsid-
edly. "There's individual evil in the church, sure, but the
major problem isn't evil, it's ignorance and incompetence
taken to a whole new level by incredible arrogance."

He went on to tell me more about the Child Nurture
Center—a gross story of filth, mismanagement, and
neglect. That spring, the ages one-to-six section was down
to just two nannies; the rest had run away, deserted. Just
two nannies, each working alone on a twelve-hour shift,

taking care of rambunctious, undisciplined little children plus some babies in diapers; about thirty in all. After several days, one of the two remaining nannies disappeared—grabbed her own kid and took off.

"Somehow," he told me, "the one nanny who was left held on for more than thirty hours alone—no sleep, no meal breaks—until one of the Central Chancery execs showed up, an arrogant twenty-year-old little bitch named Janie Blitz. Some parent had come to get her kid for parents' hour, and complained, so Janie came storming over. Gloria and I had just come back with Spirit, and we saw the whole thing. Instead of getting help for Trudy, Janie started raising hell with her, actually screaming at her, because the place was such a mess. 'Look at that!' she yelled, and pointed. 'You're so fucking lazy, you can't even put the lid back on the fucking diaper pail!'

"That's when Trudy broke. She was a big strapping girl, and had a juice pitcher in her hand. First she threw the juice in Janie's face, and before Janie could stop sputtering, bonged her on the head with the empty stainless-steel pitcher. Then she grabbed her by the hair and threw her down. After thirty hours without rest, she must have been running on fumes, but right then she had the strength of a Kodiak bear, and when Janie hit the deck, Trudy started kicking her.

"Gloria was shrieking obscenities at Trudy by then, and trying to help Janie, which tells you something about what Gloria had become. But I held her back. When Trudy got tired of kicking, she took a diaper pail, half full of dirty diapers soaking in detergent, and emptied the whole mess on Janie, then jammed the pail on her head.

"That's when I got hysterical. I laughed myself nearly sick, then let go of Gloria and left the building. I should have walked right on off the Campus, but—" He paused, shook his head. "I was too brainwashed. I hate to use the term, it's been politicized for so long, and the meaning's so vague and stretched out of shape. But it's the best term we've got.

"Within the hour, Janie and Gloria had reported me to

the Morals Police, for not rescuing Janie or letting Gloria try. And for laughing, the ultimate insult. The next day they held a Board of Review, and offered me a chance for restitution and correction: I could volunteer to serve on the SRC—that's the Spiritual Reclamation Crew, which I won't try to describe—and when I got out I'd be assigned as a nanny. Or I could be expelled—kicked out. I told them to kiss my ass."

He was shaking his head, remembering. "That sounds as if I didn't give a damn, as if I was pretty independent. And at the moment I thought I was. Then the reaction set in, and I left in shock, in grief. I'd been kicked out, lost my marriage, maybe my kid . . . And my eternal salvation. I still believed!" He looked at me via his phone screen, and shook his head with a small rueful grin.

We talked for two or three minutes more, then he gave me his name and his Denver address and phone number, and Gloria's address, and we disconnected. I had the phone print out the conversation, and gave it to Carlos the next day, along with my dictated write-up summarizing the case. In my summary, I left out the details of the Child Nurture Center, and Carlos said I did the right thing on that: We weren't hired to describe the conditions that Angela DeSmet's granddaughter lived in, and besides, Hamilton could have been exaggerating, although I didn't think so. As wild as the story was, something about the man made me believe him. Then Carlos faxed the report to Angela DeSmet, along with the paperwork, and transferred to her what she had coming back on her deposit.

And that, I thought, was the end of that. The Church of the New Gnosis might not be evil—after all, it had let Hamilton simply walk away—but it was ugly and unpleasant, and I was glad to be done with it.

I never imagined how much criminality I'd find connected with it, though I've had to rethink the word *evil* since then.

3
BUTZBURGER

It was last April, the thirteenth, that we got the real case, the case of Christman's disappearance. When a guy named Armand Butzburger came in about a contract.

He'd talked to Joe on the phone the day before, and Joe and Carlos had discussed it and decided they wanted me to do the job. I'd been raised from investigative assistant to junior investigator after I'd located Gloria DeSmet for her mother, and to full investigator after I solved the case of Arthur Ashkenazi, the twice-killed astronomer. I'd done some pretty good work in between, too, but when I picked that one apart, they decided I was a real sherlock.

So when Butzburger arrived at Joe's office for his interview, Joe called Carlos and me to come down, and introduced us.

Butzburger's a wealthy "New Gnu"—people pronounce it "New Guh-new"—a polite name for a Gnostie, which is pronounced without the G. And what he told us was that Ray Christman, the Gnostie guru, hadn't been seen in public since last October or maybe September. Within his church, Ray Christman had been a highly visible man, but now and then, for whatever reason, he'd disappear from the Campus for a few weeks or even a month or more, so for a while, people didn't think anything about it.

Then, in December, the church held its annual big Christmas event at the New Palladium in Hollywood. A really great-looking woman named Marcy Mannheim conducted the opening ceremony. Which was something Christman traditionally did. The proceedings were always taped, and the tapes sold for twenty bucks each. Every New Gnu was expected to buy one. Butzburger had brought his with him, and played it for us on Joe's wall screen.

What Mannheim said to the crowd was, "In October, Ray went to stay at the Ranch, to do concentrated research on Freed Being. And after a while"—she paused there to tighten their attention—"after a while, things began to break for him." She paused again, and the place exploded with applause and cheering. She let them clap and shout for maybe a minute, then with a motion, cut them off. Like she'd pulled their plug. "Finally," she went on, "early in December, Ray left the Ranch for a location where he could continue his work in virtually complete solitude, in an environment totally uncontaminated with activities of any kind, except for such basic matters as the preparation of meals. He has only one person with him to see to his needs. He plans to stay where he is until he's worked out the complete road, the full procedures, and the state of Freed Being is ready to deliver to the public!"

She stopped again, and for a long few seconds the place was quiet as a mortuary, as if the crowd was stunned. Then once more it exploded with wild cheering. After a few seconds of that, Butzburger turned off the tape.

"That's all of it that's relevant to my problem," he said, and looked around at us with steady blue eyes. Somehow they reminded me of the red-brown eyes of the guy at the withdrawal assistance office. "I could accept what Marcy told us," he went on. "In fact I did accept it, without hesitation. But since then? . . . Since then there's been evidence and rumor of a power struggle within the Church's top executive strata. Replete with expulsions of executives, then reinstatements and amnesties, then more expulsions. Which certainly supports the power-struggle rumors."

His eyes moved to me and stopped. "To appreciate that,

you need to realize that within the Gnostic community, rumors are rare. We are not—*not*—a gossiping people. So this has concerned me. It's been three and a half months since the Christmas event, and nothing more has been heard from Ray, at least not publicly. And if he was around, even on a remote island in the Indian Ocean or someplace like that, he'd know, be psychically aware of, anything like a power struggle within his Church. And take immediate and effective steps to end it.

"This does not seem to have happened, and I'm troubled by it. It may seem unreal to you, *but Ray Christman is the hope of mankind and the world,* so I want you to find him for me, and find out whether he's all right." Butzburger's gaze fell away then. "It may be that I'm simply lacking in faith," he added slowly, "and that what I'm doing here is harmful to his cause. I'm not as—perceptive as I should be; I'm well aware of that. But I've decided." He looked back up at me, then at Joe. "I realize that this is a very difficult undertaking. It may well prove impossible. But my attorney tells me that Prudential is the best investigation firm in the country, probably the world, and very ethical. So if you're interested in the case, I'm ready to discuss an agreement."

That's when I left the room; the negotiating aspects weren't anything I needed to sit through. Prudential has a standard contract with standard clauses. Individual agreements can vary within limits, but we're expensive. That's why most of our contracts are with corporations and government agencies, especially the city and state. Documented reports would be sent to Butzburger at regular intervals and sometimes in between.

I figured he must have deep pockets, and wondered how someone like him got mixed up with something like the Church of the New Gnosis. I'd thought of it as an outfit that attracted the weak and wishful, not the strong and wealthy. I knew it had wealthy members, but to the extent I'd thought about it, I'd assumed they were playboys and playgirls who'd inherited their money. Butzburger didn't seem to fit that image.

❖   ❖   ❖

I went to my office and started calling stuff up on my computer from the L.A. City Library, mostly articles in the *L.A. Times*. I read about 800 to 1,200 words a minute, maybe the most useful single skill I have, and I was getting quite an education. After about half an hour, someone knocked at my door. It was Butzburger; he wanted to know if I'd have lunch with him, his treat.

He'd already called a cab. We rode to downtown Hollywood, to Musso and Frank's Grill. It's a place where you're apt to find yourself at a table near some holo star. But we didn't; he'd reserved a small private room. He wanted to ask questions, to get a better feel for the kind of guy who'd be working for him. Until I'd finished my ranch-size prime rib, though, all he made was small talk. Then, while we waited for dessert, he asked about my earlier case involving the church. Without naming names or going into the matter of the Child Nurture Center, I gave him the picture.

"So your experience is very limited," he said.

"With the church, right. Most of what I know, I have from news articles. I was reading one of them when you knocked." He nodded. I could see he wanted to say something and was trying to decide whether he should. Or more likely how. Finally he asked for my initial view of the case.

"Usually," I told him, "we go into a case with definite evidence of a crime, and a set of additional information that seems pertinent. And work from there. This time we don't have much, which is going to make it tough. And what will make it tougher is that the church is— It's been described as impenetrable, and that fits my experience. Mine and others'. If the church is right, and Mr. Christman is holed up in some out-of-the-way place doing his research, they're not going to give me his address. So the best way to approach it is to look for evidence of kidnaping or murder."

Again Butzburger nodded. "There is evil on this planet, Mr. Seppanen, and the Church has many enemies. People, governments—forces that want to harm it. Destroy it if they can, legally or otherwise. Thus it has to be impenetrable. Impenetrable and formidable."

There was that word again: *evil.* "Right," I said. "And those enemies are another part of the problem. If he's not lying up somewhere, then it seems highly probable that someone's killed him."

Butzburger's face pinched a little.

"As you said," I went on, "the church has a lot of enemies. It was born with enemies, and it's created a lot more, with lawsuits, the breaking up of families . . . things like that. There are a lot of people who'd like to see Ray Christman dead. So the opening question becomes who had the resources and the opportunity.

"I presume that Mr. Christman went around well guarded. The buildings on the Campus have guards at the entrances. That I know. At least the Neophyte Building does. And that nine-foot chain-link fence around the parking lot, with the razor wire on top, is obviously HardSteel. Plus I noticed men on the roofs who aren't up there to enjoy the view. So he wasn't all that vulnerable."

I was thinking out loud, feeling my way through the situation. "The Institute of Noetic Technology might have the necessary resources. They certainly regard themselves as the church's enemy, and when they lost that lawsuit against the church, and their appeal, they probably figured they had no further legal recourse. If they still wanted revenge, they'd have to get it some other way.

"Then there's the COGS, the Church of God in Science. Or actually its various and apparently numerous extremist groups. There's got to be some well-heeled people among them. They'd be nearly impossible to investigate, because the extremist groups don't have formal memberships. Mostly they seem to be ad hoc groups, and they're all hostile to anyone who asks questions. We can assume that various local police agencies throughout the country have moles in them, along with the FBI, but they certainly aren't going to give us any information about Christman, assuming there is any and they have it."

Butzburger was taking it pretty well. He looked serious but not upset. "My guess," I went on, "is that neither of those groups has the expertise necessary to get to Mr.

Christman and kidnap him. But presumably they have the money necessary to contract the job out to some underworld outfit that does have that expertise. And it would make sense for them to contract with an L.A. mob—people who know the city. So one thing I'll do is talk to information sources in the underworld, and see what they may have heard.

"Then there are the families of converts who've broken their family ties and joined the church. Especially those who've joined church staffs. How many centers are there, worldwide? Seventy-eight?"

"Something like that."

"So the number of hostile family members has got to be large," I went on. "Again though, the only way they could get at Christman would seem to be through the underworld.

"But why would any of these want Christman to disappear quietly? It would be a lot easier to have him ambushed, or his office bombed—something like that."

I paused, examining the man sitting across from me, his face, his eyes. "I'll look into all those possibilities as best I can. But I'll tell you, Mr. Butzburger, if Mr. Christman has been kidnaped or quietly killed, it's likeliest to have been by some faction within the church. They had access to him. They knew his habits, his patterns of movement, his vulnerabilities. They could approach him without arousing his suspicion.

"You talked about a power struggle in the hierarchy. I can imagine a faction that is less interested in saving the world than in getting rich and powerful." Actually I could imagine both factions like that. "And the Church of the New Gnosis has a large income, even if the published estimates are high by a factor of ten. Maybe one of those factions feels that they could really take over if Christman was out of the way."

Butzburger didn't argue—he didn't even look as if he'd like to—and that was the end of our business conversation. All that was left was dessert. I don't think he enjoyed his cheesecake.

4
TAILED?

Back at the office, I phoned a few information sources. Most of them, though, I'd have to go out and contact personally. Almost all were loners on the fringe of the underworld, who lived with their ears open.

The best of them wasn't part of the fringe. She was on the inside—a Korean-American woman, "Miss Melanie." She was one I'd have to talk to in person. Melanie runs a large stable of expensive call girls—Asian, Eurasian, Anglo, Afro-American, and Chicanas. She even had her own clinical service. She also had the protection of the Korean mafia, probably paying for it with the services of her girls and with information the girls picked up. Information about rip-off possibilities, underworld activities—things like that. Occasionally she helped us out, for a healthy fee, with information about people or groups in competition with the Koreans.

One thing she never did though, she told me once. "Melanie," she said, referring to herself in the third person, "never does blackmail." It would kill the goose that laid the golden eggs.

When I'd finished my phone calls to information sources, I called up the directory to see if Gnostic Withdrawal Assistance still existed. It did. The same guy answered, and he still did business on the same basis at the same location. I told him I'd be there that afternoon, and that he probably wouldn't recognize me.

Then I had Larry, in our technical section, make me up—nothing ambitious, but misleading—and fit me out with some clothes. He darkened my complexion and my hair, and gave me brown eyes and a mustache. And a driver's license with a Turkish name. No one was going to talk Turkish to me, that was almost certain, and if I wanted to, I could swear in Finnish and pretend it was Turkish.

The makeup job didn't take long. Larry is fast. Afterward I called Tuuli, my wife, and told her I'd be home late. Probably very late. Then I went to Gnostic Withdrawal Assistance, and said I wanted to know about another missing person. He agreed to give my name and number to two recent exiles, plus Fred Hamilton again; Hamilton wasn't at his old number anymore. I also told him what I'd told Tuuli—that I'd be home late. They could leave a message on my phone.

The rest of the day I spent talking with assorted bartenders, pimps, hustlers, bail bondsmen, pawn brokers, and Miss Melanie. I wasn't optimistic, but I needed to cover all the bases. I stopped at Melanie's last. She gave me tea, and we agreed on charges.

Then I drove back to the office to get my personal car. It was full night by then, though with the sky-glow from street lights, headlights, windows, and signs, night in L.A. isn't very dark. Not like Hemlock Harbor, Michigan. As I drove my car out of the company lot, I noticed another, a late-model sea blue Hyundai, stopped across the street in the entrance of the Beverly Drugstore parking lot. The driver, it seemed to me afterward, had been black, with a close beard. I paused and waved for him to pull out first; he'd been there ahead of me. But he didn't move, so I pulled out. When I turned east on Beverly, so did he, which didn't have to mean a thing; I barely noticed. But when I turned north on Fairfax and he turned too, I wondered, so I doubled back west on

Rosewood; if he'd done the same, I'd have been pretty sure. But he didn't. He had the chance but continued north on Fairfax.

He could have been innocent, or he could have recognized that I was testing him. Whatever. He was gone.

5
HAMILTON

Two calls were recorded on my phone when I got home, with numbers to call the next day, a Saturday. They were from two of the ex-Gnosties, but not Hamilton. I didn't really know why I wanted to talk with Hamilton anyway. He'd been out for three years. I guess because I'd liked his frankness and intelligence when I'd talked with him before.

Tuuli would bawl me out for working on weekends if I didn't really have to. So I waited till she went out for groceries, then called them back. The first exile had worked on the church's in-house magazine, and simply deserted. He was totally soured on the church, but totally devoted to Christman. When I told him the missing person I was interested in was Christman, he told me he was sure that Christman was too psychic to be abducted or physically harmed! His view was that the great guru had withdrawn from the church "to punish it for its degeneracy and aberrations."

He hadn't heard anything about a power struggle, though he was aware of the rash of expulsions and cancellations. I got the impression he wasn't very bright.

The second exile was a "technical compliances enforcer," who got kicked out when he refused to coerce the San

Diego church to suspend counselors for what upper management had decided were technical errors. I had no idea at all what he was talking about. My reading hadn't dealt with "technical" aspects.

He was aware of two factions, one led by Lon Thomas, president of the church, and the other by a Frank Evanson, who was "the director of technical practices." The guy was very cynical about both the church and Ray Christman, whom he considered had abandoned "his crusade" and was only interested in how rich he could get. Nothing I'd read, including Christman's book for beginners, had said anything about a crusade, either.

The guy believed that Christman was probably dead, most likely assassinated by an insider with a grudge. He didn't think that either faction would have Christman killed, even if they wanted to, because "with Christman dead, the great moneymaking machine will grind to a halt." The claim that Christman had gone off to do research, he said, was a fraud, to hide his death. "But it won't work forever. When the church doesn't come through with procedures leading to Freed Being, people will get smart and see through it, and leave."

Killed by an insider with a grudge! He'd only been guessing, but it could be. And the church would probably hide it. I had virtually zero chance of finding out, from an organization like the Church of the New Gnosis.

When Tuuli got home, we took a commuter airbus to Santa Barbara. I love L.A., but in Santa Barbara the air is softer than anywhere else in the known universe. We strolled around and snacked and shopped, neither of us actually buying much. Tuuli likes to look, and I kind of do too. One place we went was Nielsen's Dairy, where we sat outside under an awning and had about a dozen different flavors of rich, rich ice cream. I could almost feel myself getting fat. Tuuli can eat like that and stay tiny, but that's not how it works with me at all.

When we got home, Fred Hamilton had called and left his number. A local number. I called him right away, Tuuli notwithstanding. He was living in West Hollywood, working as a stockbroker, and admittedly was out of touch with what was going on in the church.

I asked him how a would-be abductor might have gone about getting his hands on Christman.

"Look," he said, "I have a friend with me now, from out of town. Will tomorrow be all right? I'd like to meet you. We'll eat out somewhere, on me."

"Sure." Obviously he'd come a long way from the Gnostie exile who needed to bum a phone call, to ask his parents for bus fare.

"There's a little place on La Cienega," he said, "near Willoughby. Called Yolanda's. It's hard to miss; got a conspicuous sign, and tables with awnings out front for nice weather. Suppose I meet you there at noon, for brunch?"

"Um. Would earlier be possible? On Sundays my wife and I usually eat lunch together at home. It's gotten to be sort of a tradition."

"Actually, earlier would be better for me, too. My company's heading out early tomorrow, flying back to Seattle, so I'll be up at seven anyway."

We settled on breakfast at eight-thirty. It turned out to be a good hour; there weren't a lot of people there, and most of them were eating outside. We took a booth in a back corner. Yolanda's was a health food kind of place, though the food turned out to be excellent. I ordered black coffee, a stuffed bell pepper, and buttermilk, trying to make up for yesterday's ice-cream binge. "Real buttermilk or cultured?" the waitress asked. When I lived with my half brother, Sulo, after dad and mom were killed, I used to drink real, homemade buttermilk. Eila made it when she churned butter. I hadn't realized you could get it in L.A. It came from Altadena Dairy, the waitress said. She looked Hispanic, so I told her, "Real then. *Leche cuajada.*"

She laughed. "I think I'd better bring you *suero de mantequilla,*" she said.

Which left me unsure whether I'd made a real mistake, or if it was a matter of dialect. L.A.'s got about every

Spanish dialect there is, plus usages all its own. While we
waited, Hamilton and I talked, and I told him what I had
to work with. Mainly speculations.

He stirred honey into his herb tea. "Christman has, or
had, three residences," he said, "each of them well guarded.
He moved from one to another at irregular intervals by
sky limo. The main one was a luxurious penthouse apartment at the Campus, on top of the Administration Building. He was there more than anywhere else, sometimes for
extended periods. His office was in the penthouse too. It
would be nearly impossible for outsiders to get at him
there; there were too many people around. Including his
bodyguards, who were chosen for utter loyalty and obed-
ience. They were security-checked on the psychogalvanometer. He dressed them well, in civvies, and they were
trained to be totally unyielding. They carried guns, too. I
know that for a fact, because I saw one of them take off
his jacket in the restroom, and he was wearing a pistol in
a shoulder holster. Supposedly they practiced on a pistol
range somewhere beneath the Admin Building."

The theory of a gangland hit, never very compelling,
began to shrivel.

"Another place he lived is called 'the Ranch.' It's out
in the Imperial Valley, backed up against the Vallecito
Mountains, southwest of the Salton Sea. Supposed to be
forty acres. I was there a few times when I was a courier
in the church's Executive Communications Section. It was
surrounded by a twelve-foot chain-link fence—HardSteel
topped by razor wire—with little towers at the back cor-
ners where they weren't conspicuous. Watchmen sat in them
with radios and guns, watching the fence. At night there
were lights here and there along it so they could see if
anyone came up to it, colored lights so they wouldn't seem
like a security thing, although they were.

"Inside the fence it was beautifully landscaped. Had been
when he got it. All the way around, there were rows of
Washingtonia palms—the real tall, skinny ones—alternating
with tall, stout date palms. And irrigated Bermuda grass
lawns, and marvelous gardens. Fountains played constantly,

and there were pools with exotic carp, red and white and gold. At night, colored lights would play on the fountains, except when Ray was stargazing. Then they were turned off.

"A really nice place. Makes being rich seem worthwhile. He'd go there off and on in the winter, though we never knew when in advance. Especially when L.A. had one of its stormy, rainy winters. On a February day when it was gray and wet and chilly at the Campus, it'd be sunny and warm at the Ranch. Maybe a little windy. He'd host rich churchies there, rich members, especially Europeans or Japanese or Brazilians, when he wanted to pitch some expensive project to them. He always preferred to spend other people's money.

"He'd had an observation deck built on the roof of his residence there—we called it 'the hacienda'—with an expensive telescope, and he'd go out and stargaze at night." Hamilton laughed. "I remember being shocked at a thought I had: *If Ray can leave his body*—that's the soul going for an outing, you understand, the body being left to run on automatic—*if Ray can leave his body like that, which was supposed to be nothing for him, he should be able to go out into space and look at any star he wants to, from as close as he'd like. So why use a telescope?*"

Hamilton chuckled. "At the time it seemed like a terrible, heretical thought.

"There was a bigger tower near the back, screened from the hacienda by tall date palms. It was said to have electronic scanners, and supposedly surface-to-air missiles in case of aerial attack. That could have been a rumor, of course, the part about the missiles. It's hard to know."

I interrupted. "I've been told by a church member that in the church, rumors are rare."

Hamilton laughed again. "That may be true of rumors about controversial or negative matters; it's considered evil to pass along bad rumors. But there were always rumors about what wonderful things Ray was doing or was going to do. Churchies feed on them; they're nourished by them. They don't think of them as rumors.

"His third residence is called 'the Hideaway,' on 160

acres of private land inside the Willamette National Forest. In Oregon, in the Cascade Mountains. I was there just once, as a courier. There's a log lodge in virgin forest, beautiful, and the whole place is surrounded by a security fence. I guess you know how tough it is to get through a HardSteel fence, and any disturbance of it—someone climbing it, or a tree falling on it, anything like that—would set off alarms and flashing lights in the guardhouse. And of course, there's the usual razor wire on top.

"The fence is patrolled twenty-four hours a day, or it was, by armed patrols with German police dogs." He chuckled. "Makes Ray sound paranoid, and I guess he was, at least a little. But apparently people did try to get in. Supposedly several were injured on the razor wire at different times, trying to get over the fence at night. At least that's the story. Guards picked them up and called the sheriff, and meanwhile their injuries were treated in the little clinic at the lodge. When the sheriff got there, he hauled them to town.

"Ray didn't spend a lot of time up there; it was too far. But now and then he'd go, maybe during a bad hot spell in summer. And when there was a storm on the sun, and northern lights were forecast. Ray loved the northern lights. I think he got high on them. Oregon's a lot farther north, and there's no light pollution at the Hideaway. The word was that he'd fly up there to watch.

"There was a stony ridge that sort of wrapped around where the buildings were, with a foot trail up to the top. He'd had a little observatory built up there for stargazing. I've seen it. I guess Ray had a thing about the stars.

"He seldom traveled, except between those places. So if anyone kidnaped or killed him, it was probably at one of them, or traveling between them. Unless he changed his habits since three years ago."

The waitress brought our food while he was telling me about the observatory, and we pretty much stopped talking to eat. When we were done, we skipped dessert. He sipped his tea and I worked on a refill of my coffee.

"Fred," I said, "I'd like to ask a personal question. Or

maybe several of them. Tell me to stuff them if you feel like it."

He grinned. "Shoot."

"How much do you make a year now?"

"Huh! It's hard to say for this year. A hundred and twenty thou last year."

A hundred and twenty thou. About two and a half times the national average for families. "I haven't talked to many New Gnus," I told him, "and most that I have talked to, worked for the church as staff members. I got the impression, though, that they weren't too bright. But the guy at Gnostic Withdrawal Assistance . . . ?"

"Gerald. Gerald Williams."

"Gerald not only seemed smart; he had something. Had it together, you could say. That's the impression I got. And a wealthy guy I talked to yesterday, who's a totally dedicated New Gnu, or seems to be, made somewhat the same impression. And today, you. Why the difference?"

Fred grunted. "First," he said, "there are simply differences between people, for whatever reasons. In the church as well as out. Also, strange as it may seem to you, Ray's counseling procedures do help people. They don't do everything he claims for them, by half, but they help. A lot. And a lot of staff members never get any of them. I did, and Gerald did, because we managed to get ourselves trained as counselors, and counselors are allowed time to counsel each other.

"Most members *not* on staff have had quite a lot of counseling. That's where probably ninety-nine percent of the money comes from. They tend to be in good shape, mentally and emotionally—except in matters concerning the church. Concerning the church, they tend very strongly to be obedient, even robotic."

Robotic. I remembered the staff member I'd talked to in the Neophyte Building. She didn't think; she recited.

"And then there's the matter of in or out," Hamilton went on. "For most of the time I was in, ten years, I was a good little robot. I believed what I was told to believe, and rejected what I was told to reject. In the midst of a

whole lot of evidence to the contrary. Sometimes—quite
often, actually—I noticed the contrast between what I saw
and the way things were said to be or supposed to be. And
I always found an excuse for them. Then, for a while, I
was a sort of secret questioner. Finally the effects accumulated, and I got myself kicked out.

"Within days after leaving, I began to see a lot of things
more clearly. More freely. It was like I'd been colorblind,
and was starting to see color. People who've been in the
church, who've gotten counseling and then left, tend to do
better personally than before they'd gotten in. Sometimes
a lot better."

"Do many of them leave?"

"Martti, *most* of them leave. A big majority of them.
The biggest product of the Church of the New Gnosis
is ex-members."

That was something I hadn't been aware of. Somehow
it made me feel better about the church; it was less a trap
than I'd thought. My coffee was cold, and I signaled the
waitress for a refill. When I had it, I asked, "How much
money do people usually spend on counseling?"

"In my case, nothing. I discovered New Gnosticism as
a college senior, a finance major, and quit before I graduated, to join staff. I didn't have any money. But there are
lots of people, wealthy people, who've spent more than a
quarter million." I sat stunned. *A quarter million!* It seemed
impossible, even considering prices of up to a thousand
dollars an hour I'd read about for counseling. "How . . . Why
does anyone spend that much money on a cult?"

He smiled a small smile. "There are enough unusual
truths, or what feel like truths, in the books and introductory lectures, to get you curious. Maybe even hopeful; even
excited. Me, I got excited. And particularly if you're dissatis-
fied with your life, or the world, you may decide you want
to look into it further. Then, if you get some counseling—
The results of getting counseling, particularly the more basic
levels, can seem miraculous: old fears and worries gone,
old grim moods, old regrets, old grudges, old psychosomatic
conditions. Gone! Crap you thought you were stuck with

for life! So you think, *Jesus! This stuff works miracles!* And you keep expecting more. Ray was always promising more and more up the road."

Fred had started quivering, trembling, as he talked about it. It was pretty strange, because his voice, his eyes, seemed perfectly calm.

"While at the same time," he went on, "he fed us a line that this was all part of a crusade, that the human race was doomed unless we got everyone in the world into the church. And that, of course, was going to take *lots* of money and *lots* of dedication. The church was an embattled army fighting to save humanity. And like any army, ours had to be *obedient. Unquestioning.* Also, it could be destroyed from inside, by subtle deviations in teaching and procedures. So absolute orthodoxy was vital, and continuous vigilance— an uncompromising ruthlessness with anything done differently than Ray said."

With that he stopped, sat dead in the water for a minute, then took a sip of tea. "Sound like anything else you ever heard of?" he asked.

To some degree or another, it seemed to me, most cults were like that; some mainstream religions were too. "It must be a relief to be out of it," I said.

His smile was rueful. "It is and it isn't. Being out has left a hole. For me, dealing stocks is a way to get money. Beyond that, it's neither satisfying nor important. I'm looking for something that is. And that's not easy, when you've been burned like I was."

We didn't say anything more for a couple of minutes. I started wishing I'd ordered dessert. Finally I asked, "Do you have any thoughts about what may have happened to Ray Christman?"

He shook his head. His eyes focused again, and he came out of whatever he'd been in. "No. No I don't. Every possibility I can think of seems unlikely. He may have simply taken off with a bunch of the loot, to live somewhere as an anonymous rich American. That's probably the best bet."

That stunned me. It seemed so damned logical! And

obvious! And I hadn't thought of it before. "Tell you what," he said, and he sounded all business now. "I'll give you the name of a woman, an ex-churchie like me, who may be the best-informed person there is on the church. Outside its upper executive levels. She has sources everywhere, sucks in contacts and information like a black hole. The difference being, she'll let it back out when she feels like it.

"Even churchies talk to her. She's probably the only outie I know who has information sources inside. And she's never been expelled—kicked out. It's supposed to be automatic to expel anyone as evil who openly quits the church, but she's never been expelled."

He gave me the phone number and address of a woman called Molly Cadigan, a business consultant who worked out of her home. "She's informal," he said, "and may not make a great first impression, but she's smart. I've seen her in action. The first time I met her, she gave me some free advice, and it worked like a bomb. I cashed in. Since then I buy her advice, and it's always good. She's not in it to get rich, either. She doesn't go looking for business. She's content to make a comfortable living, and lives the way she pleases, does what she likes.

"She's a well of information, not only about the church, but about its enemies. And so far as I know, she doesn't sell that kind of information—not to individuals. She gives it away. Although she might charge a corporation like yours."

He emptied his cup and didn't pour any more. Apparently we were about done.

"She was an early member," he continued, "one of the founding members. Before that she was a Noetie—one of Leif Haller's followers. Beginning in her teens. But she was always self-determined. She quit the Noeties when Haller began to demand conformity. Later she quit the church for the same reason.

"Since I've been out," Hamilton went on, "I've met a lot of ex-churchies, some of them oldtimers like Molly. And they tell stories. One of them is that Molly was Ray

Christman's girlfriend, once upon a time. That may be why she never got expelled."

I left the restaurant knowing that Molly Cadigan was someone I wanted to talk to.

6
MOLLY CADIGAN

Reading the *L.A. Times* at my desk the next morning, I found an item that jarred me. *"Gerald Williams, owner and operator of a firm called Gnostic Withdrawal Assistance, was arrested yesterday on a charge of possessing for sale a quantity of crack cocaine."* Crack has long since been out of style, but it still has its users.

Anyway that rocked me back in my chair. Williams a pusher? I didn't believe it.

He was being held in lieu of $50,000 bail.

I got on the phone to the LAPD and identified myself, explaining that Williams was an information source for me in an investigation. I asked to speak to the officer in charge of the case. A Lieutenant Emiliano Gonzaga accepted the call. My name was familiar to him. He told me they'd gotten their tipoff from a teenaged kid named Joseph R. Minnis.

"I can't help but wonder," I said, "if Joseph R. Minnis isn't a Gnostie. Or was put up to it by the Gnosties."

"You're not the first to wonder," he told me. "We're looking into it. So far as we can determine, Minnis isn't a Gnostie, but he is a street hustler on the make.

"We found the package in Williams' restroom cabinet, with the extra soap, scouring powder, and TP. And failed to find his prints on it, or anyone else's. It could have been left there by anyone. We've also verified that he lets street people use his restroom. If we don't get firmer evidence against him today, we plan to release him late this afternoon."

Gonzaga paused and grinned. "Incidentally, my office has taken half a dozen calls like yours. Williams has lots of friends."

I hadn't foreseen that, but it didn't surprise me. "Thanks, Lieutenant," I told him, and we disconnected. I felt pretty burned. I was sure the church had set Williams up, and right then I really wanted to get something on them: hopefully Ray Christman's murder. Assuming, of course, that Christman had been murdered.

When I'd finished the paper, I called Molly Cadigan's number and caught her at home. I explained who I was, and told her I was investigating Christman's disappearance. We agreed to meet at her place at ten o'clock, which gave me plenty of time. Briarcliff Drive is in the Hollywood Hills, but it's not one of those winding little goat-trail streets that appear and disappear up there. It's easy to find and keep track of.

So on a hunch, I went out of my way to swing by the Campus, and parked in the church's lot. I stopped in at the Saints' Deli to look at the notice board. Sure as hell, there was a *Times* fax right in the middle, with everything else moved back a little to draw attention to it. Next I went into the Neophyte Building and found one on the notice board in their reception area, edged with red tape to make it hard to overlook. A typed note beneath it read: "This is the kind of person who attack Ray adn the Church. And this the kind of thig that happen to them." Replete with typos and poor grammar on church notepaper. I wondered how the church could favorably impress someone like Armand Butzburger. If someone typed for him like that, he'd fire their ass in a minute, I was willing to bet.

When I came out, I saw a guy across the street and down a ways, sitting on the edge of a planter lighting a cigarette. A lightish-brown black guy with a short beard. Minutes earlier he'd been going into the deli when I was just about to leave. I couldn't help wondering.

So I sat down on a bench and pretended to check through my pocket notebook, waiting to see what he'd do. After a minute he got up, crossed the street, and walked into the Neophyte Building. I put my notebook back in my pocket and went to my car, where I sat and waited. Five minutes later he came into the lot and drove away in a somewhat beat-up red Chevy. Not a sea blue Hyundai. False alarm, I decided, and left.

Next I drove past Gnostic Withdrawal Assistance, which was pretty much on my way. There was space at the curb, so I stopped by. The place was open, with a white guy at the desk now. He wasn't as big as Williams, but he made the same kind of impression: straight, competent, fearless. I introduced myself; his name was Eric Fuentes.

"Gerald may be back pretty soon," I said, and told him what Lt. Gonzaga had told me.

He laughed. "It figures. The church's been caught in enough dirty tricks that people distrust them automatically."

Then I told him about finding the *Times* faxes at Saints' Deli and in the Neophyte Building. He gave a wry grin. "Right," he said. "It's the Disinformation Section in the Division of Public Relations. That's the way they operate. They're in charge of dirty tricks."

He was matter-of-fact as hell about it. I was surprised he didn't look mad, and told him so. "It's a waste of energy to get mad," he answered, "and a bigger waste to stay that way." He grinned again. "I admit I was steamed when I got here this morning and found a copy taped to our front door. And to most of the front windows along the block." He gestured at his waste basket. "I ripped 'em all off." "They actually have something they call the Disinformation Section?"

"Yeah. It's not shown on the open T.O., the table of organization that the public sees, but it's there, part of the Information Department, Division of PR."

"You must be a Gnostie exile."

"You've got it. I was a case reviewer in the Technical

Division. Got in a row with Evanson himself, and told him what I thought. A year earlier I'd have said 'yes sir,' and done what he ordered, regardless of my own judgement. My eyes had been opening since a friend of mine got kicked out by a kangaroo court."

And apparently all in the name of saving the human race. *The more I hear about them,* I thought, *the less I like them.* I wondered if Fuentes' friend was Fred Hamilton.

I looked at my watch then. It was 9:37, and I'd rather get somewhere early than late, so I left. I got there early enough that I sat in the car and listened to KFWB News Radio for a few minutes. At 9:58 I knocked at Molly Cadigan's door. A young woman opened it, wearing blue jeans, a red-and-white checkered blouse, and a small apron. I decided she must be family. "My name is Seppanen," I told her. "I have an appointment to see Ms. Cadigan." She took my card and peered at it, then turned.

"Molly!" she shouted, "it's Mister—" She stumbled and looked harder at the card. "Mr. Seppanen to see you." She said the syllables well enough, but put the accent on the second, even though I'd said it for her. That happens a lot. "Come right in, sor," she said and, turning, led me through a foyer and the living room, then into a hall, chattering as we went. Her speech was so Irish, I could hardly believe it. She gestured me into what had probably been a large bedroom originally. As no one else was there, she waited with me. It was an office now, with a big heavy table, desk, built-in bookshelves, and a Hewlett-Packard Executive VIII, about right for the Mount Wilson Observatory. Wide old-fashioned French doors stood open, with a balcony outside. The morning haze had burned off, and beyond the wrought-iron railing was a long view across the L.A. Basin, burnished by April sun and framed by the tops of eucalyptus trees lower on the ridge.

The spell was broken by the sound of flushing, and a moment later Molly Cadigan stepped out of her private bathroom. Behind me the girl left the room, leaving the door ajar. "Nice view, eh, Sweetbuns?" Molly said.

Not exactly a formal opening. "Yeah," I said, "it's beautiful."

Molly didn't sound Irish any more than most Americans who have Irish names. I decided I'd been met by a domestic instead of her daughter or niece. Cadigan was a big woman—six feet and 240 pounds, at a guess, and maybe fifty years old. With red hair that would have been carroty before it was diluted by encroaching gray. "Sit down," she said, and motioned to a chair. "You like coffee? Or tea?"

I sat. "Coffee," I told her.

She went to a stainless-steel urn on a sideboard. One of the spigots showed coffee in the glass, the other hot water, both near full. This, I thought, is a serious coffee drinker. The Insulmugs she filled held about a pint; she put one down in front of me. "Cream and sugar?"

"Both." My diet needed a break.

She put them on the table by my mug. "Doughnuts?"

I hesitated.

"They're good for you," she honked. "Chockful of vitamin sucrose."

I poured cream in my coffee—real cream by the look of it, and decided what the hell. "A doughnut would be nice."

"KATEY!" The abrupt volume almost made my ears ring. "BRING SOME DOUGHNUTS FOR MY GUEST!" Then to me: "You like chocolate?"

I sipped my pale brown coffee. It had hair on its chest. "Chocolate's my favorite," I told her.

"CHOCOLATE, KATEY!"

She looked at me again and sat down, picked up her own mug, and sipped the strong brew straight. Her eyes were interesting. Redheads most often have blue eyes, or green. Hers were chestnut brown, almost the color of Gerald Williams'.

"So you're interested in what might have happened to Ray Christman." I almost missed what she said. I was trying to picture what she might have looked like maybe twenty-five years earlier, to attract the sexual interest of the young guru. He was still a good-looking guy in news pictures as recently as a year ago.

"Uh, yeah. I'm accumulating a lot of information, but none of it points anywhere yet. One informant says Christman may simply have blown with a ton of money, and be living somewhere as an anonymous rich American."

She snorted. "Not likely. Ray was broad-spectrum greedy. He wanted a lot of things in life, and one of them was admiration—or adoration. He wanted to be something very special, and be appreciated for it."

She pursed her lips thoughtfully. "Try this one for size. Ray liked to live well—good food, good booze, good-looking women, and he smoked like a fireplace with a dead buzzard in the flue. He stayed in halfway decent shape with steam baths, vitamins, massage, occasional dieting, and periodic fits of riding an exercise bike while reading.

"He may have just dropped dead. Stroke, heart attack, something like that. If he did, and it wasn't in public, Lonnie and Evanson would sure as hell try to hide it. Ray Christman, dying of a physical illness? It would ruin his mystique! The church would have to cover it—smuggle the body out, dispose of it, and release some kind of cover story."

Katey came in with the doughnuts, each about five inches across and loaded with chocolate frosting, a whole damn platter of them, about a thousand calories each, mostly fat. She set them down between Molly and me, then left. I eyed them carefully, then took one, broke it, and dunked. I was pretty sure Molly Cadigan wouldn't mind my dunking. It tasted as good as I'd known it would.

"What do you think of the theory that someone inside the church killed him?" I asked.

"Hell, honey, anything's possible, but that's one of the less likely. I knew Ray when he was still young. Knew him well; you could even say we were close friends. People were already claiming he was psychic, but that was bullshit. He ran a bunch of interesting procedures on himself after that, but I'll bet you dollars against rabbit turds he wasn't any more psychic a year ago than he was in 1990.

"What he was was damned observant. He noticed things that even I didn't, and I'm one of the most observant people I know. He could pretty much read your emotions,

even if you were good at hiding them. By things like slight
eye movements, pupil dilation, subtle color changes in your
skin and the white of your eyes. Along with more obvious things like facial expression, fidgeting, and sweat. He
taught me some of it. If someone around him was hostile
toward him, or was trying to conceal things from him, he'd
know it, Sweetbuns, he'd know it."

I knew some of those techniques. My dad taught them
to me when I was still a preadolescent. They were part
of what made him such a good lawman. But I couldn't
do the sort of thing with them that Molly Cadigan was
claiming for Ray Christman, not reliably, and I doubted
that Christman could either.

"Incidentally," she said, "if you want to know what he
saw in me, that's me over there. And that's Ray's Corvette
behind me." She pointed at a framed photo on the cluttered wall, showing a long-legged, shapely young woman
in shorts, with a pretty face and hair like red gold. The
car was an old gas-driven machine from before geogravitic
power converters. And scarlet! Tuuli would love it.

Molly kept talking. "He used that talent to play people.
It helped make him such a great salesman. And cocksman.
Like I said, he loved the ladies, but he didn't waste his
time or cause upsets by making passes at someone who
wasn't already interested. Or at married women. He isn't—
wasn't a bastard, just self-indulgent. And most of the
people around him, including Lonnie Thomas, damn near
worshiped the man.

"So no, I don't think someone inside killed him. Not
unless they'd been PDHed, and killed him without any
advance awareness themselves of what they'd been pro-
gramed to do." She paused. "You know what PDH stands
for, don't you?"

I nodded; I'd had a period of reading spy thrillers. PDH
meant treatment by *Pain*, *Drugs*, and *Hypnosis*. To condition someone to do something, usually murder someone,
when triggered by some word, or maybe music, or something that happened. I didn't know whether such things
were possible, except in theory.

"It wouldn't be easy," she went on. "It may not even be possible to PDH someone that precisely, not without leaving them visibly strange, anyway. Maybe, just maybe, some outfit like the OSS could, but I can't see them taking Ray Christman or the church that seriously. I think they got over that sort of bullshit with Leif Haller and his Institute of Noetic Technology."

Which reminded me: Hamilton had said Molly'd been a Noetie first. "Could the Noeties have had someone kill Christman?" I asked.

She frowned. "Maybe, but I doubt it. Like I said, lots of things are possible, some of them things neither of us has thought of and probably won't.

"I was a Noetie once myself, but back in Rochester, New York, where things were different than here. And I'm way out of date on them. Matter of fact, I don't know who isn't. But I know a couple of people who may have kept some attention on them. They might have some insights for you."

She gave me two names, with addresses and phone numbers. One was a Dr. Winifred Landau Sproule—Molly gave me all three names plus the title, as if that was how the woman was referred to. She'd not only been a member of the Noetie's board of directors. Later she'd been on the board of directors of the Church of the New Gnosis, and a math professor at LACC. Now she was a research associate at the Hypernumbers Institute—the so-called "Beverly Glen Church by the Numbers." She'd also known Ray Christman "as well as anyone had," according to Molly. The other name was Olaf Sigurdsson, whom I'd heard of, a well-known psychic. Like Winifred Sproule, Sigurdsson had worked directly with the Noetie founder, Leif Haller, and eventually became estranged from him.

"They may not be any help to you," she added, "but they're interesting as hell, both of them. And who knows?"

Yeah, I thought, *who knows?* "Well then . . ." I started to get up.

"Just a minute."

I paused.

"Do you think you might try to interview anyone in the church? Lon Thomas maybe?"

"It's crossed my mind." I used her line then. "Who knows?"

"Sit down, Sweetbuns." When I had, she went on. "What do you know about church staff? And the Campus? The actual physical property?"

"The property's four square blocks, six or seven buildings, and some parking lots. And the staff? There's a lot of them, and they aren't very smart."

She snorted. "Don't underrate them. They work incredibly hard, and do what they're told. More than a few of them are even bright; they just have a blind side. They're also loyal as hell. If Lonnie Thomas tells them a cow turd is cheesecake, they ask for seconds. Otherwise most of them wouldn't be there. They'd have seen through it and blown." I found my hands breaking another doughnut. My third? Fourth? I dunked it and took a bite, remembering the things Fred Hamilton and Eric Fuentes had told me about being on church staff. Molly opened a drawer of hanging files in her desk and handed me what looked like a folded-up road map. "The latest table of organization of the church," she said. "Of the Central Chancery—the central management organization that is. Could be useful to you, and I've got a couple others."

I started to open it. "Don't look at it now," she told me. "It'll take too long, and I've got to get some phone calls made this morning. Besides, you're not going to understand a lot of it. I just want you to have an idea of how big and complicated an outfit we're talking about.

"Meanwhile, Sweetbuns, if you decide to talk to Lonnie Thomas, and if by some quirk he agrees to see you, be careful."

"I'd probably do better to talk to someone lower on the totem pole," I said. "High enough that they might know something, but not that high."

She shook her head. "Nobody's going to talk to you about anything except registering for church services or joining staff. Except Lonnie. Even Ray never gave interviews; not since the early days. Said he was consistently misquoted, and his facts altered or used out of context. Which was true. If an outsider wants an interview with someone in the church, it's Lonnie or no one. Usually no one."

She cocked an eye at me. "And if you plan to join staff and snoop from inside, forget it. Anyone who wants to join staff gets grilled on a sort of lie detector first, a psychogalvanometer. You'd never pass.

"If Lonnie does give you an interview, be damned careful. There are interconnecting utility tunnels all over beneath the Campus. Some have dead ends used for storage rooms, full of junk and the personal stuff of people on staff, but mostly they hook up. If you know your way around, and some staff members do—the security people do—you can go between any two buildings there without ever sticking your head above ground."

"So?"

"So if Lonnie Thomas decides you're a threat, you could be quietly drugged, taken underground, and brought out through some manhole by the light of the moon. Slid into the back of some staff member's old van, and given a free ride out to the Ranch, where they could grind you up for fertilizer."

I stared at her. As far as I could see, she was serious.

"Do you think they'd actually do something like that?"

Her eyes were steady as a lioness'. "Damn straight they would! So don't give them an incentive. Don't even hint you're investigating the possible death of Ray Christman. Because if they think he's dead, and they think you might find any real evidence, they're going to be scared spitless."

Her eyes had narrowed, the pupils glistening out at me through the slits. Her voice, normally loud, lowered almost to a whisper, pulling me into it. As if it was important that I listen and understand.

"If the word gets out," she went on, "it will do two things. It'll do more than hurt the church's income. It'll slowly kill the church itself."

I thought then that I knew what she was getting at. Some of the staff members, maybe most of them, felt at a gut level that they couldn't survive outside it. It was their family, their home. Their cocoon. Williams and Hamilton and Fuentes, even Molly Cadigan, had left because they were disillusioned. If they got kicked out, it had been only the formal, final act. But for those who weren't yet disillusioned . . .

Molly wasn't done; she talked on relentlessly. "And to almost all of them," she said, "even Lonnie Thomas I suspect, reality and the alternative futures of mankind are exactly the way Ray Christman described them."

Her eyes burned me like lasers as she finished. "The ones who know their cover story is only a cover story are already scared. They're scared because Ray isn't with them anymore. They're scared because Ray won't be developing new procedures to bring people to Freed Being—or more to the point, bring *them* to Freed Being. They think of the church as the only salvation of mankind, and that its failure will damn us all forever. It's crazy, but that's how they see it."

The chills still hadn't gone away entirely as I walked to my car.

7
A TAIL VERIFIED

As I drove away, all I could think of was how crazy people could get in the grip of religious fanaticism. By the time I got back to my office, I'd gotten things at least partway into perspective again, but there were some things I wanted to ask Hamilton about.

As soon as I got back, I keyed Hamilton's office number. He was busy; his secretary said he'd call back at lunch time. So I keyed the number Molly Cadigan had given me for Doctor Winifred Landau Sproule. Sproule had turned off the vidcam on her phone, leaving me to guess what she looked like. She sounded too young to be a veteran of the Noeties in their prime. We only talked for a minute or so, but I got a mental image of someone slim and blond and beautiful. She gave me an appointment for 9 A.M. the next morning. Then, so I wouldn't be talking to her cold, I keyed the library and called up an article on the life of Leif Haller, serialized by the *L.A. Times* in 1990, updated and published as a small book twelve years later. The writer had done her homework, traced Haller's roots and talked to scores of people who'd known him before he got famous.

It was one of the more interesting lives I've read about.

❖   ❖   ❖

Leif Haller
The Early Years

Oscar Leif Haller, founder of the Institute for Noetic Technology, was born on Valentine's Day, 1930, on a farm near Opdal, Wisconsin, to Britta Augustsdatter Haller and Johan Ola Haller, Norwegian immigrants. Among his peers, the child would insist on being called "Leif"; he despised the name Oscar, and rarely even used the initial.

Almost from the beginning, Leif Haller was an energetic dynamo, but not hyperactive. His schoolmates would remember him as always in control of himself, and generally of the situation. For even as a child, a child smaller than most, he had charisma. In the one-room country grade school he attended, he was a leader, full of ideas, and able to dominate in his boyhood disputes.

He matured early. He was shorter than average, of medium frame, and sinewy muscular. By age fifteen, despite his youth, he was locally renowned for the amount of heavy work he could do in an hour or a day. By his sixteenth birthday, Haller was in trouble with three different families regarding their daughters. This seems to have been less a matter of adolescent horniness than of a desire, a need, to dominate.

But he was already careful in matters that could seriously complicate his life. He impregnated none of the girls he entertained in the back of his father's 1938 Chevrolet sedan; he had an older youth buy condoms for him.

He excelled in class from the beginning, through his high intelligence, his energy, and his determination to be superior. He read voraciously. At age thirteen, in the tenth grade, he read his new history textbook on the evening of his first day, and claimed never to have looked inside it again. No one doubted him. His memory was remarkably responsive. He got an A in the course, as he did in every other course he took. Math he did with only quick and partial homework, enough to get the feel of procedures, and earned a perfect score on almost every quiz and test.

In high school he did not participate in sports, although he'd been outstanding in playground sports in grade school. He was small, of course, and there were a lot of chores to do on the farm. And as he told at least two friends, he'd outgrown athletics. Instead he read his way through the village library. Beginning when he started high school at age twelve, he'd go home from school at four o'clock, do chores, including milking several cows by hand, eat supper, and often bicycle five miles of gravel road back to Opdal, to the library. Sometimes he was the only person there besides the librarian. He'd return the books he'd borrowed at his last visit, usually six or eight of them, browse the shelves for an hour, and start home with another load. In winter, when the gravel road was snowy, he'd jog or ski in, if he couldn't borrow his father's car.

Years later he'd be remembered as the first person in Opdal school to use a book bag—an old skier's knapsack.

Among much else, he read H.G. Wells' *Outline of History*; the books and essays of Elbert Hubbard; and of all things for a boy in an ethnic farm community, the Harvard Classics. Norwegian was the language at home, and he read Ibsen in the original Dano-Norwegian. He read Nietzsche and Kant, Freud and Jung, Kierkegaard and Swedenborg, Ramakrishhna and Yogananda. He read Plato and Alfred Korzybski. Intellectually further afield, he even read Heinrich Harrer and Alexandra David-Neel on Tibet. The librarian in Opdal was delighted to have a young reader with such an avid desire to learn, and through inter-library loans, ordered whatever he requested that her shelves did not have.

Perhaps most impressive of all, for someone so young, he became the devotee of none of the great men whose books he read. He read critically, absorbing and analyzing, gradually evolving his own basic cosmology, his own metaphysics. Listening to ex-schoolmates reminiscing on his boyhood, one might wonder if he hadn't been born with his philosophy and metaphysics. The closest thing he had to a real confidant was Morten Jacobsen, an older boy on a neighboring farm. Jacobsen, who would later become Brigadier General Morten V. Jacobsen, USAF, recalled that once, while they were pheasant hunting, Haller told him: "I'm going to be the most powerful man in the world. A superman. I will hold all its knowledge, and learn to do things no one else can do."

"And I believed him," Jacobsen told me chuckling. "There was something about Leif Haller that when he said something, you believed him."

In September 1946, at age sixteen, Haller enrolled in the University of Wisconsin on a full scholarship. For two years he took math and German, physics and chemistry, a course in each, every semester. He also took philosophy, including logic and the philosophy of science, and he took history. And at the end of two years selected his major—economics! At age twenty he graduated *summa cum laude* with a grade point average of 3.96, and went to New York, where he was employed in a trainee position in the brokerage firm of Abbott, Bourne, and Masswell.

According to the firm's personnel files, Leif Haller performed his duties exceptionally well, and was three times promoted. But business success was not what he was looking for. The experience was useful, as was the modest investment portfolio he acquired, but after two and a half years he quit, having arranged employment as a staff assistant to Congressman Harvey Lingdal of Wisconsin.

The congressman might not have hired the energetic youngster if he'd known of Haller's association with witchcraft on Long Island, in a coven that ritually used drugs and hypnosis in an era when drug use was rare. Haller and his Long Island friends saw witchcraft as a way, or hopefully the way, to expand their individual powers. Hypnosis and drugs were tools in their witchcraft.

Leif Haller had no more intention of climbing to power via a political ladder than he'd had in doing it via the stock market. Later he'd tell friends he took the job for the knowledge, experience, and insights it could provide. He was already fixated on becoming the world's most powerful man by other means: He intended to develop psychic powers to go with his remarkable intelligence.

By the time he moved to Washington, he was already disenchanted with witchcraft. It's not clear how much he'd ever really expected of it. After his Long Island experience, he still considered that there was validity in some of its principles, but he'd concluded that the subject was based too largely on erroneous theories, and too cluttered with superstitions, to be useful as it stood.

Besides, it is clear that he planned to build his own system. He would write that its two branches, theory and practice, would grow simultaneously and in parallel, practices being based on theory, with further theory growing out of experience with practices.

The Making of a Guru

Haller soon found his job as a congressional staff assistant too demanding on his time; sixty- and eighty-hour weeks left far too little time for study and experimentation. So after five months he left the capital and went to Los Angeles, there to try his hand at applying the procedures he'd concocted.

The first thing he did was grow a beard—a rarity at the time. It's been suggested he grew it to camouflage his youth, but more likely it was to project a specific image. People who'd known him as early as his university days say he looked more mature than his years. While he grew his beard, he worked as a warehouseman for an auto parts chain. Finally, suitably bearded, he rented a tiny office on Melrose Avenue, and opened for business as a mystic counselor, under the name Swami Suvarnananda; *suvarnananda* in Sanskrit meaning Bliss in Gold. (Haller's humor could be sly or broad; in this case it was both.) For a time he made a sparse living at best, perhaps converting investments to cash when necessary. Some of his clients were deeply troubled; some had little money, but needed repeated counseling sessions.

He regarded these as necessary learning projects, and tried to see them through to successful conclusions, continuing to work with people who could no longer pay. Later he would say that it was during his Swami period that he refined his cosmology and his theories (he called them "the laws") of the soul and mind, as well as his basic principles of counseling.

With experience and a modicum of success, he moved to a better office, shared a secretary with a chiropracter, billed himself as Dr. Karl Mogens, psychoanalyst, and affected a cultured Danish accent. The diplomas on his wall, he once said, were the best that money could buy. As the good doctor, he had numerous rather impressive successes, and through word of mouth developed a profitable practice. Within six months he'd moved to a still nicer office, with a secretary of his own.

In working out his early procedures, Haller borrowed heavily from the work of others. He was influenced by Freud's early work in regression, work done before Freud became fixated on sex as the key to the psyche. And by Jung's work. Though Haller rejected Jung's concept of archetypes, he adapted his use of the psychogalvanometer in compiling and evaluating, with the patient, lists of psychologically charged words as a wedge and lever in analysis. He was also strongly influenced by Alfred Korzybski and Edgar Cayce. Some of these works he'd read in his teens, others in the UCLA library. Later he would mention reading case histories of idiot savants. There is no evidence that he borrowed any practices from witchcraft.

It seems clear that his tenure as a swami and bogus Danish analyst was the first project in a long-term plan. It also seems clear that the plan was to culminate in himself as superman, surrounded by an expanding corps of supermen who would be subordinate to himself. The phase after the swami/Mogens phase was the establishment of the Institute for . . .

There was a knock at my door. It was Carlos, with some questions about a case I'd handled earlier. As he was leaving, Hamilton called; it was his lunch break. "Is this a good time?" I asked him. "It may take twenty or thirty minutes."

"Go ahead," he said. "What you're doing is more interesting than eating at Hannery's. If necessary, I'll catch a sandwich and juice from the snack machine later."

I told him what Molly Cadigan had said about the leaders of the church believing in Ray Christman's theories on reality and the alternative futures of mankind—some kind of doom on the one hand and presumably a golden age on the other, with the church being the difference. That they were scared because Ray wasn't around to feed them new procedures and keep the thing going; that basically they were fanatics who might go off the deep end if they thought someone was going to show that Christman was dead.

"Does she have something there?" I finished. As I said it, I remembered what Hamilton had told me about a hole in his own life, a sort of pointlessness, since he'd left the church.

It took him a minute to respond. "She has a point. Three kinds of people get to the upper echelons of the church. One kind is cynical predators. Another is dedicated fanatics. I'm not sure which kind Lonnie Thomas is; some of each, maybe, incompatible as they seem. And the third kind is people who honestly believe but don't behave like fanatics, people who can get things done and who can get others to get things done, in spite of confusion and stupidity.

"As for their running scared . . . With due respect to Molly, I doubt it. Worried maybe, but not scared. They've been without Ray Christman for about half a year now, and I think they've probably gotten used to the situation. And I saw no evidence that Ray was conceived by the Holy Ghost and born unto a virgin. What he did, other people should be able to do, especially when they have his lead to follow. I suspect that before long they'll start coming out with new procedures they've invented themselves, and say that Ray sent them. And the faithful will cheer themselves hoarse, and start transfering credits to pay for them.

"Whatever; Molly's point is well taken. If I were you, Martti, I'd be careful not to let the church know what you're interested in."

We disconnected then, and I sat there sorting out who I'd told. Nobody in the church. The biggest danger seemed to be that Armand Butzburger might get a guilty conscience and unload it on his confessor or whatever they have.

At quitting time I got in my car and drove east down Beverly. I'd only gone half a block when I saw a guy behind the wheel of a parked DKW sport coupe. I'd have sworn it was the same guy I'd seen that morning across the street from the Neophyte Building, but wearing a white soft cap now—a cap like a lot of merchant seamen wear, with a small, snap-down bill and a button on the top. And it occurred to me that someone didn't need to drive the same car all the time. Suppose he'd been hired by the church. He could take a different car every time out. He'd parked it nose-on to a loading zone, where he could pull out quickly. And sure as hell, he did.

So I drove east all the way to LaBrea, catching sight of him pretty often, then south, and pulled into a parking lot at a Denny's. I went inside, and walked right through the kitchen and out the service entrance, with the chief cook yelling at me. Then I slipped around the side of the building and peered over the shrubbery. I could see the DKW in a bank lot across the street, where the driver could watch for me driving out.

I waited till the light at the intersection turned red, stopping the traffic flow, then I trotted out and across the street, hand inside my jacket on the butt of my Walther 7.65mm.

The DKW backed, U-turned, and burned rubber out another entrance. There was no question at all about it now; I'd had a tail. And he knew that I knew. I watched his disappearance with a big rock in my stomach.

8
WINIFRED SPROULE

My wife is self-employed, a professional psychic with a reputation that lets her charge fairly big fees. Psychics have been big in L.A. since the plagues at the turn of the century, and the business is growing. Anyway, while Tuuli isn't awfully busy, she makes a good income. Generally she arranges things so she can sleep late—commonly till nine. By which time I've been at the office for an hour, which means I either fix my own breakfast or eat out. Most often I eat at Morey's Deli, down the block from the office. It's not that I don't like to prepare meals; I just don't like to eat by myself. Besides, there's less traffic earlier.

But on the day of my appointment with Winifred Sproule, I ate at home. I was trying to make up for all the fat, chocolate-frosted doughnuts I'd eaten at Molly Cadigan's the day before, so what it came down to was low-fat cottage cheese, Rye Krisps with nothing on them, and slices of raw turnip (try raw turnips; they're mildly sweet), all washed down with a big glass of Altadena Dairy's real churned buttermilk.

I can enjoy a meal like that without getting carried away. Probably because it's not sweet and not salty. Some foods send me into a feeding frenzy. Chocolate! God!

The only thing wrong with breakfast that day was, I

had the TV on to the morning news. Which featured a
trashing. Trashers had damn near destroyed a senior
citizens' center in Burbank the night before. After dis-
abling the alarm system, which had taken some know-how,
they'd poisoned the shrubbery and lawn, slashed and
hacked the furniture, knocked holes in the drywall, spray-
painted obscenities . . . and waited till they were ready to
leave to break the windows; the noise would bring the
beat cops.

The police estimated the trashers must have carried out
the whole thing in under ten minutes. As if they'd drilled
it. Something like that always rouses a terrible urge to
homicide in me. Which scares me, because I almost always
carry a gun. I imagine myself shooting half a dozen of them,
gut-shooting them, then going around kicking the wounded,
busting ribs and stuff like that. Bad stuff. It makes me
remember . . .

So I turned off the TV and did the drill my therapist
gave me after mom and dad were killed, to settle me down.
It usually only takes a minute or two. Then I went down
to the parking level, got in my car and left.

The Hypernumbers Institute is in Bel Air, of all places,
on a little goat-trail street called Chikaree Lane that snakes
along the top of a ridge in the Santa Monica Mountains.
I went the back way, via Mulholland Drive and Beverly
Glen. I hadn't realized the neighborhood was a security
neighborhood, but Dr. Sproule had let the gate guards know
I was coming, so my Prudential ID got me through.

The institute sprawls along the upper slope, with a great
view across Stone Canyon to the west. A rambling, two-
story building with cedar siding, it could easily pass for
some holo star's western-style mansion. Tall Mexican pines
shade it, while rhododendrons stand guard. The receptionist
called and told Sproule I was there, then gave me directions to her office. Somehow I'd expected to see students
trooping through the halls or standing around drinking
coffee, chatting. Instead it was quiet. The few people I saw
looked as if they had things to do.

Winifred Sproule's office was on the second floor. Most

of her west wall consisted of sliding doors, one-way Klearglass that opened onto a balcony with view. They were open when I walked in, open to birdtalk and a warm April breeze. Sproule had gotten up when I entered. I'd visualized her pretty well—blond, slim but well-built, and all-round good looking. Also elegant, in spite of, or maybe because of, the short, slit, Singapore skirt. The kind of elegance you see in old 2-D movies with European leading ladies. Dietrich. Garbo. She could easily have passed for the proverbial thirty-nine, but I judged she'd be in her late forties. That seemed like a minimum, if she'd been a high-ranking Noetie while Leif Haller was still alive and publicly active.

"I'm Martti Seppanen," I said.

She gestured. "Have a seat, Mr. Seppanen." She sat down herself. Elegantly. There was no desk between us; it faced a side wall. She was only about five feet from me, close enough to make me edgy at first. The office wasn't that small, and I was strongly aware of her crossed legs, which were elegant too.

"You said you're investigating the disappearance of Ray Christman. For whom, may I ask?"

"A private individual."

"I see." She lit a cigarette, the smoke wisping upward into an air cleaner. Even so, I got a whiff. It wasn't tobacco or weed. Maybe one of the herbals you can buy, supposed to be relatively harmless. I didn't know much about the different brands. I'd still been a kid when the government made it illegal to advertise them. This one had an apricot-colored filter tip.

"How can I help you?" she asked.

"I've heard you were once on the Gnosties' board of directors. And on the Noetie board of directors before that. Is that true?"

"They're both true, but neither was a position of any influence. That's one respect, one of several, in which Ray was like Haller at that time. Both kept the power—all the real power—in their own hands. A directorship wasn't even an honor, really, though they treated it as one. We rarely even had meetings. All they wanted a board of directors for was a list of names to put on legal papers and letterhead. Names with a Ph.D., MD, or DD appended, or some such. I had a doctorate in math."

I revised my estimate of her age up another notch—not easy to do, considering her looks. Or maybe she'd been a child prodigy. "But I suppose you're knowledgeable about them," I said.

She shrugged. "About current situations, no. If you're interested in organization and philosophy, yes. History definitely." Even her raised eyebrow was elegant. "Ask your questions and we'll see."

I'd been reviewing what to ask the evening before, and on the way over. Basically I was groping, fishing for leads and trying to evaluate the too numerous possibilities. What I could most hope to get from her were insights into the church and the Noetics, and possibly more contacts. I still couldn't discard the possibility that the Noeties had done Christman in. They'd had a serious grudge. And if the story was true about Christman and her, she'd have insights into him, too.

"Of the members of the Church of the New Gnosis," I said, "what proportion had been members of the Institute for Noetic Technology?"

"Over the long term? A tiny percentage. The institute was already declining when the church began. But the church *began* quite largely with disaffected members and ex-members of the institute."

"The institute's suit against the church was for copyright infringement. . . ."

"And was quite properly rejected by the court."

I wondered what made her so sure. "Did the church borrow *ideas* from the institute?" I asked. There's no legal protection for ideas by themselves.

"Your question would better be phrased, 'Did Ray Christman borrow ideas from Leif Haller.' The answer is no. Leif insisted otherwise, and I have no doubt he believed it, but by that time he was borderline psychotic. Ray didn't even know much about Leif's ideas. He'd never been connected with the institute, or interested in its technical procedures. Though the source of his own ideas had been."

"The source of Christman's ideas?"

"Right. Ray's cosmology was not his own, and the basis for his procedures wasn't either. But neither were they Leif's."

I gawped. The booklets I'd bought from the church, and material I'd called up from the library, credited all of it to Christman, or blamed it on him. "Tell me about that," I said.

"First of all, almost anyone's ideas derive to some degree from other people's. You borrow, and you build from there: revise, rearrange, and add on. Haller, for example, openly borrowed from others, bits and pieces, major ones. He added his own ideas, and integrated all of it into a functional whole, Noetics I. Which wasn't as good as he claimed, of course—nothing was—but overall it was new and remarkably effective. Later he erected a shaky additional structure on it—Noetics II—that promised more and delivered less. Considerably less.

"Ray, on the other hand, borrowed a whole system intact from someone else, reworked it to make it easier to understand, then designed an organization for large-scale application. And told people that all of it was his. The person he'd borrowed from had been associated with Leif Haller, and some of Leif's ideas were implicit in what Ray borrowed. But they weren't basic ideas, just rules of application. That's where most of the similarities lay that inspired the suit—in the rules of application."

Christman had borrowed someone else's system and never acknowledged them! That could be a motive for murder! But I stayed with the Noetie matter just then. I could come back to the other.

"The institute claimed that the copyright infringements had materially damaged it," I said. "If we change 'copyright infringements' to 'lawful borrowing of ideas,' did Ray Christman actually rob or otherwise harm the institute?"

She reached, stubbed out her cigarette, then leaned back

in her tiltback chair. Not only her legs were nice. It was hard to keep from staring, and she knew it. "The institute had begun to shrink, or at least had quit growing, before Ray ever started his church," she said. "Charisma doesn't necessarily include charm, and Haller's heavy-handed arrogance had turned off too many people. And especially to people close to him, it was more and more apparent that he was becoming a mental case. Also he'd made too many claims and promises for too many years without coming through.

"As Ray's church grew, Leif came to hate him, first for cutting in on his game, and secondly for the cardinal sin of being more successful at it. The church simply speeded the institute's decline; people left more readily because they saw an alternative.

"And now, what had been a network of nearly a hundred Noetic centers worldwide, recruiting members and delivering counseling and training, is down to one, just one. A two-story building in Santa Maria. There's not much left except a few sour, hard-bitten loyalists to the memory of Leif Haller."

If they'd shrunk that much, they might be hard pressed to finance a contract on Christman. On the other hand, there'd been stories, when I was a kid, that the institute had procedures that could produce super intellects and psychic powers. I had a friend who used to fantasize about that, said that when he grew up, he was going to get in on it. I mentioned this to Sproule, and asked if there'd been anything to it.

She laughed wryly. "Not really. I said that Leif had made too many promises and claims without coming through. His early procedures and their results—Noetics I, that is—got people excited and enthused. And that, along with his charisma, made them ready to go along with him on other things. Noetics II was a much larger, open-ended set of procedures, with a foundation of untested and unlikely theory. By that time Leif was too enamored of his own intuition. The only test was application, and when it failed, he blamed other things, not his intuitions."

"Isn't that more or less what happened with Christman's work?"

"More or less, yes. But in developing his applications, Ray Christman took a lot of liberties with the theories, which makes it impossible to evaluate the theories from his results.

"And in comparing the two men, there's the matter of intentions. Their work was directed at different goals. Leif wanted to be superman—actually more than superman—and to surround himself with a corps of supermen. What he called Metapsyches. Ray, on the other hand, wanted to save humanity, which required, he felt, that we all rise above our physical selves and be what he called Freed Beings.

"They both had a lot of success with their beginning procedures, which were designed to rid people of fixations, phobias, psychosomatic ailments, things like that. Even neuroses, quite commonly; sometimes even psychoses. You get rid of someone's eczema and asthma, and they see other people around them losing their stutter, for example, or their fear of flying, or their inferiority complex . . . If you do that for someone when all the medical profession did was ease them more or less, that someone's going to look at you as a magician. And of course the medical establishment will look at you as a dangerous fraud. Not every doctor, not every psychiatrist, but the establishment as a whole: the AMA, the APA. Partly because they've seen too many charlatans; it wasn't entirely self-interest.

"Meanwhile a lot of people are going to be impressed by Uncle Frank, whose arthritis went away at the Noetic Center. They're not going to pay much attention to Dr. Pokefinger when he says it's all a fraud." She paused, looking me over. "It freed me of some troublesome problems, though I do retain a foible or two."

I wondered if she could read people like Molly claimed Christman could. "So what went wrong?" I asked.

"Basically they hit limits. It's as simple as that. When they cured someone's arthritis and recurrent migraines, or his compulsion to window peek or fondle little boys—when they cured something like that—they had a saner, healthier human being. What neither of them succeeded in doing was to produce a Metapsyche or a Freed Being, at least not stably. Nor even that intermediate phenomenon, a reliably psychic human.

"You might have psychic experiences during and after their procedures, especially Ray's. Sometimes even verifiable psychic experiences. Even on the lower-grade procedures. And when you did, it had a real and powerful effect on how you looked at the world afterward. But you were still a human being. You still had foibles, problems, and limits. They never took us beyond that."

"So it was a matter of overreaching," I said. "They weren't actually phonies."

"Certainly not to begin with. I have no doubt that Haller deliberately lied from the beginning, but I'm also convinced that he thought he could come through in the long run. Toward the end . . . Who knows what he thought and felt, in seclusion back in Wisconsin? He used to claim that his procedures, fully and properly used, could cure virtually everything. Said it off the record, of course, so the AMA and FDA couldn't hit him for it. Publicly he only implied it. Yet he became a physical wreck himself, years before the Great Flu killed him."

She paused, glancing at the coffeemaker on her worktable. The pitcher on it held only water, presumably hot. "I'm a hell of a hostess," she said, and got up. "Would you like coffee? Tea?"

"Coffee," I told her, and she mixed two cups of instant. "Honey?" she asked. I told her I'd take mine plain.

When she sat down again, she changed direction a bit. "If you want to see some reliable psychics, visit a home for the retarded that has some idiot savants, hopefully one that does more than calendar computations. You've heard of psychic photographers? There's a boy—a young man now—who's a ward of the Savants Project at the University of Minnesota. He does some marvelous things."

I'd read a book about a psychic photographer named Ted Polemes, who'd been studied by the University of Nebraska med school, fifty or so years ago. Intriguing. But

I was looking for insights into the Christman case, not psychic photography. "That would be interesting," I said, and got back on the subject. "Who was the person that Ray Christman got his ideas from?"

"There were two of them, a husband and wife: Vic and Tory Merlin. Apparently they'd dedicated themselves to metaphysical and psychic research."

"And Christman didn't tell anyone? Except you?"

"So far as I'm aware, I'm the only one."

"Why you?"

She didn't answer right away. She sipped coffee, then lit another cigarette. "I was Ray's girlfriend for a while," she said at last. "I was with him for more than a year—longer than any other I've heard of. I've always been sexually attractive, interested, and talented. And Ray . . . Besides charisma, he had a large, strong body, something that's always turned me on."

She looked thoughtfully at me. I squirmed.

"Every now and then," she continued, "Ray would get a letter from Vic Merlin, updating him on what the Merlins were doing. Some of these were fifteen or twenty pages long. I remember the first one he got while I was with him. When he saw it, he dropped what he was doing and canceled an appointment. When he'd finished reading it, he was so enthused, he gave it to me to read. That's how I learned about them.

"The first time I read it, I understood almost none of it, so he gave me a stack of older letters, a couple of hundred pages, with marginal notes in Ray's handwriting. Reading them in chronological sequence, and being a fairly advanced counseling student, they made a certain amount of sense to me, but a lot of it was still a mystery. Ray told me to read them again in a week or so, and I was surprised at how much more I got out of them the second time. It was as if exposure started a subliminal mental ferment, and out of that grew a sense of what Merlin was communicating. Reading it a third time, I found myself saying 'of course.' It was beginning to seem obvious.

"Actually, that's what got me hooked on Charles Musés'

work with hypernumbers, and eventually brought me here. I'd read some things on hypernumbers years earlier, and while it was interesting, I hadn't found it at all compelling. But the Merlins' work in metaphysics, on what they called 'the reality matrix' and 'the parts of man,' complemented it and gave it additional meaning for me."

"If the subject is that abstruse," I said, "how was Christman able to use it?"

"That was where Ray's contribution came in. He saw his function as translating Vic Merlin's stuff into teachable statements and procedures. I asked him why he didn't let others get it the same way he did, from repeated readings of Merlin's writing. His answer was that people wouldn't do it, and he was probably right.

"On a couple of occasions that year, he rented a plane and flew to Arizona to consult with the Merlins, go over things with them. It was all very secret. He flew himself; he was a licensed pilot. He'd be all excited at the prospect of seeing them. Ray could be like a child. I suspect they gave him counseling sessions while he was there. Once I asked to go with him; I wanted to meet these Merlins. Ray wouldn't take me. Said he didn't want any distractions. There should be only himself, and Vic and Tory."

I'd forgotten to drink my coffee. Now I took a sip; it was tepid. "What did the Merlins think of his using their stuff and not giving them credit? Did he pay them for it?"

Sproule looked surprised. "I don't know. I never wondered. They kept sending him stuff though. There may have been some kind of payment."

She went on to tell me how Christman got connected with them. "He'd never been interested in philosophy or psychology," she said. "He'd been a hot-shot salesman— in his own words, he 'could sell sand to the Arabs.' By age twenty-six, he'd parlayed his salesmanship into a chain of computer service centers in the west, and gotten hooked on golf. The way he told it, he was one of the world's worst golfers. Then someone suggested he see Vic Merlin, that Merlin could sit down with him and perform some psychic voodoo, and it would help his golf game.

"Ray had always been interested in the idea of psychic powers, so he went to see Merlin. After that he had no more trouble with his golf game, because he lost interest in it. Merlin had blown his mind, and had also blown his muscle spasm problems; he never had another muscle spasm.

"So he attached himself to them—he insisted that Tory was as powerful as Vic—and read their foot-high stack of 'research notes.' He also had them teach him some of the procedures they used. The result was the Church of the New Gnosis.

"There was one thing about it that troubled Ray, though," Sproule went on. "It hadn't developed in him the kinds of powers he insisted the Merlins had: telepathy, clairvoyance, out of body travel . . . That sort of thing. He put a lot of importance on things like that, believed it was part of what mankind needed to be saved. I think the lack must have troubled him more as time went on—made him fear he might fail. That may have been why he got more interested than ever in money and adulation, the last few years. They helped him feel successful. That's still the dark side of American culture, though it's lost ground since the plagues—the idea that money is success and success is money."

That was effectively the end of the interview. Sproule didn't know the Merlins' address. They lived on a ranch somewhere. But she told me someone who might know: Olaf Sigurdsson. Molly Cadigan had already given me Sigurdsson's address and phone number.

Thanking Sproule I got up, and she stepped over to me, so close we almost touched. "It was my pleasure, Mr. Seppanen," she purred, putting her hand on my arm. And then, more softly, "If there's *anything* else I can do for you, I hope you'll let me know."

That's when I discovered how sexually overwhelming a woman can be. I managed to get out without stumbling over my feet.

9
OLAF SIGURDSSON

Outside the Hypernumbers Institute, I called up the Los Angeles grid on my car computer, and keyed in the address Molly Cadigan had given me for Ole Sigurdsson. I'd intended to talk to him anyway, about the Noeties. Now it seemed he might also be able to tell me something about the Merlins, including how to get in touch with them. I wanted to see him as soon as I could.

If Ray Christman had been paying the Merlins for their ideas, paying them some agreed-upon rate, then they might or might not have a motive for killing him. It depended partly on how much they valued public recognition.

And if Christman flew to Arizona from time to time to see them, flew there alone without telling anyone, they certainly had the opportunity. My heads-up display showed Sigurdsson living in Bel Air, not far from where I was, and a Bel Air address meant he had to be pretty damned affluent. It was hard to visualize a psychic having that much money, unless . . . Maybe he could predict stock prices—things like that.

I keyed in his phone number and got a bowl-cut security man. "You've just dialed Laura and Ole's number," he said. "Neither is at home now; you've got Bel Air Security. We're being recorded. How may I help you?"

"What would be a good time for me to try again? My name is Seppanen, and I want to speak with Olaf Sigurdsson. I was referred to him by Dr. Winifred Landau Sproule."

"Right, Mr., ah . . ."

"Seppanen," I repeated.

"Seppanen. Right. Would you care to leave your phone number?"

I gave it to him. It occurred to me that Sigurdsson might be aware of Tuuli as a psychic, and feel favorably inclined toward fellow psychics, so I went on. "That's the residence of Martti Seppanen and Tuuli Waanila." I spelled them for him. "I'll call again at about nine."

"Oh! Martti Seppanen! I'm sorry! Certainly, Mr. Seppanen." People sometimes recognize my name, usually from media coverage of the case of the twice-killed astronomer. It's kind of a kick when it happens.

When we'd disconnected, I keyed the office. We carry beepers, but it's company policy not to use them except for urgent messages. In our work, beeping can be a nuisance, even a danger, so we check in from time to time. Fidela told me I hadn't had any calls, and Carlos and Joe hadn't put a come-in on me. Then I went to the gym for a couple of hours. I left the Nautilus alone, worked hard on my flexibility and forms, sparred awhile, and finally beat and kicked hell out of first the heavy bag and then Big Dummy, the response mech. After that, and ten minutes in the sauna, I ate a green salad and a bowl of rice and beans, and took my coffee black. All in all, I figured, I'd almost made up for Molly Cadigan's chocolate doughnuts.

Afterward I keyed up the public access information on Olaf Sigurdsson. He was no kid. He'd been born near Eskifjördur, Iceland, on 8 February 1928, which made him eighty-four years old. His profession was listed as psychic consultant, and there was a published biography on him by Laura Wayne Walker.

Tuuli and I ate supper at home that evening: broiled walleye with lemon, microwaved potatoes, barely cooked mixed veggies ... You get the picture. I can eat all I want of stuff like that. I've discovered it's good, too, but it pains me to see Tuuli eat butter brickle ice cream for dessert while I finish off with fat-free fruit yogurt. She says she can't help it if she can eat the way she does and stay trim. She's right, and I'm glad for her, but it hurts.

I told her I was trying for an appointment with Ole Sigurdsson, and right away she wanted to go with me. She'd never met him, and wanted to. I told her I had nothing against her meeting him, but not when I was on official business. It wouldn't be professional.

We were about ready to have a fight over that, when the phone rang. I answered. The man on the screen was elderly, his face strong-boned and hawk like. "I'm Olaf Sigurdsson," he said. "And you're Martti Seppanen."

"Right. With Prudential Investigations and Security. I'm not looking for your services as a psychic, Mr. Sigurdsson. Not just now. What I would like is your views on the Institute of Noetic Technology. In connection with an investigation. I'd like to talk with you; tomorrow. If possible."

"Ja-ah?"

It came out as a question, as if he wanted to know more about it, or what else I was interested in. I didn't intend to mention my interest in the Merlins yet. Sproule had said he was a friend of theirs. I'd bring them up when I was with him; make it seem as if my interest was incidental.

"Yes, sir," I said. He had an eye like a hawk, and it was looking inside me, right over the phone.

"Do you vant to know v'at I charge for consulting vith police? Or investigators like you?"

I said yes. It wasn't as high as I thought it might be, but I'd prefer not to pay it out of my own pocket.

"You'll have to make it this evening, though," he went on. "My vife and I are leaving town tomorrow."

"I can be there in under an hour."

He nodded, then looked at me silently, as if thinking. Or looking into my head. Disconcerting. "And bring your vife. Ve have heard of her."

I glanced at Tuuli. Where she stood, she'd shown in his screen too, though out of focus. She was grinning. "Fine," I said. "We'll both be there."

Sigurdsson's place was modest for Bel Air, but the location was something else, on top of a ridge. Sigurdsson himself answered the door, a tall, rawboned old man who still stood straight.

His eyes settled on Tuuli right away. Men generally find her interesting. She's small, dainty actually, but nicely shaped, with a face that's delicate and pretty. She's been described as elfin. Her hair is tan and so is her skin. All over; it's her natural color. Her eyes are green and tilted. She's Lapp on her mother's side, and Finn on her father's.

I introduced us. Sigurdsson's eyes shifted to me while I spoke, then turned back to Tuuli. It wasn't as if he was an old lecher. It was more like a—like a personnel examination. After four or five seconds he nodded, as if he approved of her.

"Laura vill vant to meet you both v'en ve're done vith business," he said. "She is in her office, marking up a shooting script. Yust now she's executive producer for a picture that the director is trying to run up the costs on."

He led us down a hall to a comfortable room like a small living room, that obviously served as his den. Against one wall, a brick stove had been built that could be used for heat in chilly weather. I'd never seen a brick stove before. It had a steel plate in the top that you could cook on, and looked as if it burned wood. There was also a table painted like a couple I'd seen in old Swede farmhouses back in Ojibwa County, with chairs to match. The couch he motioned us to was high enough and firm enough for comfortable sitting.

"Coffee?" he asked.

We both said yes. He put on a red-laquered percolator with something written on the side in a foreign language, Icelandic I suppose.

"So," he said, looking me over, "v'at do you vant from me?"

I told him I was investigating the disappearance of Ray Christman. That the Institute of Noetic Technology, or people inside it, were suspect, and I wanted to know more about it. A woman named Molly Cadigan had suggested I talk to him, had said he might be more up to date than she was. That I'd read a *Times* article on the institute, dated 1993, and a brief biography of Leif Haller which had information about the institute as it had been years ago. And that I'd talked with Winifred Sproule.

"Vell," he said, "I ain't much more up to date than that. But I'd be surprised if the institute vas up to getting Christman killed. If any individual Noetie vas, it vould be Haller himself."

"And he's dead," I said.

"Do you know that?"

That stopped me. "According to his biography," I answered, "he died of the Great Flu in December '99, and was buried in a mass grave near Eau Clair, Wisconsin." I looked at the circumstances that would have prevailed then. I didn't know how big Eau Claire had been, but big enough to be a well-known name throughout the region—forty or fifty thousand maybe. That mass grave would have been one of many for Eau Claire, each with maybe a hundred or even five hundred bodies. There'd have been no autopsies, no embalmings, little if anything more than an identification by whoever discovered the body or brought it in. Even my home town, Hemlock Harbor, had mass graves, and it only had some four thousand people before the Flu—twenty-eight hundred afterward. They bulldozed a trench, lined the bodies out in it, limed them heavily and covered them up.

I changed tack. "As a psychic, does it seem to you that Haller's alive?"

"I don't get anything vun vay or another on that."

"Do you get anything on who's responsible for Christman's disappearance?"

He stood silent for a minute, frowning, then grunted and shook his head. "Nothing on that either. How long has he been missing?"

I gave him a rundown on what Armand Butzburger had told me. Meanwhile the coffeepot had been perking, and when I'd finished, Sigurdsson got up and poured three mugs. I had mine with honey and cream, the cream out of a little oak-veneer fridge built into his oak bookcase. He didn't have anything to say till he'd served all three of us.

"So he has been missing probably since October. More than six months. Then I vould guess he is dead. But that's only a guess. And considering v'at the church is like, I vould guess that somevun or some group inside it killed him."

"I don't suppose it would do me much good to interview Lon Thomas?"

Again he grunted. "From v'at I've heard, he vouldn't give you an interview. And if he did, v'at makes you think he'd tell you the truth?"

"I consider myself pretty observant about things like that. I think I'd know if he was lying."

"Don't be too sure. I vas never in the church, but I have friends that vere, three or four of them that vere pretty high up. Thomas is sharp—maybe not intelliyent, but sharp—kvick, avare. And he came up through their PR division. The people in public relations there do lying drills till they can say anything to anyvun, straight-faced and vithout blinking."

My first reaction was, it sounded like a myth, the kind that can grow up about a mysterious organization or secret government agency. But even as I thought it, I realized it was possible, and might well be true of an outfit like the Gnosties. I nodded. "Who are these three or four people you mentioned? I'd like to talk with them."

"There vas three of them. Two died in the plagues. The other vun you already talked to: Vinny Sproule."

"Ah."

"So," he said. His eyes, I'd thought, were gray. Now I decided they were blue. They looked into me, steady and disconcerting. "There is something else you vant from me. V'at is it?"

"Dr. Sproule mentioned a couple named Vic and Tory Merlin."

His gaze never changed, he didn't nod, his eyebrows didn't arch. He simply said, "O-oh?"

I hadn't intended to say what I said next. It just sort of blopped out. "She told me that Christman's ideas came from them. That he simply adapted them for teaching and application."

"She is right about v'ere his ideas came from. His ideas about reality and people and how to help them. But Christman did more than adapt them. Overall he changed them. Not on purpose, I don't think. He didn't fully understand them. He changed importances, left important things out . . . Made a dog's breakfast out of them, if you vant to know. Except the easy stuff, the beginning stuff. He got that pretty good."

"Could you tell me how to get in touch with the Merlins? Give me their phone number?"

He pursed his lips. "Tell you v'at. I'll give them your number, and tell them v'at you're interested in. If they vant, they can get in touch vith you."

And that's as far as I got. Sigurdsson turned his attention to Tuuli, and they talked for a few minutes while I sat there like a lump. If he'd been forty years, or maybe even thirty years younger, I'd have been jealous. Tuuli gave him her card, and he talked about the Merlins, whom he called the most powerful psychics he knew of. Then he buzzed his wife, and she came in, a really good-looking lady in her sixties, I judged. Probably twenty years younger than her husband. She and Sigurdsson and Tuuli had a good time yakking for another half hour, but I had things on my mind, and didn't add much to the conversation.

I needed to talk with Lon Thomas. I'd been afraid of it, afraid of him, been holding the idea down, mostly refusing to look at it, telling myself he wouldn't say anything useful. After a few minutes we got up, shook hands and left. As we drove away, Tuuli was full of the evening, full of having had a conversation with Olaf Sigurdsson! And of how friendly and charming Laura Sigurdsson had been. She was so full of it all that at first she didn't seem to notice

I was only half with her. When she did notice, she laid a hand on my arm.

"Thank you, Martti," she said softly in Finnish. "Thank you for taking me along."

I hadn't had much choice; Sigurdsson had almost ordered it. But she wasn't expressing thanks; she was expressing affection. Love. She didn't do that a lot. Of course, lots of times I wasn't very loveable; I was inconsiderate and unreasonable, and took too much for granted. We both did, as far as that went.

I'd turned onto Mulholland Drive by then, headed east. We came to a place—a public overlook—with a great view of the billion lights of the San Fernando Valley, and I pulled off the right of way into one of the diagonal parking slots there. Then we just sat holding hands and looking. We didn't even neck. I can't say personally what L.A. was like in the smog years. But with Arne Haugen's geogravitic power converters powering everything from cars to cities, from desalinization plants to transmountain water pipelines, L.A.'s got to be one of the most beautiful cities in the world. Especially at night, from the Santa Monica Mountains.

We'd been there about three or four minutes when a Buick pulled up behind us, blocking us in. Both of us stiffened; I thought of the guy who'd tailed me. I had my 9mm Glock in the door pocket and my 7.65 Walther under one arm. Presumably Tuuli had the little .25-caliber Lady Colt I'd given her in her shoulder bag. There were at least four guys in the Buick. Three piled out with wrecking bars and hammers in their hands. Trashers. Two of them came to my door and one to Tuuli's, all of them grinning, probably high on something.

My window was open—Tuuli had run hers up—and one of them stuck his face in. "Hey! You!" he said. "No fucking in the car! Unless you're gonna pass it around!"

Now I knew which one was the ringleader. The others laughed at his wit until I pointed my Walther at him. He backed away quickly, both of them did, but not any quicker than I keyed the door open and stepped out.

"You pull a gun on someone and you can go to jail!"
He half yelled it; the other half was whine, high and nasal.

I answered by shooting once, blowing the Buick's right
front tire. Their hands were already up. Now they reached
higher, stretching. "On your bellies!" I said, twitching my
gun at the two in front of me. They went down as if their
knees had melted, very cooperative, hands wide. Meanwhile
I'd heard Tuuli's door close. I glanced back and saw the
guy on her side backing away. She'd have her Lady Colt
in her hand. I pointed the Walther at the guy still in the
Buick, behind the steering wheel; his hands were up by
his ears. I stepped to where I could see his other front
tire, and shot it out. That left me with seven rounds. "Out!"
I told him, and out he got.

"You got a trashing tool in there?" I asked. He nodded.
"In back?" Another nod. "Get it out! Carefully, or I'll put
one of these right through your spine." He gave a little
half sob, opened the back door, and brought out a short-
handled sledgehammer.

"Whose car?" I asked.

"My old man's."

"*Your what?!*"

"My father's."

"He know what you use it for?"

"He thinks I'm at Sepulveda Mall, ice skating."

"Hon!" I said. "Cover those three!"

"I am!"

I had the driver get back in his Buick and drive it ahead
a few meters, out of the way, then get out with his hammer and lie down by the other three. "Hon," I said, "back
out and then back east down the road a hundred feet or
so." I was assuming none of the punks had read my plates,
and I didn't want them to. When she'd done it, I had the
four of them get up, watching them closely. I decided that
none had a gun actually on him, though there may have
been one in their car. They were dressed in the Valley
Smooth style, tights with a codpiece, and not even pocket
space for a handkerchief. "Pick up your tools!" I told them.

They did.

"Now trash the Buick!"

No one moved. Then I fired a round close, very close, to the head of one of them, the one nearest the car, the driver. He may have felt it zip past his ear. Whatever. He flinched and yelped. "The next one," I told him, "is right through your face."

It was really real to him now that he could die, bleed out his life right there, right then. He stepped quickly to his father's car, smashed a front window, then stopped and looked back at me. The others were moving reluctantly. "That's a start," I told him. "Keep it up."

Meanwhile Tuuli had come back and handed me the Glock. I stood there like John Wayne, a gun in each hand. The driver sobbed again, not weeping but in frustration, and again he swung, this time with more force, putting a large dent in the door. The others joined in, and in a moment they were all hammering away.

That's what they were doing while we backed off to my car and got in. I presumed the shots had been heard, and three should have been enough for someone to get a directional fix on them, more or less. I accelerated hard past the trashers, wanting to get off Mulholland onto Beverly Glen Boulevard, the quickest way into the anonymity of Valley traffic.

As we wound down the hill, I was shaking, telling myself it was all right, that no one could identify me. That they'd had it coming; that they were lucky I hadn't leg-shot them. They weren't really hard cases, but up there with the two of us alone, if we hadn't been armed, they'd hardly have settled for trashing our car.

But I didn't really calm down all the way home.

Our building loomed square and shadowed behind its sentinel date palms and the row of tall, vine-covered Mexican pines along the curb. The place had never looked so good. I stopped, put my key card into the slot, and when the cover raised, keyed in my code number. Through the open window, I heard insects or tree frogs or something chirring in the darkness, and a mockingbird tried a tentative half bar. Voices murmured on balconies, and someone laughed softly. The door swung up, and I rolled down the ramp and inside. Al, the guard covering the garage that night, waved from his booth.

I never even thought about Lon Thomas or Vic Merlin. When we got to the apartment, Tuuli and I were in one another's arms almost before the door closed.

10
TWO APPOINTMENTS

The next day I slept in till after Tuuli was up. She fixed our breakfasts, then left for an appointment in Thousand Oaks. If I hadn't had the Christman case in mind when we got in the night before, I did now. And I knew what I wanted to do next. I'd pretend to be a freelance writer, and get an interview appointment with N. Lonnberg Thomas, President of the Church of the New Gnosis.

I wasn't sure what I might accomplish, the case was still so amorphous. But church factions were suspect, and I needed to poke around and see what I could learn.

I spent a couple of hours at Gold's, doing Choi Li Fut forms followed by a Nautilus workout, had a good lunch at Morey's, then went to my office, where I created a fictional résumé of imaginary publication credits, and printed it out. Next I tried to foresee what questions Thomas or his secretary might ask before giving me an interview, and how I'd handle them.

Then I called the church, got a receptionist, and told her I wanted to speak with N. Lonnberg Thomas. When she asked what the call concerned, I told her my name was Martin Eberly—Eberly's my mother's maiden name— an identity I have official-looking documentation for, from driver's license to credit cards. That I was a freelance writer preparing an article on the church, and wanted an interview with Reverend Thomas at his earliest convenience. I'd gotten a lot of adverse statements about the church, I said, and felt I should hear its story from its own president. Particularly since I had an uncle in Detroit whom the church had relieved of his eczema and asthma.

"Give me your phone number," she said, "and Reverend Thomas can call you back."

"No," I told her, "I'm not willing to do that. My experience has been that all too often such return calls are never made. They get postponed and then forgotten. Tell Mr. Thomas that the article will be written, whether or not he talks with me."

She put me on hold for forty minutes, which didn't bother me. The executive director of a controversial outfit like Thomas' would receive more than a few calls from writers and would-be writers. One way to thin them was to leave them on hold for extended periods. While I waited, I read my new *ASI Journal*.

Suddenly I had only a dial tone, which did irritate me. I dialed again. This time I was only on hold four or five minutes before Thomas' personal secretary came on the line, a sound-only connection. She asked a few well-designed questions, then somewhat to my surprise gave me an appointment to talk with Thomas the next afternoon at 1:30, in the Administration Building on Campus.

It had been easier than I'd expected. After that I went to Carlos' office and we talked about the guy who'd tailed me. We couldn't see anything to do about it. And the guy knew, now, I was onto him, which could well be the end of it. There was no strong reason to think the church was responsible, or anyone interested in the Christman case. In our business you offend people from time to time, and some of them get resentful. I knew that better than almost anyone, from when I was a kid. You can also draw the attention of the police or other investigation firms, who may suspect you of operating in an area they're interested in.

❖   ❖   ❖

It was that evening at home that I got a call from Vic Merlin. From the way he talked, I guessed he'd been a Texas country boy who'd read a lot and gone to college, then lived somewhere else. He called me Martti right away. Visually he made a very different impression on me than Sigurdsson had: he made me think of a slightly built, elderly pixie who'd grown up on grits and beef instead of herring and mutton. I told him what Sigurdsson no doubt already had—that I'd gotten his name from Sproule, and that I was investigating the disappearance of Ray Christman. I ended up with a date to meet him at the airport in Wickenberg, Arizona, in two days, at 2:30 P.M. From there he'd take me to his place.

"And Martti," he said, "Ole told me your wife is Tuuli Waanila." He pronounced it to rhyme with vanilla. "Why don't you bring her along, too? We-all would like to meet her."

I threw a glance in her direction. She'd been listening from her easy chair, and now was nodding enthusiastically. But the invitation had made me uncomfortable. "I don't know," I said, "she's pretty busy lately." Her expression changed instantly, and she started to get up, as if to come over. "Just a minute; let me talk to her."

I touched the *hold* key and, turning, reminded her that the Merlins were murder suspects. That I was investigating them, and they could be dangerous.

"Martti," she said, "I want to go." Her voice was not pleading; there was steel in it, honed to an edge. "If these people are more powerful than Ole Sigurdsson, I want to meet them."

I didn't find her logic compelling. I'd met Sigurdsson, and he hadn't done anything psychic at all. I was willing to bet the Merlins wouldn't either. On the other hand, her tone of voice was compelling as hell. I shrugged, and opened the line again. "She says she can make it," I told him. "She looks forward to meeting you. Ole made you sound pretty interesting."

The way he grinned out at me from the screen, I wondered if maybe the hold hadn't worked, and he'd watched and heard. But it had worked. The screen had been blank when I'd turned back to it.

After a minute we disconnected. I couldn't help but wonder, though, what Vic Merlin's real reason was for inviting her.

11
LONNIE THOMAS

Considering what Molly Cadigan had said about the church being dangerous, and how Fred Hamilton had agreed with her, and that I'd been followed lately, the next day I took a company car with Colorado plates. In California it's now legal for licensed investigation firms to register a vehicle in more than one state, as long as one of the states is California. I parked in the big lot on Campus, and arrived in the lobby of the Admin Building at 1:20, ten minutes early.

The receptionist—smiling, good-looking, and wearing a space-cadet uniform—called to a tall, skinny, teenaged kid wearing a uniform and a complete set of pimples. I guessed his IQ as about equal to his weight—in kilos, not pounds— maybe sixty. He led me to an office. The plaque beside the door read simply CENTRAL COMMUNICATIONS. Inside, a not so pretty and sure as hell not smiling young woman wearing a dictation headset sat typing rapidly at a computer. Without slowing, or even looking at me, she told me to take a chair. There was a reading rack, but all it held was church promotion, and booklets supposedly written by Ray Christman.

I took one of the booklets, titled *The Freedom Road*. Beneath the typist's fingers, the keyboard sounded like a popcorn popper having an orgasm. I'd never seen anyone type so fast; I had to watch. Her fingers were a blur. How many typos per minute, I wondered? She sat ramrod straight, and while she typed, smoked steadily on a cigarillo, letting ashes dribble on her lap. Finally it was down nearly to the filter tip. She stopped just long enough to put it in a big ashtray that needed emptying—didn't even take time to butt it out—then lit another and started typing grimly again.

I wondered how the hell many letters or pages she typed in a day. There was a graph taped to the wall—hand-drawn!—showing an ascending curve. From where I sat, I couldn't see what it said, and it was behind her so I could hardly go over and look at it closely. Pages typed per day or week, maybe.

I gave my attention to *The Freedom Road*. The damned thing actually made sense, if you accepted the underlying premises. It made a certain amount even if you didn't, as good promotion should.

One-thirty came and went, and 1:40. By then she'd lit still another cigarillo. If Hamilton had been truthful about that ten dollars a week, she had to borrow to keep herself in smokes. Maybe they gave bonuses for production. "Does Mr. Thomas know I'm here?" I asked.

She actually stopped typing to look at me. As if I'd crawled out from under a rock. "He knows." Then she jabbed, and jabbed is the word, an intercom key and spoke to someone on her throat mike, an exchange of maybe eight seconds. "He'll be a few minutes late," she told me. "He's with someone important."

Having put me in my place, she began typing again. A couple of cigarillos later, another uniformed, teenaged boy hustled in with a large styrofoam cup of coffee for her; she accepted it without thanks or even a look, took a sip, then typed on furiously. I wondered how many empty styrofoam cups were in her wastebasket.

At 1:52 another young woman hurried in, a girl, really, in a form-fitting uniform guaranteed to raise your body temperature. Her eyes were on me as she came through the door. "Mr. Eberly? Come with me."

I followed her down the hall to a small elevator foyer, almost trotting to keep up. She poked impatiently at a button, as if pumping it formed a vacuum in the shaft that would pull the elevator in against all resistance. It arrived and took us to the seventh floor, where I stepped out into a penthouse with the quiet of sound insulation and the feel of humidified air conditioning. There she led me down a short hall to an office suite with no plaque on the door. Probably the only office up there, I decided. This had to be the penthouse that Hamilton had said held Christman's apartment and office. Apparently Thomas had moved in, at least into the office. As if he didn't expect Christman back.

I found myself in a small reception room. The receptionist was a tall and very handsome Hispanic lady, maybe forty-five years old, with raven hair, and the first smile I'd seen since the receptionist in the lobby. She too wore a headset, but not a uniform. There was a couch and a matching chair by one wall, and she gestured. "Please have a seat, Mr. Eberly. Mr. Thomas will be with you in a minute or two." I sat. She turned to a computer and began to type. I'd have thought she was really fast, if I hadn't been watching the typist downstairs. After a moment, a silent printer kicked a sheet of paper out into a basket beside her. She scanned it, then put it atop a stack on her desk and continued at her keyboard.

I took the compad out of my attaché case, put it in my jacket pocket to have it handy, then reopened *The Freedom Road* and began to read again. At 2:09, a buzzer *brrrrted* at her from her computer. She picked up a privacy receiver and listened, then got up and looked at me, smiling again. I got the impression that the smile was genuine, that she was actually friendly. And more—that she was somewhat the kind of person the church claimed to produce! "Mr. Thomas will see you now," she said, and led me to the door of what turned out to be a large, richly furnished office. When I stepped in, she stepped back out and closed the door behind me.

Thomas looked skeptically at me, and motioned toward

a chair across a desk from his own. "All right, Mr. Eberly," he said when I'd sat down, "what do you want to know?"

He was a large man, about six-four and maybe 270 pounds—overweight but not obese, more beef than pork. I judged his age at forty-five. Like the typist's, his ashtray was full of butts.

"First, let me say I'm recording this." I touched my attaché case. "So I won't have to rely on notes."

He nodded curtly.

"Is it true that the Church of the New Gnosis has a standing offer of refunds for services given which the parishioner considers unsatisfactory?"

He could see what was coming. His face took a "that again" look. "That's right. And it's an offer we make good on."

I spoke carefully. "I've had people tell me they've applied for refunds and gotten the run-around. Endlessly. What's the truth about that?"

"The truth is that a parishioner has to go through certain steps for a refund. We try to determine what, if anything, went wrong. If the fault was ours, we try to ensure that it doesn't happen again. It's a necessary step in quality control. We're the only church I know of that has a quality control division and offers refunds. Mr. Christman realized when he established the refund policy that it invited trouble. But he considered it the only ethical thing to do."

I jotted notes in speed-writing, as if I was doing more than chumming the water for serious fishing. "Two people have told me they've been trying to get refunds for more than a year, and have been sent to one office after another for a long list of approvals. From people who were 'in conference or out of town'—that sort of thing. After having had appointments with them. Do you know anything about that?"

"Mr. Eberly, fewer than two tenths of one percent of the people who receive services from the church apply for refunds. So. What sort of person does request one, do you suppose?" He paused, then answered his own question.

"The malcontent, Mr. Eberly, the troublemaker. The compulsive liar. Someone who wants something for nothing. Gnosis isn't for everyone—we don't deceive ourselves that it is. But even people who resign from the church seldom request refunds, often despite extreme pressure from family members, and often under the influence of the psychiatric establishment or predatory lawyers. Until you realize these simple facts, you'll have difficulty writing a factual account of the church."

I nodded, wondering if that figure, two tenths of one percent, was correct, or something he'd plucked out of the air. In my business, you learn that some people create lies as easily as they breathe, and I remembered what Ole had said about lying drills. And Thomas' eyes didn't tell me a thing.

"I've also been told," I said—actually I'd only read it—"that Mr. Christman ordered the church to frustrate all refund requests until the requester gave up. What truth is there to that?"

Thomas' lips thinned and tightened. "None. That is patent slander. For years Mr. Christman has paid no attention whatever to the financial activities of the church. They distracted him from his key and vital function, his central purpose—his research. He established basic financial and other policies years ago, and left management to the managers he appointed, and their successors."

Now it was time to bring up serious business. "Is it true that threats have been made against Mr. Christman's life?"

He handled it without blinking. "Of course. Any major public figure, especially one who runs counter to various establishments, receives threats. He'd have felt he wasn't doing his duty if he didn't get death threats."

"You feel no concern then for Mr. Christman's safety?"

He sighed, an act somewhere between impatience and being worn out by stupid questions. "Mr. Eberly, I can't imagine they could even find Mr. Christman to harm him. Even I don't know where he is. He has retired to carry on his spiritual researches in virtually complete seclusion.

His written message to me was that he'd employed three persons to see to his personal needs."

Three persons. That was up two from the "message" read at the Palladium. "He must have financial needs," I said. "How does the church get money to him?"

"Mr. Christman was a wealthy man before he established the church. He then sold his business and converted the funds into more fluid and convenient investments. My impression is that many of them survived the Crash of '96, and subsequently became profitable again. The key point is, he receives no money from the church, none, and never did. I presume he lives on investment income."

Not for the first time I wished we had a contract with the state or city for some aspect of this case. Then I could use the State Data Center and maybe track down his whereabouts from credit flows. If he was still alive.

"Not long ago," I said, "the church was the victor in a lawsuit brought against it by the Institute of Noetic Technology. Is the institute a possible danger to Mr. Christman in his retirement?"

He stared at me for a long moment. Something was going on with him, but I didn't know what.

"Mr. Eberly," he said slowly and deliberately, "this interview is wasting my time. Either you don't grasp what I tell you, or you ignore it. Write your book or article and send me a copy of the manuscript, and I'll either critique it for you myself, or have one of our attorneys do it."

He stood up. "And now— And now, Mr. Eberly, I want you off these premises."

At that point something flared in him, a focused anger. Generally when someone gets mad, it splashes; his anger was as hard and sharp as a laser. "*AND I MEAN NOW! GET YOUR . . .* "

He mixed his obscenities in unlikely combinations, leaning over his desk at me and pointing at the door. At the time it shook me, shook me deeply, and it takes a lot to do that. If it had come down to it, if he'd attacked me physically, I could have stomped the seeds out of him without any trouble at all. And looking back at what happened and what didn't, I think he suspected as much, or knew it, but it didn't matter to him.

At the time though, like I said, it shook hell out of me, and it was more than fear I felt. It was the sheer blasting force of his anger. It knocked the breath out of me. I backed out of his office door, then turned and hurried through his secretary's office and into the hall. I didn't even pause to see what kind of look she had on her face.

I didn't slow down in the hall, either, or wait for an elevator. Both cabs were down, so I used the stairwell. The crash-door at the bottom opened into a first-floor corridor. I followed it to the lobby, and went out the front door into the bright April afternoon. The entry guard paid no attention to me at all, just chewed his gum. Pausing, I pulled myself together, relieved to find my attaché case in my right hand, then strode north down Kinglet Place toward the parking lot. My personal antennae were up even higher than usual, and I was aware that someone was walking behind me, not quite as fast as I was. Not trying to catch up, but there. There was no reason there shouldn't be, of course. People walk on the sidewalk all the time. I angled across the street, looking both ways as I did, and catching a look at the person behind me. He was neither black nor bearded; one of the uniformed teenagers I'd seen earlier, running errands in the Admin Building.

I took another look when I turned in at the parking lot gate. He'd stopped at the sidewalk to the Neophyte Building, not seeming to do anything, just standing there as if waiting, or listening to the birds.

A minute later, as I stopped my car to pay the gateman, I saw the kid still there, watching the gate now. He saw me, then looked the other way and started to walk back toward the Admin Building. That, it seemed, was a signal. There was a parking lot across the street, with a sign that said STAFF ONLY, and by the time I'd rolled out into the street, a veteran white Dodge Westerner was nosing out. I turned north and so did it.

It hadn't been near enough that I knew what the driver looked like, beyond being white and beardless.

I drove to the next cross street, Villamere, and turned west. I'd gone maybe half a block when the Dodge turned west too. I stayed on Villamere west to Vermont, and turned north. So did he. Vermont had a lot a traffic, but he stayed near enough to keep me in sight, and when I came to the on-ramp to the Hollywood Freeway east, I took it. He did too. He still had me in sight when I exited onto the Harbor Freeway south. He did the same. Which almost guaranteed he was following me: If he'd wanted to go south on the Harbor from the Campus, it would have been shorter and quicker to take Wilshire.

But how could Thomas have gotten someone on me that quickly? Or had he set this up before he had me brought to him?

So far I hadn't tried ditching the guy behind me. Now I did, changing lanes, ducking behind delivery trucks, then making a last-minute move into an exit lane and onto the Santa Monica Freeway. And saw no more of him. I'd tried not to be too obvious about it; hopefully they wouldn't realize I knew I'd been followed.

I exited the Santa Monica onto LaBrea and drove back to the office. Why, I asked myself, had I been followed? The likeliest answer was, to find out where I'd come from. That could mean where I worked out of, or where I lived.

My tail should have seen my Colorado plates. Which should put them off. But would it? I couldn't be traced by them. The owner's—the firm's—address was confidential, available only to California and Colorado motor vehicle departments and to law enforcement agencies.

Did the church know that private investigation firms could use out-of-state plates? It had worked its way into detective dramas on TV and holos, much to Joe's disgust. And Prudential was the biggest and most prominent investigation firm in California; it would be the logical place to start checking. The Colorado plates would have to come off, just in case. Because Thomas could be dangerous; I felt sure of it now.

12
VIC AND TORY

The next day Tuuli and I drove to the Hollywood-Burbank Airport, and from there took a skybus to Sky Harbor in Phoenix. After a thirty-minute wait at Sky Harbor, we took the mail-stop shuttle that serves Wickenberg, Lake Havasu City, and places north from there. Places that didn't have scheduled air service in the days before AG.

All to the good, right? Skybuses can be small and still economical to operate, which means you can have a lot of small ones with frequent departures. Also they're a lot cheaper to build than airplanes were. They land and take off vertically, make slow and almost silent approaches, and they're a lot cheaper, easier, and safer to fly than the big, clumsy, noisy, polluting airfoil craft of six or eight years ago. And they don't require roads, runways, or large fields. All in all they're like a clean, superfast bus service, which is why people started calling them skybuses.

Almost no one today wants to go back to the old ways of travel. Or telephoning. Or going to the library or heating a building, or . . . You name it. The problem is, you never have a chance to get used to things. You learn a trade today, and it may disappear tomorrow. Not mine, but a lot of them. Forty or fifty years ago, a guy named Toffler wrote a book called *Future Shock*. I read it about the time—about the time my folks were killed, and it was old then. If he wrote it today, he could call it *Now Shock*. And twenty, twenty-five years ago, a science fiction writer named Vinge—Vernor Vinge—wrote about a future when things changed so fast that people—biological people—couldn't handle it anymore. Well, I'll tell you what. When the research in nanotechnology breaks through the barriers it's run into . . .

Sorry. That's not what you're here to record. Blame it on the Veritas. So. Where were we? Oh yeah. Tuuli and I were going to visit the Merlins. Vic was waiting for us at the Wickenberg airport. He turned out to be a sprightly old guy. I'd have judged him at a lively seventy-five and been short by ten years. He was also taller than I'd expected, but thin: close to 6 feet and probably 130 pounds. But in jeans, a twill workshirt, and work boots, he looked lean and wiry, not frail. He shook my hand with a strong grip, and appreciated Tuuli with his eyes. I could tell she loved him right away.

My first impression was, he'd never murder anyone.

He led us to his pickup and we sped away from town, at first on a highway, then on a narrow blacktop road too minor to rate a center stripe. The air was dry, the April sun bright, and the desert had more vegetation than you might think. It was dominated mainly by what Vic identified for me as mesquite—broad, thorny, 6- to 10-foot shrubs—and in places by what he called creosote bush. There were also lots of spiny cane cactuses 3 to 5 feet tall with big pink flowers, and similar ones so thick with stiff pale spines, they seemed to wear a white aura. He called both kinds chollas. There was a scattering of saguaro cactus, too, some of them 30 feet tall. Vic said they were getting toward their upper elevation limit there. Graceful ocotillas were scattered almost everywhere. Shrubs I guess you could call them, thorny shrubs without twigs or branches, their leaves tiny and sparse, but bright green. Their spiny, sprawling, multiple green stems grew from a common base, to spread 20, maybe 30 feet across, each stem ending with clusters of vivid red flowers.

I could get to like that country, at least in the spring.

After a while we came to a mailbox that read VIC & TORY MERLIN, and from there left the blacktop for a private road that obviously had never known an engineer or road grader. In about a mile of gradual climbing, we reached a range of hills that, farther on, grew to a long low mountain, and the road entered a small canyon. A little brook trickled down it, among rounded stones, with groups of distorted old cottonwoods along its banks. During the occasional storm, according to Vic, the brook could become quite a stream, though most of the time it was dry.

About a mile up the canyon we came to their home, a low, pink-tan adobe ranchhouse with narrow, deep-set windows. Behind it, a windmill pumped water to a tank on a roof-high timber platform, the water supply for the house. They had a GPC-driven pump that did their pumping when the wind was down—gravity is always there, and as cheap as the wind—but Vic said they enjoyed having the windmill do it.

Tory was on the porch to greet us, a small woman, not much bigger than Tuuli. Her hair was still red-tinged, though she was probably as old as her husband. Her eyes were chestnut brown like Molly Cadigan's, and just as direct and powerful. But her look was less aggressive than Molly's, more calm and—*knowing* is the word, I guess. I don't believe anything could flap her—not the arrival of the angel of death, not the end of the world. According to Winifred Sproule, Ray Christman thought Tory was as powerful as Vic. I wasn't sure what Christman meant by powerful—I wasn't sure what *I* meant by powerful—but it seemed to me that if anything she might be more powerful than Vic. And I got that impression just in the minute or so between being introduced on the porch and her going into the kitchen to check on the coffee. She seemed to me like someone who could pretty much control whatever went on around her, if she wanted to.

The living room was big, the ceiling supported by *vigas*, rough-hewn timbers with axe marks on them. More than a century old, I'd guess. One wall had a wide adobe fireplace.

Tuuli and I had taken seats on a comfortable benchlike sofa that might have been made of local cottonwood, upholstered with big fat cushions. Vic sat across from us in a wicker rocker that would have seemed old-fashioned to my dad, who was born in 1917.

"How did you know about Tuuli?" I asked.

He grinned at me. "We've got friends who keep up to date on psychics and who did what." He turned to Tuuli then. "We first heard about you after you took care of the poltergeist that Emmy Raye Crockett had trouble with, after she bought that mansion at Pacific Palisades."

I looked at my wife. She'd never told me anything about a poltergeist! It must have been before I'd met her. And for Emmy Raye Crockett! Doing a successful psychic gig for a major, free-talking country-western star must have gotten important word-of-mouth promotion, as well as publicity in the New Age magazines and newsletters.

"How'd you handle that?" he asked.

Tuuli blushed, something I'd never seen her do before. "I'm not sure," she said. "Well, I guess I am now, partly, but at the time . . . When the dishes started to fly, and the ashtrays and books, my hair stood out like this." She held her hands a foot from her head. "So I admired it. I thought, *you are amazing! Truly marvelous!* And I meant it, because it was. It really was.

"When I thought that, I could feel the change, from anger to something else—pleased pride. No one had admired her before! Ever! I say 'her' because she'd been a woman, I could tell; an old woman who'd lived unappreciated and scorned, and died neglected. Then she picked up a heavy glass tabletop and threw it in the fireplace. It broke in a thousand pieces! After that she stopped. Emmy Raye told me the ghost had never thrown anything heavy before. Mostly it hadn't really thrown things at all, just knocked things over and blew curtains— things like that. When it threw the tabletop, it felt to me as if it had already stopped being angry and was just showing off. I don't think it had ever admitted to itself how powerful it was."

My hair was standing up just hearing about it. For a minute there, *psychic* felt really real to me. I didn't doubt it had happened the way Tuuli said. It wouldn't be like her to exaggerate. Until after I started dating her, psychic had never been real to me at all, even though the firm hired a psychic consultant now and then; that's how I got to know Tuuli. And sometimes we'd gotten useful information from them. Now I asked myself what kind of world she lived in, where you communicate with ghosts. What was it like to have dishes and books and tabletops flying around? Tory had come back from the kitchen while Tuuli was talking. "Then what?" she asked.

Tuuli shrugged. "After a few seconds the poltergeist went away, and that was the end of it."

"How could you tell it had gone away?" I asked, "if it had already stopped throwing things."

"She wasn't there anymore. I could tell. I couldn't feel her anymore."

I let it go at that and turned to Vic, moving the conversation in the direction I wanted and needed. "According to Winifred Sproule, you're psychic. And you knew Ray Christman personally. Could you concentrate on him and find out whether he's alive or not? And where he is?"

He laughed. "If you want information like that, ask Tuuli here. Or Ole. I don't compete with folks in the consulting business."

His answer should have irritated me, but it didn't. I did wonder though whether he could but wouldn't, or would but couldn't. I changed the subject again, telling him what Sproule had said about his being the source of Christman's theology. That's the word I used: "theology." He grinned at it.

"I did send him write-ups from time to time. I needed to write it down anyway, so all I had to do was mail photocopies. A lot of it there isn't words for, of course, or familiar concepts to frame it in, so he'd fly out here now and then to go over it with us. But a lot of it he never fully got, and what he taught, and the procedures he applied, were his own, not ours."

"But wasn't your material the basis of his . . ." I had to grope for the word. "His cosmology? And his, ah, technical procedures? That's what Sproule said."

He nodded. "Yep, that's right. When Ray first decided to start a church, he wanted us to go in on it with him. We'd be the spiritual leaders, and he'd be the executive director, in charge of management and promotion. But it looked to us like the wrong thing to do. For one thing, we'd lose too much freedom."

"So what did you get out of it? If I may ask. What did he pay you for it?"

Tuuli's sharp elbow dug hard in my ribs.

"We never asked for anything; we didn't really need it. But when he came out, he always left us a check. Usually for twenty thousand." He turned to Tory as if looking for help in remembering. "That time he was here when we had snow on the ground, that was fifty thousand. And the time we took him up to visit the kachina in Mount Humphrey—" He looked back at me then. "Say three hundred thousand over the years."

A lot of money maybe, but not much from an operation that according to an *L.A. Times* estimate had grossed more than half a billion by 2006. Which brought to mind the question, where was all that money? Even if a lot of it had been lost in the worldwide Crash of '96 . . . The church was listed as the owner of a lot of real estate, but supposedly that made up no great part of the total. The *Times* had compiled a chart listing the property values, and the church had never built a new building. Its specialty was buying properties from owners who were in a serious bind for money. It would offer them twenty to forty percent of the listed value in instant cash, take it or leave it. It was impressive how many had gone for it. Christman had gotten the Campus for only eight mil. The land by itself had been worth more than that.

"Didn't that bother you?" I asked. "I mean, he made millions on millions, got a lot of recognition . . ."

"Nope. We didn't need the money. I'd done pretty well as chief technical editor for Bourdon Electronics, and

before that from Viggers Technologies in Maryland. And
I'd helped finance a few small but promising businesses." He grinned again. "The owner of one of them
introduced me to Ray. Before I was fifty, we were living
off investments.

"Now and then I'd do counseling on somebody with a
lot of money, like Ray. One of them signed this place over
to us; these eighty acres plus the buildings. Just gave them
to us. The entire ranch is half a million acres, and he'd
decided to run the whole spread from his headquarters over
by Yellow Jacket. Actually I was still working for Bourdon
then. Getting this place was what decided me to quit and
work full-time on my research." He laughed. "Research,
naps, and puttering around the place."

"What kind of research?"

"Nothing that science would recognize. I'd been a Noetie
counselor before that, and before that I'd been interested
in the mind and what the science fiction of that time called
psionics. I'd had experiences that gave me something to
work with, and training and experience in science and
technical editing that gave me a viewpoint.

"There were problems, of course. The experiences had
mostly been personal, or even subjective. So I went into
it subjectively. I couldn't see any other way. Sometimes I
use the psychogalvanometer and ask myself questions, to
get me into it. Other times I start out with meditation.
Usually not like in yoga though; generally I meditate *on*
something. Not *think,* just put my attention on it. Then,
after a while, things are likely to happen; I follow where
they lead me, and watch or experience the results. After
that I do the best I can to sort it out. Put it in words and
diagrams like the ones I gave Ray. It's not always easy."

He gestured. "Tory gives me an anchor—Tory and sometimes the boys. Bails me out when I get in over my head."
He grinned again, ruefully this time. "There were times,
early on, when I foundered. They gave me an external
viewpoint then. Seems like they'd get a sense of what was
going on when I didn't." He paused. "Been interesting."

He'd been leaning forward while he talked. Now he sat

back. "No," he said, "we live the way we like, and like the way we live. We do what we want, when we want. And we don't do without. Sometimes we don't see anyone for a week or two, until we go to town. Our nearest neighbors live seventeen miles from here. Now and then one or both our boys will drive out from Phoenix with their wives for a weekend. Other times friends will drop by, with or without their bodies."

With or without their bodies! I wondered if he was serious. Tuuli thought so. She was listening intently.

"Ole flies out from L.A. once or twice a year," Vic went on, "and now and then the Diaconos fly down from the Rim. It's a good life, and public attention would have spoiled it."

I got the message, and believed it: the Merlins were happier without recognition. Another dead end, I decided, but I still might get some useful insights out of the trip.

"Look, people," Tory put in, "I've got a big pot of coffee and a tray of chocolate-chip cookies in the kitchen." She looked at me. "Guaranteed not to add weight. If y'all are interested, we'll go out there and you can help yourself."

We trooped to the kitchen behind her. Again there were rough-hewn roof beams, and a big adjoining pantry in which I could see a freezer. Besides freezer, fridge, electric range, microwave, dishwasher, and all the rest of the modern stuff, there was a tall 'dobe fireplace built into a corner, with two pot hooks for cooking! There were even two black iron pots on a mantel, and a woodbox to one side. With wood in it, I had no doubt. On the table, a glass cream pitcher was full of what looked to me like real cream, and the sweetener was sugar cubes, not low-cal powder in envelopes. The cookies had calories written all over them. I took three. *They're not as fattening as Molly Cadigan's chocolate-glazed doughnuts,* I told myself. *They weren't cooked in deep fat.*

Back in the living room I asked, "What did you hope to learn from your research?"

"Whatever there was to know. I was exploring."

"Didn't you have a hypothesis?"

"Two of 'em. That there was something to find—something to learn—and that I could learn it."

"Such as?"

He grinned again. "How the odds and ends of unexplained observations and experiences relate to one another, especially the ones that science doesn't like because they don't fit orthodox scientific paradigms: things like clairvoyance, telepathy, telekinesis, psychic photography, firewalking. . . . I figured if you poke around in things like that, some of them might come together for you.

"I ran into anomalies, of course, and things I could only see vaguely." He chuckled. "There was a time, twenty-five years ago, we thought we'd gone far enough, we could tie the rest of it up pretty fast. Have us a tight, inclusive theory; a sort of metaphysical universal field theory. That was after we debugged the surprise generator."

I didn't know how to take that, especially the thing about a surprise generator. Metaphor I suppose.

His laugh was relaxed and self-amused. "There were more barriers left than we'd imagined. Then Arne Haugen turned physics upside down without any metaphysical research at all. With just . . ." He paused and laughed. "*Just* his native inventiveness—the meeting ground of physics and the subliminal mind. And of course the engineering knowledge and money that made it work.

"All we contributed here was, we'd debugged the surprise generator. Which had to make a difference." He raised an eyebrow. "That was up in your part of the country."

Surprise generator again. I had no idea what he meant by that. Or how he knew, or *if* he knew, what part of the country I was from. Actually, his comment almost slipped past me. I'd started feeling groggy; something about the subject was getting to me.

I straightened, pushing the grogginesss away. "Dr. Sproule told me that when Christman changed your stuff, she thought he screwed it up. Ole thought so too."

Vic laughed again, as if that didn't bother him at all. "Ray's idea was to create a religion with it, train a lot of people to go out and help others to be freed beings. His

problem was writing it up and teaching it. He felt folks
had to *understand* it before they could know it; grokking
it wouldn't do. And of course, he didn't understand it
himself, actually, any more than I do."

I stared at him. He got to his feet then, took a ruled
pad from a big old-fashioned desk, and drew a quick diagram, then brought it over and, kneeling, showed it to Tuuli
and me, pointing with his pencil and explaining.

To me it was just marks on paper, and I got to feeling
weirder and weirder. It was a little like when I was thirteen and climbed this big willow tree on a cutbank on the
Hemlock River, at the edge of town. Bobby Latvala had
spiked pieces of one-by-four on the trunk for a ladder, and
you could jump off branches into the water. The highest
branch you could get out on to jump was fifty-three feet
above the river, measured by Jimmy Dobrik's mother's
clothesline. The first time I went out on it to jump, it felt
like my knees were made of water—as if I was going to
faint and fall off. Physically that's a little like I felt when
Vic was explaining his diagram—like I was going to faint
and fall a long way. Nothing was coming through mentally
at all.

"Vic," Tory said, "I think that's a little steep for Martti."
That did come through, and I was aware of her eyes on
me. "Martti," she told me, "get up and walk around the
room. Look at things. Touch them." I did, and felt better
right away. Then we all refilled our coffee cups and I got
a couple more chocolate-chip cookies, and they asked Tuuli
about what it was like growing up in Lapland.

After a little, I brought the conversation back to Ray
Christman, more or less. "So all this information and theory
you developed—what good does it do? If Christman got
it wrong and you're not doing anything with it yourself?"

"It doesn't have to do good. The bottom line is, we had
fun doing it, Tory and the boys and me. Especially me. And
Ray had fun with it in his own way. Beyond that, he gave
half a million people enough of it that it's making a useful difference in their lives and their environments. And
it's percolating into the overall body of the New Age

174 John Dalmas

movement, with all its interests and information, its mythologies and misinformation from a lot of different directions.

"Folks need a new paradigm, you see. One they can relate life to. Even before Arne Haugen introduced his geogravitic power converter, things were changing so fast in people's lives that a lot of them were having trouble coping. Then along came the GPC, and the incomplete theory that Haugen based it on, and all of a sudden, science had the breakthrough it needed to start simplifying a lot of things, and integrating them into new and more powerful conceptual models. And engineers had a whole new information set to play with. Play and build with. And boy have they ever!"

He paused to dunk and eat another cookie. I matched him; I'd forgotten all about calories.

"So things got to changing faster than ever," he went on, "and people are having more and more trouble with the changes. They feel like the world's getting away from them."

I nodded. "That's why the government passes laws to slow things down, some things."

I thought of the agricultural preservation acts that restrict the use of food factories in the United States and a lot of other countries. The geogravitic power converter changed agriculture as drastically as it did transportation. Desalinized seawater was nearly as cheap as river water now, and pumping it long distances over mountains is economical too. Though to call the machinery "pumps" is stretching the term; they just create localized energy fields where uphill is downhill. And there was storm control that grew out of the same theories, and the advances in molecular engineering. Along with genetic engineering, they'd changed farming so drastically my dad wouldn't have recognized it, and he'd been dead less than twenty years.

But it was still farming. People still lived on the land and worked the soil, even if a lot of it was under cleartents that covered acres of ground. The unrestricted development of food factories would wipe out most of it, something a whole lot of people weren't ready to face yet.

That's the kind of thing I meant when I mentioned government restrictions.

"Right," Vic said, "the government does hold back some changes. But even so, they're coming faster than ever, and a whole lot of people feel anxious. Some get to be activists for some cause, trying to increase their control of things. Some take drugs, trying to relieve their anxieties. Others look for deeper meaning in consciousness clubs, dream networks, or just life itself. Or join churches or cults. A religious cult, if it's not a con, is just a church outside of what folks are used to."

He stopped to eat another cookie, chewing and sipping thoughtfully. "More of them might join cults, except they've learned not to trust 'em. So there's getting to be a lot of New Age eclectics, borrowing from this belief and that philosophy and these other sets of practices—puttin' them together in a system that makes sense to them. People leave groups like Leif's and Ray's, and take with them what they learned there, and gradually it spreads.

"Leif borrowed a lot from psychiatry and psychology— culled it, tested it, and unified it. And added his own ideas. Some of them, especially dealing with application, have worked their way into psychology and psychiatry in a sort of reverse flow. You can find quite a few psychiatrists now, and clinical psychologists, who'll treat you with what amounts to Noetics One, which are the levels that bite best. Especially when they're not loaded up with Leif Haller's cosmology and megalomania. Even his cosmology can be beneficial; it can break older false realities, and give you food for thought."

I interrupted. "You're talking about Noeties. What about Gnostic procedures?"

"They've barely begun to influence psychology and psychiatry. They're less familiar seeming."

Tuuli broke in then, and what she said startled hell out of me. Shook me! "I want to— I want to realize my potential as a psychic," she said. "I know there's more. I can feel it. Will you be my guru? You or Tory?"

She hadn't asked me about it or even warned me. As

if she was independent, unmarried. Vic wasn't grinning now. "We're not in the guru business, Tuuli," he answered softly. "If we were, we'd sure like to have you, but we're not. Tell you what though. Before you folks head back to L.A., we've got something to give you. Each of you."

He turned his attention back to me then, and after a few thoughtful seconds picked up more or less where he'd left off. "The big breakthrough in philosophy won't come from people like Tory and me. Not directly. It'll come from the scientific establishment."

I stared at him.

"Physics and math. It started long before Arne Haugen, but he shifted it up a few gears. And it's changing a lot more than the way we travel, and power our factories, and raise our crops. Physics has been turned on its head, and it's growing a new cosmology. Now we've got theoretical constructs like the omega matrix and the Meissner-Ikeda Lattice. Interest in hypernumbers theory is getting to be respectable; it's spread beyond the Institute. And Ali Hasad's *Limited Theory of Generated Reality* is gaining supporters in mainstream physics. In a decade or so there'll be a new model of reality to orient on, compelling enough and simple enough that it'll change how people look at things. And sooner or later it'll give rise to a psychology that'll compare to present-day psychology the way chemistry does to alchemy."

He stopped then and picked up his last cookie.

I knew this wasn't just a pause. He'd finished. I ate my last cookie too, and finished my coffee. As far as I could see, I was done there.

13
MERLIN THE MAGICIAN

Before I could say anything about going home though, Tory invited us to stay for supper, and she seemed to mean it. Vic said they were having friends down from "up on the Rim"—that's the Mogollon Rim, the rim of the Coconino Plateau—who looked forward to meeting us. It would have been rude to insist on leaving sooner, and besides, I could see that Tuuli wanted to stay. Really wanted to.

Then Vic asked if I'd care to take a hike around, and that seemed like a good way to use some of the time.

"You want to come?" I asked Tuuli.

Tory spoke before Tuuli could. "I'd planned to show her some things around here."

So Vic and I went alone, hiking a path that slanted up the canyon side to the top, stopping to rest when we needed to. A couple of times we passed what seemed to be pieces of airplane, and when we got to the top, sure as hell, there was a whole damned propellor stuck upright in the ground. When I asked about it, he said the plane had belonged to "the Four," and had blown up. I got a strange chill when he said it, and didn't ask for an explanation.

We sort of moseyed along up there in late-afternoon sunshine and a mild breeze. The temperature must have

been about 75 degrees. We talked about everyday kinds
of things. He asked about my family, and I got carried away.
Told him about my dad having been Ojibwa County Sheriff
for twenty-five years, and a deputy for ten years before that.
That he'd married my mother when he was sixty-one, and
they'd had Elvi and me. I also told him a couple of stories
I'd heard of things dad had done as sheriff. I was still a
preschooler when he'd retired.

Dad was a pretty remarkable man, born on a homestead
in a Finlander colony in Upper Michigan, and went to work
in the logging woods when he was fourteen, instead of
going to high school. I didn't mention how he died though,
how they both died. I'd learned years before that I couldn't
trust myself not to break down. The last person I'd told
was Tuuli, and I didn't tell her everything. My sister Elvi
and my half brother Sulo did it for me.

Vic was from Texas; he could even talk Tex Mex. His
dad had been an oil field worker, a roustabout, and Vic
had too, after high school. Till he had enough money to
start college, where he got his bachelor's in chemistry. He'd
started on his master's in biochem, but washed out by
getting a C in physical chemistry. He'd switched to science
education then, to finish his degree, but taught only briefly
before getting a job with Viggers.

While we walked, a Dodge Skytote came in from the
northeast; its driver saw us and put down on the ridge. It
had DIACONO'S SPIRIT LODGE painted on the side, in script
resembling the Devanagari of India. A big, powerfully built
guy got out, and a woman as good looking as it's possible
to be at sixty. With them was what I took for a Hindu,
small, hardly bigger than Tuuli, looking totally incongru-
ous in Levi's, a chamois shirt, and a very large hat. I stood
back and watched while all three of them, laughing, hugged
and kissed Vic as if he were a favorite uncle they hadn't
seen for years. My family had had a lot of affection among
themselves, but its men didn't kiss each other, or their wives
in front of anyone. I'd always felt uncomfortable, seeing
men kiss each other, but for these people it seemed natural.

When the hugs had been distributed, Vic turned to me.

"Frank, Mikki, Bhiksu, I'd like you to meet Martti Seppanen, the visitor I told you about from L.A. Martti, this
is Frank Diacono, and this pretty lady is his wife Mikki."
He chuckled. "And this rawhide buckaroo is Bhiksu. Frank
and Mikki and I are old friends from way back; Frank
helped me debug the surprise generator, and Mikki saved
his life on the lake ice. He'd been shot, and like to have
froze unless he bled to death first. Bhiksu's an old friend
too, who came to Arizona three years ago. Bhiksu's all the
name he uses. I think he's on the run from somewhere."

Something about Vic's monolog had made my head spin,
but pressing the flesh cleared it. Frank Diacono's grip was
as strong as mine, and his strength seemed to flow through
it into me.

"Glad to know you, Frank," I said. "And Mikki. And
Bhiksu." It seemed to me I knew Diacono's face, and his
wiry hair, half gray now. Knew it from when he was younger
and I was a kid. The name rang a bell, too. It would come
to me.

Then we all got in the Skytote and floated down to the
house. As soon as I got out, I could hear two women
laughing in the kitchen, and for a minute thought someone else had arrived while we were gone. It turned out
to be just Tory and Tuuli; I'd never heard Tuuli laugh like
that before, or look so beautiful.

Supper was a ranch-style meal: steak, chili, and coffee,
plus a salad with boiled eggs and home-sliced cheese on
top of lettuce and slices of cucumber and tomato. There
wasn't any dessert, but when we went to the living room
afterward, there was a tray of brownies, and two battery-
powered thermal coffee pitchers to supplement the pot.

I really can't tell you what was talked about. I started
feeling groggy early on, a grogginess I decided later was
protection against mental or psychic overload. Tuuli, though,
was taking it all in. I have a sort of vision of her there,
laughing and lovely, her tan cheeks with a pink underglow.
Before I conked out entirely, I was in a sort of weird
falling-asleep state, with Bhiksu seeming to float in the air,
glowing a violet blue. That was the last I remember until

I woke up in darkness, having to use the *hyysikää*, the bathroom. It was half past one, and the house was quiet. The only light came from the bathroom door, standing slightly ajar down the hall. When I was done and came back out, there was Vic, sitting in the wicker rocker, almost invisible in the dimness. I wondered if he'd been there all along.

He stood up, and without saying anything, beckoned. I didn't know what else to do, so I followed him down the hall to a corner room. He opened the heavy wooden door and closed it behind us.

It was an ordinary, if undersized, bedroom with no bed, only two kneeling chairs, well upholstered. He gestured at one, and I knelt-sat down on it. He sat down facing me about six feet away, and spoke. "Remember I said we had something to give you?"

"Yeah."

"Tory gave Tuuli hers while you and I were up the hill."

I nodded. Something had happened, that I knew.

"I thought I'd better give you yours tonight, so you could sleep on it."

I had no idea what he was talking about, but for whatever reason, it was okay with me.

"I want you to just sit there and look at me, while I look at you."

We did, and I felt tension gradually developing. Then something began pulling inside of me, twisting, and suddenly I felt as if the whole world was dying. I could feel my face screwing up, and then the tears started. I was a grown man crying, crying right in front of someone, another man, and I couldn't stop, didn't want to stop. I keened and swayed and sobbed, and then a stranger thing happened. Much stranger. I seemed to be outside myself, in a back corner of the room, up by the ceiling. I watched myself cry, and as I watched, felt a strange warm affectionate feeling, tinged with amusement. And at the same time still felt the grief and the bitter bitter loss. It was as if I was two people, one watching the other.

It went on like that for several minutes—long enough

that my shirtfront was wet with tears. Then it eased, and I realized I felt—clean. Drained but totally clean.

"Well," Vic said quietly, "shall we call that a done?"

I nodded. It felt done to me.

"Then how about we have a bite to eat?"

I followed him to the kitchen and sat watching him fry bacon and eggs at two in the morning, the bacon in an electric skillet, the eggs on an electric grill. The sound of sizzling was an aesthetic masterpiece. Frying bacon had never smelled so good, and things had never looked so sharp and clear before. I couldn't remember feeling so relaxed. While the eggs and bacon fried, toast popped from the toaster, four slices, and I helped butter them. Then Vic poured a tall glass of milk. Neither of us said anything till the bacon was crisp, perfectly crisp. Then he sat me down and put the whole batch in front of me, enough to feed a family.

"That's yours," he said. "I'll make some more for me."

Salivating like a rabid wolf, I started eating. It was marvelous. I scarcely thought, just savored the food, and the smell and sound of more bacon frying. Vic settled for two eggs, with bacon and toast in proportion. When we'd finished, we put jackets on and walked outside to look at the desert sky awhile. Living in L.A., I'd forgotten how many stars there are to see. *Linnunrata,* the Milky Way, was a broad white swath across the sky, and mentally I reached, glorying in it, high as a bird.

Back inside I lay down on the couch again, not to waken Tuuli. Vic went on to bed. I wondered if I'd go to sleep, and in a minute or two was drifting off, remembering Tuuli's laughter when I'd come back from the hill. Then I slept and dreamed, though I don't remember what.

I awoke to a kiss. Tuuli was kneeling beside me, and sunlight was glowing through the windows.

14
PIE ARE SQUARE

We flew out of Wickenberg at noon for L.A. It was another beautiful April day. I didn't feel as strangely marvelous, or as marvelously strange, as I had in the kitchen with Vic, and maybe I never will again. But I felt more relaxed than I was used to—than I had since I was sixteen. Since before dad and mom were killed, and I shot and stomped their murderer.

I can talk about it now. I still feel—not grief, but the memory of grief, a shadow of it. And the rage is gone, the rage and shame I worked to hide for so long, suppressed for so long.

On the flight home, Tuuli and I talked more than usual to each other, and without the sharp edges that sometimes were there—that often were there beneath the surface. Also, I came away with Frank Diacono's business card:

Frank Diacono
(602) 555-3443
DIACONO'S SPIRIT LODGE
Long Valley Route
Box 146
Pine, Arizona 85544

And an invitation: "If you ever need a place to get away to, give us a call. We can pick you up at Flagstaff or Phoenix."

The next day I caught up on office work, especially reading. Joe subscribes to a clipping service that faxes us clipsheets on crime and criminals in California, Nevada, and Arizona, covering both English and Spanish-language newspapers. And I turned in my expense account for the weekend—airfare, not including Tuuli's, my mileage driving to Hollywood-Burbank, and airport parking.

I also worked out at Gold's. I didn't buy Tory's comment that her brownies and chocolate-chip cookies were non-fattening. Although I hadn't gained any weight over the weekend, which didn't hurt my feelings.

Most of the next two days I spent contacting my informants and learning nothing. Just after I got back to the office on Wednesday, Tuuli called. The WorldWide Films Theatre was showing a Finnish film about the Lapps, and she wanted us to go that night. I told her sure. After that I dictated an interim report on the case, for Joe's editing and initials. He'd send clean copy to Butzburger, recommending the investigation continue. It was too soon to give up. Butzburger, of course, might feel differently, and it was his money. Also he might not like what I'd learned about the source of Christman's ideas.

The report didn't take long. Then I left early, to get home before the rush hour traffic.

We took Tuuli's little red Sportee, and stopped at a restaurant on Hillhurst near Sunset, called Pie Are Square. We eat there now and then. As we followed the hostess, we passed close by a table where three people sat, wearing the sky blue uniform of Gnostie staff. One of them laid his eyes on me almost as soon as we came in, and said something quietly. The other two glanced at us then. As we walked toward them, Tuuli started talking Finnish at me, telling me to talk, but to speak Finnish, not English.

So I did, asking her what was going on. She told me she felt danger. I didn't know whether she was being psychic or if it was because the Gnosties were looking at us. We talked Finnish all the way to the corner booth we went to; she wanted the Gnosties to think we were foreigners. I sat where they couldn't see me. That was her idea too. A couple of them could see Tuuli, but she wasn't worried about that. A few minutes later, Nerisa, our usual Filipina waitress, came over and took our orders. A couple of minutes after that, Tuuli saw one of the Gnosties beckon to Nerisa and talk to her, but nothing more happened.

When we left, two of the Gnosties were still at the table, talking over coffee. Tuuli hadn't noticed when the other one left, or if he'd just gone to the rest room. One of the two gave me a glance, but that was all, and I told myself that if there'd been any danger, it was past. We went out to her car and drove to the movie.

15
INDIAN'S STORY

A couple of days later I stopped at Morey's for breakfast, and while I was eating, a guy called Indian came in. He'd taken to wearing his hair in a Mohawk, exposing the skull patches he'd had put on for electronic brain stimulation. Indian's a Loonie who works as a casual for Yitzhak's Transit, just down the street from Morey's. As a casual, some days he works and some days he doesn't. He turns up at Yitzhak's at 7:10 for muster, and if they don't have a job for him that morning, he stops in at Morey's for coffee and a glazed doughnut. He's been doing that for at least as long as Prudential's been in the new building.

He's a big, rawboned Angeleno, not an Indian, though he claims to be a quarter Chippewa. His hair's sort of sandy brown, and his mustache is red, but if you dyed his face and hair, he might pass.

He saw me when he came in, and when he'd gotten his coffee and doughnut, he came over. "Hey, Martti!" he said. "I ain't seen you lately! You're looking good, man! Like the spirits are bein' good to you!"

I told him Tuuli and I had gotten out of town last weekend and it had done us both a lot of good.

"I seen you and her a couple days ago at that pie place on Hillhurst. Me and Moonbeam were across the street in the ticket line at SF Adventures, to see *Time Drifters*. And I seen a little red Ford parked at the pie place, and I said to Moonbeam that it's the kind your wife drives; I wonder if they're havin' supper there? And a little later, sure enough! You came out and drove away."

"Yeah," I told him, "we went to the WorldWide to see a movie."

He broke his doughnut in half, dunked a piece, and took a bite. "You know what else I saw?"

He said that quietly, looking around, which caught my interest. It was out of character for him; Indian's usually very open. "Right after I first saw your car, some New Gnu in uniform came out and stopped behind it. And wrote down your license number."

Yitzhak's a New Gnu, a politer term for Gnostie, and most of the people who work for him are New Gnus. According to Indian, they're a good bunch to work for and with, but they don't have any tolerance at all for outsiders talking about the church, because it catches so much bad-mouth.

"Writing down our license number?"

"That's how it looked. He stopped behind it and it looked to me like he was writing it down in a pocket notebook or something."

That actually gave me a cold chill. "Huh! That's weird. Why would he do that?" Because there was no way he could have known it was ours. He couldn't have seen us get out of it from where they'd been sitting. "Maybe he was getting the number of the car next to it," I suggested.

"Might be. Couldn't be sure from where we were."

I spent most of the day on other things, and before lunch took time for an hour's workout. I seemed to be dead in the water on the Christman case.

That afternoon I got a phone call from Molly Cadigan. "You alone, Sweetbuns?" she asked. I told her I was; actually Carlos was in my office at the time.

"I had a lunch date this afternoon with a friend of mine. In the Saints' Deli. The Gnostie hangout on Winderly, across from the Campus. While I was waiting for her, I looked at the notice board." She paused for effect. "And saw your picture."

"My picture?!"

She held it in front of her vidcam, a printed church circular with a composite computer sketch of me. A pretty good one. "I recognized you right away," she said. I couldn't read much of it on the screen, only the heading: *Security Division. FOR IN-HOUSE DISTRIBUTION ONLY.* "It orders anyone who recognizes you to notify church security," she told me.

I thought, *Judas Priest! What does this mean?*

"It says *In-House Distribution Only,* which is ominous by itself," she went on. "If they didn't have something unpleasant in mind, they wouldn't have said that. Obviously some dimwit on church staff posted it in the Saints' anyway. So I took it down."

Obviously she had. "Wasn't that sticking your neck out?" I asked her.

"Sweetbuns, my neck's been out so far for so long . . . But if anyone had noticed, they'd have squawked. And I'd have jumped all over them, because the thing says In-House Only." She paused. "What'd you do to stir them up?"

"I'm not sure," I told her. "I did get an interview with Lon Thomas. Under an assumed name. I told him I was writing a book."

"*Hah!*" She barked the sound. "I'll bet he had someone research the name and found out you weren't legit! Look, Sweetbuns, take my advice. Stay well away from the Campus. Lon Thomas doesn't play with a full deck. He's smart, but he's crackers, too."

She didn't have to convince me. When we'd disconnected, I sat back wondering if one of those might get posted in Yitzhak's. Not likely, but . . . Occasionally there was a guy or two from Yitzhak's besides Indian that ate at Morey's, and they'd recognize the picture.

"Sweetbuns?" Carlos said. One eyebrow was cocked halfway up his forehead. He couldn't see my phone screen from where he sat.

"It's just something she says," I told him. "She's twenty years older and twenty pounds heavier than me."

He grinned. "If you say so. You're wondering about Yitzhak's now, right?"

"I was, yeah."

"Penny and I are going to put some stuff in storage," he said. "I think I'll walk down to Yitzhak's. I suppose he sells storage boxes. And while I'm there, I'll browse their notice board."

That's Carlos for you. He didn't get to be supervisory investigator by being slow.

After Carlos left, I recalled Indian telling about the Gnostie staff member writing down our license number. I thought I knew why. Tuuli had a Finnish-flag bumper sticker, with "Suomi" written on it. It's unlikely he knew that Suomi meant Finland, and even less likely that he recognized Finnish when he heard it. But we'd been talking a foreign language, and he could easily have recognized the sticker as a flag. Flag stickers aren't rare with a generation that's gotten interested in their ethnic roots.

And if they'd questioned Nerisa about us, she might have said that ordinarily when we came in, we spoke English. Even Tuuli doesn't have much accent.

All in all I didn't feel too comfortable.

16
WRONG TARGET

That was on Friday. On Sunday I slept in, and Tuuli and I had breakfast together. We figured that after we'd eaten, we'd go to the L.A. Zoo. It's in Griffith Park, built against the foot of the Hollywood Hills, and if the winter rains have come through, the hills are exceptionally beautiful in spring. The zoo itself is sort of overgrown with tropical and subtropical plants, its paved paths leading around through them. Just for starters, there are albino tigers, pens with goats that children can get in with and pet, and an African bull elephant that dwarfs the Asian elephants. He wears a huge leg chain bolted to a steel post set god knows how deep in concrete.

Our plans got altered though. We had the TV news on for breakfast, something we seldom do. It's bad for the digestion. Maybe Tuuli's psychic power was operating subliminally. She's the one who turned it on.

The feature story was a bombing the evening before, and the building bombed was the apartment house she used to live in. Worse, the specific apartment bombed was on the southwest corner of the second floor, the one that used to be hers. It killed an Armenian immigrant family: Barkev Boghosian, his wife Sophie, their two children, and Boghosian's mother. It also killed a person

189

in the apartment below. A still picture showed Boghosian as a husky, thirtyish guy who worked for an import-export firm.

A neighbor reported having seen a man, with a package "as big as a suitcase," ringing the Boghosian's doorbell a few minutes ealier. The man had worn a brown shirt and trousers like a deliveryman's uniform. Apparently the package had held the bomb.

It could have been a coincidence, of course, but right from the start, neither of us had any doubt that the bomb had been meant for us. For me specifically and for Tuuli by association. I put it together for her this way: The Gnostie that took her license number had then reported seeing us at Pie Are Square. Maybe he'd even been sitting in his car watching, and saw us come out and drive away. We'd been speaking a foreign language, but according to Nerisa were able to speak perfectly good English.

Tuuli admitted that she hadn't sent her change of address to the Department of Motor Vehicles after we got married, and she hadn't had to reregister her car yet, so their records still showed the old Hollywood Boulevard address. Someone in the church either hacked or bought their way into the DMV's computer and got that address; not an easy thing to do. The guy who delivered the bomb would even have been met at the door by a burly guy with a foreign accent, though presumably that made no difference in what happened.

Thomas would have watched this morning's news, or maybe last night's, and read the morning paper. And he'd know from the DMV records that Tuuli's car wasn't registered to any Boghosian. Besides, except for the build, Boghosian's picture didn't look like me. He'd know they'd hit the wrong target.

When I'd run through it, we sat looking at each other over our coffee. "How'd you like to take a vacation in Arizona?" I asked her.

"If you'll come with me."

"Honey, I can't; I've got a case. This is the best lead I've had on it, and if I solve it, I'll have the people who want to kill me. This is real evidence, circumstantial but real, that the church is behind Christman's disappearance."

"Let Carlos handle it."

"Honey, Carlos is good, very good, but he's not as good as I am. The firm will rent me a room somewhere; maybe a series of rooms. You can go stay at Diacono's. I'll bet the firm will cover the cost. If they won't, we'll cover it ourselves."

She looked thoughtful. I could almost see the wheels turning: she was thinking about studying or whatever with a guru. She'd already told me that Bhiksu was psychically very advanced, and had done some remarkable things that evening at the Merlins', after I'd fogged out and gone to sleep.

I remembered the dream that maybe hadn't been a dream.

She'd also told me that Mikki was a psychic whose powers had been expanded and stabilized by Tory and Vic.

A lot of people, Tuuli said, had occasional psychic moments, probably most people. With some of them, these were explicit, but mostly they were vague, like a notion with no apparent source. With her, they were only occasional, unless she deliberately looked for one. Then she'd often get something, often sharp and clear.

And one of the things they did at Diacono's Spirit Lodge, she said, was train people in that sort of thing—people with a talent for it. My natural tendency was to be skeptical, but if believing would get Tuuli out of L.A. for a while, great. Besides, I couldn't doubt that Vic had some sort of power, not after what he'd done for me. And apparently Tory did too.

After a minute, Tuuli nodded. "All right. I have appointments with clients on Monday and Tuesday. Surely the people that want to kill us won't have our new address by then, will they?"

"I've assumed they got your name and old address from DMV. And now that they know the address was wrong . . ."

Suddenly I realized there was something I needed to do. Right away! I got up from the table and called GTE. Had them remove both of us from directory assistance—Tuuli's business listing as well as our residential listings. I used my investigator's credentials to have it done immediately. In fact I didn't disconnect till it was done. The big question was, had it been in time?

Tuuli hated to have her listings removed, but she recognized the need. If Thomas or whoever hadn't checked yet, being unlisted would stall them for a while, maybe quite awhile, and we could get listed again when it was safe. There were phone books, of course, but most people didn't have one. If your phone wasn't computerized, you got the books free, white and yellow pages separately. Otherwise you had to order and pay for them. Presumably the church didn't have phone books, and wouldn't think to check one anyway. If someone wasn't in the electronic directory, they'd rarely be in the book either.

Of course, if they'd already checked . . . "Hon," I told her, "I think you should leave today. Call and notify your clients that you've had an emergency of some kind."

She frowned, considering. "This *is* a security building," she countered, "and Prudential has the contract. I don't like to be driven out of my home by some criminal. And I hate to lose business."

"There are worse things to lose. And building security isn't intended to prevent determined terrorist-type attacks. It's to prevent nuisance entry and discourage crime on the premises. Utilities people, delivery personnel, clients who come to see you—anyone who seems to have a proper reason to enter—they let in."

I shifted my approach then, and phoned the Diaconos to ask how much they charged. Frank answered. For Tuuli, he said, they'd only charge for meals and housekeeping: fifteen dollars a day. When I objected that that seemed awfully cheap, he laughed. "We've got unoccupied rooms, and our food is nothing fancy. If it was you, we might charge twenty-five."

While we were talking, I remembered where I'd known

Diacono before. Not personally, but on television, when I'd been a kid. He'd been an all-pro NFL linebacker before I was born, and I'd seen his antidrug spots on television when I was little.

I generally liked people who fought drugs. The guy who'd gunned down my parents had been a drug smuggler dad had caught, and who'd nursed his grudge for eighteen years in prison. As if it was dad's fault, not his. He'd only had about half a minute to enjoy it before I unloaded a charge of number four shot into his back from my twelve-gauge. It severed his spinal cord. Then I'd kicked and stomped him very thoroughly to death. Something I used to revisit in nightmares.

I told Frank what our situation was, and that conceivably Tuuli's presence could be a risk to them. He grinned and said so was a tornado or Lucifer's Hammer, and not to worry about it.

She talked to him then. He finally agreed to accept twenty. She also arranged to be picked up at Flagstaff on Wednesday—made the decision on her own and without discussing it with me. When she disconnected, she turned, expecting me to blow up. "I won't postpone my clients," she said. I surprised her. "Okay. I'll call Joe and tell him what's happened. I'll ask him to intensify security here for a couple of days. If we have to, you and I can pay for an extra guard or two."

Joe agreed without hesitating. He'd add a third guard on each shift, seasoned people with superior ratings, and send out a scanner they could use to check packages. Then I called the building manager and had him take our names off the directory. I told him we'd had some harassment calls.

We did get to the zoo that day, only later than we'd planned. By the time we got back, I'd thought of something else I needed to do. I'd called myself Martin Eberly for my appointment with Lon Thomas. Presumably he'd checked afterward, when he'd decided I might be a threat, and concluded that the name was false, but I wouldn't take it for granted. So I checked for possible Martin or

M. Eberlys, Eberleys, and Eberles listed in metropolitan L.A.-Riverside-Long Beach. There weren't any. If there had been, I'd have had the firm warn them of possible danger.

17
TUNNELS

On Monday I talked with Carlos about the bombing and the encounter at Pie Are Square, and he agreed it pointed to the church. Joe called the LAPD, told them the firm might have a lead on the bomber, and asked for a contingency contract on the bombing case. A contingency contract pays nothing unless you get information that at least contributes to an indictment, but it doesn't commit you to anything, either.

He had to give his reason for thinking there might be a connection, and put it in very general terms: The bombed apartment had until recently been occupied by the wife of one of his investigators, whose car the investigator sometimes used. Thus the bomber might well be connected with some case the investigator was working on or had worked on. It was a nice job of selected facts effectively worded. And broad enough not to sound promising, so they didn't ask for more details. Which also gave Joe the impression that the LAPD's theory was totally different.

Still, we had a reputation, and a contingency contract would be insurance for them, so it seemed likely their Contract Office would approve Joe's request. Which would give us limited computer access to the State Data Center, via contract ID.

Meanwhile, Joe told me to carry a gun at all times, including off the job.

Tuuli's Tuesday meeting ran into complications, and she had to meet with her client again on Wednesday. So she rescheduled to leave Hollywood-Burbank Airport at 4:20 Wednesday afternoon, on one of those flights that service smaller towns—in this case Victorville, Barstow, Needles, Kingman, Williams, and Flagstaff.

She'd drive her new Haugen Arrow to Hollywood-Burbank. She hadn't felt comfortable with her Sportee since the bombing, and had found a buyer for it. I was to drive it to work that morning. The buyer, a dealer from the Lower Wilshire District, would pick it up at noon. My own car was already in the security lot, at the building. I'd drive it to the room the firm had rented for me.

Life was getting complicated.

On Wednesday morning I drove my usual route to work, crossing the Santa Monica Mountains on Laurel Canyon Boulevard, through a light drizzle and mist, enjoying the way the Sportee handled the curves and how green and lovely everything looked. I didn't notice anyone following me, and I doubt there was. At the lot, I transferred my bags from the Sportee to my Olds.

I'd spent Monday looking into the department's evidence from the bombing site, and didn't find anything useful. On Tuesday I'd checked with my main informants again, with the usual lack of results. The only thing that tweaked me at all was that Miss Melanie seemed uncomfortable with me. I didn't ask her why. She wouldn't have told me, and it would have made her more wary.

Wednesday morning I worked out, then checked with more informants.

At the end of the day I drove to the apartment hotel I'd been registered at, and moved into my room there. It was getting dark before I drove to Canter's for supper; I like Yiddish food almost as well as Mexican. I did better than I sometimes do at walking out before I was stuffed, and had just reached my car when a guy with a pistol pointed at me stepped from behind a van.

"Hands up, asshole!" he said. "We want your money!"

Never get into a life-threatening fight over your wallet, sure as hell not when the other guy's got the drop on you. My hands went all the way up, shoulder-width apart and open wide. I heard someone else come up behind me, and expected him to go through my pockets. Instead, something pressed against the back of my neck, something not a gun or knife. It stung, and almost instantly I felt my mind fogging, my knees going weak. I started to fall, and he grabbed me under the arms. That's all I remember of that.

When I woke up, I was in the back of a van, parked in someone's attached residential garage. Some Gnostie's no doubt. The dome light was on, and there was a guy in the off-side front seat. I was gagged, but I must have made a noise, because he was looking back at me. My wrists had been handcuffed behind my back, and my ankles and knees were tied with duct tape. The guy didn't say anything, just put his book aside, got out, and went into the house.

I don't know what they juiced me with, but I didn't feel too bad. A little headachey, a little weak. I rolled around enough to discover that my pistol was no longer in my shoulder holster, not that I could have gotten to it anyway. A couple of minutes later he came back with two other guys. One was big, with a nasty smile. He stood in the van door, flexing and unflexing his hands in front of him, trying to intimidate me, while the third guy got in and blindfolded me. Then they threw a plastic tarp over me. A minute later I heard the garage door open, and we backed out.

As we started down the street, I heard one of them talking on the car phone, telling someone we were on our way. We drove for fifteen or twenty minutes, then stopped—I had no idea where—and the tarp was pulled off me. Someone grabbed my feet, pulled me most of the way out, and cut the tape on my ankles and knees.

Someone else grabbed my upper right arm. "Stand up!" he said, and pulled.

I was a little unsteady, but I managed. The problem was being blindfolded and disoriented, not the shot. I heard traffic sounds not far off, smelled night jasmine and damp soil. Then he told me "Walk!" I stumbled trying, and someone grabbed me to keep me from falling.

"Fischer, take his blindfold off. It doesn't matter if he sees something. Walking blind like that he'll fall down, and he must weigh 250 pounds."

Two hundred thirty, I thought. *At most.* I felt someone untying the blindfold, and when he pulled it off, I realized at once where I was: at a service entrance to one of the Campus buildings. I could see a residential street maybe 120 feet to my left, with apartment houses on the other side.

And it didn't matter if I saw things! That could only mean one thing. I yelled as loudly I could, louder than you'd think. The gag was effective against speaking words, but when it came to an animal-like howl . . . The big guy slugged me in the gut, doubling me over, then uppercut me, hitting me in the forehead. I went down like a stone, and he kicked me once in the side. When I looked up, he'd stepped back. He had a police baton in one hand, and the guy in charge was swearing at him in a hard-edged undertone.

"Miller, you goddamn fucking idiot, if you kill him, Lon will have your balls on a stick! You'll be lucky to get assigned to the SRC! He wants information from this guy."

"Whaddaya mean? I had to shut him up!"

"You did that when you hit him in the gut. If you hit him with that goddamn billy club, you could kill him."

"Shit! You couldn't kill him by hitting him on the head with a crowbar."

"That's backflash, Miller! Once more and I'll see you before a committee! And when you talk to me, call me sir! Now get him inside!"

He took a key ring off a clip on his belt and unlocked

a pair of double doors, holding one of them open while the other two guys dragged me inside, into a dimly lit corridor. The door clashed shut behind us. After he'd locked it, he spoke to me. "Can you stand up?"

I grunted, nodding my head.

"Help him!"

Fischer and Miller lifted me by the arms. I stood there for a second, steadying myself. Actually, Miller didn't seem particularly strong. He'd been getting by on big.

"Okay," the leader said, "let's go."

We went down the corridor, turned left down another, and entered a large dining room at the end. It was unlit except for city light shining like a full moon through large windows. Open windows; night jasmine overrode the smell of floor-cleaning compound. Three people were sitting at a table near the front, looking at us. The light was too weak to show their facial features from across the room, but the big one had to be Lon Thomas. The others were probably bodyguards, I told myself. My keepers led me to him.

It was Thomas, all right. As for the bodyguards— One didn't seem to be. He was a thin, tallish guy with some kind of instrument on the table in front of him. The other was a woman, young and good-looking in a hard, lipless way, but a bodyguard sure enough. One of her hands rested on a machine pistol, an Uzi. Anyone who'd carry one of those where an ordinary pistol would do, is at least a little crazy.

Thomas looked me up and down, then nodded. I noticed Miller rubbing his right fist. I hoped he'd broken it; sprained it at least.

"He yelled," my captor told Thomas. "Right through the gag."

Thomas grunted. "So that's what that was." He looked at the quiet one, Fischer. "Mr. Fischer," he said, "go outside and see if anyone's poking around who seems curious about the noise. If there is, tell them someone was, uh, preparing to braze a door handle and burned himself with the torch. Be casual but convincing. At this hour, I doubt anyone would investigate, but let's not take anything for granted."

Fischer left. Thomas was looking at me again. "So. Mr. Seppanen," he said. "You see, I know your real name. I am going to have your gag taken off so you can answer some questions. If you become abusive or refuse to cooperate, I'll have to have you disciplined and perhaps injected. If you cooperate, we'll finish our business here and I'll have you returned to your car."

Yeah, I thought. *Dead. The victim of a mugging, no doubt.* A clock glowed pale on a wall: It was minutes after two in the morning.

"Miller, be prepared to, um, punch Mr. Seppanen in the abdomen if he becomes unruly. Hard enough to subdue him. Collins, take his gag off."

Collins took the gag off, and I stood there working my jaw from side to side. Thomas looked at me thoughtfully. The bodyguard hadn't moved, as far as I could tell. I'd a lot rather have Miller mad at me.

"We'll have to have his hands in front of him. Collins, do you have the key to his cuffs?"

"Yes, sir." Collins took the ring of keys from his belt clip again and held one up.

"Mr. Seppanen," Thomas told me, "get down on your knees."

I did. Collins took the cuff off one wrist, had me put my hands in front of me, then chained them together again. With the cuffs over my shirt sleeves—that was Thomas' order. Then Thomas had me stand up and sit on a chair across the table from the thin man, whose instrument panel lit his face a ghostly blue.

Thomas looked at him. "Will there be any difficulty getting reads with his hands manacled?"

"There shouldn't be."

"Fine. Mr. Seppanen, please pick up the electrodes and rest your hands in your lap." The electrodes were a pair of metal cylinders. I picked them up, wrapping my hands around them.

"Very good. Now please don't move any more than you

must, and don't touch the electrodes together. The instrument is a psychogalvanometer. I presume you know what that is?"

"It's used in polygraphs; it measures electrical resistance across the skin."

"Very good." He turned to his technician. "Selkirk, talk the dial down into range."

"It's there now, Mr. Thomas."

"Oh? Well then, we'll begin." Thomas turned back to me. "You are a man of exceptional self-possession, Mr. Seppanen. My congratulations."

He wanted to keep me calm, to make the galvanometer readings as meaningful as possible. "Thanks," I said.

His eyebrows lifted. "Well then, let's begin."

It was a short interrogation. First he asked me some ranging and calibration questions: My name, where I'd grown up, if I'd ever committed a sex crime, any other crime, things like that. And what, before my present assignment, I'd thought of the Church of the New Gnosis.

His first meaningful question was what, specifically, I was investigating. I told him: the disappearance of Ray Christman. That we suspected he was dead or kidnaped. Thomas didn't look surprised or angry, but the question seemed to introvert him. He didn't ask who our contract was with.

Then he asked who my suspects were, and I told him: the Noeties, the COGS, factions within the church, and the various and numerous people with grudges against it. I didn't mention the Merlins; I no longer suspected them.

The guy with the psychogalvanometer never said a word; presumably he would have if he'd had any meaningful instrument readings.

But to me, Thomas' response was especially important: He looked thoughtfully past me and said, "How could any Noeties or COGS have gotten to Ray? It would have been virtually impossible. Surely you considered that?"

"They could have hired professionals. Some underworld outfits are pretty resourceful."

"If they only wanted to assassinate him, yes. A sniper,

someone with a military mortar, that kind of thing. But I can't accept that that sort of people—any sort of people—could have secretly abducted him."

"Which brings us," I said, "to the major reason for suspecting someone in the church."

Thomas shook his head, a strong, decisive rejection. That's when I told him we'd been bogged down badly on the case, and if something hadn't developed soon, we might have dropped it, or mothballed it. But then someone had bombed Tuuli's old apartment. That must have been done by the church, I told him, and told him why. I thought he'd deny it, but he only frowned. I also told him we had a contract with the LAPD to compile evidence for an indictment on the bombing, which was true as far as it went.

His face turned wooden. "Thank you, Mr. Seppanen," he said. "You have been very helpful. I'm going to have you returned to your car. We have nothing to fear from your investigation, because Mr. Christman's retirement was entirely his own decision. And I can absolutely assure you we had nothing to do with any bombing. Also, I assume you are astute enough to realize that there is no way you can prove that this little discussion ever took place. As you said, in the Church we are a very close group. 'Impenetrable,' I believe the media have called us."

As I put down the electrodes, Thomas looked past me. "Mr. Collins, take Mr. Seppanen to the security entrance and hold him there till a vehicle comes for him. I want you to see personally that he arrives back where he came from."

Fischer had come back, and Collins told him and Miller to take my arms. Then Collins, with a gun in his hand, led the three of us into and through a big kitchen to a service elevator. He pushed a button, the door opened, and a few seconds later we were on our way down to the basement.

I didn't like the look of the room at the bottom. The floor was smooth-finished concrete, sloping to a central drain, and there was a large meat-cutting table near the middle. The ceiling was low, and there was an overhead track with rolling meat hooks that led to what appeared to be a reefer door.

Collins turned. By the light of the fluorescents, he looked as pale as anyone I'd ever seen, as if he might faint or puke, but his face was set. He pointed his gun at me. "Miller," he said, "I know you'll be disappointed if you don't get to do the honors."

Miller let go my arm and slugged me in the kidneys. Except he didn't, quite. He'd been just high, banging me in the floating ribs from behind. It hurt all right, but not as much as I pretended. Then he stepped around in front of me, police baton in one hand. He could just as well have clubbed me from behind, but he wanted me to see what was coming, which was stupid—right in character.

Miller was just slapping the baton against his left palm when I stomped down as hard as I could on Fischer's instep. He let go my arm with a yell. At the same instant I launched a flying sidekick that took Miller in the breastbone. In the gym I'd have been criticized for it; it leaves you vulnerable to a quick counter. But Miller wasn't quick, and it slammed him backward into Collins, who swore as his gun went off, possibly into Miller. The greater danger had been that, with my hands manacled in front of me, I might have lost my balance after the kick, but I didn't. I was on Collins before he could recover, kicked the side of his knee, and about the time he hit the concrete, kicked him *hard* in the gut, then the ribs. He rolled into a ball, a natural reaction, and stepping around, I kicked him once more, in the neck. He stiffened with spasm, then went slack.

I knelt, grabbed his gun, and spun to see what Fischer was doing. What I saw was the elevator door closing. So I put the gun on the butcher table, fumbled the key ring off Collins' belt clip, and put it between my teeth. Then I picked up the gun again and looked around. At that moment I was really scared, for the first time that night. I felt trapped down there, and remembered Thomas' bodyguard with that damned Uzi. Thomas was probably

armed, too. Then I saw a door at the back of the room,
ran to it and opened it. There was a narrow staircase
leading downward, and I remembered what Molly Cadigan
had said about utility tunnels connecting the different
buildings. I started down, and a pneumatic closer closed
the door behind me.

The tunnel was about ten feet wide, dim and chilly, with
ducts and big pipes overhead wrapped with insulation. Here
and there was a single fluorescent tube for light. It took
precious seconds to find what I assumed was the right key.
I put it between my teeth, got my hands free, and took
off at an easy trot. About a hundred feet farther, I came
to a steel door in the side wall, like a ship's door, and
opened it. Inside was a lightless room with a lot of old
sheet-iron junk. I trotted on, glad to be wearing crepe-soled
shoes; they were virtually soundless on the concrete.

Pretty soon I passed a junction with a narrower tunnel, then steep steel stairs like a ship's ladder, leading up.
Presumably to some other part of the building I'd just
left. I passed it by. A ways farther was a wide door,
apparently to another tunnel, but it was locked, and I
padded on. There were more doors like the first; I
ignored them. Farther on, the tunnel I was in ended at
a cross tunnel. It was even wider, and there was another
steel stairway leading up. Hesitating, I considered. I might
still be under the building with Thomas in it—it was a
big one—so instead of going up, I turned right.

This tunnel was blocked, farther on, by a broad, heavy
sliding door. I paused and listened, but couldn't hear a hint
of pursuit. I reminded myself I'd been down there for no
more than two minutes, and maybe Thomas and his bodyguard had left the dining room when I did. Maybe Fischer
was having to chase them down. I grabbed the handle of
the door and pulled. With an effort it opened, fairly quietly, moving on wheels on an overhead track. After taking a moment to close it behind me, I ran on. A short way
ahead, the tunnel turned about 45 degrees and, a little way
past the turn, entered a sort of workroom like a large
alcove, about 20 feet wide and 40 long. Along the far side

was a bench with pipefitter's vises. Overhead were racks with a few pipes on them.

Just now, though, the room seemed to be a dormitory. It was pretty much taken up with old canvas folding cots, most of them occupied by unblanketed men and women in gray coveralls, patched and dirty. They were curled against the chill, but seemed to be sleeping heavily. A single man, also in dirty coveralls, was standing by a small and battered metal desk beneath a single fluorescent. What looked like a logbook lay open on it. I guessed he was a straw boss or something like that. He wore an orange ball cap that I took to be a badge of rank. His eyes, calm and direct, stopped me in my tracks.

"Sir," he said quietly, "this is SRC space. It's off limits to all others except security and the morals police. You'll have to leave."

I nodded, said, "Right!", and strode on through the room and out of it, prepared to sprint if the guy yelled. He didn't. The continuation of the tunnel was narrower here, not more than six feet wide, and darker, all the fluorescents dead but one. It occurred to me with a pang that the wall I could make out about 200 feet ahead might be a dead end.

It wasn't. When I got there, I found another cross tunnel, also narrow. This seemed to be neglected territory. The dust was heavy, and in the branch to my right I could hear and smell a steam leak. The only fluorescent was flickering weakly.

Suddenly I heard voices behind me, farther off than the "SRC space." I had pursuers, and they'd passed through the sliding door. I took the left branch.

And 80 feet farther came to a narrow steel door in one wall, with a simple handle. I stepped inside and found myself in an unlit vertical tube about three feet in diameter, with rungs up one side. I grabbed one, then pulled the door shut behind me, which left me in pitch darkness. Groping, I climbed two rungs at a time until my reaching hand came to an overhead. With a push I raised it— a manhole cover. I shoved it out of my way and it fell with a loud clank. Then I hoisted myself out onto a raised concrete dock at one end of a big parking lot; the lid had fallen off it to the pavement. The end I was in was walled on three sides by buildings. A ways ahead, the buildings ended and the lot widened. There were hardly any cars at this hour. Maybe 400 feet ahead, streetlights showed the row of tall palms where the fence would be. It had begun to drizzle. The dominant smell was ripe Dumpster instead of jasmine.

I'd jumped from the dock and begun trotting toward the palms, when a strong flashlight beam swept the pavement ahead of me. Security men on a roof, I realized. They'd heard the manhole cover fall. Another light joined it, swept the pavement to my right. Then someone saw me and called out. A light beam found me. I ignored it.

A voice yelled from the direction of the manhole, and I ran faster. Ahead I could see the fence—chain link topped with razor wire. The palm trees were on the inside. Breathing hard, I reached the nearest of them and began to shinny up the trunk. It was harder than I'd expected. Behind me, someone yelled "Shoot!" and someone else yelled "No, goddamn it, it'll bring the police!" When my feet were well above the fence, I jumped, pushing off as best I could, clearing the razor wire and landing heels first on the sidewalk, to crash heavily onto my back.

It knocked the wind out of me. Stunned and gasping, I rolled onto my hands and knees and looked up. They were not more than 150 feet away, running toward me. Then headlights caught me, and a minivan pulled to the curb. I lurched to my feet, ready to run again, when a voice called from the van—Tuuli's voice! "Martti! Quick! Get in." A door was open, and she had me by a sleeve, pulling. I half climbed, half fell in. Before Tuuli could close the door, the van pulled away, burning rubber.

18
COMMAND PERFORMANCE

The driver was Carlos. He asked if I was all right, and I told him I was. He didn't ask any more questions. Instead he phoned our security division headquarters, in north Burbank. Told them to send an extra crew to corporate headquarters in West Hollywood. The Gnosties were unlikely to try anything further tonight, but if they did, that's where they'd hit.

As he drove, I sat by Tuuli in the backseat, turning the interrogation over in my mind. I didn't even ask how they'd known where I was. Carlos stopped at a Denny's on Sunset, where we took a booth and ordered coffee and pie. At that hour, it was a good place to wait while the added security had time to reach headquarters.

We were almost the only customers there. It was a good place to talk, if we kept it quiet.

"So," Carlos said, "I suppose you've got questions."

"Yeah. How did you guys come to be there?" I looked at Tuuli. "You especially."

It turned out she actually had gone to Arizona. About the time the flight left Williams though, she'd had a premonition that I'd need her, that I'd be in extreme danger. Frank Diacono was waiting for her at Flagstaff. She told him her premonition, then tried to phone me. I'd already left my room, and left my beeper there. I don't usually carry it off duty. So she called the office, and the night watch forwarded her call to Carlos. They'd agreed to meet at building reception.

When she'd finished her call, Frank had flown her to Barstow himself, where she could catch a Vegas-L.A. local with almost no wait. Frank, of course, didn't have a permit to fly in L.A. airspace—those are really hard to get, for obvious reasons—or he'd have flown her the rest of the way. All the way back she'd worried about what she could possibly do when she got here. The premonition was vague. I was in danger; that's all there was of it.

When she got with Carlos though, it seemed to her that the danger was or would be at the Campus. So they'd driven there, and she'd told Carlos, "Park here." "Here" being at the curb about forty or fifty meters from where I eventually came over the fence. That had been about midnight; they'd had more than a two-hour wait. She smiled at me, then reached and patted Carlos' cheek. "And you never complained a bit," she said to him. "I'm not sure you even doubted."

He laughed. "No comment," he said. Carlos Katagawa was seldom the inscrutable Oriental, regardless of his Japanese ancestry. "Actually I assumed it was genuine when you first talked to me on the phone. I've seen you operate before, remember. But I admit feeling spooky about sitting there at the curb with nothing happening. What good could it possibly do to wait there? Next to a nearly empty parking lot!" He sipped coffee and looked at me. "That's quite a lady you married. So. Now it's your turn to talk. How did you get into a situation like that?"

I put off answering till we got to the office, where I could talk to the computer terminal, to a confidential fail-safe file, telling him pretty much what I told you. Adding that I might have killed Miller; a kick like that to the sternum would shock the heart, might even stop it. Or Collins' shot may have hit him. Collins might also be dead, though I doubted it. I might have broken some of his ribs, though, so he could have a punctured lung.

"We've got grounds to call in the LAPD now," Carlos pointed out.

"No, I don't want to do that. I'd rather we each tape our statements of what we saw and heard, and duplicate the files into two or three legal repositories for use as depositions when the time comes. I'm not out to bust the church hierarchy, necessarily. I want to find out what happened to Christman."

Carlos raised an eyebrow. I suppose he figured I'd *want* to bust the hierarchy, after what had happened. "If we get a few people indicted," he said, "and some hotshot LAPD interrogators talk to them awhile, maybe they'll tell what happened to Christman."

"I don't think they would, Carl. I don't think even Thomas knows what happened to Christman."

He didn't say anything, just waited for me to explain. "It's the questions he asked me: Thomas seemed unwilling to accept that Christman was really dead. He argued that the Noeties and the COGs couldn't possibly have killed him. Which tended to load the case against him. Why would he do that? And who was he trying to convince? Me? He never intended for a minute to let me out of there alive.

"No, he was thinking out loud. My best judgement now is that he doesn't know what happened to Christman, and wishes he did."

"Okay, then why is he trying to kill the investigation? Or at least the investigator."

"If Christman's dead, he doesn't want us to find out. Plus I don't think he's all there mentally.

"Now here's a question for you: According to the *Times* article, Christman had things set up so the church paid him essentially all its income beyond strictly budgeted operating expenses. If it wanted money for any extraordinary project—something not budgeted as routine operating funds—they had to ask him for it. That seemed to be his major form of control after he turned the executive functions over to his bureaucracy. And considering how rich he apparently was, he really didn't spend a whole lot on his personal life.

"The same writers estimated that, by 2006, the church's long-term gross income had certainly surpassed 200 million. I called up the hypertext on that, and their estimate was based on a lot of hard information and some rough assumptions. So say its long-term gross income was half a billion by last fall, when Christman dropped out of sight. That's church income. Then add whatever earnings that money had accumulated!"

Carlos' pursed lips formed a thoughtful *O*, a silent whistle. Tuuli wasn't saying anything either.

"It'd be interesting to see Christman's will," I went on. "Who'd get his money if it was legally established that he was dead? That's a piece of information that might break this case. But it's my impression that as the law stands, it's information we can't get at, without compelling evidence that Christman is dead."

Carlos nodded. "So what do you want to do?"

What I did was call church security; it seemed like the only office they'd have open at that hour. A stoney-faced woman answered, and I told her I wanted to talk to Thomas. She told me he wasn't available.

"He is to me," I said. "Tell him Martti Seppanen wants to talk to him."

"Mr. Seppanen"—she got the name right, first shot—"it is three-forty in the morning. If you want to speak to Mr. Thomas, you'll have to leave your . . ."

I interrupted her. "You're damned well aware that someone escaped from the kitchen about two-fifteen this morning, and left two guys badly injured or dead. He got away through the tunnels, across the parking lot, and over the fence."

She actually changed expression slightly. "I don't know what you're talking about."

"The hell you don't! The whole thing is over an investigation of whether Ray Christman is dead or alive. Lon will want to talk to me. He wanted to so badly earlier, he had me kidnaped. Now get him on the goddamn screen or we'll go to the LAPD with everything we've learned. We've already got an investigation contract with them."

The stone face slipped a little more. "Just a moment," she said, and put me on hold. I glanced at Tuuli; she looked impressed and—proud.

I winked at her, and she grinned. "Thanks for saving my ass, babe," I told her. "It's all yours now." It was my version of Bogart as Sam Spade. Of course, in those ancient movies they'd never have said *ass*.

It took a few minutes before Thomas came on the screen. He looked like hell. I suppose I didn't look too good either. I spoke first. "Thomas," I said, "I want to do two things for you."

He stared.

"First I need to tell you that this conversation is being recorded. I want you to know that I and the two witnesses who picked me up have just recorded and safe-stored our separate statements of what each of us saw and experienced tonight. They've been covering me since I left my office—actually since the bombing. They witnessed the assault on me outside Canter's Restaurant, and followed my kidnapers.

"Your people didn't do that bad a job of searching me, incidentally. It's just that my shirt is an ultrawave transmitter. When your goons got me down in the meat-cutting room and Miller told me what they were going to do to me— Well, it's all in the net now, in triplicate safe-files, along with your interrogation."

Thomas' face had looked a little puffy when he'd come on. It had shrunk since then. "We don't particularly want to bust the church," I went on. "Like I said a couple weeks ago, I have an uncle who swears it turned his life around, even though he quit it years ago. Probably saved him from cirrhosis of the liver. All we want to do is find out what happened to Ray Christman. And we want your cooperation. If you did nothing criminal to him, you're clear.

"On the other hand, if you try to interfere, your ass is in the fire, along with the church. Our depositions are coded to several keeper keys in the law enforcement net. If anything happens, the LAPD, the county prosecutor, and the FBI will have them, and you know how they'd love that. Incidentally, those statements also cover what we know about the bombing of the Hollywood Boulevard apartment and the murder of the Boghosians."

He was still staring haggardly at my image on his screen. "I'll tell you something else," I said. "Yesterday we were a little afraid of you people. Now we've got you by the balls. But we don't particularly want you scared of us; we just want you to act rationally, and cooperate.

"I'm going to ask you a question now. But I'll preface it by reminding you of your rights: you don't have to talk. Anything you say may be held against you in a court of law. So. What do you know about the disappearance of Ray Christman?"

There was a long pause; when he spoke, his voice was husky. "Nothing," he said at last. "If I did, I'd probably tell you. But I really honest to God don't know."

"All right, Mr. Thomas, I'll let it go for now. Where have you taken the two goons who were going to murder me?"

Another long pause. "Presbyterian Hospital."

"What names are they under? I'll be checking with Presbyterian."

"Their own names: Collins and Miller."

"What first names?"

"Miller is—Clark Miller, I think. And James Collins."

"Thank you, Mr. Thomas. We'll be getting in touch with you from time to time. Make sure your people put us through. And Mr. Thomas—I am not a vengeful person. Only one with a professional responsibility."

I broke the connection then and sat back, feeling I'd handled an awful lot awfully well. Carlos shook his head. "My what marvels our radio people have come up with! A shirt-transmitter! And ultrawave yet!"

"Make you a bet," I said. "I'll bet he doesn't check it out to see if it's possible."

After she and Carlos had recorded their statements, Tuuli and I drove home. Actually she drove; we used her car. An investigative assistant would pick mine up at Canter's. We felt pretty confident that Thomas wouldn't try to hit any of us now. That had been a major purpose in calling him and saying what I'd said. Meanwhile, Carlos had told me to take the day off, and the next day if I wanted to.

At that hour, Tuuli and I had Laurel Canyon Boulevard almost to ourselves. Dawn was graying the sky, and a cool green smell blew in on us through my open window.

"What was it like, your premonition?" I asked.

"Just a realization. A realization that you were in danger."

"No voice? No vision?"

She shook her head. "Would you still like to spend a week in Arizona?"

"I would, but it can wait a couple of days. Or longer if you want."

"Not today?"

"You and I are going to spend today alone," she purred, and put her hand on my leg. "I suppose you're so tired, you'll want to go straight to sleep when we get home."

I laughed. "Not to sleep. Only to bed. After a hot shower."

"Good," she said. "That shower is going to be crowded though."

19
SHOPPING PSYCHICS

Needless to say, we were both asleep an hour after we got home. Tuuli woke up first, not long after noon, and it was the nicest day, I think, of my whole life. We'd never been so relaxed around each other, or *talked* so much. And we didn't cross swords even once.

The coffee took a beating, but we drank hers. Tuuli always drinks decaf at home, but I'd never thought it was anything for me. As a young kid I'd drink coffee with my dad. He liked his sweet and strong, so strong the spoon would stand straight up in it—not really—and mom made it the way he liked. He was easygoing, never bossy to her, but she liked to please him, make him happy. He was sixty-one and she was twenty-five when they got married, a strange but happy story, right up to the bloody end.

Huh! Look at that! I can actually talk about it now.

Me, on the other hand—I'd been, if not actually bossy, at least judgemental, and Tuuli had . . . But I'm getting off the subject.

Like I said, we loafed around and talked a lot that day, and I asked her way more about psychics and being psychic than I ever had before. I'd always felt uncomfortable about it, a little edgy maybe, but that day I was really relaxed. Like Winifred Sproule, she mentioned idiot savants,

and said that some of the more capable psychics had been
either neurotic or more or less retarded. Ole Sigurdsson,
she said, had supposedly been kicked in the head by a horse
when he was a child, and it had left him both feebleminded
and psychic. Then, when he was pretty much grown, he'd
come to America with relatives, and en route had somehow lost his feeblemindedness.

I told her it was hard to think of Ole as having been
feebleminded. She agreed, but said she'd read it in his
biography, written by his wife Laura, before they were
married.

Anyway, for some reason the conversation reminded me
of the psychic photographers Winifred Sproule had mentioned, and when I went to work the day after that, it was
on my mind. I didn't know why. And not only psychic
photographers, but psychics in general. I still didn't have
a real lead on what had happened to Christman. Could a
psychic help me?

I hadn't asked Tuuli: She knew the problem, and nothing
had come to her or she'd have told me. I'd asked Vic, and
he'd seemed to dodge it, while Ole'd said he "didn't get
anything" on it.

I knew there was a compendium of psychics put out
some years ago by a university. It had added respectability
to the field, and boomed the growing post-plague interest. So, from the office, I phoned Winifred Sproule. I
figured she might be able to discuss and evaluate it better
than an electronic or even a human reference librarian.

It turned out she had it on her shelves in hard copy:
*A Catalog of Significant Confirmed Psychics in North
America*, compiled by a Dr. Norman J. Gustafson and Dr.
Lisabet V. Mitchell, and published by Washington State
University Press. She said I could come in and borrow it
if I'd like. I told her I'd just call it up on my computer,
from the L.A. Library tank. The truth was, I was a little
afraid of Dr. Sproule.

The title page read "Copyright 2008, 2009, 2010, 2011,"
so it was updated regularly. I read the Introduction first.
There was, it said, a companion publication, in three

volumes, on exposed fraudulent psychics. Three volumes of case histories! And those were only "a representative sample."

The "confirmed psychics" volume, on the other hand, was thin, 115 pages exclusive of the stuff up front. Even that length was due partly to multiple listings and even more to extensive appendices—hypertext in the computer edition—that summarized briefly the more important studies made of the individual psychics.

It didn't include those idiot savants whose only known talent was calendar computations. There was disagreement as to whether or not calendar computation was actually psychic.

The first list was alphabetical, and I checked to see if Tuuli was included. She was. So was Ole. The Merlins weren't, or Bhiksu, or Mikki Diacono. Maybe they hadn't come to the compilers' attention. After each name on the alphabetical list was a list of talents verified for that person, and reference codes to appendix material. Cross lists were by talents, and state or province. Under any particular talent, the people were listed in a consensus order of reliability: a 1 rating was highest, and according to the introduction, no one had rated a 1 except some idiot savants.

I looked under *psychic photographers*. The best, according to the book, was a Charles Tomasic, originally of St. Cloud, Minnesota, and currently the ward of Dr. Clarence Hjelmgaard, Savants Project, Department of Psychiatry, College of Medicine, University of Minnesota. I called up and read the hypertext on Tomasic. He was born in 1993, had an IQ of 64, etc. His photographs were more reliably clear than those of any other known psychic photographer.

And his most notable performance had been to produce photos of a crime in progress, that had occurred ten months earlier. A vagrant in Willmar, Minnesota, had been accused of molesting a retarded, ten-year-old girl, then killing her. He'd been found guilty, and Tomasic had seen the sentencing on television. Even at the sentencing, the murderer had continued to insist he was innocent. Tomasic, then sixteen

years old, had been angrily indignant at this, and insisted
that Dr. Hjelmgaard expose a pack of Polaroid at him.

As usual, none of the exposures showed Tomasic. The
first several were "whities," as if shot at the sun, but two
were clear shots of the crime—the molestation and the
murder. When compared to the garage where the crime
had occurred, the pictures were an exact match, even to
the '02 Plymouth sedan parked there, though Tomasic had
never seen the place, apparently had never even been in
Willmar.

I sat back and stared at the screen for a minute. The
thing must have been kept quiet at the time, or the
papers would have publicized hell out of it. I could see
a rationale to that. Tabloid-type publicity would be bad for
a research project, and reporters would have hounded poor
Tomasic out of his skull.

Meanwhile though— I called Fred Hamilton's number.
"Do you have time to talk?" I asked him.

"Will ten minutes do?"

"How would you like to fly up to Christman's Hideaway that you told me about? In Oregon. We'll fly over
it, and you can help me case the place. You said he had
an observatory on a hill. That might be where he was
most vulnerable to abduction. I want to size it up."

He didn't answer for a moment. Then: "When?"

"We could fly up Saturday afternoon, look it over Sunday
morning, and fly back afterward."

Then I told him what I really had in mind.

"Martti," he said, "if you'll cover the travel costs and
lodging, you've got a taker. I'll pay for my meals."

I told him I'd cover the meals too, and pay him two
hundred a day. It was the least I could do and be professional, and my client was responsible for expenses. I'd call
him later regarding departure time, and where and when
to pick him up.

Then I looked in the catalog for the clairvoyant rated
most reliable. His name was Seamus Waterford, and I was
in luck; he lived just half an hour down the coast in San
Diego. I called, got a sound-only connection, and five

minutes later had an appointment for that afternoon. I had
time for a tuna sandwich at Morey's, then drove to the
Tamarind Station for an air shuttle to LAX. The hourly
flight from LAX to Lindbergh Field at San Diego took
twenty-eight minutes, and a cab to Waterford's address
twelve more. I was there almost twenty minutes early, but
I'd come prepared. I sat on the edge of a big planter across
the street, and read my way into a pocket novel, one I'd
read half a dozen times before: Poul Anderson's novelization
of *Hrolf Kraki's Saga.*

Then I went and rang Waterford's doorbell. He answered
it wearing a heavy bathrobe, stocking cap down over his
ears, and a scarf! I could hardly believe it! It was hot in
his apartment—close to ninety, I'd guess.

He waved me in, a tallish, skinny Irishman with red
cheeks that made him look feverish, and tufted reddish
blond eyebrows. There wasn't a drop of sweat on his face.
I wondered if his disorder was mental or physical. I was
almost afraid to go in, as if it was catching. "Come in!
Come in!" he said with an Irish accent, and waved harder.
"Before you let in the cold!"

I went in. It must have been about 75 degrees outside, almost perfect shirtsleeve weather. Once I was in,
he relaxed. "Would you like some lemonade?" he asked.
There was a big pitcher of it, maybe three liters, half of
it ice, on a table by stacks of books and papers.

I told him no thanks. Somehow I didn't want to eat or
drink anything there.

He gestured at an ancient recliner upholstered with
something leatherlike. It looked as if it might fold up and
eat me, but I sat. After pouring himself a tall lemonade,
he sat down across from me and swigged most of it noisily
at one go, as if dying of thirst. Then he gestured back
at the littered table. "I'm writing my book," he said gen-
ially. "Now. What can I do for you?"

"Have you ever heard of Ray Christman?"

For a moment he frowned in thought, then, "The cult
leader!" he said. "I've known people he'd got in his
clutches! What about him?"

"He's disappeared. He may have gone into seclusion somewhere, or been abducted or murdered, or simply died. I hoped you could tell me."

Waterford frowned slightly for a few seconds, then said, "The man's dead. I can tell you that much. Dead long enough, he's either reincarnated—become someone else, some infant—or he's absent from the material realm. Beyond that I get nothing at all.

"Is that all you want?"

I told him yes, and wrote a credit transfer on his PC, using my company card number and intersig. A minute later I was out the door, wondering if I'd just been had. Two hundred dollars for that! Plus the time and air fare. I was in the wrong business—had the wrong talent.

20
OVERFLIGHT

Tuuli flew back to Arizona on Friday afternoon. On Saturday, Hamilton and I rode an AirWest express flight to Portland, then Oregon Air to Eugene. The office had already chartered an outfit at Eugene to fly us over the church's property in the mountains east of town.

The pilot assigned to us knew about the Hideaway and where it was. When Hamilton asked about possible SAMs there, she looked at him as if he were crazy. If the Gnosties shot up an overflight, she said, even it couldn't hire enough lawyers to save its ass. Even given the near silence of modern skycraft, private property *is* protected from nuisance overflights—flights low enough or frequent enough to constitute harassment—but that protection was by law, not weapons.

Twice in the past, a pilot had been accused by Christman and the church. The first time, the court threw the case out on the basis that the church's witnesses weren't credible, and this was upheld by the appeals court. A result, I suppose, of the church's reputation for public lying, and for using the threat of costly litigation to intimidate. The second time though, the evidence was electronic—radar and radar-directed video photography—as well as visual. The same court fined the same pilot, and told him another such instance would bring more than just a fine. It would confiscate his skyvan and operator's license, and lock him up.

Our first overflight was 2,500 feet above the lodge, and we saw no sign of occupancy except for a surface bus—a crew bus—and what Hamilton said were the caretaker's house and the security barracks. The next pass was at 1000 feet. We didn't see any sign, IR or otherwise, that a security patrol was out. No radar was operating, either. In fact, there was no electronics at all operating on the ridge. It looked as if a skycar could land on it at night and never be noticed.

And most important, *what appeared to be the boundary fence ran along the ridge crest, which was about 100 feet wide. The fence was only about 30 feet from Christman's observatory.* Yes, the pilot said, property lines sometimes ran along a ridge top. She called a topographic map onto her screen; the land on the other side belonged to the Willamette National Forest.

Which meant we could land on the ridge without trespassing on church property.

21
A REVIEW FOR BUTZBURGER

Butzburger came into my office on Monday morning just as I was getting ready to call Dr. Hjelmgaard at the University of Minnesota. "Mr. Seppanen—Martti," he said. "I'd like to stand you to lunch today and discuss some aspects of your investigation."

Considering what it had already cost him, and how far I seemed to be from the information he wanted, that was understandable, but I didn't have to look forward to it. "Would it be all right to talk about them now?" I asked. "My terminal gives me access to things I might want you to see, and you won't have to wait."

He nodded, looking as if he preferred it that way himself. I guessed then that he was going to be critical, and the invitation had been to soften the criticism. "Yes, that would be fine, Martti. If you'll agree to have lunch with me afterward." He sat down in a chair beside my desk. "I'm concerned with the lack of progress thus far. Not that I'm criticizing you for it. You and Mr. Katagawa made clear at the beginning that progress was likely to be slow and uncertain, and I can understand why. But— Last Friday I found an expense statement for consultation with a psychic, a Mr. Waterford. And there'd been one earlier with a Mr. Sigurdsson. Under the best of circumstances, I'd feel uncomfortable about paying money to psychics. In a situation where progress has been so slow, it occurred to me that it might have been a matter of desperation." He shrugged slightly. "If things have gone that badly, it might be well to discontinue the investigation."

"I understand," I said. "This morning Mr. Keneely told me to report to you today on a major—call it 'a happening'—last week. Beyond that, a new possibility occurred to me, and I spent the weekend in Oregon, checking its feasibility.

"But let's talk about the psychics first, because frankly I'm surprised it bothers you. I thought the church considers psychic powers real, and teaches that a person can learn to use them."

He nodded, looking slightly troubled. "But what it takes to *become* psychic," he said, "these gentlemen very likely have never experienced. I'm assuming that neither of them is a member of the church."

"The church says that the only way to psychic power is through its training?"

"To reliable psychic power, yes. First through its counseling services, which remove the deep spiritual traumas that foul the channels, so to speak. The individual parishioner may have sporadic psychic experiences even during early counseling, but only sporadic. The channels are opened further by advanced counseling, which prepares the parishioner for the training that programs and exercises those channels."

Then he added, almost apologetically, "The procedures are still incomplete. As of now, the ability varies considerably between individuals."

I was tempted—well, not tempted, but it crossed my mind—to ask him how advanced Lon Thomas was. Thomas showed all the perceptual sensitivity of a stone. Instead I said, "I have something here that may interest you." Then I rolled my chair to one side so he could move in beside me, and called up the WSU catalog of psychics. "When you've read the introduction," I said, "I'll show you what I have in mind."

When he was done, I called up the material on Charles Tomasic, the psychic photographer. As he read, Butzburger commented that he'd read about a much earlier case, Ted Polemes, who'd been studied at the University of Nebraska. Polemes had produced remarkable pictures, but was very inconsistent, and showed little control of his talent. When Butzburger had finished, he looked at me. "And your plan is to . . . ?"

"Information I've obtained indicates that Mr. Christman's greatest susceptibility to abduction was at his mountain hideaway in Oregon, and that he was usually there when solar storms promised to provide an auroral display. He loved the aurora.

"This weekend I scouted the Hideaway from the air, visually and with infrared and electronic surveillance. It seems entirely practical to land on the ridge where he has a small observatory . . ."

Butzburger interrupted. "I've been to his lodge. There are radar installations on the ridge, and some kind of defensive installation to repel possible aerial attacks."

I remembered Hamilton saying that Christman hosted rich Gnosties at the Ranch when he wanted to pitch something to them. Apparently he'd used the Hideaway for the same purpose. "We looked into that," I said. "To date, the only response the church has made to overflights has been in the federal court at Salem, and our instruments showed no indication of even radar monitoring. As a matter of fact, the place seems nearly deserted. Inserting a rumor of radar and surface-to-air missiles could have been a useful fiction to discourage aerial snooping."

I'd expected at least some sign of annoyance from Butzburger at that, but he simply looked thoughtful. I continued. "The fence that runs past the observatory is a boundary fence. The land on the other side belongs to the Forest Service. Because landing there looks feasible, I plan to call Dr. Hjelmgaard today and examine the possibility that we can fly Charles Tomasic in there with us. And maybe get a photograph of an abduction in progress."

He shook his head, but before he said anything, I went

on. "There is another aspect of the case that came to a head last week. An attempt was made to kill me. And there'd been an earlier occurrence, a bombing, that seemed to be aimed at me."

If he'd intended to say anything, that stopped him. Then I told him of my interview with Thomas, when I'd posed as a freelance writer, and the events that led to the bombing that killed five people. That was enough to tighten his lips; he was waiting for me to accuse the church, something he wasn't about to accept.

I forestalled that, too. As I'd finished describing the bombing, I'd called up the statements recorded by myself and Tuuli and Carlos, after my run through the tunnels. Now I had the computer play them back aloud, followed by my phone conversation with Thomas. When it was over, Butzburger was in shock.

"Tuuli's recorded statement wasn't complete," I said. "Mr. Butzburger, my wife is a Laplander, and a professional psychic. She was born and grew up in Lapland, in a tough mining town in the Swedish arctic, till she was nine. After that they lived on a frontier farm in northern Finland. Her mother's lineage has a sequence of tribal shamans, and Tuuli has the talent. Mostly her clients are people in entertainment, but she's been used as a consultant on several cases by police agencies, defense attorneys, and private investigators; that's how I met her. She was in Arizona that evening, got a premonition that I was in danger, and tried to call me. I was gone. Then she called Carlos—Mr. Katagawa—and flew home. At no cost to you, I might add. At eleven that night, she showed Carlos where to park. The rest you know."

If Butzburger had backed out then, Joe would not have been happy with me. An investigator is not supposed to try dealing with a client's uncertainties. That's Joe's hat. But Butzburger had been up front with me, and I wasn't willing to put him off.

"So you think the church is . . . But assuming for some incredible reason that Lon Thomas or anyone else in the Church wanted to get rid of Ray . . ."

"Exactly," I interrupted. "Why would they abduct him at the Hideaway? I don't think the church did abduct him. What I do believe is, they're afraid we'll get evidence that he's dead. That would have a powerful negative effect on the church. And there's the matter of who or what gets Christman's fortune."

"Christman's fortune?"

"Right." I stopped there. From the way he'd said it, there was more.

"Ray Christman had no fortune."

"Oh?"

"He had no fortune. He lived in church facilities and accepted only a modest salary."

I turned to my keyboard again, dumped the memory, and called up the summary article that the *Times* had published a few years earlier, moving to the part on Christman funneling most of the church's disposable income into personal accounts. Butzburger shook his head. "That's a lie," he said, "the sort of thing his enemies write about him." But he didn't sound confident. He was reciting Christman's PR line, and maybe, for the first time, wondering. I shrugged.

"Could be it is." I called the backup data to the screen, where he could see it too. It looked convincing. "Meanwhile I'm using it as a working assumption. And if there's not any will—maybe even if there is one—the church would get none of the money. That could account for Thomas' concern. He may want Christman to show up alive somewhere."

Butzburger was gnawing on his lower lip. "That doesn't entirely make sense. If Ray is simply in seclusion somewhere, the Church would . . ."

"Get none of it anyway. True, as far as we know. We're short on information. What I've been doing is accumulating pieces of the puzzle. Some parts of the picture are beginning to take shape. Maybe some photographs from Oregon will give us a major key.

"Now if you want, I can call Mr. Keneely. He's the man you need to tell if you want to drop the investigation."

Butzburger had strong-looking hands. I was willing to bet that his early experience in construction hadn't been at a desk. Just now he was holding them in front of him, looking down at them as if searching for an answer there. "No, Mr. Seppanen," he said, "I'm not dropping out. Not now. I want to know what happened."

"Thanks. Where are we going for lunch? And when?"

I thought that might release any residual tension, and half expected him to laugh. He didn't.

"Would you prefer noon?" he asked, "or one o'clock?"

"Noon," I said. "I don't like to postpone eating."

"Noon then." He got up. "Thank you, Mr. Seppanen. I appreciate frankness and honesty in the people I do business with."

I'd recorded the meeting; it was standard practice. When Butzburger had gone, I wrote it to the case file and sent a flag to Joe's terminal so he'd know it was there.

Next I phoned Dr. Hjelmgaard: he was interested but leery, and wanted to talk to me in person. He also wanted time to investigate the firm; to see how "Charles" responded to me; and to be assured that his one-in-a-billion ward would not be endangered in any way. And he didn't want any publicity. None at all.

My lunch with Butzburger was nonbusiness. Despite being from upstate, he's a Dodgers fan, so we talked about them first, then the Raiders. Neither of us mentioned the church—we were both careful about that—and the matter of psychics never came up.

Later that day, Joe said Butzburger had told him he was glad it was me on the case, so our talk had worked out even better than I'd thought.

That afternoon, Hjelmgaard called back. He'd looked into Prudential's reputation, record, and financial condition, and been impressed. He'd also looked into my own record, came across the case of the twice-killed astronomer, and read my debrief and the prosecutor's summary report. And again had been impressed. I've gotten a lot of mileage out

of that one. He ended up giving me an appointment for
the next afternoon at 3:30—half-past one, Pacific Time—
which meant catching a morning flight out of Hollywood-
Burbank. So I left the office early and went to Gold's,
where I worked out harder than a logger on piecework.

I was optimistic about my Tomasic project. It seemed
to me Hjelmgaard would go for it, and that Tomasic would
give us something useful. I didn't have any evidence, but
that's how it felt.

22
CHARLES TOMASIC

The nonstop flight to Minneapolis took four hours, plus about thirty minutes waiting at the terminal, riding the air shuttle to the Campus Station, and walking to the ultramodern, tile-faced Steinhof Building where Hjelmgaard was located. I got to the departmental office about four minutes early, and the doctor had them bring me right over.

Being the leader of the Savant Project—they avoided the term "idiot savants"—Hjelmgaard had an office big enough to hold small conferences. He even had a silver tea service—a monument to the prosperity that had begun with the introduction of the geogravitic power converter. Hjelmgaard was a short, pink, balding blond, and wore old-fashioned on-the-nose glasses over blue eyes. I guessed his age at forty-five. He was forward without seeming aggressive, direct without being rude. After seating me and offering tea, coffee, or hot chocolate, he asked me five minutes worth of questions about myself. His questioning was skillful, and when he was done, he probably knew more about me than most people who've been around me for years.

"I think," he said, "it's time for Charles to meet you." Then he keyed his phone and waited long enough for three or four rings. "Hello, Charles. Do you remember I said a Mr. Seppanen would be here to meet you today? . . . That's right, the detective. . . . Fine. I'd like to bring him over now. . . . Good. We'll be there in five minutes."

He broke the connection. "The reason I set our appointment for three-thirty is that Charles is with his tutor till three. Usually he watches television till four, then does his homework."

Homework? I thought. The catalog had given his IQ as 64.

"He's quite interested in history and geography," Hjelmgaard went on, "but because he reads rather laboriously, with resulting poor comprehension, he listens to his homework on audio tapes designed especially for the disadvantaged. They're a little like learning tapes for the blind, but the language is simpler and the learning gradient easier. And they use visual material, computer-coordinated with maps, simple charts, and photographs or video footage. And some of the better historical and biographical documentaries. In general, our wards do quite well with them."

The apartments for the Project's savants were in a wing of the same building, across a courtyard from the office wing. In bad weather you could go from one to the other indoors, through the classroom section, which was the main or base section of the U-shaped building.

We shortcut across the courtyard, where the planters and tulip beds were splashed with red and yellow, white and violet. Some of the shrubbery was putting out new leaves. Even the young maples were tinged with green from the bud scales separating. It was about as nice a garden as you could hope for in a climate where the temperature in January averages 11 degrees. (I'm interested in weather and climate: I subscribe to the Weather Service's electronic Michigan and National Monthly Climatic Summaries, with statistics out the tubes. And to *Monthly Weather Review.* Hemlock Harbor, a lot farther north, averages the same January temperature as Minneapolis, but its winters arrive two weeks earlier, as defined by a normal daily temperature of 32 degrees, and end more than three weeks later. And it has a normal annual snowfall of 128 inches, compared to 51 in Minneapolis. We Upper Peninsulers are proud of our winters, especially when we've left them for places like L.A.)

Hjelmgaard showed me a little of the savants section in passing. They had their own dining room, a gymnasium and pool, a sort of small theater that handles TV, holos, and film, and a social room with an honest to God concert grand piano. According to Hjelmgaard, one of the savants came to their attention because he played the classics on the piano—Chopin, Beethoven . . . without ever having had lessons. And one of their wealthy supporters— a wide receiver on the Vikings—decided the kid needed a good piano to play on. Each savant also had a private room, with the exception of a pair of twins who were inseparable. Hjelmgaard said that in general, they needed the opportunity to be alone.

When we got to Tomasic's door, Hjelmgaard knocked politely, and a young man's voice called out, "Just a minute." To my ears, it could have been a teenager's, one not into cynicism or being "smooth." Then he let us in. Charles was medium—medium size, medium build, with medium brown hair in the currently mod "bowl cut." He thrust out a hand to shake. His grip was firm but not strong or assertive. "You're Mr. Seppanen," he said, putting the accent on the first syllable, where it belongs. From learning it by ear, I suppose, instead of seeing it in writing.

"And you're Charles Tomasic," I answered. "It's up to you, but I hope you'll call me Martti."

He grinned. "Okay. I'll call you Martti and you call me Charles. Dr. Hjelmgaard told me something about you. You're a famous detective."

I grinned back. "Not *really* famous. Semi-famous. And you make pictures like nobody else can."

He nodded. "Yes," he said. "Dr. Hjelmgaard says I do it even better than Ted Polemes did." He tapped his head. "That's why I don't figure things out as well as other people. Part of my brain got used to do my special thing." He looked at Hjelmgaard, who was beaming like a father. "I figured that out myself, didn't I, Clarence?"

"Yes, you did."

We sat around and talked for about twenty minutes, then Hjelmgaard excused us, and we left Charles to do his homework. "It tires him to carry on a conversation at that level for too long," Hjelmgaard said. "Then he begins to act childish, and realizes it, and tends to get upset with himself. I tell him it's all right just to be himself, that everyone has their own style, but advice like that isn't always easy to follow." He shrugged. "For any of us.

"Studying history and geography, especially cultural geography, has increased his confidence and competence in social situations. He's a very special person, entirely aside from his talent, and very interesting as well.

"He came to us at fourteen, more than five years ago. At that time his IQ was fifty-one. His father had died in the EVM plague, when Charles was only six, and his mother, who needed to work, had left him at a day care center for special children.

"His talent didn't show up until a Christmas picture— a candid shot—was taken of him with his mother and grandparents. Instead of showing them, it showed a ship at sea: a specific ship—the *Alvin S. Baker* of the Baldwin Transportation Company." Hjelmgaard laughed. "The uncle who took it couldn't imagine what had happened. The negative was a single frame in an uncut roll! So a week or so later he tried again and got an aircraft, an old Boeing 747. In flight, as if shot from above!"

Hjelmgaard chuckled. "His mother mentioned it to the director of the care center, not as something Charles was responsible for, but as a family mystery. But the director there had read an article, years before, about a psychic photographer, probably Polemes. Knowing of the Savant Project, she called us.

"Charles is not autistic, but he was a somewhat disturbed boy at that time. Then our Dr. Pendleton did a series of traumatic incident reductions on him—Pendleton was the first person on our staff trained for it—and it not only stabilized Charles emotionally; it caused an immediate eleven-point jump in his IQ. It's climbed several more points since then, perhaps due to his growing confidence."

We sat down in Hjelmgaard's office again. "Charles reacted very well to you, Mr. Seppanen, and you to him. You seem nicely compatible. What I need to know now is how, specifically, we would proceed. You said it wouldn't be necessary to trespass."

I wasn't even sure it would be necessary for Charles to leave his room, but according to Hjelmgaard, the Willmar murder case was the only instance in which he'd succeeded in producing a photo of an intended subject. He'd seen the murderer on television, heard about the crime, had an emotional response, and produced what might be termed "target photos." So we acted on the hope, if not the expectation, that if Charles was told about the presumed crime, and then shown the presumed site, he might give us a picture of the crime in progress.

The fee that Hjelmgaard named was $2,500, to be paid directly into a trust fund that the project had already set up for Charles. I checked it with Butzburger over the phone, and he agreed without even looking troubled. Apparently to him that was pocket money, once he'd decided it was all right to use psychics. And maybe he liked where this particular twenty-five hundred was going. A good man, Butzburger, in spite of his church.

We ended up with an agreement to do it in three days, or as soon afterward as conditions were suitable. Hjelmgaard was to come along too, of course. He wasn't charging anything for his time and services. All we had to do was cover his expenses. I also told Hjelmgaard I'd like to take along an ex-Gnostie, Fred Hamilton, to advise me as necessary. We called Hamilton at his office—he'd just gotten back from a business lunch—and Hjelmgaard and he talked for several minutes. Hamilton would remain behind if Charles didn't like him.

Then I called Joe. He had Contracts finalize the agreement then and there, and Hjelmgaard's computer received a copy with Joe's intersig. When I took off from Lindbergh that evening, I felt as if I'd done a really good day's work.

23
EVIDENCE—OF A SORT

I reserved two moderately priced suites in the New Black Angus Inn in Eugene, Oregon, one for Hamilton and myself, the other for Hjelmgaard and Charles. Our flight arrived at the airport a little after noon, half an hour ahead of theirs. We waited for them there and took a taxivan to the motel.

The idea was to go to bed early, because our chartered skyvan would take off with the four of us at 2 A.M., which meant that Hjelmgaard and Charles would have to get up at half-past midnight. Hamilton and I would make a preliminary overflight at eleven, to make sure there was no reason to postpone or cancel.

Hamilton and I actually did catch a decent nap. But Charles was wound up like an old clock spring, so about seven, Hjelmgaard took him to a movie. *Snow White and the Seven Dwarfs* was going around again. I'd like to have gone myself.

Our preliminary overflight showed the lodge occupied. A sky limo was on the ground beside it, while a skyvan was parked at the guard barracks. Apparently some bigwig was there, though why I couldn't guess. At that elevation, the ground was still snow-covered. A thought struck me: Wouldn't it be something if Christman was back in residence there, hail and strong. I asked the pilot if there was an aurora in the weather forecast.

She turned to me with a quizzical expression. "In the forecast?" she said, and pointed. "Look out the window."

And there it was, not a major display—as a kid I'd often seen better over Lake Superior—but there it was, some cold shimmering curtains, and sheaves of icy-looking bundles of lightspears, shifting and pulsing. I'd been looking down, ignoring up.

We flew over just fast enough not to look like snoopers, in case we were being monitored from the ground. The skyvan's computer recorded everything our scanners picked up, of course, so we could examine it more closely on the flight back to town. Among other things, it showed a small security patrol—seemingly three men and a dog—near the forest road along the property's lower edge, where there was more chance of trespass. As on our earlier trip, there was no evidence of radar or other electronic activity on the ridge, and no people on it or on the trail that climbed it. The observatory was glass-roofed and glass-walled, surrounded by a wooden walkway and railing. The telescope inside was aligned with an oblong panel that presumably could be opened. Apparently the whole building could be rotated. It was mounted on a circular metal base. Now though, it was dark and cold.

There was no question. We'd go for it as planned, making another preliminary overflight just before landing there, to be sure no threat had developed.

Back at the airport, Hamilton stayed with our pilot. I took a cab to the motel, in case Hjelmgaard needed help. He didn't really, though he'd had trouble getting Charles awake enough to get dressed. I helped Charles stumble out to the cab, where he fell asleep immediately. I began to wonder if he'd be functional, but kept it to myself. If there was a problem, it would be Hjelmgaard's to handle. Charles became more alert at the airport, and walked to the skyvan on his own, still not talking, but looking around. After we took off, I told him again what I thought might have happened on the ridge, and what I hoped he'd provide us with. He nodded without speaking, but now his eyes were bright.

It was 2:16 when we made our preliminary overflight. There was no sign of anyone outdoors now, just a pair of sentry dogs in the run outside the kennel. The sky limo was still there, and an IR reading showed that the lodge was heated to a comfortable temperature. We made our landing approach from the northeast, keeping the ridge between us and the lodge, the dark and brooding evergreen forest barely beneath us. Our pilot set us down carefully about 150 feet from the observatory. Charles still wasn't talking, but his eyes were wide and alive.

The observatory was on a rock hump, a sort of ridgetop prominence without trees, though there'd been some cut down, both outside and inside the fence. Their stumps had prevented landing closer. As we got out, I realized the sentry dogs had sensed us. They were barking in their run, maybe a quarter mile away and 400 feet lower. I wondered if the security people would let them loose. Even with the distance and the protection of the boundary fence, we walked somewhat hurriedly across the hard, crusty, frost-rimed snow till we were within 40 feet of the observatory. It had been a mild spring night in Eugene; on the ridge it was cold.

I pointed. "That's it," I told Charles, then stepped back with my repeating Polaroid. Hjelmgaard stood beside me with his own. Charles turned, faced the observatory, and stood quiet for a long minute. My shivering was only partly from the cold. Then he shifted his gaze down the path that led to it, closed his eyes and grimaced. After a long moment he gritted out: "Now!" I pressed the shutter release. "Now!" he repeated, and again, my finger keeping time. Then he turned, facing almost toward the skyvan. "Now!" I exposed a fourth frame. "Now! Now!" Two more.

His eyes gleamed as he turned back to Hjelmgaard. "That's all, Clarence," he said. He didn't sound retarded at all; at his game we were retarded.

"Thank you, Charles," Hjelmgaard answered, smiling, then looked at Hamilton and me. "Well, gentlemen." We crunched our way back to the van, where the pilot eyed us curiously as we climbed in.

Off the ground and flying back to Eugene, I turned on the cabin lights and we removed the prints from the cameras. Hjelmgaard was blasé about what we found, but Hamilton and I stared. Charles had unbelted, and crowding close, laughed delightedly, a strange sound in the chilly skyvan cruising otherwise silently above nightbound mountains. The prints looked as if they'd been shot with Ultracept 1000, instead of Polaroid, the details of faces and figures equal to film exposed in, say, overcast daylight with a proper exposure setting. Yet the background was dark with night.

The first shot showed Christman walking beside a young woman, both of them wearing down parkas with the hoods back. His arm was around her waist. Behind them to one side, you could make out a man wearing black trousers and jersey, his face and hands blackened. He was half crouched, as if just getting to his feet. The rest formed a sequence, two men grappling with Christman, Christman being injected, Christman being supported to a skyvan while the young woman was carried to it dead or unconscious. And two men pushing and pulling Christman through the door. He seemed semiconscious; his head wasn't lolling.

The final shot appeared as if taken from the rear of the skyvan's cabin. The woman was trussed up on the floor, apparently unconscious instead of dead, while Christman lay on a side seat, handcuffed and seemingly also unconscious. Three men sat across from him, looking toward him, and each face was clear. In the previous shot we'd seen four men. The fourth was either the pilot, or was with the pilot in the pilot's compartment.

"Do you know any of them?" I asked Hamilton.

He shook his head. "Only Christman."

At the airport I called a taxivan, and had it take us to an all-night restaurant off the freeway. We were too wound up to go to bed, especially Charles. He chattered about the food, and a place in Minneapolis where Hjelmgaard and his wife occasionally took him for supper, and about other pictures he'd made that he was particularly proud of. I had bacon and fried eggs, buttered sourdough toast, and tomato slices, and listened to him partly because I owed it to him, but also because he was interesting. Charles had strawberry waffles, and respectable table manners in spite of talking so much.

I looked forward to a few more hours of sleep. But more than anything else, I looked forward to getting back to L.A. and finding a way to identify the men in the pictures. The pictures weren't legal evidence of anything, but they could be a powerful wedge for breaking the case.

24
LUNCH BREAK

The effect of the Veritas had begun to fade; it showed on the aura analyzer. Now the young woman spoke, breaking Martti's groove. "This is a good place to stop for lunch, and the injection is wearing off."

His eyes had opened. "Ah. How did we do?"

"Just fine. Excellent in fact. Why don't we eat on my expense account and start again at one-thirty."

"Sounds good. Do I need a counter injection?"

"No. A bit of walking will handle what's left. Is there a restaurant you like within walking distance?"

They agreed on Canter's. It was a bit far, but she was willing and they had time.

He'd been aware of his monolog as he gave it, aware that he'd rambled, and aware that he had no will to edit as he spoke. As he went down the hall to the men's room, he was also aware that his throat felt none the worse for his verbal marathon. The effect of the Veritas, he decided. It was, after all, a sort of hypnotic.

PART TWO:
SERVICIO VIAJERO
INTERNACIONAL

PROLOG

The old man was no longer bed-bound, nor showed any obvious sign of the stroke he'd suffered some years earlier. He still did not look healthy—his face remained puffy, his eyes yellow with jaundice, and his body flaccid—but neither did he seem actively ill.

The sun was high enough that the cool of morning was beginning to dispel. Sweatered, he rested beneath a large parasol in his garden, on a light, motorized, mobile recliner. Beside him, several books lay scattered on a glass-topped table, waiting to be devoured. Another lay open, facedown on his little paunch. His lips were pursed, and a frown creased his forehead.

Most people's minds the old man could monitor undetected, especially someone who discussed or argued with himself a lot. Ordinarily he would eavesdrop from the fringes of the person's immediate mental field, but would sometimes intrude within it, to poke and pry for information, blending in as the self-generated entity the person discoursed with.

Some, though, when he intruded, would sense his presence, and almost invariably reacted sharply, repelling him, a jolting experience that snapped him back to his body. Given his poor health, he'd designed and practiced drills enabling him to better withstand ejection shock.

If he intruded undetected, however, there was then the possibility of hypnotizing the person from within, *whispering his formula directly into their mind. Subliminally at first, then more strongly as it began to influence them.*

If they were susceptible enough to suggestion. So far he'd found no firm criterion for predicting that susceptibility. Intelligence, emotional stability, strength of character—none of these assured it or ruled it out. And therein lay danger. For if, when he tried to hypnotize someone, his would-be victim discovered him, their reaction was likely to be violent. Shocking to both of them but far worse for the intruder—far worse than simple ejection shock. The first time it happened, he'd been taken by surprise, and very nearly died. The crippling effects still were not entirely gone.

To him though, the game was worth the risk. It was what he lived for now. And he was too strong-willed to abandon his plans, though he had learned caution. Besides, once a subject had been hypnotized and given an appropriate post-hypnotic suggestion, he could reenter at will to give further commands, seemingly with little or no danger.

After the shock that had precipitated his heart attack and subsequent stroke, he'd worked very carefully, improving his technique. But although his skill had increased markedly, there still was risk in undertaking to hypnotize someone from within their mind for the first time. He'd learned this the hard way, and again had lain in a coma for two days. And again, if his personal physician had not been at hand, he would probably have died. After that he became very selective, taking the risk only for compelling reasons.

Another difficulty in using his skills was the initial contact, psychically "finding" the person he wanted to eavesdrop on, or possibly control. Once a contact was made, it left him with a connection which, while tenuous and subliminal, made the person easy to reach again. But to make that first contact, he needed an intermediary, a live introduction, so to speak. He hadn't learned to surmount that requirement, though he expected to. Thus he'd found and connected with Alex DeSmet by first controlling an old student in Monterey, and implanting a post-hypnotic command to meet and cultivate DeSmet.

*Then, after cautiously infiltrating DeSmet, he'd prod-
ded and peered, and learned about a man named Kelly Masters.*

When one of his out-of-use contacts had a shock of some
sort, it sometimes caught the old man's attention from a
distance. The criterion seemed to be whether or not the
event had anything to do with his own interests. Lon
Thomas had just received not a shock, but a troubling
report, and it was that which had interrupted the old man's
reading.

It had been months since he'd eavesdropped on Thomas'
mind. He'd long since learned what he'd needed from
Thomas, and the man seemed quite able to scuttle the
Church of the New Gnosis unintentionally and unassisted,
given time. Now though— Something clearly was wrong.

Thomas was at Christman's mountain retreat. The old
man listened, then ferreted out what had preceded it.

It had begun the night before. The sentry dogs had
barked furiously and at length, and finally Thomas had
roused enough to call Security. The chief told him that the
perimeter alarms had not been triggered. The dogs' attention
had been on the ridgetop, in the direction of the observatory. Perhaps a bear was prowling up there.

Thomas had had a patrol sent out, well armed and with
the dogs. Then he'd lain back down. He was not very alert
mentally. He'd rutted till late with his latest lady, main-
taining his lust and capacity with Harem Smoke—illegal
but readily available. The result had been deep exhaustion,
and with the dogs shut up, he was asleep again as soon
as his eyes closed.

What had drawn the old man's attention was not what
had happened that night, however. It was Thomas' reaction to the security chief's report after breakfast. There were
fresh landing marks in the snow on the ridgetop, on the
other side of the fence. And foot tracks, several sets of them,
ending at a point near the observatory.

The Gnostie chief didn't know the significance of the
report, but it alarmed him in an undefined sort of way.

The old man, on the other hand, sensed in a general way what it meant, and was possessed by a cold, intense anger. Two valuable tools were endangered, tools he'd cultivated carefully and with no little risk to himself, to his life. He wouldn't take action through Thomas, though. Thomas, it seemed to him now, was nothing. A fool! Like Christman had been a fool in the last analysis.

He'd use one of the endangered tools instead.

25
CLOUD MAN AND STEINHORN

The UCLA researcher removed the syringe from the flat, velvet-lined box. She knew that Martti had stopped at the mens' room again when they'd returned from Canter's, but she asked anyway. "Any last-minute business to take care of?"

"Nope. Let's do it."

She nodded, took his hand and held the syringe against the back of it, then pulled the trigger. The syringe hissed, and she put it back in the box. Martti watched, vision already blurring. Again he closed his eyes and began to talk.

On the day after we got back, I went into Morey's for breakfast. Indian was there at his favorite table, and waved me over. There was a strong-looking guy with him I hadn't seen before. He wore well-worn jeans and a new twill work shirt. I assumed he was from Yitzhak's, probably a Gnostie.

After I'd ordered my breakfast, I went over to them. "Martti," Indian said, "meet my friend Cloud Man. He's a new brother that lives at our house. He's started working for Yitzhak, too. Cloud Man, this is Martti Seppanen I told you about." He looked at me again. "I didn't tell him anything I shouldn't," he added.

Cloud Man and I shook hands. A Loonie? I doubted it. The Loonies I'd met, admittedly not very many, didn't have Cloud Man's watchful, appraising eyes. They tended to be easygoing, sometimes spaced out.

"Nothing doing today, eh?" I said.

"Nah. The turn of the month rush is over. Him and me got in fifty-eight hours in four days; I'm just as glad it's come up slow now. A real slate pool table and two baby grands, for chrissake! The pool table took eight of us, up thirty-one steps to this house in Woodland Hills! You shoulda been there. We could've used your muscle."

"No thanks. I thought Yitzhak generally didn't hire anyone but New Gnus."

"I guess I broke the ice. Now he'll hire other guys that's religious, if they come in recommended and they ain't druggies. How you doin' with them? The Gnus, I mean."

"As little as possible." I didn't want anything more said about the Gnosties and myself in front of Cloud Man, so I changed the subject. "A slate pool table and two pianos, eh? Sounds like a workout all right."

"Yeah, and the world's biggest Murphy bed. That was on the fourth job. It must have weighed four hundred pounds, and opened out queen sized! No shit! We never did figure out how anyone got the sonofabitch into that fourth-floor apartment. It was one of those old buildings with narrow inside halls and narrow doors. We finally took it out through a bay window; used tie-straps tied together for rope. To keep it from bustin' the windows below it, we tied another rope to it, and a big guy—you know Bill Brawn? No? That's his real name! He was out on the lawn with the rope belayed around a tree, keepin' the Murphy bed away from the wall. I tell you, when we pushed it out the window, I almost shit my pants. I didn't know what would happen, whether it'd get away from us or what."

My food came, and while I ate, we talked about this and that, mostly the Dodgers. Then I left. I couldn't help wondering if Cloud Man was an undercover Gnostie. That would account for Yitzhak hiring him, and he could have been sent by Lon Thomas. *No*, I told myself, *not after what happened. Thomas isn't that stupid. And just because the*

*guy might see me in Morey's now and then, he'd be in no
position to learn what we're doing.*

So, was he LAPD? If he was, it was none of my business,
which didn't make me less curious. I spent awhile that
morning with Carlos, shuffling the photos, staring at them.
To the cost of Charles Tomasic's services, add my travel and
lodging and everybody else's, and the charter costs for the
skyvan, including Hamilton's and my earlier trip ... Alto-
gether those photos had cost Butzburger more than six thousand dollars, not including my hours. And I still had no idea
who the kidnappers were, or how to find out; only what they
looked like. The main thing I'd learned was that Christman
had been abducted, that he hadn't just run off somewhere
to a life of wealthy anonymity with a lady love.

Maybe that would be enough for Butzburger. I hoped
not. It would be worse than coitus interruptus to pull out
of this case now.

Most of that day and evening I spent on the unprom-
ising cycle of calling and visiting informants, with the usual
total lack of success. One thing had changed though.
Melanie wasn't seeing me anymore. I wasn't surprised.
Someone could easily have an informer in her place, one
she was aware of, working for someone who wouldn't like
her having anything to do with an investigator of any kind.

The next morning I slept in, then spent most of the
afternoon at Gold's, working off my frustrations. Maybe I
hoped, subliminally, that some ideas would grow out of my
sweat. They didn't. I spent the next few working days doing
other stuff, for Carlos, till he felt he had to nudge me to
get me back on the Christman case again. Nudging like
that was something Carlos didn't like to do to his investigators, which tells you something about my mental state
at the time.

Then one morning, Carlos introduced me to a new
investigative assistant who'd started with Prudential the
afternoon before. His name was David Steinhorn. He had
a strong handshake, and a face with no trace of illusion.
I judged him at thirty-something.

Investigative contracting by public agencies had been increasing, and Prudential was getting more than its share, so Joe was trying to beef up staff. Unfortunately, a lot of applicants have romanticized ideas of the business. They don't realize how difficult it can be, how double-damned frustrating, and sometimes monotonous as hell. And when they find out, they're apt to quit, after the firm has spent a bunch of time and money breaking them in. Or they're bovine—they stand the monotony all right, but they're mentally lazy. Or they're smart and interested, but lack toughness. I don't mean pushing people around; that's a good way to get off-loaded around here. They just can't face up to some of the people you have to face up to.

After returning him to the IA pen where the investigative assistants were officed together, Carlos came back looking pleased with himself.

"I think we've got a keeper," he said. Steinhorn, it seems, had brought a good record with him. In the army he'd spent four years as a Ranger, then injured a hip in a jungle drop and been transferred to the CID, where he'd been trained as an investigator. His military record had been excellent; he'd made sergeant first class before he'd turned twenty-five. A check of his CID personnel file turned up phrases like "analytical, tough, and learns quickly. Shows particular talent in the adaptation of electronic resources." Also, "Is not given to talking shop, even with his peers."

Then his wife and kid had been killed in a retaliatory hit near Salinas. He'd applied for a discharge, and it had been granted.

After leaving Fort Ord, he'd gone to Tucson, a city he'd gotten to know and like while investigating a theft ring at Fort Huachuca. He'd wanted to get a civilian investigative job, but they were hard to get at the time, particularly without a college degree in law enforcement. Contract legal investigation hadn't begun its major expansion yet.

So in Tuscon he'd taken a job as a security supervisor with Algotsson-Scherker, a Westwide construction contractor, and worked there for more than two years. The job involved the routine security of buildings, and also of equipment at company warehouses, equipment parks, and on the job. A-S' personnel records rated him highly, particularly for his "scrupulous attention to details." Carlos loved that, I was sure. It's important in our work, although in my opinion it can be overrated.

After a while he'd subscribed to a professional job-listing network, watching for a job in investigation with a company that might offer a good future. When Joe listed Prudential as hiring, Steinhorn applied. An opening-level job with us paid quite a bit less than his A-S job did, and the cost of living is higher in L.A., but as he put it in his application, "It offers a career ladder in my preferred line of work." An attitude Joe Keneely liked.

Joe and Carlos might have thought we had a good one, but somehow I didn't feel right about Steinhorn. There was something behind his eyes, as if he wasn't being straight with us. And unlike Joe and Carlos, it didn't make any difference to me whether the new positions got filled or not. So it was easier for me to feel skeptical of him.

I didn't say anything though. His employment record was excellent, his test scores very good, and so what if I didn't like his eyes? Me, a guy who'd allowed himself to get thoroughly bogged down on a case.

Looking back, I'd say my attitude just then constituted treason against myself, against my own instincts, but that's how it was.

26
COMPUTER TRESPASS

The next day it was time to make the rounds of my informants again, and Carlos told me to take Steinhorn with me, give him the feel of the L.A. underworld. It went okay. We didn't talk much, beyond line of duty, but he had a good attitude. Sometimes a person with experience thinks he knows it all, and scorns procedures different from those he'd learned somewhere else. Not Steinhorn. So I pretty much banished my misgivings about him.

The only thing wrong with the day was the continuing lack of any useful results.

That evening Tuuli called from Diacono's. She sounded great, and said she'd be coming home in three days. When she asked me how things were going, I lied: I said fine. I'd called her the evening after I'd gotten back from Eugene, telling her about the photos, so "fine" might have been believeable, but after we'd disconnected, it seemed to me she knew better. Also, I realized I was feeling sorry for myself because she wasn't home already, "when I needed her." *Yeah, you big clod,* I told myself, *what you want is someone to pat you on the head and say, "Poor thing, poor poor thing."*

✧   ✧   ✧

The next morning I looked into Carlos' office to say "*buenos dias, jefe*" or maybe "*ohaio, gozaimasu.*" Carlos wasn't there though. He'd gone to Fresno and wouldn't be back before late afternoon, and Steinhorn was sitting at Carlos' desk. I didn't think anything of it, beyond, *he's doing some flunky work for Carlos*. The sort of thing I used to do as an investigative assistant, although Carlos had never told me to use his desk and computer; I'd done my work in the IA pen.

In my office, I took my six thousand dollars' worth of photos out of the desk—or actually computer facsimiles; the originals were in the evidence vault—and stared without really seeing them. I knew right away I could look at them all day and come up with nothing. So after a couple of minutes I told Fidela I was going to take some compensatory time off, and left. I didn't go to Gold's; I drove west out Sunset Boulevard and parked in the lot at Will Rogers State Beach.

The day was overcast—common enough for the season—and the onshore wind verged on chilly, so there weren't many people there. Mostly surfers in wet suits, because the surf was up a bit. I hiked the sand for quite a ways along the fringe of the surf wash, deliberately using my eyes instead of thinking about things. Spotting the dead gull, the piece of driftwood with some old carving worn nearly illegible by sea and sand, the discarded condom, while listening to the regular, soothing rush and hiss of breakers and their backwash, and the random, counterpoint screeing of gulls. I'd discovered some years earlier, as a junior detective with the Marquette, Michigan, police force, that skiing some forest trail or hiking the Lake Superior shoreline could sometimes shake things loose for me. This was the same sort of thing.

On toward noon I got back to my car and drove south to Santa Monica Beach. There I walked around eating the local equivalent of a Dodger dog and a couple of ice-cream cones, and watched people ride the rides and throw baseballs at targets. This one girl about eleven, who should have been in school, was watching the baseball throwers. She wore as despondent an expression as I'd seen for a while. Even I didn't look that bad. So I bought three tosses, knocked down three targets, and won a fluffy, meter-long nylon or something rabbit which I handed to her, then walked away quickly so she wouldn't get the wrong idea and be scared.

After that I browsed the bookshelves at the Change of Hobbit II, and bought a couple of paperbacks—an Ed Bryant collection and a new novel by an old master, David Brin. It was almost quitting time when I got back to the office. I told my computer *"hyvää iltaa,"* and called up the Christman file, prepared to enter another null day.

Before it downloaded, a code flagged on the screen. When I'd first been with the Marquette Police Department, there'd been some factional infighting, replete with spying and even accusations of the sabotage of files. And because it wasn't all right to make a file inaccessible to the office, or try to, I'd learned to install a covert security alarm on sensitive files, something I've done routinely ever since, on general principle. *"Hyvää iltaa,"*—"good evening" in Finnish—or *hyvää päivää,* depending on the time of day, were the codes I used to identify myself and tell the computer to flag anything that might be a trespass.

And someone had activated the Christman file, called it up on Carlos' terminal at 12:27 that afternoon! Fidela would have been in the lunchroom, and a check indicated that Carlos still wasn't back from Fresno. So far as I knew, the only people who should be using Carlos' computer were Carlos himself, and whoever he might have told to use it for some reason. Steinhorn for example. Except there was zero likelihood that Carlos would have told him to do anything with the Christman file.

So. Presuming it had been Steinhorn—why would he have snooped? Curiosity?

I called up the file again, to look at it "with other eyes than mine," and see what it might have looked like to him. Parts of it were clear and detailed. The Oregon project, on the other hand, read cryptically, if you didn't already know what was going on. The entries were dated, and the photos were there, but how we'd gotten them wasn't even hinted at. The bills, the charges and times of charter flights, the trip to Minneapolis to see Hjelmgaard—all those things were there, but not the why, not what they meant. Charles Tomasic wasn't even mentioned except as Charles—"Hjelmgaard and Charles."

And since then, all the entries simply stated "null," or "nothing new."

I asked the computer for a reprise of all operations run while whoever it was had the Christman file in the RAM. It had been scrolled, stopped, and scrolled again, repeatedly. Nothing had been entered, deleted, or altered in any way, *but the computer had printed a copy of each of the photographs from Oregon!*

Perkele! Who had he sent them to? He'd hardly have faxed them on one of our office machines. There'd be a record, and he knew it. I checked anyway. They record everything sent; my expensive pictures weren't among them. But there were plenty of commercial fax machines in the neighborhood. Lots of stores have them for customer use, cheap.

It seemed to me that someone, perhaps the abductor, perhaps the church, now had copies. And someone's hair just might have been standing six inches out from their head when they saw them. The important question now was, what might they do next?

I locked my door, then took the bug scanner from my attaché case and checked my office over. Sure as hell! There was one in the thermostat control! I let it be. It could have been there for weeks or months, but I was willing to bet it had been installed that day, or at most only a few days earlier. By Steinhorn. Better let him, or whoever it was, think none of it had been discovered, neither bug nor computer trespass.

Then I walked down the hall and asked Fidela if Carlos had called in. He hadn't. So I phoned his flat and asked Penny if he was home yet. She said no, and that he'd probably stop at the office first. I told her I'd call that evening if I didn't see him sooner.

By that time it was five o'clock, and people were leaving. I called up the Christman file again and entered a null day. Which of course was a gross lie. *Because,* I told myself, *I'd just been handed a lead that might be more important than the photographs.*

I was wrong about that, it turned out. Both were vitally important.

I also decided to call Tuuli that evening and talk her into staying longer in Arizona. If Christman's murderers or abductors had those photos, things could get dangerous again.

I hung around for a little and read my messages, dictating the necessary replies or comments to the computer. Vocorders are still pretty expensive, but Joe liked to hold down the paperwork for his investigators. Everyone else was gone except floor security and the night receptionist, but with Tuuli out of town, I felt no urge to get home, and this way I missed the quitting-time traffic. Real Angelenos say the traffic these days isn't nearly as bad as before the plagues, but I still prefer to leave early or late.

Then Carlos came in. I waited a few minutes while he handled his in-messages, then asked him if he'd walk to La Fonda with me and eat Mexican. He knew I wouldn't distract him if I didn't need to—not when he was being an investigator instead of a supervisor, and working on a case of his own. So he called Penny and told her he'd be eating before he came home.

La Fonda is only five blocks from the office. It's not as good as La Casa de Herreras, but it's cheaper. And we were really going out to talk; the meal was incidental. Neither of us said much on the way. It was a pleasant evening, and the only reason I wore a jacket was to cover my shoulder holster.

Based on experience, we both ordered *enchiladas suizas.* Then, while I creamed and sweetened my coffee, Carlos asked what was on my mind. First I told him my office was bugged, and that his might be, and conceivably other places around corporate headquarters. That sobered him.

Then I told him about the trespass into the Christman file at noon, and that the photos had been copied. I could almost hear the wheels turning in his mind. "You see why I didn't want to talk about it at work," I finished.

He nodded. "And you've got some ideas about what it means."

"Right." Then I told him about Steinhorn using his desk that day. "You didn't tell him to, did you?" I asked.

He was frowning, mouth and eyes. "No. Which doesn't prove anything, but it's suggestive. What do you make of it?"

"For one thing, it's a break in the case. Also, I don't want Steinhorn to know I suspect him, or that I even know anything's wrong. I think we need to check the personnel reports we got on him against the original files, both with the army and Algotsson-Scherker. But first I think you should scan your office for bugs, because quick-checking his personnel records will require using the phone."

"I doubt that the army's files were tampered with," Carlos said thoughtfully. "These days, military storage archives are supposed to be about as tamperproof as you can find. When one of them gets compromised, it closes down the whole system, alarms God knows how many offices, and kicks in a backup system."

"Even personnel records?!"

"Once they're closed."

That didn't make much sense to me, but if that's how it was . . . That left Algotsson-Scherker's. He'd check them in the morning, he said, during A-S' office hours.

After enchiladas, we went back to the office. A scan showed no bugs in Carlos', but that didn't mean it would stay clean. He decided to check it again whenever he came in. The men's room was clean too, electronically as well as otherwise. He'd send Steinhorn out with Rossi first thing in the morning; that would keep him out of the way till quitting time. Then we could sit down and do some brainstorming.

Prudential has the security contract for our building. Ou

security crews are the best in the business. As we left, Carlos gave instructions for the swing shift and night shift to record any staff who came in, along with time in and time out. And not to tell anyone but him and me; he stressed that. If *anyone* else came in after hours "to work late," he wanted to know.

On my way home, I stopped and called Tuuli—on a coin phone, leaving no paper or electronic trail—and asked her to stay in Arizona for another week. I expected her to ask why, and I also knew that anything but the truth would sound weak. Which could start an argument. To my surprise, she agreed right away, and never asked a thing.

That got me worried. Had she found some guy in Arizona that she liked better than me? Would worrying about it keep me awake half the night?

So I stopped at Gold's for an hour and a half, to poop myself out good, then buried my nose in Hirschman's massive *Twenty Case Histories of the Post-Reform Era*— about my fifth reading of it—and around midnight went to sleep without any trouble. By that time I'd decided Tuuli wouldn't have found anyone at Long Valley, Arizona, who was stronger or smarter than me. Not that she could talk Finnish with.

27
NEW BREAKTHROUGH

I was finishing off an omelette in Morey's the next morning when Indian came in. Usually when he comes in, he's there earlier, and I could tell by his expression that something was seriously wrong. I waved to him and he came over without even stopping to order.

"Jesus Christ!" he said as he flopped down.

"What is it?"

"Cloud Man's dead! Killed! This morning!"

It turned out they'd been riding in together on Indian's big bike—an Indian Buffalo, appropriately enough—with Cloud Man on behind. They'd turned onto Hollywood from Gower and just passed the intersection with Cahuenga when a sniper had shot Cloud Man right off the bike. Indian had almost lost it; it took him forty or fifty meters to stop. By the time he'd run back to Cloud Man, cars had stopped and people were gathering. A couple of them were on their knees, trying to help. Crowding them aside, Indian knelt. Cloud Man's eyes were open, and when he saw Indian, he tried to talk to him. Indian had to get his ear down close to hear.

"My real name," Cloud Man whispered, "is Leo McCarver." He repeated it. "Leo McCarver. The guy, who shot me— Card in my wallet. Ensenada. Mexico. Warn Martti. They'll kill him too."

As Indian finished telling me, his eyes opened wide, as if only the words, not the meaning, had registered before. As if his attention had been so totally on the incomprehensible—someone shooting Cloud Man—that he hadn't really connected the words with reality. "Go on," I said. "Then what?"

That was all Cloud Man had told him; then he'd closed his eyes. Indian hadn't tried to frisk him for his wallet, because about that time two beat cops came running up. Three or four minutes later an ambulance was there, and the paramedics had gotten Leo McCarver—Cloud Man—onto a litter. Indian heard one of them say he was dead. By that time a patrol floater was there too, and Indian told the sergeant Cloud Man's name—names—and where he'd lived, and what his own name was. The sergeant had asked a few more questions, then let him go.

He hadn't mentioned Ensenada or me. Indian had driven on to Yitzhak's then, even though he'd arrive too late for muster, to tell them what happened. The jobs had already been assigned, so he'd come to Morey's.

Warn Martti. They'll kill him too! Unless Indian had left something out, those were McCarver's last words, said with almost his last breath! Why, unless he thought it was true? And where did I fit in?

I passed Steinhorn and Rossi in the lobby, going out as I went in. Rossi said hi; Steinhorn only nodded. I suppose I said something back.

Carlos' office was still clean, and I sat down next to him so we could both watch his computer screen. I told him about Cloud Man. Leo McCarver: the name meant nothing to him either. He called Algotsson-Scherker, and as you'd expect of a construction outfit, their headquarters' office was open. They opened at eight instead of nine, and they were on Mountain Time. The guy who answered connected him with their personnel office, where a Francine answered. After Carlos had identified himself and the firm, he told Francine he needed to see their personnel file on David Steinhorn.

She asked why he needed to know. When he'd satisfied her, she said, "Just a moment, Mr. Katagawa." Her attention went to her computer; presumably her fingers were giving it instructions. Then, frowning, she looked back at her vidcam. "I'm sorry, Mr. Katagawa, but we have no record of a David Steinhorn."

"You did when I checked with you a little over a week ago," Carlos said. "You may have a record of my call. We hired him on the basis of it."

Her gaze returned to her computer screen, her brows drawn down in concentration. Again her fingers wrote. She shook her head slightly, still frowning, and tried something else, then something else again, finally staring thoughtfully with her lower lip between her teeth. Then she looked out at us from the phone screen. "I'm sorry, sir. I have nothing on a David Steinhorn; on any Steinhorn; or any other name beginning with S-T-E-I-N or S-T-I-E-N or S-T-E-N."

"But you do remember my call."

"I remember your face, yes."

"Do you remember finding a file on Steinhorn?"

"I remember finding a file for you, yes sir, but I don't recall its identity."

"Okay. There's something strange here. May I speak with whoever's in charge of personnel files?"

"I'm in charge of personnel files," she said. She was still frowning. I got the notion that actually she remembered seeing the file and was wondering what the hell had happened to it. "Would you like to speak with Ms. Hawks, the personnel director?"

"If I may, please."

Ms. Hawks was a trim and handsome woman, black but with an Oriental look. Her father'd probably been a GI in Asia somewhere. When Carlos had explained our problem to her, she shook her head. "I'm sure we've had no salaried employee named Steinhorn since I came here in oh-four. And our personnel files haven't been culled since they were computerized; probably in the seventies or eighties."

"Who has access to them?"

"Various people, in read-only. Only Francine and I have access to them in edit mode. Except of course Mr. Scherker, and Ms. Lopez, his administrative assistant. And— We employ standard precautionary systems to ensure the integrity of our personnel files. To meet the legal requirements for personal privacy. Entering them illegally would require someone skilled and resourceful. And reckless."

She left it at that. The rest was understood: Such people were available for hire, operating out of homes and offices everywhere. There was a constant attrition of them, of course. Some made their stake and quit. Others got located by monitor programs and arrested; sent to work camps to chop cotton in the desert sun, or plant trees on old cutovers and burns. Hard manual labor, hot and sweaty or wet and cold. But the payoffs could be big. There were always recruits to the ranks of computer criminals. Or perhaps Lopez or even Scherker could have done it, maybe as a favor to a friend. Or it could have been Hawks or Francine, though Francine especially had seemed too convincing to be acting. Carlos decided to let be; he thanked Hawks and disconnected. Then we talked. Conceivably Steinhorn might have hacked into A-S' personnel files himself, and inserted the erroneous file. Then erased it after he was hired, to avoid someone like Hawks running across it and perhaps informing us, if they logged the personnel reference requests they received.

But if Steinhorn had the skills for that, what was he doing working for Prudential as an investigative assistant?

To both of us, it seemed a lot more likely that some-one else had arranged the false file, for the purpose of inserting Steinhorn in our office. Someone interested in the Christman case. Which could be any of our active suspects, or someone else, unsuspected and maybe unknown.

"So," I said, "assume his military record is genuine. It probably is. If he hasn't been working for Algotsson-Scherker since he took his discharge, what has he been doing?

"And Cloud Man, Leo McCarver—was he connected

with Steinhorn in any way? They both arrived on the scene about the same time. When I first met McCarver, he didn't seem like a Loonie to me. I thought he might be under-cover for the LAPD, or maybe the DEA—something like that. Whose card did McCarver have in his wallet? Apparently someone in Ensenada who might be interested in killing me.

"Why would someone, or some business entity, in Ensenada want me dead? Is there a connection with Steinhorn? And why would McCarver want to warn me, when we'd barely met? Was there a faction that wanted me dead, and another that wanted me alive and on the job? Specifically the Christman job? Because that's the only job I'm handling."

Carlos had been leaning back in his chair, listening with eyes half closed. Now he sat up and leaned toward his computer, his fingers pecking. He accessed ITT's public-access listing of private security and investigation firms in Ensenada, a hundred kilometers south of the border on the west coast of Baja. There were three firms listed that did investigations—a lot for a town that size. A phone call to a contact and friend in the PEF—the "federales," the Mexican national police—established that all of them were one- or two-man operations, probably operating out of one-room offices. That sort of thing.

"So," I said when he'd disconnected. "Where does that leave us?"

Carlos grunted. He can put considerable meaning into a grunt, but it's not always apparent what the meaning is. "Back before *La Guerra de Octubre*, there was an outfit in Ciudad Juarez, with branches elsewhere, that called itself a travel and transportation service. A charter operation. But their main activities were smuggling weapons and drugs, and sometimes they took on a murder contract. The cover allowed them to operate aircraft and trucks without mak-ing anyone curious."

His fingers moved again, calling up transportation and travel services in Ensenada. Aside from the usual travel agencies, there was an outfit that called itself *SVI*—"*Servicio*

Viajero Internacional." Then he called up the public-access records on its ownership and management. It was a partnership, the listed partners being an Aquilo Reyes, a Eustaquio Tischenberg-Hinz, and a Kelly Masters.

"Carlos," I said, "call the Data Center and get McCarver's social security number. Use the Boghosian bombing case ID for access." To our surprise, they actually had a Leo McCarver listed as employed by Yitzhak's. His SocSec number was 1487-23-8765.

"Now see if he's been in the military."

He keyed up the Pentagon, went through three connections, then made his request, listing the contingency contract we had with the LAPD regarding the Boghosian bombing. He was referred to a captain, who asked enough questions to satisfy himself that there was at least some connection between the request and the case, then let it go at that. After all, we weren't asking for access to national security secrets.

He didn't show us a readout. He read from it, apparently editing out things he considered irrelevant to our needs. McCarver, it turned out, had been in Special Forces, and discharged without prejudice in November 2007, in the middle of an enlistment.

Carlos thanked the captain and disconnected, then turned to me. "So?"

"I'm not sure. But McCarver was in Special Forces, and Steinhorn supposedly in the Rangers. Steinhorn left in February '08 and McCarver, what? Three months earlier? Let's say that both of them were connected with SVI. So how did they get recruited?"

Carlos nodded, turned back to his computer and keyed up another Pentagon office. This time he asked for the Criminal Investigation Division, and did something illegal: Citing a contract with Sonoma County, regarding smuggling, he asked for access to a name-and-number-coded list of army personnel separated since 2006, with final postings. There had been no Tischenberg-Hinz. A Captain Aquilo Reyes had resigned in August 2007, last duty post Fort Bragg, Kentucky, which would fit both the Rangers and

Special Forces. And the name could hardly be a coincidence. There was also a Spec 2 Kelly W. Masters who'd taken his discharge in 2010 at Fort Benning, an unlikely match.

Carlos looked like he does when he's on a roll though. His fingers jabbed again, calling up directory assistance. The guy he wanted was listed, and he keyed the number. While it rang, he told me what he was after. "There's an engineer I've heard of," he said, "a spook freak, who's researched and compiled a list of ex-OSS personnel. As complete as he could . . ."

The guy answered. Yes, he'd compiled such a list, including ex-Special Projects personnel from the CIA, before Haugen had split it off and reconstituted the old OSS. All in all, he said, his list included probably half its retired or otherwise terminated operatives. Why, he wanted to know, was Carlos interested? Carlos explained without being specific, and said he was interested in just two names: An Eustaquio Tischenberg-Hinz, and a Kelly Masters. He spelled the first. The guy's list had a Kelly Masters, but not a Tischenberg-Hinz. Masters had taken an early retirement in June 2007.

Only two months before Reyes had resigned his commission! Something was starting to take shape. We might have been looking at coincidences, of course, but it felt unlikely. And while it still might have nothing to do with me or the Christman case, we'd work on the assumption that it did.

Carlos decided he'd go to Ensenada and investigate SVI on the ground. He wouldn't be conspicuous. He speaks fluent Spanish in three dialects: the chicano patois of Colorado's Rocky Ford-LaJunta Irrigation District, where he grew up; the somewhat different patois of L.A.'s Mexican barrios; and the proper Spanish of educated Mexicans. And his appearance wouldn't be a problem; there's a sizeable Japanese colony in Ensenada.

He also had a friend he'd worked with a couple of times, an inspector in the PEF in Mexicali, the capital of Baja Norte. Presumably the guy would be willing to provide him with credentials for liaising with the PEF in Ensenada, if necessary.

My Spanish, on the other hand, was merely functional, so I wouldn't go with him. I'd be recognized as a gringo right away. Instead he'd take one of our junior investigators, Miguel Vasquez. Until they got back, I could fill in for Miguel, helping Ernie Johnson on a case of trespass and illegal dumping. I'd be doing legwork, that sort of thing. If anything further broke on the Christmas case, I was to go back to it. Ernie's was a case with its main features well worked out. The job was to fill in the details for litigation and prosecution. It sounded restful, compared to the Christmas case.

That evening I called Tuuli again, at the Diaconos'. Someone named Debbie answered. Tuuli, she said, was off to some place called Sipapu, with the Diaconos and a couple of other people. I got the impression it was some sort of test. I hoped she was having a good time. Meanwhile I took advantage of the opportunity to feel sorry for myself because I couldn't talk with her.

28
HARLEY SUK O'CONNELL

A couple of days later I went down to the parking lot to grab a company car and check some things for Ernie. As I started east down Beverly, a small maroon sedan pulled out of the lot across the street. So why not? A lot of cars pull out of parking lots behind me, and don't mean a thing. But this one rang an alarm in my mind, so I called Ernie and told him. He said he'd be right down.

I hoped to hell it wasn't a false alarm. At the stop light at Sweetzer, I could see the car and driver in my outside mirror, a few cars back. I couldn't actually see his face very well, but it could have been the face I remembered from a few weeks earlier, when I'd been followed two or three times. I'd almost forgotten about that. This time I wouldn't try to throw him off. To give Ernie time, I pulled into the parking lot at the Big Ekon between Fairfax and Grove, and hurried in as if to buy something. When I came out, I couldn't see my tail anywhere, but I continued east. Sure enough, he'd jogged south a few blocks, then circled north and pulled in behind me again at the intersection with Genesee. I told Ernie, who by that time was in a car and on the phone only a couple of blocks behind us.

I also told Ernie what I had in mind, so he peeled off

north on Highland. Keeping it down to the speed limit, I stayed on Beverly a ways farther, then turned north on Rossmore. When my tail and I came to the intersection of Melrose, where Rossmore becomes Vine, Ernie was only a couple of blocks west. Probably by crowding the ambers or even the reds. I stopped for a stoplight at the corner of Sunset, and took the opportunity to snap the silencer onto the Glock 9mm the firm equips each car with. When the light turned green, I continued north to Franklin, then east to Beachwood Canyon and north to Mossydale, a little goat-trail street that hairpins its way up a ridge in the Hollywood Hills. My tail had dropped a little farther back on Beachwood, as if he hadn't wanted to be noticed. The traffic had been light. I couldn't see him at all, and wondered if he'd thought better of it, but at the upper switchback I glimpsed his maroon sedan a couple of switchbacks lower, still coming.

The danger then was that I'd lose him even if he didn't quit, so on the top I stopped where he could see me from a little ways back, got out with a camera, and let it seem as if I was taking pictures of a house there, shooting over the roof of my car as if trying not to be noticed. He stopped as soon as he saw me, got out and opened his hatchback as if doing something entirely legitimate. He even took out a piece of paper and stuck it in the gate of a yard there, like a notice. He was back in his car before I was.

I knew exactly where I wanted to lead him, and told Ernie, who by now was coming up the switchbacks. There's a point—a short side ridge with a curving stub street about a block long—where couples sometimes park. I turned off on it. If my tail knew the area well, he'd smell a rat and drive right on by. It dead ends where you can look out southeast over the L.A. basin, and there's no houses on it, I suppose because of a landslide hazard. It's just chaparral brush and the overlook. The curve is near the end. As soon as I was well around it, I stopped and got out, keeping the car between me and my follower, if any. Sure as hell, there he came, and saw me as he rounded the curve. Right away he stopped and began to back.

I heard my phone. "*I see him!*" Ernie said. Then, "*I've got him blocked!*"

I could still see the maroon sedan from my end, too, and with the Glock in both fists in front of me, I started toward it. The guy got out, a bearded black, caramel brown, actually, staring at Ernie. You've seen those old Dirty Harry movies on late-night TV. Ernie looks a lot like Clint Eastwood did—like a forty-year-old Dirty Harry. He was actually mild-mannered, but he knew how to use the resemblance. He'd have his car gun too; the guy was boxed.

"Spread 'em!" I shouted, and he did, hands and feet wide, leaning on his car. Close up I recognized him—Harley Suk O'Connell, the son of a black G.I. and his Korean wife. He was a minor league gun who got hired from time to time by the black mafia. He hadn't worn a beard when he'd ambushed Tuuli and me last October, but close up I knew him. I had a memento from that time, a scar on my right cheek from a bullet fragment.

"What're you up to, O'Connell?" I asked.

"I drove up to enjoy the view."

I pressed the silencer against his ear. "This is a nice private place here," I said, "and I've got a good memory. With the silencer, this nine em-em is as quiet as the one you shot at me with. Only there's no ornamental railing to blow the bullet up; just that quarter inch of skull bone.

"So, I'll ask again. What're you up to, O'Connell? Who are you working for?"

"You won't believe me if I tell you."

"Try me."

"You know I followed you a few weeks ago."

"Right. Several times"

"I was doing a job for the Carwood Family. They hired me to do a surveillance of Melanie's house. Suspected some brother was selling her information on the family's operations, and she was passing it on to Kim Soo."

"Was she?"

"Not that I could see. But I saw you go in, so Roman hired me to follow you and see what I could learn. About what you were working on. No big deal, but you got him curious, and he likes to know. It seemed to me you were doing something on the Gnosties, but I couldn't be sure. I told him you were on to me, and he said let it cool.

"Not long after that I heard he had Melanie picked up, questioned her about stuff and let her go. No profit gettin' in a war with the Soong Family. And he never did say to get back on you. I figured maybe he found out what he wanted."

"So what happened this morning?"

"I got a different car, and I'd been busy in Beverly Hills last night. You know how it is; a guy's got to make a living. And I was driving by your place of occupation and thought I'd stop a few minutes and see if you came out. If you did, I was going to follow you. See if you'd spot me this time."

I stared at him. He was still spread, looking at me from the corner of his eye. It sounded unlikely as hell, him just happening to stop. He'd had no reason to expect me.

He must have read my mind. "See!" he said. "I told you you wouldn't believe me!"

The funny thing was, I decided I did. I didn't like him, didn't trust him. He'd tried to kill me twice, and come close. His first bullet would probably have hit either Tuuli or me, if it hadn't hit that iron railing. And apparently he'd spent last night burgling. But somehow I believed him.

And he'd been lucky for me that other time: His trying to kill me had given me the leverage I needed to complete the Ashkenazi murder case. I stepped back and lowered my gun. "I believe you," I told him. "Just don't ask me why. But do us both a favor, O'Connell. Don't try me again." Not that I'd have shot him there in cold blood, but he didn't know that.

He stared at me a couple of seconds, then nodded and got in his car. We both stood watching him, guns in our hands, as he jockeyed around and left, squeezing past Ernie's car.

Ernie looked at me. "We should have looked in his luggage space," he said. "Then held him here till the police came. He's probably got a couple months' pay worth of loot in there."

I nodded. That's what policy said we should have done. It's what the law would have us do. And it would have been a point for Prudential with the LAPD.

"I'll call them," Ernie said.

"No," I told him. "Let him go."

Ernie peered at me, then shrugged. I didn't know why I said what I had, and neither did he. But it seemed to me like the right thing to do.

29
PULLING THREADS

Carlos was in Ensenada for four days. It turned out that SVI occupied a rented floor of offices over a large clothing store. Across from it was a big furniture store with a warehouse upstairs, and Carlos managed to rent a dusty upstairs corner with two windows, pretty much screened from the rest of the loft by furniture. His cover was, he'd been hired by an absent partner in SVI, who wanted to know what went on across the street. Carlos dropped a vague hint that gun-running might be involved, but didn't make clear whether with or without the partner's approval. In any case, it could obviously be dangerous for the furniture store owner to snoop or talk.

The SVI offices seemed to be three good-sized rooms in front, with maybe two rooms and a lavatory in back. Masters' office was the smallest front room, located in a corner.

Carlos had already learned, through his PEF connection, that SVI also leased four hectares of land from a dairy farm twelve kilometers out of town. He drove past on the day they arrived. Mostly it was an equipment park. Either they didn't have a lot of equipment, or most of it was out; there was more than room to spare. It also had a big Plastosil shed where they maintained their ground- and aircraft, and maybe drilled their operations.

The farm buildings were a kilometer farther up the road, which was known as *El Camino Alfarería*, "The Pottery Road." A couple hundred feet back from the road, and just across from the SVI land, was the pottery itself, which had been closed for about a year.

The next day, Carlos and Miguel got up well before dawn and drove out the Pottery Road to a jeep trail Carlos had noticed the day before, maybe a kilometer short of the pottery and on the same side of the road. They drove back in out of sight and parked. Then they walked to the pottery, which was on a little slope, giving them a view of the equipment park and its shed.

They spent the morning watching, careful not to be seen themselves. At one point after daylight, Carlos nosed around in the building and noticed a sizeable but inconspicuous brown stain on the coarse concrete floor, pale from washing. Basically the stain existed in the pits in the concrete, and it could have been anything. Including old blood. He also noticed a mop in the restroom and, checking it out, found the mop strings stained pale brown. With his pocketknife, he trimmed about half an inch off the strings, and bagged the trimmings.

All they learned from watching the shed and equipment was that the four men there didn't have much to do, that day at least. A resonance scanner, aimed at a window of the shed's office, found them playing cards most of the morning. A skyvan came in at 10:25, carrying two men who left for town after giving instructions about a skytruck they'd be taking out that evening.

Back in town that afternoon, Carlos called his connection in Mexicali, and Miguel was able to pick up a kit from the PEF's Ensenada office for collecting samples of bloodstains—in this case from the pits in the concrete. He drove out again at dawn the next day and collected his sample as soon as it was light enough.

Between he and Miguel, they also got telephoto footage of people arriving at and leaving the SVI offices over two-plus days. And eavesdropped on conversations in Kelly Masters' office. Mostly what they heard didn't mean much to them because it lacked context. But they did hear Masters' half of a phone conversation with "Dave." Masters was interested in "Seppanen," with whom Dave worked. There was no doubt at all now that Steinhorn was part of SVI.

Carlos didn't get any explicit information on the Christman case, but he arrived back tentatively pleased. We screened his video footage and compared the faces with the pictures Charles Tomasic had given us. And found matches for two of the three faces in Charles' pictures. Carlos had also left the mop trimmings with Skip at the lab, along with the putative blood residue from the pottery floor. Charles' pictures had no value as courtroom evidence, but if—*if*—the blood could be identified as Christman's . . . Assuming it was blood.

I was just getting up to leave when Skip came into Carlos' office. "It's human blood," he said. "They seem to have mopped before the blood dried, and didn't use any cleaning compound. If you can get me some blood, tissue— maybe hair from a presumed victim, I can hire a DNA match made at UCLA."

The only possibility I could see was that Winifred Sproule just might have a keepsake of some kind. Or know of one. I couldn't imagine her keeping a lock of anyone's hair. My office being bugged, I called her on Carlos' phone. She said to come out and we'd talk; she'd treat me to lunch.

Come out. She'd treat me to lunch. It gave me an erection. I was glad Tuuli was coming home the next day.

Sproule, though she still came across sexy, didn't make a move on me, and to my dismay, I found myself disappointed. And while she had no keepsakes, she did have some information. Christman had had a vasectomy—"the better to tom-cat around"—as she put it, and before the operation he'd had a sperm sample stored. She also gave me the name and maiden name of Christman's ex-wife, along with the street she'd lived on in Phoenix, twenty years earlier.

❖   ❖   ❖

Back at the office that afternoon, Carlos sicced an investigative assistant, Bridges, onto tracing down Christman's ex-wife, who hopefully would know the name of the sperm bank. Where hopefully Christman's sperm were still happily hibernating. Even though he'd sent Steinhorn off with Rossi again, Carlos made sure that Bridges knew damned well not to mention the assignment to anyone, in or out of the firm.

Meanwhile there was the question of getting access to the sperm. Needless to say, while some of our own people have law degrees, Prudential has a high-powered law firm on retainer, so Carlos called them. There was, it turned out, a legal precedent. If we had a contract with some law enforcement agency to investigate Christman's disappearance, and assuming no one contested it, we should be able to get a court order for a microscopic sample. Enough to test for a DNA match.

Unfortunately—so we thought—none of this fell within the jurisdiction of the City of Los Angeles. Or the county, or the State of California, as far as that's concerned. And at that time the feds rarely contracted investigations. So Carlos got on the phone and called the Lane County Sheriff's Department in Oregon. The receptionist said that Sheriff Savola was on another line, if we cared to wait. I told Carlos that Savola was a Finnish name—Americanized Finnish, shortened from Savolainen. I went to school with some Savolas in Hemlock Harbor.

Unless he was totally divorced from his roots, Savola would recognize my name as Finnish too. So when he came on the screen, Carlos introduced both of us to him, and told him I was the investigator. And that I had evidence which might lead to an indictment for an assault on Ray Christman, assault leading to kidnaping. We believed it might have taken place on the church's estate in Lane County, and we'd like a contingency contract for the case, to give us access to information we couldn't get otherwise.

Savola pointed out that interstate kidnaping was a federal offense, and as such an FBI responsibility. Which of course was why I'd talked in terms of the assault. It was the junior of the two felonies, but it came under the sheriff's jurisdiction. I told him I'd run onto the evidence while carrying out two other investigations, one private, the other for the City of Los Angeles. If the feebs, the FBI, started an investigation of the Christman disappearance, they'd pull the rug out from under me and the firm on both of them. But if we could present major evidence that certain persons had abducted Christman, the government would have to pay us our costs and a reasonable fee, which could be substantial.

I watched Savola while he thought it over. Not every county sheriff feels friendly to contract investigation firms, but most of them feel even less friendly to the feebs, who can be really arrogant and overbearing toward local agencies when their interests overlap. Besides, Joe Keneely has carefully nurtured Prudential's good name, and this wouldn't need to cost Lane County much if any money.

"Seppanen, eh? I've read about you." It had to be the twice-killed astronomer again. As Joe likes to say: "The best promotion is outstanding work properly publicized." Savola ended up saying okay, if our terms were suitable. Carlos transferred the call to Joe, and twenty minutes later we had another contract we could use, registered in the National Law Enforcement Network. It didn't mention kidnaping.

As Joe put it: "Ah, the marvels of electronics, the Network, and a good reputation."

While we waited, I got a bright idea for my next action. My office was still bugged, and I needed to use the National Law Enforcement Network, which meant I couldn't do it from home. So I sat down, called up the army's CID headquarters in the Pentagon, and instead of telling them orally what I wanted, I wrote it. Including: "My office is bugged, and I need to pretend I don't know it. So I'm writing this." I figured a little drama might help get me what I wanted. Then, still writing, I identified my firm, myself, and the contract, and indicated that at least two of our suspects were ex-Rangers. What I needed, I told the guy, was a printout, with photos and certain other particulars, of all Rangers who'd served in the same company as Captain Aquilo Reyes, and who'd resigned or failed to reenlist between 2007:1:1 and 2008:12:31.

He checked me out on the Network first, then agreed. It turned out there were sixteen of them, including Steinhorn. Eight had been unmarried, and three had Hispanic names. Two of the sixteen photos matched faces in Carlos' videotapes from Ensenada. A third matched a face in Charles' photos. Of those three, all had been single at the time of discharge.

Then I went home. I decided to start with the eight who'd been single. I'd gotten their addresses at the time of enlistment; now I called up local directories and got the phone numbers for those addresses. At six of the eight, someone answered, none of them the subject. Only two knew, or admitted knowing, the person I was calling about. I pitched myself as an old army buddy trying to get in touch, and got addresses for the two; neither was in Ensenada.

Then I called up the Ensenada directory; two of the others were listed there. That left me with four to go. I called up the directories for their pre-enlistment home towns, then called the listed numbers. I put on a mild Finnish accent, in case people were suspicious that I was police. People don't usually associate foreign accents with police, except in some places Hispanic or Oriental accents.

One number got me an L.A. family. My man, Robert Myers, was their son. Until recently he'd lived in Ensenada, Mexico, they said, where he'd done security work and traveled a lot. But three weeks previous they'd called him and gotten a recording in Spanish. Their college-student daughter told them it meant the number was out of service. So they'd written to him. The letter had been returned: he was no longer at that address, and had left no forwarding address.

I promised them I'd let them know if I learned where he was, and the daughter gave me the names of three L.A. friends of his. The directory gave me numbers for two of them. The third was a Jesse Johnson. There were eight Jesse Johnsons listed, along with maybe thirty J. Johnsons, so I skipped him. At one of the two numbers, for an Osazi Gorman, a woman answered. She was suspicious and hostile, and said her husband didn't know any Robert Myers.

At the other number, a man answered. He told me he'd heard, a week or so earlier, that Robert was in town, but he hadn't seen him. And if his parents hadn't seen him, then . . . After a long hesitation, he suggested I call Osazi Gorman. There was also an Arnette Jones who was more likely than anyone else to have seen him, but Jones had no regular address. He hung out around Lafayette-MacArthur Park a lot, and was easy to recognize. An ex-Colorado State basketball player, he was seven feet tall and usually wore a feathered headdress.

You work at UCLA, so you probably live in Westwood, and might not be familiar with those midtown parks. They've pretty much been taken over by street people and assorted characters, many of them doing drugs. Was Myers in trouble? Maybe on drugs and gotten fired? Or run away? If SVI was smartly run, and it probably was, they wouldn't keep someone on the payroll who used drugs. He might blab; even sell information. Or had Myers gotten crosswise of them for some other reason? In either case they might not want him running loose.

Had Leo McCarver been another runaway from VSI?

It was conceivable that Myers was still with them, had gone underground for them on some job, though my gut reaction to that was rejection.

But the real question was, could Robert Myers give me any information regarding Christman.

30
MACARTHUR PARK

I'd planned to eat breakfast at home the next morning. I got up more than early enough, showered, shaved, and being alone in the apartment, turned on the radio. The first thing I heard was a news item about a newly reported development by a Brit research project. They'd built what they called a spatial transposer, and tried to move a rock from one side of their lab to another with it. Somehow it was supposed to relocate without moving through the intervening space! They transposed it, all right, but it arrived as a little pile of molecular dust.

Back to the drawing board. Yeah. But when they perfected it, and they probably would ... What a terrorist could do with something like that! Or a dictator, or anyone else who was ruthless. What price peace then? Or privacy? What would happen to wilderness areas? Wildlife refuges? Homes? Convents for chrissake! Let alone what it would do to people's sense of what kind of universe they lived in. This report by itself would stimulate a new spike of craziness for the newscasts to tell about.

With that on my mind, I finished dressing without noticing. The next thing I knew, I'd put on my shoulder holster and was shrugging into my jacket without fixing breakfast. To hell with it, I decided, I could eat at Morey's.

Tuuli'd be flying home later that day, and maybe the world would seem right again.

I left for work. Twenty minutes later I was driving south on Fairfax, still thinking about the spatial transposer and half listening to music on the radio. Then KMET interrupted with a special news bulletin. According to the station's traffic floater, a huge explosion in Van Nuys, a couple of minutes earlier, had done massive damage to an apartment building in the vicinity of Woodman Avenue, south of Ventura Boulevard.

My stomach spasmed and I jerked over toward the side of the street, braking, almost hitting a parked car and damned near getting rear-ended. Horns blared. For a minute I just sat there, till someone got out of a car and came over to see if I was all right. He thought I'd had a seizure of some kind, which I guess in a way I had. I thanked the guy, and told him I'd be all right; that I'd just heard on the radio my apartment house had been blown up. Because I had no doubt at all what building it was. A day later, Tuuli would have been there asleep when the place blew. If I'd eaten at home as planned, I'd have been there. Meanwhile, the building security guys were ours. Had been ours. I realized then that I'd heard the explosion and ignored it, dismissed it. As if it might be some demolition contractor bringing down an old high rise.

I drove on to work but didn't go to Morey's. Breakfast didn't interest me then. Instead I went into the lobby, pressed the *up* button, and waited for an elevator. When one arrived, who should step out but Rossi and Steinhorn, getting an early start on their day. I took myself totally by surprise. I slammed Steinhorn right between the eyes, driving him back into the elevator cab, stunning him and breaking his nose. Grabbing his feet, I dragged him back out in the lobby, got in the cab, and started upstairs, leaving poor Rossi staring, his lower jaw hanging down on his chest. Steinhorn was bleeding all over himself.

When I got upstairs, I didn't know what the hell to do, so I just sat down in reception. A minute later Joe came out of his office looking terrible. He saw me there, and asked if Tuuli was still out of town. He'd just gotten a call from one of the night guards who'd gotten off duty at 6:05; at the apartment. He'd stopped for breakfast at a Clancy's a few blocks from there—had finished eating and was drinking his coffee—when a huge explosion broke all the tempered glass windows in the restaurant.

He'd had a feeling it might have been "his" building, and had driven back, bleeding from glass cuts. It had been a car bomb, apparently on the entrance ramp to the underground garage. The whole front half of the building was rubble; there was even major damage to the building across the street. No way the entrance or garage guards could have survived. The hall man might have, possibly, if he'd been in the back of the building.

When he'd finished telling me, Joe went back into his office. Meanwhile Rossi had come up, and heard most of it. "Your partner," I told him, which made no sense to him at all. Made no sense, period. I started down the corridor, thinking how many people must have been killed. Most wouldn't have started for work yet. Kids wouldn't have left for school.

Rossi followed me into my own office. I knew what I had to do. First I removed the bug from the thermostat control; no use playing that game anymore. Then I called Tuuli. I told her what had happened, and to stay where she was a while longer. All after telling the computer to charge the call to my home phone, so the call and destination wouldn't be registered in the office computer.

When I disconnected, I told Rossi his partner was a plant, then asked myself aloud: "Why in hell have I been screwing around trying to get a line on Robert Myers, when one of the murderous assholes was sitting right here in our offices? And I knew it!" And I'd left him downstairs! I should have put him under citizen's arrest! Rossi said he'd told Steinhorn to go to the building infirmary, which was on the ground floor, so I called there. They hadn't seen him. I wasn't surprised. He'd realized his cover must be blown, and taken off. All the satisfaction I got from it was what Rossi told me: Steinhorn had been bleeding badly from the nose, and his eyes had started to swell.

Meanwhile I still had the lead I'd dug up the day before: Robert Myers. Carlos wasn't in—he was flying to Fresno that morning—or I'd have told him what I had in mind. So I clipped a gadget pouch on my belt, with some stuff I'd need, then told Fidela where I was headed, and left.

I took Sixth Street east toward downtown, and parked in the shade in the big lot at the First Congregational Church between Commonwealth and Occidental. Then I crossed the street to Lafayette-MacArthur Park, and started circulating. It's an open-access park south of Sixth Street, a mile long and half as wide. That's a lot of city blocks, and it always has a lot of people. Even finding someone seven feet tall and wearing a feathered headdress could take awhile.

The eastern section north of the lake is sort of a bivouac for street people—a lot of Plastosil bubble tents that the city set up, with interspersed latrines and showers, and stand-up mess tents with rice, beans, bread and cheese, and whatever produce is a glut on the current market.

There aren't as many street people as there used to be, and they're different from the street people of the eighties and nineties. A good job is still a problem for the functionally illiterate, but they're a lot less common than they were years ago. For a lot of today's street people, it's the rate of change that's gotten to them, and they've opted for days in the sun, with music or drugs or both, till they get bored with it or maybe die. When the weather's nice, there's a sense of fun and laughter. When it rains or a Santa Ana blows in, those who stay tend to get gloomy and suicidal, or surly and mean. Sort of a manic-depressive subculture. But this day was beautiful—sunny, temperature about 75, and a light breeze.

I'd been walking around for the better part of an hour, when I saw a small crowd on the west shore of the lake, gathered around some drumming and chanting. I drifted over. In the center of them, some guys, mostly blacks, were bounding up and down in a Watusi-looking dance. One of them was going so high, he looked like he was on a pogo stick. He wore a feathered headdress that added an extra foot to what was already way more height than anyone else there. *Arnette Jones,* I decided, and moved in closer. Maybe Robert Myers was one of the other dancers.

He wasn't. He was sitting cross-legged, slapping the bongos. I recognized the face from his picture. He was a caramel-colored, average sized, athletic-looking black. The dance was nearly over by the time I moved in. A tallish, lean-looking guy was doing a sort of rap counterpoint to the chant in some African-sounding language. He changed tempo, speeding up and raising his pitch; the drums crescendoed; then everything stopped, the dancers streaming sweat.

I'd already gone over and squatted down beside Myers. He looked at me, not very alert, under the influence of some chemical, hopefully New Orleans Sugar. It's supposed to be big with musickers, and they can shake it off if they need to. "Robert," I said quietly, "I'm trying to bust Kelly. For the abduction of Ray Christman. And for Christman's murder, if that's what he did to him."

He turned to me, coming back into the world a bit.

"Steinhorn's in L.A.," I went on. "Steinhorn and others. They've already killed McCarver. Maybe you knew that."

He shook his head.

"They don't wish you well, either. Kelly's gone kill-crazy, and if I could find you, his guys can. This morning he car-bombed the apartment house I live in. Lived in. It killed a lot of people; it's not known how many yet. If my wife had been in town and I hadn't gone out for breakfast, she and I would be dead now. That's what they had in mind."

I held his eyes. "If you're willing to give me your deposition regarding SVI and Christman, I can hide you where you can't be found. Not in the time Kelly will have. Because with your statement we can nail the sonofabitch. And as far as I'm concerned, you won't have to name any other names than Kelly Masters."

He was looking at me, apathetically but taking it all in.

With the music and dancing over, the crowd was dispersing. Arnette Jones and another dancer were standing by though, to find out what was going on between me and their buddy.

"Robert, you want us to run this shark?" Jones asked. In street argot, a shark's a detective.

Myers shook himself, physically. "No," he said, looking up at Jones. "I told you I was in deep shit. Maybe the shark's got a ladder for me to climb out with."

I took the minicam out of my pouch and found his face in the viewfinder. I was going to get his statement now, before anything happened, before anything ran him off. I deliberately didn't read him his rights. It might spook him. Of course it would make him hard to prosecute, but if he netted Masters and company for us, that was fine with me. Joe and Carlos would understand, even if they weren't overjoyed. And if the prosecutor's office bitched, their heart wouldn't be in it. They're not what you'd call naive, and they've negotiated more than a few plea bargains.

"All right," I said, "if you'll speak slowly and clearly, starting with your name . . ."

He took a deep breath. "My name is Robert Fielding Myers. I was copilot of the skyvan that forcibly removed Ray Christman from Church of the New Gnosis property in Oregon about 7 October, 2011." He sounded like someone trained on being debriefed. I wondered if that was his Ranger training, or something the SVI taught its people. "Mr. Christman and a female companion were abducted by personnel acting for my employer, Servicio Viajero Internacional, of Ensenada, State of Baja California del Norte, Mexico. I'd been briefed as an alternate to the abductors, but I wasn't used in that role. I was the copilot.

"The managing partner of SVI, Kelly Masters, was the pilot. Masters is an ex-OSS officer. Christman was flown to Mexico alive and in constraints, to a place about twelve kilometers from Ensenada, arriving there at approximately 0230 hours, Pacific Time.

"After we arrived, I went home to bed. The next day

I was told that Christman and the woman had been taken to a shut-down pottery works across the road, where they were killed, then cremated in a large pottery kiln. Their ashes, I was told, were dumped in a manure pit on an adjacent dairy farm, and covered with manure."

Myers hadn't changed expression during his recital. "How did they kill him?" I asked.

"The plan had been to resedate him, then suffocate him. But because Christman was a large man—this part is hearsay, from, uh, one of the guys there—because Christman was a large man and it was uphill to the pottery works, they decided to have him walk there before they resedated him. They didn't want to carry him. They told him they planned to hold him for ransom. Inside the plant though, he started to fight and kick, as if he realized what they had in mind. Maybe the kiln was on and he could hear the gas flames, I don't know. Then Mr. Masters shot him and they cremated him. While he was in the kiln, they suffocated the woman, and when they finished cremating Christman, they cremated her. And that's it."

"Thanks, Robert." I popped another microcube into the minicam and started making a copy. "That seems to cover it. We got samples of the dried blood from a mop, and from pores in the concrete. Your statement should clinch it. Now let's get you out of here."

I got to my feet and helped him up. Jones and the other dancer had heard the whole thing. I wasn't very comfortable with that, but I couldn't see what harm could come of it. There hadn't been anything I could do about it anyway, not and get Meyers' statement.

It seemed to me I was up against something worse than just a commercial murder operation. Something more evil had reared its head this morning. Now, as Myers and I crossed the grassy park past one of the slender, HardSteel pylons of the Wilshire Monorail, we were escorted by one medium-sized and one very tall black man, both seeming dedicated to Myers' survival.

I decided that when I got to the car, I'd transmit a copy

of Myers' video statement to Joe, with a recommendation that he transmit copies to whoever—the feebs and Lane County, I suppose. Promptly, before Masters tried blowing up our office building. These new semi high-rises, built to current earthquake specs and with key structural elements made of HardSteel, could stand a lot. But a delivery van loaded with high explosives rammed into the entryway? Or a well-trained hit team with assault rifles and grenades, preceded by a couple of pleasant-looking guys with Uzis in their attaché cases and pistols inside their jackets? Guys who could take out the lobby guards before the man at the desk could hit the switch that locked the elevators and stairwell doors?

Sure I was paranoid. I'd earned it.

As far as that was concerned, my escorts, my Choi Li Fut, the Walther under my arm, and Myers' undoubted close-combat skills wouldn't mean a thing against an armed hit team with orders simply to kill. My real security lay in staying on the move, location unknown.

Shortly we were walking along Sixth Street, striding out, unconsciously hurrying. A block ahead, just across from the handsome, vine-grown privacy wall of the Frederic Knepper Village greenbelt, stood the First Congregational Church. Its parking lot was surrounded by a waist-high, ornamental stone wall overgrown by ivy.

I stopped. "Just a minute, guys," I said. The lot would be a perfect ambush site. But hell! That was silly! Who'd know I left the car there? All I'd told Fidela was, I was going to Lafayette-MacArthur Park, and I was reasonably sure no one had followed me.

Unless . . . Had Steinhorn been carrying a key to one of the vehicles? Each company vehicle was fitted with a 360-degree, narrow-band pulse beacon, so they could be located in emergencies from our office and from our other vehicles. Joe had a policy that you left them on except under certain conditions, unusual and specified. Some of our vehicles were kept in the outside lot, and when Steinhorn left the building, he could have . . . But hell, he hadn't even known I'd be going out that morning! And given Steinhorn's appearance, the gate guard would have called the office. Policy was to report anything unusual. And the office would have let me know.

But if someone cut me down with an assault rifle as I entered the parking lot, all that logic wouldn't mean squat. Paranoid was the word all right, but just the same . . . I looked at Jones. "Arnette," I said, "there's something I need you to do."

He looked at me suspiciously. I opened my gadget pouch, took out the minicam, then popped out the backup cube I'd made and handed it to him. "I want you to take this to the nearest police station. Tell them Martti Seppanen from Prudential gave it to you. In case anything happens to Robert and me." I repeated my name so he got it. "And tell them what it's about. So they take the time to listen to it."

He put the cube in his pocket, but stood as if unwilling to leave Myers. He still didn't trust me. A thought came to me then, and I looked at the other guy. The thought was of the biggest eager beavers in L.A. television news. Taking out my minicam again, I popped in another microcube for copying, then stood there watching the red light blink. When it quit, I took the cube out and held it up, looking at the other dancer. "I need someone to get this to KCBS-TV for me. To the news director."

He was a slim muscular black with sharp, pretty much Caucasian features. Just now he was grinning. He knew exactly what I had in mind. "I'm your man, shark," he said.

"You know where it is?"

"On Sunset, where it crosses the one-oh-one." His accent struck me as Jamaican.

"Good. When this gets aired, the danger of Robert and me getting hit goes way down, quick." I put it in his outstretched hand.

"It's done," he said, and started to turn away. I put my hand on his arm.

"What's your name?" I asked.

"Duncan."

"Thanks, Duncan." I put out a hand and he shook it.

"That's all right," he said. "You have good luck, eh?" Then he took off at an easy lope, presumably for a monorail station a couple of blocks west.

Arnette hadn't been happy; now he looked resigned. "All right," he said, "I'll take this one to the Rampart Station. It ain't far." He too left us then, jogging northward up Hoover to bypass the privacy-walled Alvarado Village. By that time Duncan had reached the corner of Occidental, where the parking lot began, and was crossing Sixth against the light, through a gap in the traffic.

"Okay, Robert," I said, "let's go." If there was an ambusher behind the stone wall . . . Hell, I thought, it's just your nerves. And I was right. When we walked through the entrance, we were the only ones there. I looked the vehicle over. It had been locked, and still was. Had someone rigged it to blow up? I looked it over, through the windows and underneath. Nothing. Still, I was pretty uncomfortable, inserting the Ferroplast key into the slot, and even more so pressing the latch release and opening the door. Then Myers and I got in. I shut off the beacon, activated the motor, drove out of the lot, and started west on Sixth, feeling a lot better.

Until, in an approaching car, I saw two faces I knew. One was Steinhorn; he was driving despite a swollen nose and two swollen eyes. The other was Kelly Masters; I knew his face from Carlos' video footage. I saw Steinhorn's mouth open as if shouting, and Masters turned. His eyes latched onto me like something—evil, as if he were memorizing my face. All this in about two seconds; then they were past me.

In my rearview mirror I saw Steinhorn try a U-turn to come after me. The move depended on other cars swerving or braking quickly enough to avoid hitting him. Two of them didn't. He sideswiped one of them, and at almost the same moment the other one broadsided him. I was just coming to the intersection with Vermont Avenue. I turned north, my heart rate about a hundred and sixty.

31
THE WORLD TURNED
UPSIDE DOWN

I'd planned to drive to the office and deliver Myers. I'd also figured to call Joe and tell him what I'd learned. But that morning's bombing, and the encounter with Steinhorn and Masters, had shaken me. I didn't trust my assumptions anymore. It might be dangerous to go to the office. It was hard to imagine that SVI would start an actual shooting war with us, but they'd already blown up a building and killed a lot of people.

Tooling north up Vermont, I decided to leave Robert off somewhere first. If there *was* an ambush waiting for us near the office, I wanted him safe. Molly Cadigan's wasn't too far; I'd see if she'd keep him for a few hours. When the police got the cube, SVI would soon be out of business.

I turned the short wave on to the police band. It was way too soon for Arnette to have arrived at the LAPD's Rampart Station, but when they broadcast a bulletin to watch for SVI's people, I wanted to be sure to catch it. Maybe, I thought, I should call LAPD headquarters and tell them about Masters. Maybe they could pick him up at the wreck. I'd do that, I decided, at the next stop light, when I had a break from dealing with traffic.

As luck had it, the next several signals were green. I was on the Hollywood Freeway overpass when a police broadcast grabbed my attention. It wasn't what I'd expected. Three cars were ordered to watch for, and arrest for questioning, a black Hispanic male named Hector Duncan, height about five-eleven, weight about 170, believed to be on foot in the vicinity of the CBS studios on Sunset Boulevard. And to bring him downtown to detective headquarters!

"Hector Duncan?" I said aloud. The description and locale were right. "Are they talking about our Duncan?"

Myers nodded, forehead furrowed. I thought: *What the hell?!* Had they picked up Arnette on his way to the station? Maybe he'd seen a patrol car and flagged it down. *But why arrest Duncan?* The same call would alert the beat officers in the vicinity. KCBS building security would get a call, too.

Seconds later they broadcast an all-cars bulletin to arrest for questioning Martti Seppanen, white male, age 33, height about 6 feet, weight about 230, hair brown, eyes blue, build stocky and muscular, last seen driving an aquamarine four-door Ford sedan traveling west on Sixth near Vermont, license plates unknown.

They hadn't learned that from Arnette. The only ones who could have told them that were Steinhorn and Masters! I had gooseflesh crawling over me in waves, and I expected to hear sirens and see flashers coming behind me any minute. I got myself together and had the car's computer copy the microcube into memory.

Luckily for me, the LAPD is chronically undermanned. We reached the Hollywood Hills with no sign of having been spotted. I'd just started up Hollycliffe when we heard a patrol car report that they had Hector Duncan in custody and would be heading downtown on the one-oh-one.

If they had Arnette and Duncan both, then they also had both of the microcube copies I'd sent. Most importantly, they had the one I'd sent to KCBS.

When I got to Molly's place, I drove a couple hundred feet past it and turned up a little dead-end lane, parking by a "For Sale" sign on a picket fence. Then we back-tracked to Molly's on foot. When I rang her doorbell, I half expected a uniformed policeman to answer. That's the shape my mind was in. Instead I heard Molly's voice trumpet, "NEVER MIND, KATEY! I'VE GOT IT!" Seconds later she opened the door. "Martti!" she said, as if I was an old and dear friend. Then Myers registered on her. "Both of you! Come in!" She bustled us through the door and closed it behind us, then we sat down in a sunroom with a view across the L.A. Basin. "So," she said to me, "who's your friend? And what brings you here today?"

There was something about that brass voice, red hair, and complete integrity that settled me down. I introduced Myers, then I told her about his statement, and Arnette, and Duncan, and seeing Masters—all of it, wondering if I was giving her too much too fast. She grew a crease between her eyes, and clenched her jaw, jutting her chin out.

"You know what the hell's happened, don't you?" she said when I'd finished.

"Masters and the LAPD have something going together."

She nodded. "Damn straight they do! That's the only explanation. D'you have the foggiest idea what?"

"I think so," I answered. And told her, the picture developing for me as I talked. The biggest crime organization in L.A. is the so-called Spanish mafia. It's bigger than the Sicilian or Korean, even bigger than the black. None of them is actually an organization. Each is a group of so-called "families," with loose agreements on what are sometimes called franchises. Anyway, in the Spanish mafia, the three biggest, most troublesome dons had disappeared during the past three years, which had thrown the families into serious disarray. With discipline impaired, factions distrusting each other, fighting each other, it wasn't surprising that their morale, security policies, and agreements had gone down the tubes. The LAPD had arrested dozens of family members, and the prosecutor's office had sent most of them to prison.

In major crime syndicates, the leaders, the dons, are

protected by layers of underlings—protected from violence, protected from informers, protected from getting their own hands dirty in ways the police could use to put them away. And if the heat did get bad, they'd bop across the border into Mexico. Take a vacation for a few weeks or months till things cooled off.

But starting two years ago, Luis "El Grande" Lopez, Eddie "Yaqui" Macias, and Johnny "Numero Uno" Guzman had dropped from sight, one after another, as if on one of those vacations. Only they hadn't reappeared. After this long, it was doubtful they'd be back, doubtful they were alive. Matter of fact, I'd pretty much forgotten about them.

How it looked to me was, the LAPD had gotten used to hiring Prudential, for example, to handle a lot of their more demanding investigation load. It was more economical: didn't require as much staff, as much organization, as much facilities—as much pressure. Now, it seemed to me, they'd gone a step, a long step, further. They'd hired an Ensenada-based criminal organization, SVI, to assassinate selected underworld leaders who seemed legally untouchable.

I asked Myers if I was on the right trail. He smiled a small, wry smile. "I'm your witness on that, too," he said.

"What're you going to do about it?" Molly asked.

"First of all, I was hoping you'd hide Robert here till I can pick him up again. He's our principal witness. Beyond that, I've got some resources I have to check with before I can make any explicit plans."

It was about a minute till noon then. Molly turned her TV on to the KCBS noon news, to see if, just possibly, Hector Duncan's microcube had somehow gotten through to their news people. Instead of hearing about SVI though, and the murder of Ray Christman, we watched footage of an apartment building—my home—the front half of it a pile of broken concrete. Police with dogs poked around for possible survivors while equipment and workmen moved rubble. The anchorman, Bart Weisner, said nothing at all about Kelly Masters, but he did say that the police were seeking an unnamed resident of the building for questioning.

I was willing to bet that I was the unnamed resident. They'd have a hard time making that stick. I had witnesses to my arrival at the office at a time that wouldn't allow my being the bomber. So they weren't thinking clearly. There were people at the top, in the LAPD, who were sweating, making poor decisions they'd play hell backing out of. And this had to be something that only a few were involved with. Now things were getting out of their control—Masters was going psychotic—and every time they did something to cover it—gave some weird order—the people around them would wonder. It wouldn't hold together long. Their only chance, not very good, was to get rid of me as soon as possible, and hope everything would settle out again.

Now, with Molly using my minicam, I recorded briefly what had been learned in Ensenada, and what I'd heard on the police band afterward, including the pickup of Hector Duncan. Concluding with what I suspected about unidentified LAPD officials and the SVI. Robert verified it. Then I used my last spare microcube to copy Myers' earlier statement, with my own as an addendum.

As long as my car was parked where it was, our hiding place was compromised. So leaving the cubes with Molly, I drove the car to Ralphs' Market at the corner of Western and Franklin, and left it in the parking lot. According to Molly, the store was open around the clock. A car parked there could go unnoticed for days.

Then I hiked back up the hill. She'd offered me the use of her second car, an old Dodge Town Van. I also borrowed a Dodger cap her son had left at home, and a denim work jacket she wore in cool weather, for walking, or for working around the yard. Plus I got a microcube mailer from her.

I drove the old Dodge down the hill. I wanted to mail the cube to Bart Weisner at his home, rather than the studio, but I didn't know his address. It wasn't listed in the public directory. So I stopped at Ralphs' lot, got in the company car, and used its computer to access the State Data Center—via the office mainframe, of course—ther used the Lane County contract to access Weisner's mailing address. I was in luck: it was a 90027 post office box.

I didn't know whether the LAPD was monitoring the firm's computer or not, or even if they could. But if they were, they could use the call to locate the car; the boys in blue might arrive soon. So I got back in the Dodge and left. At the nearby Los Feliz Post Office—90027— I addressed the mailer, and dropped the microcube in the chute. Weisner's postal box was in the same building. If he picked up his mail that evening, he'd get it then. Otherwise, surely the next day.

Unless, of course, the police read the call, realized which "Weisner" I was interested in, and got a federal court order requiring the branch supervisor to turn it over to them. Which might—should—require convincing answers to some awkward questions.

I drove back to Molly's. I still didn't know what I was going to do next. I'd had ideas, but none of them felt good.

Molly and Myers and Katey and I sat around playing cards for a while, with the radio tuned to KFWB News. All we heard of any relevance was that the body count at the apartment was up to thirty-three, and so far no one had been found alive in the rubble. At about two-thirty, Myers started yawning. I lay down on one sofa and he on the other, and went to sleep.

The clock read 1640 when I woke up from busy dreams. I couldn't remember what they were about, but I'd awakened with the germ of an idea. After buckling my shoulder holster back on, I found the *hyysikkään*, then went to the kitchen for a drink of water. Molly heard me and came out of her office.

"So," she said, "what's happening?"

"I think it's time for me to move."

She started rustling around the kitchen, got out a plate of the great temptation, brownies, put them on the kitchen table, and was in the middle of pouring coffee when she stopped abruptly, scowling.

"Get your goddamn ass out of my space!" She didn't yell

it, just said it loudly and firmly, with a distinct tone of annoyance. It embarrassed me, even though she wasn't looking at me when she said it. Then she finished pouring, and sat down as if nothing had happened.

"Reel your eyes back in, sweetbuns," she told me. "I wasn't talking to you." She tested her coffee with her upper lip, and sipped. "Now and then," she went on, "someone, some entity, some being, will show up in my space. If I don't like the way they feel, I send 'em packing. And if they don't git when I tell 'em to, I blast 'em. That gets rid of 'em every time."

"You mean—ghosts?"

"Not usually. Not in the usual sense. But someone without a body, or out of the body."

I got a rush of chills. "Do you know who it was?"

She snorted. "Don't know, don't care." She dunked a brownie and bit it in two. "D'you feel like telling me what you're going to do? Or would you rather keep it to yourself?"

I shifted my attention to my present problems. "Keep it to myself for now."

We sat there eating brownies and sipping coffee. Molly's blast had wakened Myers in the next room. He'd peeked in worriedly, saw us talking normally, and after a trip to the bathroom, joined us. Neither Myers nor I had much to say, and Molly wasn't being talkative either. I finished my coffee and stood up. "It's time for me to go," I said to her. "If you'll let Myers hide out here temporarily, the firm will pay. Fifty bucks per diem. How about it?"

Molly scowled. "For a couple of days tops; I'm not into house guests. I don't even let my kids stay more than two or three days."

"Is that okay with you, Robert?" I asked.

He nodded.

"Good. If I'm not back day after tomorrow . . ." I looked in my billfold; I didn't have a lot of cash, but enough to give Myers a hundred. "Catch a flight out of town, to Phoenix maybe, or San Francisco, and tell your story to the FBI."

He nodded again.

I got the jacket and Dodger cap that Molly had loaned me, and went out to her old Dodge. She'd been damned generous to someone she hardly knew. Then I got in and started it up, but before I could drive away, it seemed to me someone was there, watching me. So I looked in the back, and saw no one.

Then I got out and looked in the enclosed luggage compartment. As I closed the hatchback, I suddenly realized.

"Get your goddamn ass out of my space!" I didn't shout it, but it slashed out of me with snap and anger. Waves of chills washed over me then, as intense as orgasm, and after half a minute, when they'd settled out, I realized there was no one there but me.

But there had been! I didn't doubt it. I hoped I'd blasted him out of his ectoplasmic socks.

32
PICTURE AT A PARTY

I got back in the Dodge and drove down Hollycliffe to Bronson. In some respects, Los Feliz and the I-5 Freeway was the most logical route to take, but Los Feliz was continually patrolled because of speeders, so instead I took Franklin west, and then the Hollywood Freeway. The freeways were safer for me than surface streets. They were patrolled by the California Highway Patrol, and I was pretty sure the bad apples in the LAPD wouldn't invite the CHP in on their game. They could order their own officers without questions getting asked, at least out loud, at least for a while. But the CHP or the sheriff's department would want explanations.

I crossed Cahuenga Pass and left the Hollywood for the Ventura Freeway westbound, then exited onto Coldwater Canyon and drove north. LAPD territory again. I hadn't gone far, hadn't crossed Tujunga Wash yet, when I heard a siren growl, the sort of little growl patrolmen use to get your attention. I looked in my rearview mirror, and sure as hell, there he was, coming up on me from behind, flasher spinning.

I'd been careful not to speed or break any other traffic laws, and it was still daylight, so it couldn't be a taillight out or the telltale wrong glint from an out-of-date license sticker. The first thing they'd want was to see my driver's license, and even if they didn't remember the all-cars bulletin, they'd check the name on their computer. Standard practice. And there I'd be.

I didn't think it all out like that, of course; that's simply the data I acted on. Instead of pulling over, I swerved through a short gap in the oncoming traffic. Horns blared; tires squealed. Someone sideswiped me and caromed into the police cruiser. Someone else broadsided me. I was pretty well shaken up. There were other crashes, half a dozen or more, then relative quiet. Molly's van was on its left side, and the right side was smashed in, so I unbuckled, crawled quickly to the rear and out the back door, which had sprung open. I needed to separate myself from the Dodge, hopefully before the patrolmen worked their way to where they could see me get out of it. The scene was turning into an ants' nest. People were running over, helping people out of smashed cars, and for half a minute I pretended to be part of them. The patrol car was on its side, too, and it looked as if the officers hadn't been able to get out yet. There were enough smashed cars there, and stopped cars, that it looked as if I'd get away with it. And I didn't even seem to be injured, just shaken up.

I walked over to the sidewalk, where a crowd of people stood staring at the wreckage. There were too many of them to have gathered since the pileup; they'd been there before. Mostly they were young; we were right next to Valley College. A small group of them, about eight or nine that seemed to be together, started walking away then, and I joined them. I didn't want to be around when more police arrived.

"Quite a pileup," I said to a couple of them, a guy and a girl.

"You ain't just glibbin'," the guy answered. "I wonder what started it?"

I shook my head. "No telling. Someone lost control, I suppose. Went to sleep, maybe. What's the crowd about?"

"We just left the ball game. We beat Pierce."

"Pierce? Are they good?"

"They're the defending league champions."

"Huh! That's pretty good! Now what? Parties?"

"You got it."

Of the group I'd attached myself to, one or two looked to be still in their teens, but most were in their twenties. We crossed Tujunga Wash on Victory Boulevard, and after a few more blocks turned north on a residential street, and went in a small house rented by several of them. Someone got a jug of wine out of the fridge and poured. Someone else went out for more. Three or four other people came in, one of them with a giant bag of tortilla chips, and opened it. A joint got passed around.

I didn't drink or toke or add to the conversation, just threw in a ten when someone else went out to get a bushel of chicken wings from Colonel Sanders. The conversation soon left baseball and went to psychic stuff. Since the 2006 Stanford study of psychic phenomena, interest had surged on campuses.

The place was getting crowded. A girl who came in about the time the chicken wings arrived was a psychic photographer with a different shtick. Instead of people pointing their cameras at her and getting strange results, *she pointed her Polaroid at other people.* And my being a total stranger, she asked if she could take my picture.

"What does it do?" I asked. "Capture my soul?"

She laughed. "Maybe, in a sense. Usually I get a picture of the person surrounded by their aura."

"Kirlian photography?"

"No," someone else said, "better than that. Manuela uses ordinary Polaroid color film and gets the auras on that!"

"How does it work?"

She shrugged. I was standing; she was sitting on a tall kitchen stool. "Stand still and I'll shoot you," she said, so I did. After a few seconds she pulled the picture and stared at it. "Huh!" she said, "I never got one like this before." Two or three people looking over her shoulders seemed impressed too.

"Here." She handed it to me. It showed me, all right, but not in real time, and there wasn't any aura. *It showed*

me standing behind Molly Cadigan's Town Van, peering in
through the opened luggage doors. While from close
behind me and a little to one side, an old man watched.
Dimly you could see right through him! The farther down
you got from his head, the more transparent, the less *there*
he looked, but from what I could see of his feet, they were
well above the pavement. His face was clear enough though,
and from his expression, he did not wish me well.

Others crowded around to see. "How'd you do that,
Manuela?" one of them asked.

"Darned if I know. I'm not sure it was me, this time.
It felt as if someone, some spirit, was helping." She laughed
then, pointing at the photo. "Not that one though. *That*
is an evil spirit."

I just kind of sat there a while. This "evil spirit" was
the wild card, the joker in the deck. Somehow it seemed
to me he was behind the whole thing—Kelly Masters
jumping into the scene, the apartment building blown
up . . . The police recognizing Molly's van this evening, for
chrissake! Though how someone like that communicated
with people . . . But hell! Who else or what else knew I was
using it?

Besides Molly. It could have been Molly. I couldn't have
that though. I'd always been a good judge of character, and
Molly wasn't someone who operated like that. She'd
have . . . Geez! They'd trace her van and know where it
came from! They'd probably been there already, and picked
up Myers! I should have called! Where in hell was my
head?!

"Can I use the phone?" I asked, loudly enough that
whoever's place it was would hear. "Local call," I added.

"Go ahead," a guy said.

It was an old-fashioned voice-only phone. "Katey," I said,
"is Molly there?"

Molly's voice came in then, on an extension. "Martti?
Where the hell are you?"

"I'm not exactly sure, but I'm all right."

"The police just called, said my car was in a wreck.
Totalled. I told them I'd loaned it to a friend. They said

the driver was trying to elude a police cruiser and caused a pileup. They couldn't find him afterward; thought he must be wandering around hurt. They wanted to know your name, so I told them. Then I took Robert to stay with a friend of mine. A guy named Casey Jones. You want his number?"

I got it, memorized it, thanked her, and hung up. I didn't call Myers though. I just sat there awhile, not really thinking, just sort of mulling, turning over the same spadeful time after time and coming up with nothing. Finally I decided it was time to carry out my earlier plan, the one I had in mind when I'd left Molly's. I got up from my chair, Manuela, the psychic photographer, watching me. "You leaving too?" she asked.

"Yeah. I've got things I need to do."

She stood, and picked up her gadget bag. "So do I. You driving?"

"No. My car's in the shop. I'm walking."

"Maybe I can take you somewhere." She didn't wait for an answer, just went to the door with me and out into a lovely spring evening. It was nearly dark. "D'you know the spirit that helped me take the picture?" she asked.

"I'm not sure what you mean."

"It was a woman."

"Small?"

"Physically? Smaller than me." Manuela was a petite chicana, not a lot bigger than Tuuli, with small bones and fine features, about five-three and maybe a hundred pounds.

"How do you know?"

She shrugged. "You either know or you don't. Do you live around here?"

"Not close. I— I lived in the building that got bombed this morning."

Her eyes widened. "Jesus! Did you—lose anyone?"

She was thinking about the spirit, the female spirit she thought had helped her get the picture. I shook my head. "Acquaintances. My wife's out of town. Have you heard of Tuuli Waanila?"

"*She's your wife? Tuuli Waanila's your wife?*"

"Right."

"It must have been her then. Congratulations! . . . And to think I was going to make a pass at you!

"So where can I take you?"

Rather than tell her where I was headed, I had her drop me off at the Hollywood-Burbank Airport terminal. It wasn't that I didn't trust her. It just seemed wisest to keep things to myself. After she drove away, I turned and started walking. I had maybe a mile to go.

33
SETTING THINGS UP

Where I went was our security headquarters in an industrial section of north Burbank. It's where security crews are dispatched to short-term jobs. Prudential gets a lot of those: the grand opening of a new mall, a big celebrity party—that sort of thing. Guys logged in there by phone or radio when they reached the job, and it's the place they called their reports to at the end of their shifts. There are always guys without assignments, and it's where some of them would hang around and wait, reading or watching the tube, playing cards or pumping iron. At intervals, guys got physical exams there from a staff paramedic. Who also checked them for overweight. Joe doesn't mind a little overweight, luckily for me, but he won't stand for his guys getting actually fat. I knew some of the guys, and all of them knew who I was—sort of a celebrity investigator. I knew the senior sergeant in charge: Wayne Castro. "Martti!" he said when I came in. "How the hell are you?" It was obvious he didn't know I was in trouble. "What are you doing here amongst us peasants?"

"Is there a place we can talk, you and I? Privately? I'm on a case."

"Sure." He got up from his desk. "This way." They have

a little debriefing room, and he took me inside. "How can I help?"

That's the attitude that made him senior sergeant in charge.

I wondered how private we really were there. Was that old man floating unseen beside us? I'd felt him before when he was. Hopefully I'd feel him if he was again.

"First I'm going to tell you what I've got in mind," I said. "If it sounds doable, I'll call Joe and check it out with him."

To begin with, I gave him the picture in brief, then told him what I had in mind. He turned really sober, but didn't let it throw him. After asking a few questions on details, he said it sounded doable—scary but doable. With Joe's approval. He'd have to call in some guys listed as occasionals—mostly off-duty sheriff's deputies and police from outlying communities, who moonlight with us from time to time.

I wasn't going to call Joe from there. If his house phone was monitored, they'd get my location. Instead I borrowed a company car and drove a few miles to North Hollywood, where I called from an outdoor booth at a shopping center. I caught him at home.

"Joe, this is Martti."

"Martti? *Sinulla on musta rupinen perse!*"

I should mention that Joe grew up among Finns in Iron Mountain, Michigan, and learned to talk a little MichFinn as a kid—enough to play with—back when it was still spoken quite a bit. What he'd just said was crude bordering on obscene—totally out of character for him. It was also totally non sequitur. He was trying to tell me something was wrong, that he didn't trust his phone. Which meant I couldn't talk freely. Then he went on. "Do you know the police are looking for you?"

I wished he spoke enough Finnish that we could talk about my plans in it. Unfortunately he couldn't say much more than thank you, give me a beer, shut up, and a dozen or two other phrases handy for teenagers. "Yeah," I said, "I heard it on the police band. Look, I'm at Meredith's, in the Valley—you know Meredith—and I have to make this fast. What I want to do is spend a bunch of company money. *Minä valehtelen.*" (It means I'm lying; I figured he'd catch that one. He knew *sinä valehtelet*—you're lying.) "Maybe up to the max for my working account," I continued. "I need to leave town, do some stuff in Mexico. Fight fire with fire, so to speak. Make it all right, will you? Authorize it. I'm short on cash."

"Now look!" he said, "I'm not financing you for setting any bombs in Ensenada! The smart thing to do is give yourself up. You know that, don't you?"

"There's a time and place for everything, Joe. I'm going to do what I do with or without your help."

"It's your ass, Martti. *Minua on nälkä.*" Which means "I'm hungry," another total non sequitur. Hopefully he'd try to get in touch with me on a safe line.

"Thanks for the help, Joe," I said sarcastically. "And the same to you." I disconnected, then hurried out, got in the car, and headed back to the security office. I wasn't sure what he'd do. But he and I didn't have any mutual friend named Meredith. Meredith was the street the security office was on, a connection I was betting he'd made. If he didn't—well, we'd see.

While I drove back, another possibility occurred to me: What if it was Steinhorn monitoring the calls? If it was— He hadn't been with us very long, but maybe long enough to recognize the allusion to "Meredith's." The Burbank PD was independent, but the LAPD just might ask for their help, if they were worried enough.

When I got there, there weren't any police cars or barricades. Joe had already called from a shopping center and said he'd call back. About ten minutes later he did. I gave him a rundown on what I'd learned—from Myers, and about seeing Masters and Steinhorn together . . . all of it with him recording. Including where Myers was hiding out. And told him what I wanted to do. He was spooked by it—so was I— but he approved. If we didn't get Masters soon, the guy might cut out and we'd never see him again. That or he'd do something even crazier than he already had.

Then he talked to Wayne, among other things telling him to follow my orders. Before we disconnected, he told me "Martti, for God's sake try to avoid bloodshed."

Joe doesn't take the Lord's name in vain. He really meant it. "I promise," I told him. "No bloodshed if I can help it." That had been my dad's working principle, too. I'd try, but I wasn't sure how avoidable it would be.

34
AMBUSH!

After our talk with Joe, Wayne phoned off-duty personnel and occasionals until we had a team of twelve men, including ourselves, that he thought were up to the job. All of them were police or ex-police, and several were ex-military as well. We even had an ex-Ranger and an ex-marine. He made it clear there might be shooting, and got only five refusals: four claiming other commitments, and one because of the 4 A.M. check-in.

I'd have preferred more time to sleep myself, but operating considerations dictated starting early.

Then Wayne and I worked out our plan. Normally you'd plan first and then decide on team size, but our team had needed to be nailed down before it got any later. Besides, the plan was simple. The main thing was to go over it on paper and try to foresee all the potential problems. Wayne called a couple guys back, and arranged to hire their personal vehicles as well. Meanwhile he sent two on-duty standbys to corporate headquarters in West Hollywood, to pick up an unmarked sedan with my access card. All the vehicles in Burbank had the company logo, so they wouldn't do for this job.

We both stuck to drinking decaf while we talked. The security office has a bunk room for men on standby, and we wanted to get what sleep we could. But when I finally lay down at 11:30, my mind was full of the uncertainties. Our plan had some serious holes, but we couldn't see any feasible way around them. The last time I looked at the clock glowing on the wall, it was 1:10, and the guy on the desk woke me at 3:20. I took a quick shower, first with near-scalding water, then with water as cold as the L.A. Water Board provides in May. Then I dried myself with a rough towel and made the best of it. When the first of our team arrived, I was breakfasting on a Peanut Plank out of the snack machine, and a mug of sweet coffee fortified with instant to make it stronger. Actually I felt alert, even a little wired.

First we briefed our team on the mission, stressing that anyone could still opt out without prejudice. No one did.

The sun was barely up, and there was very little traffic when we left in two private vans. Plus Wayne's personal pickup, and the unmarked company car—with the locater *off*. Everyone but me had Glocks as side arms. In addition, there were eight twelve-gauge pumpguns loaded with buckshot, and two spare box magazines for each. Since they've come out with a good automatic tube loader, shotguns have regained a lot of favor for police work. Actually I couldn't imagine needing to reload—if there was any shooting, it would be brief—but it seemed foolish not to take them. Two men carried car killers—lightweight, 50mm, low-muzzle-energy rocket launchers, only twenty-eight inches long. They'd been designed after the massive civil demonstrations and street fighting during the Great Crash. Wayne brought along a Colt Suppressor, a police version of the old Colt Commando. It's a fully automatic .22 caliber carbine, also only 28 inches long.

On the road, the weapons were stashed out of sight. As for me, I carried only the Walther in my shoulder holster. I wanted to seem unarmed.

We didn't want to look like a caravan, so we strung out. I led off, and each vehicle kept only the vehicle ahead of him in sight. It was a short drive to the Golden State Freeway, then north to the Valley Freeway and west out of the city, out of the LAPD's jurisdiction. From there we took a state road north to Fillmore—a small town by southern California standards—where we broke up to eat breakfast in two different restaurants, in three seemingly separate groups. I was the only one of us who went to breakfast armed. If we'd met the SVI there, we'd have been in real trouble. From Fillmore, we drove north a few miles into the Los Padres National Forest, to a picnic area Wayne knew. At that hour, no one was there but two drifters sleeping in the back of their eleven-year-old Ford pickup. It was a beautiful May morning, and I hated to do it, but I hassled them out. I had leverage: the area was posted against camping, I'm built like a wrestler, and there were two other guys in the car with me. Then, consulting with our ex-Ranger and marine noncoms, we decided on our ambush locations. The wooded picnic ground was strung out along a nearly dry creek. We chose the down-road edge; that way, if any early picnickers arrived before things got interesting, they'd be farther up the creek, hopefully out of harm's way.

By the time all assignments had been made, it was almost 8 o'clock: nearly time to call Joe at the office. I was depending on the phones there being monitored by either the LAPD, or hopefully the SVI. My bet was the SVI, using access provided by the LAPD; their conspiracy had to minimize officer involvement. The more they involved honest cops, the more likely that questions would get asked. Questions without safe and convincing answers. Then someone would call Internal Affairs, and the fat would be in the fire.

At 8:05 I got back in the company car and keyed the phone. Dalili transferred me to Joe without even checking with him. Obviously he'd told her to expect my call.

"Joe," I said, "I've had second thoughts since last evening."

"What do you mean, 'second thoughts,' Seppanen?"

"Tuuli got back last night. She doesn't want me to go to Mexico. So we're hiding out. We're in a National Forest campground about an hour from town. She's freaked, afraid I'll be killed, scared the SVI will track me down. I know this is a lot to ask, but— Could you send a couple guys out as bodyguards? From the security division? They wouldn't have to be top men; she won't know the difference. I'll pay for them myself if you want."

Joe put on a testy voice. "Damn it, Seppanen, you're stretching my patience."

I put a little edge on my own tongue. "Keep in mind what happened to our apartment house."

Long pause. "I don't know. You're a fugitive . . . How long do you want these guys?"

"A day or two. Yesterday I recorded a statement from a runaway SVI man, a guy named Robert Myers. It tells all about the SVI abducting and murdering Christman, and fits our earlier information perfectly. I've got it on microcube; it's in my pocket right now. The thing is, I sent a copy to KCBS-TV, via a runner named Hector Duncan. The whole thing ought to be playing on the noon news today—the evening news anyway. I'm surprised it wasn't on yesterday or this morning. I suppose they're doing some checking, to make sure it's not a hoax.

"After I sent off Myers' statement, he told me the LAPD is involved with the SVI. The SVI's terminated some heavy dons for them, in the Spanish mafia. He didn't know what the payoff was. Not cash, I wouldn't think. Probably privileges and an information pipeline. That's one reason Tuuli's so scared; the LAPD involvement."

"Huh!" Long pause. "Martti, you'd better not be lying to me. Okay, I'll send three good men. But if it comes to a face-off with the police, they'll have my orders to lay down. You got that? Now, where to?"

I told him. We were camped at the Rito Oso Picnic Area north of Fillmore, on a spur road off Forest Road 14. There were directional signs. Joe said the guys would get there about 11 o'clock.

Then we disconnected. He'd done a good job of acting. We both had.

Wayne had one of the guys drive back to where the spur ad met Forest Road 14. The directional sign there had another sign hanging from it that said NO CAMPING, which contradicted my story, and we wanted it out of sight when the SVI arrived. Assuming they came. When he got back, we moved all the vehicles but the company sedan to the back end of the picnic area, where they couldn't be seen from the ambush zone. Then I had the men take their positions.

One of the considerations was that the guys would get sleepy. So Wayne was up the road a ways, hiding in a thicket of chaparral oak, watching. He was an inveterate varmint hunter—he lived in the Simi Valley near the edge of development—and carried a crow hunter's call in his glove compartment. When he saw someone coming, he was to caw three times, pause, then repeat, to alert us so everyone could get prone and ready. The guys were stationed in pairs, responsible for keeping each other awake.

I sat at the first picnic table, 60 or 70 feet from the road and next to a chimneyed stone fireplace I could duck behind. Then I waited, reading a copy of *Sports Afield* that Wayne had had in his pickup. Reading a bit and thinking a lot. Any battle plan, even a simple one like ours, is based on assumptions, and battles are famous for not going as planned. Things come up. Things go wrong. Everything goes to hell and confusion. If you've read much history, you know that.

The SVI might not have heard my talk with Joe, and the LAPD might not get the word to them. Hell, no one might have been monitoring at all; we could have been talking to ourselves. Or Masters might smell a rat and stay away, or send in a whole squad of men. Hopefully he'd come in personally with only two or three guys, and that would be all. But he might arrive with a squad, and send scouts in first, and we'd think the scouts were the whole party. Then we'd have the rest of them down on us after we'd committed ourselves, and the shit would hit the fan.

That was my biggest worry—that he'd send in scouts first. After all, most of his guys were ex-Rangers or ex-Special Forces, and if he didn't think to send out scouts, they'd remind him.

But then, if they were only expecting a guy and his wife, why send scouts?

Unless Masters smelled a rat. Back to that again. The stuff was running in circles through my mind. I'd read a little, then discover I didn't know what I'd been reading—that I was too busy worrying. A time or two I was interrupted in all this by crows cawing, but it was never three caws, then pause, then three more. It was always some other pattern, and answered from somewhere else—genuine conversations among genuine crows. They helped keep everyone more or less alert.

In my planning, I'd figured the SVI people might come out in ground cars, but I'd allowed for the chance that they'd fly to Fillmore in a floater or maybe two, which would be a lot quicker. Then fly in the rest of the way at near road level, in order to follow the signs. They'd surely have flown to L.A., and Masters no doubt had an LAPD temporary permit to operate out of the city's various shuttle fields.

At 9:12 by my watch, I heard Wayne's crow call, and my guts tightened. I was glad I'd taken time to relieve myself at the restaurant. Ten or twelve seconds later, an eight-passenger skyvan floated into sight, just centimeters above the road. I recognized the driver as Masters; this was no scouting party. Steinhorn sat next to him in front—I could see his black eyes—and there were several guys behind them. They saw me almost at once and stopped in the road. Masters gave an order, then got out, leaving Steinhorn in front. I got up slowly, staring as if I'd just then realized who they were. Three guys got out of the back, carrying old AK-47s. Masters himself held a .45 caliber service pistol pointed loosely in my direction.

The hair bristled on the back of my neck.

"Mr. Seppanen," Masters said with exaggerated courtesy. "I'm delighted to meet you at last."

I dropped the pretense. "The feeling is mutual, Masters. Please drop your weapons. My people are all around you, ready to blow . . ."

That's all I got out. Masters raised his automatic with

both hands and I started to throw myself behind the fireplace. There was a lot of gunfire—the boom of the .45, the brief vicious sound of AK-47s, the heavier boom of shotguns, and the *swoosh-whump* of two car-killers hitting the engine compartment, all of it seeming simultaneous with a stunning pain in my head, a searing pain in my buttocks. Somehow I was still conscious, even though my vision had turned off. Someone was shouting "Jesus Christ, guys, hold your fire! Hold your fire!"

By that time it had already stopped. Voices called sharply; I don't recall what. Then someone right next to me said "Shit! God *damn* it! He took one right in the head!"

It hurt, all right, and my butt felt like someone had run a red-hot poker through it from one side to the other. I couldn't see anything, but for some stupid reason tried to get up. All I accomplished was to nearly pass out.

"Hey, he moved! He's alive!"

I wanted to say "Hell yes I'm alive," but didn't. It occurred to me I might vomit, and choke on it.

The next thing I was aware of, an indeterminate time later, I was on a stretcher, being loaded by paramedics into a floater.

35
LEGAL WRAP-UP

I was more or less conscious in the ambulance at first. I was aware of a paramedic saying, "I don't think his wound is that serious," and then, "Him? We may lose him." And realized vaguely that I wasn't the only casualty in the ambulance. When they were satisfied my skull wasn't fractured, they shot me up with something, after which I didn't remember anything for a while.

Actually they evacuated four wounded in two ambulances: me and three of the SVI people, while two lay dead back in the campground: Masters and one of his men. We got out of it so cheaply because our men were shooting at seen targets while Masters' men weren't. In fact, only two of Masters' men fired their AK-47s, a short burst each, one apparently while already hit and falling.

In my case, a .30 caliber slug—technically a 7.62mm from an AK-47—had hit the right side of my head at an angle. It tore its way *across* the top of my skull *beneath the skin,* and exited the other side near the top, actually creating a shallow groove in the bone. A weird wound. A doctor told me later it was remarkable I'd remained even semiconscious. I guess he doesn't know Finns, or half-Finns in my case. Another bullet had penetrated both buttocks from the right side, damaging nothing but meat. It seems that the lower half of my body never reached the shelter of the fireplace.

Joe told me about it in the hospital, after I woke up. He was also the one who told me that Masters was dead. Steinhorn had shot him in the back of the head, and Masters' .45 had kicked out one shot that went God knows where. It turned out that apparently none of Masters' guys had been very eager for this mission, and except for Steinhorn's shot that killed him, the men still in the skyvan hadn't shot at all. They'd come to the conclusion, the last few days, that their boss had gone bonkers. They'd stayed with him as long as they had because of old loyalties, and because they were in so deeply themselves.

Steinhorn had shot him hoping to prevent a firefight. For his troubles, he took some buckshot through the open door, in the left arm and leg, and in the guts.

Meanwhile the cube I'd mailed the day before made the KCBS noon news. So did the shoot-out at the Rito Oso Picnic Area, and the apparent LAPD involvement with SVI. Joe posted guards in my hospital room, more than anything else to protect me from possible news cameras. He loves publicity for the firm, but tries to keep his investigators' faces off the tube, for obvious reasons.

The survivors on Masters' team verified just about all our conjectures, mine and Carlos', and explained some things we'd missed. For example, what the SVI was all about, or had been to start with. While in the OSS, Masters had developed a dedicated hostility toward terrorists. Then he'd inherited investments that would enable him to live more than comfortably without working, so he'd taken an early retirement. But not to play golf. He and Reyes, along with a well-to-do veteran of the Mexican Foreign Service, started SVI as an aberrated expression of idealism, to assassinate and otherwise terrorize terrorists. Masters and Reyes had recruited men they'd known from the Rangers, Special Forces, and OSS.

It was about the time they'd contracted to abduct Ray Christman that Masters began to change. We got some insight into that because the PEF raided SVI's offices late

on the day of the shoot-out, and arrested Aquilo Reyes.
Reyes was an American citizen, originally from Casa
Grande, Arizona. According to him—and this was validated
by computer records of SVI and Security Pacific Bank—
Christman's death was contracted for by Alex DeSmet, a
retired OSS official, and one-time mentor and patron of
Masters in the agency. That's right; that DeSmet. Fred
Hamilton's ex-father-in-law.

According to Reyes, Masters was at first unwilling to
even consider the contract, though he pretended to, to
avoid offending his old boss. Such a contract was very much
at variance with his principles. But it troubled him to refuse
the man who'd done so much for him, troubled him enough
that he'd talked about it repeatedly to his partner. Masters also said that such a proposal was totally out of character for DeSmet, and wondered if the older man was
having psychological problems.

I'd have wondered too. DeSmet's behavior certainly didn't
sound like the man who'd dismayed his wife by refusing to
be upset when their daughter joined the Gnosties.

Then one day, DeSmet flew back down to Ensenada in
his private plane. The two of them had played a round of
golf, then eaten supper together, and DeSmet made his
pitch again. In the morning, Masters agreed. From that day
on, according to Reyes, Masters was a different man. The
change was mostly subtle, but on occasion it was glaring:
He would do and say things that were very unlike him. The
mission to stop Prudential's investigation was an example.
Reyes had objected vehemently, but Masters had been the
managing partner. After Masters and his team had taken
off for L.A., Reyes had called Tischenberg-Hinz, and they'd
talked about dissolving the partnership.

I could see Steinhorn's motivation now. His family *had*
been killed by terrorists. He'd been ripe for recruiting.
Then things had gone sour, gotten worse and worse, and
at the end he'd done what he could toward making it right.

As far as the LAPD connection was concerned, five
second- and third-echelon officials had knowingly and

deliberately conspired with the SVI to have the three racketeers murdered. In the project to kill the investigation, they'd operated through several lower-ranking officials who were aware that the orders they were carrying out were illegal, but didn't know the details. A total of eleven officials are in prison on assorted convictions of criminal conspiracy, racketeering, and murder.

Aquilo Reyes, Eustaquio Tischenberg-Hinz, and most of their agents, have been tried and sentenced by the Mexican government on a variety of charges.

Prudential collected the agreed-upon nominal fee from Lane County, and a sizeable fee from the feds, based on a previous court decision. We got substantial payment from the city of Los Angeles for exposing the criminal activities in the department, and settled for goodwill from the Mexican government, which legally owed us nothing. We also collected the completion fee from Butzburger, who came to the hospital and wished me well.

Finally we collected headlines galore. Prudential is now, beyond a doubt, the most famous investigation firm in the world. Joe's having to turn down contracts, while he recruits and reorganizes for a larger scale of operations. He's rented another floor in our building, too. I ended up with a promotion to senior investigator, and mixed emotions. For one thing, terrorism, foreign and domestic, is a curse of our times. And while SVI's activities were themselves a kind of terrorism, they may actually have had the effect of reducing terrorism overall. It's hard to honestly know. At any rate, their original impulse was understandable.

A couple of days after the shoot-out, I had an orderly wheel me in to visit Steinhorn. There was a pair of federal marshals guarding his door. I thanked him for not letting Masters kill me, and he said someone had to do something before things got any worse. After that I apologized for sucker punching him, and he told me to stuff it, that a sucker punch was the least he'd had coming. Then he kind of half grinned, we shook hands, and I left. I couldn't think of anything else to say, and he had stuff on his mind. He's in prison now in Mexico.

Tuuli got to the hospital on the night of shoot-out day. She'd learned about it not by any psychic route, but on the six o'clock news from Phoenix. The only (possibly) psychic element in it was, she'd never watched the six o'clock news in Arizona before. She "just happened to turn it on that day." When I asked if she'd influenced the psychic photographer, she said, "What psychic photographer?," and made me tell her about it.

Oh, and DeSmet suicided the evening after the shoot-out—shot himself through the brain. Sad. He'd been an able man, and apparently a good one, a decent one, most of his life. But that's history now. I've got a new case, not as interesting as that one, but nowhere near as dangerous. So. Are we done? . . . Good. Then if you can give me the antidote, I'll get out of here and go to Gold's for a workout. My damn weight's slid up five pounds again.

PART THREE:
CLIMAX AND
COMPLETION

PROLOG

Her crepe-soled nurse's shoes stepped quietly on the closely fitted flagstones. It was past time for her employer's breakfast, but sometimes he'd lose himself in contemplation or a book, neglecting to come in at nine o'clock to eat. And if he was meditating, it would be worth her job to disturb him. She didn't expect to find anything wrong, despite his generally poor health. He'd simply been preoccupied lately.

When she saw him on the ground, half out of the arbor, she hurried to him, knelt in brief examination, then as fast as her overweight, middle-aged body would take her, ran back to the house to get help.

The physician left the room thoughtfully. He'd done what he could, and considered the prognosis favorable. Next time—who knew? He'd once wanted a brain scan done on his patient, but the man had refused, absolutely, and it seemed now there'd been no tumor, for that had been years earlier. Beyond that, he had no explanation for the seizures. Possibly someone else might, but his patient had expressly forbidden him to bring in consultants.

He had no illusions that he was medically up to date. As up to date as many, no doubt, but . . . Not much of his reading was professional these days. Hadn't been for years.

His patient's reclusiveness went beyond a simple

preference for privacy. It seemed to reflect some pathological condition, although he was brilliant beyond a doubt.

Being a house physician for a sometimes crochety recluse was not what he'd visualized as a student, many years earlier. He hadn't known himself well then, hadn't foreseen his susceptibility to alcohol, and eventually cocaine. Or how he would ruin his marriages—one, two, and three—and allow, even cultivate the decay of his practice.

Then his patient-to-be had found him. No doubt through agents. He was aware, vaguely, that the man had people elsewhere who served him, though as far as he knew, they never came in person. The man, whose health had already been poor, had sat down with him as a friend, not a patient. Had charmed him, impressed him with his knowledge—its breadth, its depth—and his insights into many things. And in a short series of ever-stranger visits and gentle questionings, had given him to see things he'd never imagined. Until he became aware that he no longer wanted to snort white powder or drink amber whiskey.

Only then had his friend asked him to be his private physician. At a salary ridiculously low for a doctor, but impossible to refuse. He wasn't young himself, though less old than he looked, and his "future" was past. And after all, the man had saved him, from himself and his addictions. With a signed contract in hand, he'd saved him from his creditors as well, by a remarkable display of bargaining. He'd paid them off in cash, thirty to sixty cents on the dollar!

Besides, the man had a remarkable library, and the doctor had one addiction left—books. Between the two of them, they read enough for fifty ordinary people.

But they rarely talked anymore as friends. They seldom had, once their agreement was signed.

Looking back a few days later, the old man considered himself lucky to have come through alive. He'd been unconscious for more than twenty hours. The mind he'd been in *was one he'd felt secure with, one he'd come to control more completely than any he'd associated with before. But to be in it at the moment of violent death . . .*

Never had anyone interfered so utterly with him before. Never. Not Christman, not anyone. Christman had cost him more, far more. But in terms of personal interference . . .

And to develop one's powers, one must uphold one's integrity.

Christman he'd killed personally, so to speak. He'd been there, willed the trigger pulled, seen the dismay on Christman's face. He'd be more circumspect in handling this man—use a throwaway resource, some potent underworld group, set it in motion and allow it to operate. And if it failed, use another. There was no hurry. And he needed to husband his physical strength, the health that remained to him. While he developed his powers further, sufficiently to renovate the difficult husk he occupied, rejuvenate it.

He chuckled. He would rejuvenate it; he was confident of that now. He'd made major progress recently in his ability to psychically tinker bodies. He could even kill now without an intermediary, if the person's consciousness was sufficiently weakened. He'd tested that, first with comatose, then semi-comatose bodies. It involved manipulating certain gross physiological functions. To rejuvenate a body, of course, would require more subtle, intricate, and knowledgeable manipulations. He'd hypnotize his physician and question him, have him help design a program. Presumably it would take time, and no doubt numerous steps. But he'd always been patient, he told himself. Almost always.

36
GRAND CANYON;
THE BARNEY TRAIL

October 2012

It was Indian summer in Flagstaff, Arizona. With Tuuli
beside him, Martti Seppanen turned their rented Ford
travel van north on US 180, here called Humphrey Street.
In less than a minute they were out of the downtown
business district, driving through a pleasant residential area.

This was the Coconino Plateau, which at 2,100 meters
and higher was a land of coniferous forests. To their left,
intermittently visible between shade trees, was the low,
pine-clad mesa called Mars Hill, with its observatory domes
and comblike arrays of antennae. Northward, the street led
the eye to a pyramidal mountain peak that loomed bare-
topped above forested slopes. To Martti, Tuuli seemed
energized with an expectation he didn't really understand.
"Those peaks," she said, "are the eroded rim of an ancient
volcano. Did you know that?"

"Nope. No I didn't."

"It's supposed to have been twenty thousand feet tall
before the top blew off, a very long time ago. Can you
imagine? And this is what's left. Humphrey Peak is the

highest part of the rim, 12,680 feet. An Indian spirit lives in it. I've met him."

Martti said nothing. Nothing came to him.

"You can't see Humphrey from here," she went on. "Agassiz and Fremont are in the way, with the ancient crater in between. Twenty thousand years ago it held a glacier. Now it holds patches of aspen, and great heaps of rock."

He'd seldom seen her so talkative. She paused, then began to recite:

> Primal mountain bursting long ago,
> rupturing the darkness with your might,
> shrouded with clouds of ash and fumes
> that glowed and flashed and shuddered
>   in the night,
> high shoulders flowing red with molten rock,
> with heat and sullen light.
> Is that you?
>
> Is that you
> so calm and clean beneath the sky,
>   slopes serene in snow
> and forest frosted white?
>
> Ah, I know you in many moods,
> green, with branches dripping rain,
> yellow with aspen
> or blind with blizzard.
>
> I know you now.

She looked at her husband expectantly. "Nice," he said. It seemed to him he should say more, but didn't know what. After a moment he asked, "Who wrote it?"

"I don't know. Frank recited it when he and Mikki hiked me up the mountain to meet the Indian spirit. He wrote it down for me when we got back to Long Valley."

Indian spirit. Was there really such a thing up there?

He supposed there was, if Tuuli said so. And if there was, she'd probably have felt it; maybe communed with it. The old-time Lapps, it seemed to him, had missed a bet in having had only male shamans. He wondered if he could ever sense a spirit, then remembered the visitor he'd felt in front of Molly Cadigan's that day, and wondered if it qualified.

While they'd talked, they'd left the town behind, for what a sign told them was the Coconino National Forest. For some miles its pines alternately crowded the highway and stood back behind meadows of tall grass that formed vistas, provided scope. Here and there was private land, subdivided and built upon, but mostly it was forest. There was no hint of cloud, but autumn haze softened every view. Then the highway climbed a long tapering skirt of the mountain, to top out on a higher level of the plateau. Here for a few miles the land was an old lava flow, its forest thin and scrubby, its black and rugged bedrock showing often through short bunchgrass.

From this, the highway emerged into a long meadow that gave them another vista. Martti pulled off at a tiny roadside chapel, a rustic, cross-topped A-frame. Here there was soil again, and the grass stood tall, cured pale yellow by late summer's freezing nights.

Tuuli was out of the van ahead of him, beaming at what she saw. They'd driven half around the mountain, and looked southward now at its north side. A band of yellow aspen clothed its lower slopes, and nearer, bordering the meadow, tall stands of it glowed red-gold in the late sun. Above the aspen zone was a forest of dark spruce, and above timberline a thin covering of snow bequeathed by an early October storm. Tuuli's hand found Martti's, and she stood close, leaning against his arm, her head against his shoulder.

It seemed to him he should say something, then she said it for him: "It's beautiful."

"Yeah," he said, "it sure is." They stood a minute longer, then got back in the van and drove on. They'd traveled little in their year of marriage. Actually they'd been married on a trip, but it hadn't been a vacation in the usual

sense. After he'd solved the case of the twice-killed astronomer, Joe had given him administrative leave and sent him
out of town to avoid the cameras. The case itself hadn't
drawn nearly the attention the Christmas case had, but
Martti had drawn a lot. In that earlier instance, the detective had become the focus of attention. In the Christmas
case, the case itself, with its sensational elements, had
become the focus, with the media only secondarily interested in the detective.

At any rate, it was their first vacation trip since their
honeymoon, with the Grand Canyon, Tahoe, and Yosemite
the principal points they planned to visit.

After leaving the meadow, they passed between two
cinder cones and dropped back to a lower level, perhaps
7,000 feet, driving for a time across a broad plain sparsely
grown with juniper; a rather bleak plain, scarred for a short
distance by some abandoned effort at development. Some
miles farther, the scrub began to change. Pinyon pines
became prominent, looking like some needle-bearing
orchard in drastic need of tending. Then ponderosa pines
again, their trunks straight, their bark rusty yellow. Soon
afterward, the van entered Grand Canyon National Park,
following the highway to Grand Canyon Village.

Because it was late, they went to the Visitors' Center
first, before it might close, to register for their wilderness
hike. While Tuuli held their place in line, Martti browsed
brochures and maps, buying a plastic topographic map from
a dispenser. After a few minutes, they met with the ranger
on duty.

"Where do you plan on hiking?" the man asked.

It was Tuuli who answered. It had been her choice,
based on discussion with the Diaconos. "The Barney Trail."

The ranger smiled slightly. "Have you ever been on the
Barney Trail?"

"No, but I've hiked with people who have. I hiked with
them to Sipapu and other places. They recommended it
to me."

The official face turned condescending. "I'm familiar
with the trail to Sipapu. It is *not* the Barney Trail."

Martti interrupted. "Did anyone say it was?"

The ranger's eyebrows registered surprise at the response.

"We didn't come in here to listen to sarcasm," Martti went on. Though he spoke quietly, he drew the attention of half the room. "We came in to register and get advice. If you want to advise against it, good enough, but mind your manners. And if you refuse us, you better be ready to justify it in a hearing, because I guarantee there'll be one."

Martti Seppanen had a lot of presence when he chose to. The ranger was blushing now, and Martti was starting to. This was the sort of thing that once would have made Tuuli furious with him. She hated scenes. And ironically, he rarely created one, except in reaction to what he took as a slight to her.

The ranger rallied. "No offense intended, sir. I only want to impress you both that the Barney Trail is dangerous. There are places where it may slide beneath your feet, for example. But the most serious risk is getting lost. Old Man Barney roughed out that trail a hundred and twelve years ago, carved it out just enough to lead burros over it, loaded with packs of ore. He last used it in 1907, before the canyon became a national park." The ranger's color was back to normal now. So was Martti's. "Since then it's washed out or slid out in numerous places, and it's entirely unmaintained. Today it's used about once a week. You can easily stray off of it onto some game trail. More than a few people have gotten lost hiking old prospector trails in the Park, an experience more than just frightening. Some have died. There's usually no water till you get to the bottom, to the river. And the hike back out involves climbing 5,000 feet—about a mile—in places up very steep slopes.

"Also we don't go in looking for people simply because they fail to check back in. Most people don't take the trouble to. So someone has to report them missing. Perhaps the sheriff's department, when their car is reported abandoned."

His eyebrows stood high, questioning. Tuuli smiled at him. "Thank you, Mr. Kensington." She'd read his name badge. "My husband and I both grew up in the backwoods, he in northern Michigan, I in Finnish Lapland. I've hiked a great deal this year, and he's a Choi Li Fut black belt who trains regularly, so we're reasonably fit. I believe that with a map to orient on, we'll be all right."

Martti wrote their names and address on the register. She hadn't gotten mad at him, and for the manyeth time, he reminded himself of how much she'd changed since their visit to the Merlins. And even more since her long stay with the Diaconos. He still hadn't fully adjusted.

"Will you be camping?" the ranger asked. "Or do you plan to stay in the village tonight?"

"In the village, at the Harvey House," she said.

"Well then, have a good stay and enjoy your hike. I'm sure that experienced people like yourselves won't do anything reckless."

As they walked to their car, they agreed to go find the trailhead while it was still daylight. That would allow them an early start in the morning. They drove slowly along the narrow blacktopped road, past landmarks the Diaconos had told Tuuli about, until she said, "There!" Martti slowed, his eyes following her pointing finger, then pulled off onto the shoulder. "That tree with three small blazes, one above the other," she told him. "There should be a footpath there, maybe hard to see. The trailhead should be only about a hundred yards in. It's marked by a small sign."

They found the path, and then by the canyon's rim, the sign—a printed, legal-sized sheet, laminated and framed. Martti read it aloud:

!!WARNING! USE THIS TRAIL AT YOUR OWN RISK!!

DO NOT HIKE IT WITHOUT FIRST REGISTERING AT THE NATIONAL PARK VISITORS' CENTER IN GRAND CANYON VILLAGE.

THE BARNEY TRAIL IS AN HISTORIC PROSPECTOR TRAIL. IT IS NOT MAINTAINED OR

PATROLLED, AND IS DANGEROUS TO HIKE.
IN PLACES IT DISAPPEARS; ONE CAN EASILY
GET LOST. IN PLACES IT IS TREACHEROUS;
ONE CAN EASILY HAVE A DANGEROUS OR
FATAL FALL. THE TRAIL IS STEEP; ONE CAN
EASILY BECOME EXHAUSTED AND COL-
LAPSE. THERE IS NO WATER TO BE HAD
ABOVE THE RIVER; ONE CAN EASILY BE-
COME DEHYDRATED AND DIE, ESPECIALLY
IN SUMMER, WHEN AIR TEMPERATURES
IN THE CANYON COMMONLY EXCEED 100°
(38° C).

DO NOT ATTEMPT TO HIKE THE BARNEY
TRAIL, OR ANY OTHER UNMAINTAINED,
UNPATROLLED TRAIL, IF YOU SUFFER FROM
A HEART CONDITION, OR ANY OTHER CON-
DITION THAT RENDERS YOU SUSCEPTIBLE
TO COLLAPSE. DO NOT ATTEMPT TO HIKE
THIS TRAIL IF YOU ARE NOT IN VERY GOOD
PHYSICAL CONDITION.

THE NATIONAL PARK SERVICE IS NOT
RESPONSIBLE FOR THOSE WHO CHOOSE TO
USE THIS TRAIL. YOU USE IT AT YOUR OWN
RISK. DO NOT USE IT WITHOUT FIRST REG-
ISTERING AT THE NATIONAL PARK VISITORS'
CENTER IN GRAND CANYON VILLAGE.

IT IS ILLEGAL TO CARRY FIREARMS IN
THE PARK. IT IS ILLEGAL TO DAMAGE
PLANTS OR WILDLIFE.

THE RULE CONCERNING TRASH IS: IF YOU
CARRY IT IN, YOU MUST CARRY IT OUT. DO
NOT LEAVE TRASH IN THE CANYON. DO NOT
BURY TRASH; WILD ANIMALS WILL SMELL IT
AND DIG IT UP. BRING YOUR TRASH OUT
WITH YOU.

Martti finished reading with an irritation he knew was unreasonable. A reaction, he realized, to a public agency telling him what was good for him. *Mainly they're just informing people*, he chided himself, *and reminding them about decent ethics.*

He looked at Tuuli. "What do you think?"

"I think," she answered, "that after we've eaten, we should drive back out here and sleep in the van, instead of the hotel. We'll get to sleep earlier, and get an earlier start in the morning. And save ourselves money."

It was barely breaking dawn when their travel alarm woke them. Though the morning was near freezing, inside it was snug, thanks to the small electric heater powered by the GPC. After taking turns at the chem-pot, they washed in the tiny sink, being frugal with the water. Then they breakfasted on trail rations—rye wafers spread thick with liverwurst; rice-balls; freeze-dried pineapple slices; and a handful of raisins, washed down with decaf.

Finally they donned sweaters and shouldered their daypacks. It occurred to Martti to take his Walther, but he recalled the regulation against firearms in the park. Leaving it in the door pocket, he locked the van and they left. Dawn had lightened enough that even in the woods they followed the path without trouble, then started down the Barney Trail. It angled downward into a steeply descending side canyon, Barney Canyon, and was difficult at first. Wherever possible they clutched shrubs. To lose one's footing there would be to slide, maybe bounce, down a steep rocky slope, certainly to injury, and possibly death.

Yet mostly the going was not as tricky or treacherous as Martti had expected. For a time, Barney Canyon was roughly V-shaped, its slopes steep but not precipitous, with patchy shrubs. In places the trail was plain to see, still showing the signs of Old Man Barney's pick-and-shovel work. Martti thought what a tough and patient man the prospector had been, a glutton for danger and the hardest kind of labor. And wondered if, in fact, Old Man Barney had been old at the time, or if he'd been young, and the appellation added later.

Ahead of them the slope steepened, while the ridge crest above descended faster than they, in a series of great rugged steps. Before long, the crest met the trail, to form a long, nearly level "backbone" 10 to 20 feet wide on top, leading out to a crumbling sandstone "chimney." From the backbone they looked out across the miles-wide Grand Canyon. The terrain below them was wildly broken—a confused jumble of time-eroded ridges, chimneys, and arroyos. The sun was newly risen, and the pinnacles and upper walls of the opposite rim were washed with pale rose.

To the east they heard a distant commotion of raven voices. A great clamoring flock, diffuse and disorganized, was flying westward down the canyon toward them, and Tuuli and Martti, hands joined, stopped to watch. The flock flew pretty much at the same level as the crest they stood on, and as it approached, its noise differentiated into separate voices, deep and harsh: "COR-R-R-RP! COR-R-R-RP!" with now and then a single liquid note, as if a stone had been dropped into a deep well.

The point of the flock crossed ahead, then the flock proper was passing close around them. One great black bird climbed past them not four meters distant, gaining altitude, its wings, spreading some 40 inches, sounding a sharp *whoosh! whoosh! whoosh!* as they thrust the air. The flock passed and passed. Two crossed the crest just ahead and some 20 feet higher, flying parallel perhaps 15 feet apart. Abruptly and in unison they folded their inside wings, slipping sharply down and toward each other, then spread them again, rolling sideways, their bodies touching in a playful feathered kiss before they flew on.

Then the flock was past. The earthbound humans watched it draw away, Tuuli radiant, Martti humbled. After another minute they turned and hiked on.

Another van drove eastward from the village, a larger and more expensive machine, also with California plates. When it came in sight of the travel van, it slowed, to pull

off the blacktop across the road from it. Four black men
and a woman got out and walked to Martti's vehicle. "It's
theirs, all right," the leader said. "Got to be." He turned
to one whose eyes showed oriental ancestry. "Harley, open
it up."

Harley Suk O'Connell took a flat kit from a jacket
pocket, removed a tool, and worked with it on a lock. After
a few seconds the door opened for him. The leader climbed
inside, checked the glove compartment, then the driver's
door pocket. He found the Walther, and after removing the
cartridges from magazine and chamber, replaced the magazine. "Just in case," he said grinning, and got back out.

One of the men was dressed differently than the others, in denims and work boots. He was tall, lean, and very
dark, with exceptionally long hands. The leader turned to
him. "What's next, Cowboy?"

Cowboy beckoned with his head, then turned away
without speaking and strode into the woods, the others
trotting to keep up. In a minute they came to the trailhead
sign that Martti had studied the evening before. Cowboy
stopped and began to read silently. One of the others
scowled. "Read it out loud, Cowboy," he said.

Cowboy looked at him. It was clear he didn't like the
man. "Read it yourself."

The man tightened. "I don't read shit like that."

"I'll bet you don't."

The man's face twisted in anger, and the leader inter-
vened. "Lionel, Cowboy, cool it, both of you!" he said, then
read the sign aloud himself. When he'd finished, he grunted.
"It's like the ranger said when he talked to Seppanen yesterday: You could get lost and die down there."

Eyes hooded by blued lids, the woman looked down the
trail. "And they went down anyway?"

"Looks like it." He turned to Cowboy, who was examining the ground.

Cowboy nodded. "Fresh tracks. One set is small."

The leader looked where Cowboy was pointing. All he
could see was that the ground was scuffed. "You ready to
go down there now?"

332 *John Dalmas*

The man shrugged. "Why not?"

They went back to their van, where Cowboy opened the luggage compartment and belted on his canteen and heavy Colt .44 revolver. Then he took his rifle out, an old .257 Sako with scope and a silencer—a high-velocity, flat trajectory sport rifle with a clip of soft-point bullets. Finally he saluted the leader. "See you later, Jamaal." He looked at the others. "Harley, Naylene. Lionel. Quite a while later, unless they change their minds and don't go all the way down. That may be what they'll do."

He slung the rifle across his back, and the others followed him back to the trailhead. He started down, and they watched till the canyon wall curved and Cowboy passed out of sight. Then they returned to their van again. It was still chilly on the rim, and they sat inside to stay warm.

"How come," said Lionel, "that Cowboy talk like he does? He don' sound like no brothuh."

Jamaal looked him over before answering. Not many blacks talked like Lionel anymore. It was out of style, though he tended to slip into it himself a bit when talking with Lionel. "Cowboy's from Wyoming," Jamaal said. "He's a cowboy. He didn't grow up around brothers, except his family. Everyone else was white around there."

Lionel already knew Cowboy's origins. Simply, his considerations of race didn't allow for such anomalies—for any anomalies. He couldn't handle them; forgot them, or failing that, ignored them. Now he dismissed Cowboy from his mind. "We should have killed 'em last night. Found out what room they in, snuck up there and killed 'em then."

"We're supposed to kill them where no one will know," Jamaal said patiently. "If we can. That's why Terence hired Cowboy. Seppanen's a shark, you know that. Works for Prudential, and Terence doesn't need Prudential on our ass. That's why, when I heard Seppanen and that ranger, I decided we'd do it down there." He gestured toward the canyon. "Down there, if Cowboy does his job right, nobody'll find the bodies. And the rangers won't know they never came out. Likely Prudential won't even know they were here, unless Seppanen called and told them. And why would he do that? He's on vacation."

Jamaal was as much reviewing things for himself as talking to Lionel. Terence would like the way he was handling it, he told himself. There'd likely be a bonus for him when they got back.

Meanwhile Lionel sulked. "That's roach shit, bein' scared of Prudential."

"When you tell Terence he's roach shit," Jamaal said dryly, "do it when I'm not there. You'll be lucky if the worse he does is whup your ass. He's not bein' roach shit; he's bein' smart. He's avoidin' hassles with no profit in them."

Lionel subsided, scowling, then looked toward Harley, who was smoking a cigarette in the driver's seat. "Hey, gook eyes," Lionel said, "what you thinkin' about?"

Harley didn't even turn around. "You don't want to know."

Lionel bridled at that. "What you mean, I don't want to know? I asked you, didn't I?

"Lionel!" Jamaal snapped, "shut your mouth." Jamaal wished he'd argued when Terence had assigned the man to him. Lionel had tried repeatedly to pick a fight with Harley. Without his own repeated intervention, they'd have fought by now, and one of them might be dead.

Cowboy was worth ten Lionels. Jamaal had no doubt that Cowboy would kill the Seppanens that day, and leave them where they'd never be found.

With the ravens gone, Tuuli and Martti set out again. The trail dropped down off the crest along a tilted unconformity, a ledge widened by Barney's pick and shovel till it reached a slope less precipitous. Then it wound down into a broad cove that fanned into a set of descending draws divided by low broken ridges. Martti and Tuuli were far below the rim now, and the morning was no longer chill. In places the ground was clothed with brush, and there were piles of boulders. Once they startled a small bevy of mule deer, and once a family of desert bighorns that clattered noisily away across a scree slope.

Lizards scooted out of their way. Twice they found their path dead-ending: They'd gone astray onto a game trail— deer or bighorn or wild burro—and had to backtrack.

Finally they came to a sandy canyon bottom, nearly level among towering rocks, and as narrow as an alley. After a little, it opened onto a low dune, with the Colorado River surging past, wide and powerful, a violent, booming rapids not far upstream. They stood on the dune, watching, holding hands again. After a minute, Martti looked at Tuuli. "Shall we eat lunch?"

She nodded, smiling. Lunch might not have been the best word for it—her watch said 10:14—but they'd started at daybreak. When they'd eaten, they lay down to rest before beginning the steep hike back. Then she grinned, run her fingers along his thigh and kissed him, and instead of napping, they made love on a poncho, the sun warm on their limbs and bodies.

Afterward they lay there for a bit, Martti looking at her covertly. Her eyes were closed, her lips parted and smiling. She'd definitely changed. When she'd first come back from Long Valley, he'd thought it wouldn't last, but it had. She didn't get mad as easily; he wasn't sure she got mad at all anymore. And he—somehow he didn't put his foot in his mouth as much as he used to. It was as if her new patience, her new tolerance, had rubbed off on him.

Except it wasn't patience or tolerance; not with her. It was more basic than that, he told himself. It was as if— as if she had a new viewpoint. That almost whatever he did was fine with her. Like his flareup at the ranger, the day before. She laughed more these days, too, a lot more. She was more demonstrative, and more admiring in a comfortable way. Certainly she was more affectionate. A year earlier she'd never have initiated sex on a sand dune.

Sex was better too, their foreplay more relaxed, more *loving*. He felt less urgent, and . . . It was as if she could read his sensations as well as her own, building him, holding him, even slacking him a bit till she was ready, then— crescendo and climax! It seemed to him now that that, in fact, was exactly what she did—read his sensations.

After a few minutes they dressed again, then shouldered their packs and started back. Soon they were climbing. It was hot, 5,000 feet below the rim, perhaps 90 or 95 degrees, and they sweated. But it wasn't a problem. Mostly they were shaded by the rim high above, the humidity was low, and he kept to a pace that it seemed to him they could hold all the way, given occasional breaks.

At one point, hiking along a winding stretch through thick patchy brush, they rounded a turn to find five wild burros staring intently at them, not a hundred feet distant. For several seconds both sides stood unmoving, then the jack snorted and wheeled, and all five galloped off, disappearing into the brush.

It was on the easier stretches, topographically speaking, that Martti had the most difficulty. These tended to be brushy and have numerous game trails, making it harder to distinguish the trail proper. Often he wasn't sure, and on several occasions they'd cliffed out or otherwise dead-ended, having to backtrack.

They were perhaps halfway up, and he was beginning to feel he was off the trail for sure, when he topped a rise and saw the proper trail well off to his left. *With a seated rifleman watching it, some hundred yards from where he stood!* Martti hissed for silence, holding his hand back to warn Tuuli as he knelt, then slowly lowered himself onto his belly. The man, a black, was downslope of them and a dozen yards to their side of the trail, sitting against a tan rock, inconspicuous in a khaki shirt and faded jeans. He was watching downtrail, his rifle across his knees. From where he sat, he must have seen them half a mile back, hiking along a ledge there, and was waiting for their reappearance at much closer range. Even here they were within his peripheral field of vision. If his attention hadn't been so strongly on the trail, he might well have spotted Martti.

Lucky I lost it, Martti thought. He examined the terrain above the man, for the possibility of bypassing him. There wasn't any. Whether deliberately or by chance, the man was well situated to prevent it. Behind him the east wall of the canyon became too steep to walk on, except for the trail itself.

Besides, Martti told himself, *he's not here alone. Not if he's mafia. There'll be more of them above, probably two or three more, probably watching our van.*

The van! He'd left his gun in it! He was so used to carrying his Walther, it was natural to react as if armed. He tapped Tuuli's shoulder and they backed away on their bellies till they could stand unseen. The rifleman must expect them any minute, would soon get restless, perhaps start looking around.

Martti removed his pack, took out his binoculars, and looked the man over, then put them back.

"We need to go back to the river," he murmured, "and see if we can get out of here by working our way along the shore. We're not going to bypass this guy. The tricky part will be that ledge section we crossed back there. He'll see us for sure, and we'll be going the wrong direction for him. And his rifle's got a scope and silencer." In answer, Tuuli took off her pack and, reaching inside it, brought out her Lady Colt. Martti stared, not at it but at her. She'd never liked carrying it, yet here, where it was against the law . . .

He took it, ejected the magazine and checked it. It was full, seven rounds, and there was another in the chamber. But it was a minimal weapon, small caliber, short barrel, low muzzle energy—a weapon intended for close quarters, for intimidation as much as violence.

"Thanks." He paused for a moment as a plan took form, then handed his own pack to Tuuli. "Go back to that rocky hump," he said, pointing in the direction they'd come from. "Then crawl up on the top till you can see him—him and the slope in back of him. I'm going to work my way as far past him as the terrain allows, then try to close in on him from behind. When I can't get any closer safely, I'll wave to you. When you see me, wait a couple of seconds, then yell that the trail has disappeared. He'll think I'm somewhere behind you. That's when I'll move in on him, close enough for a good shot."

She doesn't even look frightened for me, he thought. *Attentive, serious, but not frightened.*

She turned away and started walking, crouching a bit. Martti went the other way. After a long bypass, he crawled to the crest again and peered over. He'd worked his way past and above the rifleman, who was again some hundred yards distant but facing somewhat away. The biggest danger was that the man would hear his approach.

Martti slipped over the crest and began his stalk, keeping the rifleman in sight. He too would be visible, if the man turned, but more or less obscured by branches and brush.

At 50 yards he reached his last cover. There, standing where Tuuli should see him, he waved his arms, then stepped back into cover. Short seconds later he heard her voice, distant but more clearly than he'd expected, and through a screen of branches saw the man move a few yards—enough that there was brush between him and the location of Tuuli's voice. He was on one knee, rifle ready, prepared to fire or move.

Crouching only slightly, Martti advanced across the open slope, silently cursing the slight hiss of sand moving beneath his boots. The Lady Colt was clenched in his right fist. At 25 yards he saw the man's head start to turn his way, and launched himself. The response was immediate; the man began to rise, turning. Martti's first shot missed, and his second. The rifleman was still pivoting, rifle butt under his arm as he fired off balance toward Martti, the sound harsh but not loud, muffled by the silencer. Martti's third shot hit him high in the chest, knocking him on his back, feet in the air, sending the rifle's second shot skyward. Martti's fourth missed. His fifth struck the sprawling gunman in the left calf, plowing upward into the knee, and Martti heard him roar. On his back, rifle barrel between his knees, the man got off a third round. By that time, Martti was only 8 or 10 yards away, dodging to his right, and the little Colt's sixth round took the rifleman through the temple. He went slack.

Martti straightened, breathing hard, as much from spent tension as from running. From the hole in the man's head, he was clearly dead. Looking up, he saw Tuuli and waved, then walked over to the second man he'd ever killed, the first since he was sixteen and killed his parents' murderer. He found himself calm, and wondered if it would hit him later.

The dead man lay within plain sight of the trail. Martti stripped to avoid getting blood on his clothes, then lugged the corpse over the little ridge from which he'd first seen him, leaving it in the draw on the other side. Vultures and ravens would find it, but well out of sight of anyone on the trail. Next, the two of them picked up the spent cartridge cases, all except two of Martti's which they couldn't find. Then, while Tuuli spread dust over the blood where the rifleman had died, Martti picked up the rifle, using his shirt to avoid leaving his prints on it, and left it by the body. Finally, with branches cut from a shrub well away from the trail, they brushed out the signs of disturbance as best they could. The site wouldn't stand a close inspection, but it was a dozen yards from the trail. A passing hiker would notice nothing.

When they'd finished, they discussed their next action. Tuuli recognized the dead man as someone she'd seen in the Visitors' Center. He'd been with other people, including a woman. Except for the woman, that fitted Martti's theory that the rifleman was part of a hit team. The others, presumably waiting on the rim, might well have heard the shots from the little Colt. For which he had only two rounds left; Tuuli had brought no extra cartridges. He'd thought of taking the dead man's big .44, but decided not to. Best not to have it, especially as conspicuous as it was. If the body was found, let its weapons be with it.

At any rate, it seemed out of the question to hike up and confront the others on the rim. He and Tuuli would be exposed and helpless on the last leg of the trail.

On the other hand, he suspected that the people after him had expended their one trail-wise man. They were almost certainly inner-city people, and unless one of them had been in the military—the infantry or marines—they'd be unlikely to venture far down the trail looking for him. Not if they'd read the warning sign.

So they started back down toward the river. If they could find no way to follow the shore, they'd hide out there. Perhaps some rafters would come along and pick them up, though it might be too late in the season for rafters. Otherwise they'd wait as long as they dared without food, then he'd hike out.

37
CLOSE ENCOUNTERS
OF THE WORST KIND

Though the canyon bottom was in shadow, it was still daylight when they reached the river. Reached it to find a rafting party policing up the foot of the dune, the beach so to speak, after taking a break there. Feigning a limp, Martti went to the man in charge. After a short discussion and the exchange of a fifty-dollar bill, Tuuli joined the group on one raft and Martti those on the other. Less than an hour later they were let off near the mouth of Bright Angel Creek.

From there it was only a few minutes' hike to Phantom Ranch, with a lodge and cabins. The last string of saddle mules had started up the Bright Angel Trail three hours earlier.

Again Martti and Tuuli consulted. To set out for the south rim this late, even on the well-marked, well-maintained Bright Angel Trail, seemed ill-advised. It would be dark long before they reached the Tonto Platform, halfway up, and they'd already hiked a lot of miles, including halfway back up the Barney Trail.

So Martti used one of the ranch's public phones and called Joe's home, while Tuuli stood by to ward off anyone who might otherwise overhear. It was 6:10, Pacific Daylight Time, but Joe wasn't in yet. She expected him any time now, Eleanor said. Martti left the phone number, and ten minutes later Joe called back. Martti explained the situation to him, all of it, pointing out that it wouldn't be safe to try reaching the car without an armed escort. And with the dead man in Barney Canyon, he didn't want to involve the police. It would complicate things all to hell.

Joe called up the Department of Justice atlas on his computer, and found a solution: He'd phone the Coconino County Sheriff's Department—presumably they'd have a floater within reasonable distance of the park—and ask them to pick the two of them up at Phantom Ranch. They could drop them off at Tusayan Flight Services, just south of the park boundary. The justification would be that Martti was urgently needed in L.A. There'd been an unexpected development in an investigation he'd been working on.

Meanwhile Joe would send a party of security men there in a skyvan from L.A., not to bring them home but to help them recover their car. They could overnight at Tuba City, twenty minutes away by skyvan, an hour and a half by road, then rent a road vehicle in the morning, and the whole party would come back for the travel van. Hoping the hit team hadn't trashed it.

It turned out to be not quite that simple. The sheriff's department had to get Park Service permission to fly into the canyon and pick them up. But that took only minutes, and it was still dusk when the floater arrived. Fifteen minutes after that they were at Tusayan Flight Services.

Harley Suk O'Connel pulled the roadvan up in front of Tusayan Flight Services, and stopped. The five of them got out and walked to the door. Jamaal started to open it, then closed it again and stepped back.

"They're here!" he hissed. "Both of them!" He shooed the others away with flapping gestures.

"Who?" O'Connell asked.

"Seppanen! And his wife!"

"Shit!" grunted Lionel.

"How did they get here?" Naylene asked.

"How would I know?"

For a long moment, all Jamaal could think was: *Cowboy's dead all right!* That and his quarries' escape and presence here, broke his confidence that he could kill them quietly. Then from somewhere, some hidden level, a purpose clicked in. The bottom line was to kill Seppanen; that was clear and compelling. And obviously Seppanen was armed. He'd have the pistol they'd heard in the canyon, and Cowboy's too now.

"Back to the car," he said.

He opened the luggage compartment, then a locked chest that sat in it. Inside were four Uzi submachine guns. He handed one to Lionel, then took out another. "Harley, with Cowboy gone, one of these is yours."

"I don't need it. I got my heart gun." He patted his jacket, over the snubnosed .32 concealed in a shoulder holster.

"Take it!" Lionel said, and pushed the Uzi at him. "I know you just hired on to drive, but I'm not leaving them a crack to get out of. There's got to be a back door to this place. I want you there to cover it."

"What about the pickup you called for?"

"I'm calling Terence to cancel it. We'll kill everyone here, then you'll fly one of those. By yourself." He thumbed toward three charter skyvans parked at the end of the building. "Let them think we left in it. The rest of us will drive back."

"There's going to be roadblocks on every . . ."

"God DAMN your black ass, O'Connell! Do what I tell you!"

The intensity of Jamaal's sudden anger, and the illogic of his decision, shocked O'Connell. Jamaal had always been a cool head, always thinking, rarely making a mistake. But this? No way in hell they'd get away with it. He reached and accepted the Uzi, thinking that when it was over, maybe he'd sneak off in the dark. He'd have a better chance hitchhiking, for chrissake. Naylene could fly, if that's what Jamaal wanted, though whether she could navigate was another matter.

THE PUPPET MASTER 343

Naylene could also shoot, and that's what Jamaal was interested in now. She'd been included to make them more convincing as tourists, but she could kill without scruple. She'd proven that in the past, and they'd all been checked out on the Uzis. Jamaal waited till O'Connell had disappeared around the back corner, then he led the other two toward the door.

The terminal's waiting room was 80 by 40 feet, with restrooms, an office-ticket area, and the baggage room at one end. At the other was a food service, closed at this hour.

The only scheduled flights this late in the season were daylight sightseer flights over the canyon, and this evening there was only one employee on duty. Counting Martti and Tuuli, the number of nonemployees was four, all awaiting pickups.

They might have napped, but the seats weren't well suited to it, so they simply sat, talking occasionally in murmurs. Silently Martti puzzled over who'd put out a contract on him, and why. After a little the door opened, catching Tuuli's attention, turning her eyes to it before it closed.

"Martti!" she hissed, "they're here!"

He looked at her.

"A man just looked in the door, then closed it. He was in the park information center with the gunman in the canyon!"

"You're sure?"

She nodded vigorously.

He patted his jacket pocket, feeling the Lady Colt there. Two rounds.

"Should we sneak out the back?" she asked.

This, he thought, *would be a good time for her psychic ability to turn on and come up with something.* He shook his head. "They may have someone outside the door, waiting to blow our brains out." Getting to his feet, he walked over to the service counter, Tuuli following, and spoke to the night agent.

"Do you have a gun?" he murmured softly.

"A *gun?*"

Martti grabbed a handful of shirtfront and jerked, hushing the man. "Christ, man! Keep it down! A guy just looked in the door, then backed out—a member of the black mafia in L.A. I'm an investigator. It's likely they're looking for me, and they won't be leaving witnesses."

The man stared, paling. "You serious?" he whispered.

Martti hissed his answer: "*Goddamn it! Do you have a fucking gun?!*"

Eyes large, the man shook his head.

"Great. Mine will have to do then." Martti gestured toward the other waiting couple, who sat next to each other, reading. "Get them in the baggage room and on the floor. Quietly! Hon, you too."

He took the pistol from his jacket pocket and stood with his back to the counter, both doors within his peripheral vision. The night agent hustled the other couple into the baggage room, Tuuli following. When nothing happened right away, Martti wondered if he'd done right not to try the back door. Another minute passed. Then the front door opened and Jamaal stepped in, Uzi poised. The empty seats held his attention for a moment, and perhaps, coming in from the dark, the light was a problem. Martti drew down on him. "Drop it," he said.

Jamaal blinked as if confused, then jerked his weapon toward Martti, who fired. The Uzi spewed a short burst that chewed the floor as Jamaal fell. A muffled scream from the baggage room didn't register on Martti's attention. Naylene stepped in behind the fallen Jamaal, and while her eyes sought a target, Martti shot her too. Even so, she fired a short burst that splintered the counter beside him.

The Colt empty, he'd started toward them to get a fresh weapon when Lionel came in, stepping over the bodies. "Shark," he said smirking, "you a dead muhth . . ."

There was a shot from the back door, just one, and Lionel fell too, a bullet through the middle of his forehead. The Uzi fell from his hands unfired. Martti spun.

Harley Suk O'Connell stood there, his .32 caliber lowered. He beckoned. Martti went over to him, unsure what the situation was.

"That's all of them," O'Connell said. Then, "I owed you, Seppanen. I'm out of here now. Tell the blues it was you killed them. I mean it! I'm staying clear of L.A. after this, but even so, if Terence finds out what I did, I'm a dead man."

He turned and disappeared. Martti started over to the three on the floor. "Tuuli!" he called, "you can come out now! All of you can; it's . . ."

Suddenly his jaw dropped, then his face contorted in pain, and with a terrible grunting cry he fell to his knees, clutching at his chest, and pitched forward onto the floor. Tuuli rushed toward him screaming; a slashing, thrusting knife of sound: "OUT! OUT! OUT!" Dropping to her knees beside him, she cradled Marti's head in her lap. After a minute he opened one eye and looked at her. "Look who loves me," he murmured, and chuckled, then shuddered and closed the eye again. "Just let me lay here a few minutes and I'll be all right."

A sky ambulance arrived from Grand Canyon Village about five minutes later and took Naylene away, unconscious and in critical condition. She wouldn't live to answer questions. By that time Martti was walking around, no longer even shaky. Martti, Tuuli, and the night agent stayed to wait for the sheriff's deputy.

38
CLOSURE

Their three-man security escort arrived from L.A. while the deputy was still asking questions. When the deputy left for Flagstaff, they drove to Tuba City with their escort, and checked in at a motel room. Physically and emotionally spent, they fell asleep without rehashing the events. The next day their escort drove them back to the park as planned, where they found the travel van undamaged, though the car gun was gone. From there, Martti and Tuuli drove south to Williams, then west and north to discover Las Vegas.

On the road, Martti asked questions. The first was: Why had she taken her Colt into Barney Canyon with her? At best she didn't like to carry it, and in the park it was illegal.

She hadn't even thought about it at the time, she said. Probably it was a psychic impulse acting subliminally.

He mulled that over, unsure that something acting subliminally qualified as psychic, then decided he might be placing improper constraints on the concept.

He remembered vaguely her crying "OUT! OUT!" during his seizure at Tusayan. What, he asked, had she meant by that?

There'd been a being, she said, someone not in a body,

346

enveloping Martti, stopping his heart. An enraged someone. She'd attacked it, thrown her intention at it like a war
axe, and it had withdrawn as if snapped back to its body
by some great rubber band. She'd gotten a sense of someone insane, whether chronically or in temporary rage she
didn't know.

"Could it come back and attack one of us again?" The
thought made him uncomfortable.

"Possibly, but not soon."

He wondered how she could sound so sure of herself,
but didn't question her on it. Again he brought up the
psychic photographer in North Hollywood, and the picture
she'd gotten of him with the spirit behind him. And what
she'd said about someone acting through her when she took
it. Some woman, physically small. *Had* that someone been
Tuuli?

Tuuli laughed. It could have been, she said, she could
have been acting subliminally. She'd like to meet this
psychic photographer.

He'd driven nearly to Hoover Dam before he asked the
next question: Could anyone learn to be psychic like she
was? Perhaps by going to Spirit Ranch and being taught
there?

She shook her head. Even if everyone had the potential, which she wasn't sure of, it didn't seem doable yet to
teach it broadly. Besides, in his way he was already psychic. Look at the "coincidences" and "lucky hunches" that
had been so important in his life.

He left it at that. It made as much sense to him as any
of the rest of it. He thought about asking her whether she
read his sensations when they were making love, but
decided not to. Best not to mess with a good thing. Maybe
that was subliminal too, and talking about it might kill it.

Two nights and a day in Las Vegas were enough for both
of them. Martti was no gambler, but he'd urged Tuuli to
try, wondering if her psychic power would bring a payoff.
She was willing; willing and curious. She made a bit on
the slots, a bit on the wheel, and somewhat more on the

crap tables—enough to cover room and meals, but not a lot more. Nothing conspicuous.

They spent a short day driving to Tahoe, and a night there at Rollins' Casino Hotel. They liked the lake best, and the forest and mountains.

Yosemite was beautiful, even the thick flurry of snow—great wet flakes that met them on the pass, pelting their windshield, melting on the highway. The stands of red fir, so straight and clean, so uniform and dense, were the most handsome forest he thought he'd ever seen. When they visited Tuolumne Meadow, late that day, Tuuli said there'd been a strong but peaceful spirit living there in the past, but it had left. She didn't say how she knew, but he decided that if she said so, it was probably true.

For some reason he wondered about later, he asked if the trees and mountains had spirits of their own. She said they did, but those she sensed here were simple spirits of little force or reach, not the sort that had dwelt in the valley, or in Humphrey Peak or Sipapu.

The next afternoon they were driving west on Highway 46, through the hills and vineyards southwest of Paso Robles, when they saw a funeral procession approaching. A small one: a hearse and four cars. Tuuli was at the wheel, and pulled off on the shoulder to watch it pass, regarding it thoughtfully.

Martti saw the goose bumps on her forearms, and when the procession had passed, asked "Why the stop?"

"I needed to see that," she said. "That funeral procession. It's the reason I wanted to take the coast route south, instead of I-5."

He remembered their discussion about the route, before they'd left Yosemite. They'd decided on I-5, then somehow ended up on this road. "And you knew there'd be this funeral procession?"

"Not consciously."

Subliminal again.

"I remember thinking at the time," she went on, "that my reasons felt like rationalizations, and I wondered what the real reason was."

"Who died?"

"Ask me who killed him."

"Who?"

"I did. At least I caused the shock that killed him. I think his health was already weak though."

Martti stared at her.

"You asked whether the spirit that attacked you at Tusayan might attack one of us again. He won't."

He. "You mean . . . That was him? In the hearse?"

"That was his body."

"How could you tell?"

"You know or you don't. Besides, he was with it, so to speak. Not in it, but with it. Sort of surrounding the hearse. He's going along with it to the crematorium."

She'd said it as matter-of-factly as if discussing a trip to the supermarket. She started the van then and pulled back onto the highway. He wouldn't ask how she knew. She'd only say "you know or you don't."

"It's not so uncommon for someone to have an attachment to their body after it's died," she went on. "For a little while. That's one reason it's cruel to mutilate a corpse."

"What about cremation?"

"Formal cremation is all right. It's dignified and clean."

"And you say he won't attack one of us again."

"Right. We touched when he passed. Communicated. He's not interested in that game any longer. At all."

Neither spoke for a while. Tuuli drove well and fast, yet her eyes seemed to rove the countryside, drinking in what she saw. Finally Martti asked, "What kind of life is it that's lived subliminally? Wouldn't it be like going along for the ride? Being a spectator while your subliminal self does the driving in a closed-off compartment?"

"It's more like piloting a spacecraft," she said, "setting the course while the computer does most of the navigating and runs the systems. You can change your mind about

where you're going, though. The main decisions are yours."
She chuckled. "And the computer is part of you, anyway."

She glanced sideways at him. "That's how you walk, you
know. Your leg movements, your eye-foot coordination, all
those things are subliminally controlled. You tell your body
where you want to go, and how fast, and it takes you."

He nodded, marveling as he often had at this quadri-
lingual person who'd grown up partly in an arctic mining
town, and partly on a backwoods farm in Finnish Lapland.
Who'd come alone to America at age eighteen to work as
a domestic, with no one to turn to for help and counsel.
And who, at age thirty-one, spoke American fluently, even
colloquially, and made more money than lots of engineers.

He wondered what course she was flying, and what role
he played in her trip. *Or for that matter,* he thought, *what
course I'm flying. Do I even have a destination?* Inwardly
he grunted. *If I do, it's subliminal.*

His thoughts went to the hearse. "The guy—the being
in the hearse," he said, "*with* the hearse . . . What'll he do
when his body's been cremated?"

"He'll leave. Go to the other side, the astral universe
you might call it, and review his life and actions. That's
probably the basis for the concept of purgatory. Eventually he'll recycle; be born as someone new."

"Why did he act like he did? Why did he try to kill me?"

"He was angry; psychotically angry. He'd controlled
DeSmet, and Masters, and the one in charge of the hit
team at the airport. And probably others. He'd taken them
over." She glanced again at her husband. "You know who
he was, of course."

Martti nodded. "I think so. Leif Haller."

It seemed to him there was no other explanation. If he
was right about that, then in a way, Haller had been
Christman's murderer, though it was beyond proof. He'd
killed Christman and maybe Cloud Man, and all those
people in the apartment house. Haller. So intelligent, so
hard-working and charismatic, yet he'd failed. Pretty much
all down the line, really.

Or had he? Even before he'd taken up murder, he'd had

an impact on a lot of lives. Apparently a good impact in many cases. Like Christman had. And provided a place for people who were looking for one.

But that hadn't been much of a funeral procession. Back in '95, when his dad and mom had been buried, more than a thousand people had turned out, a sixth of Ojibwa County. The funeral service had been held on the courthouse lawn, because no church in Hemlock Harbor was nearly big enough. Even so, they'd spilled over into the parking lot. If his dad had known in advance, he'd have been embarrassed.

Martti wondered how Leif Haller would have felt, in the heyday of his Institute, if he'd known his funeral procession would be only four cars and a hearse. Of course, almost everyone thought he'd died in Wisconsin a dozen years earlier.

Ray Christman's memorial service drew thousands of the faithful, even though his dying, his murder, had broken his image and shown him fallibly human. They still thought of him as the inspired genius who'd given them the new gnosis. In the case report, Prudential hadn't included the role the Merlins had played in Christman's church. Martti had checked with them. Both had said no, and it wasn't actually pertinent to the case anyway.

Who would know when Vic Merlin died? Who outside his circle of friends? Not many. And the Merlins' wouldn't care, he felt sure of that.

Maybe, Martti thought, he should spend some time with the Merlins, or the Diaconos. They were obviously remarkable people with remarkable abilities. And good people. If he did spend some time with them, would he change the way Tuuli had changed? How changed was she, though? Now that he stopped to look at it, she wasn't basically changed. Just overhauled, tuned up. . . .

Maybe someday he'd do it, spend a couple of weeks with the Diaconos. A weekend with Vic, anyway. But just now he'd live his own way. Maybe that's what he was supposed to be doing. Anyway he was good at what he did.

Subliminal! Hmm!

He looked at fame again. *Actually,* he thought, *I'm kind of famous. Semi-famous. A semi-famous detective. Dad and mom would have been proud. When I die, it'll probably even get mentioned in the newsfax—maybe even on television—unless there's a major earthquake that week, or a revolution somewhere.*

He didn't give a damn about fame, though, he decided. Well, maybe a little bit; it was handy sometimes. He had friends—not a lot, but as many as he wanted—and an interesting job with lots of independence. And most of all, Tuuli loved him. She'd even killed for him, in a manner of speaking.

Tuuli reached over and patted his knee.

THE CASE OF THE DUPLICATE BEAUTIES

A NOVELET

PROLOG

The male presenter chuckled at a witticism, then announced: "And finally Elena Marquez, for her role as Lupe, in The Last Apache."

Abruptly center stage disappeared, displaced by a holo of the Chihuahuan Desert. Half a dozen Apache warriors stood in a loose row, moccasins over their calves, thighs and torsoes bare, stoic faces painted for war. Their hands held lever-action Winchester carbines. A large white man stood facing them, hands on cocked hips, inches from low-slung pistols. Beside him, face smudged with ashes, was a lovely, black-haired young woman of mixed race, her eyes defiant as she stared at the Indians. Her deerskin shift was tattered and revealing.

"Nana," the white man drawled, "there's only six of you left. The army's watching every waterhole from here to the Jornada del Muerto, and General Miles' Apache Scouts are hunting your tracks. The best thing for you to do is cross the border back into Mexico."

Old Nana spoke without gesture, without head movement. "She goes with us," he answered. His broad face was lined, eyes hard, unyielding. "For her father's treachery."

The white man opened his mouth as if to speak again,

but the woman stilled him with a sharp gesture, and taking a step toward the chief, spoke in rapid, fluid Apache. Subtitles flowed across the base of the holo, but her imperious face, her expressive voice, her presence made them almost superfluous. When she finished, the scene froze on her for a moment, then the desert disappeared, the presenters applauding with the audience.

The man picked an envelope from the podium and held it up. "And now for the winner," he said, handing it to the woman. Smiling she took it. "The winner," she began, tearing open an end, "is . . ." She drew out a sheet of paper, unfolded it, then looked up as if with delight. "The winner is Elena Marquez, for her role as Lupe, in The Last Apache!"

The orchestra began to play the theme music from the film, and as heads turned and hands clapped, the cameras shifted to a gorgeous young woman rising to her feet in the audience. Smiling, sure of herself, she moved down the aisle, strides strong but feminine, and swept across the stage as the applause swelled.

She'd almost reached the podium when she stopped. More than three thousand viewers watched from the seats, and some 500 million more on holovision and television worldwide. Abruptly her eyes widened, her hands flew to her temples. Her mouth squared to scream, and the sound of it erupted, shocking in its raw horror. She fell writhing and thrashing to the stage, as if in an epileptic seizure. Her screams were answered from here and there in the audience, and guards ran onto the stage from the wings, tried to corral her flailing limbs. Seconds later a doctor hurried out, bag in hand.

Someone in the control booth had the presence of mind to key the curtains closed, and a moment later killed the backstage cameras. In a hundred million living rooms worldwide, the view switched to the stunned attendees in the auditorium, most with expressions of shock, horror, or fear.

Someone else had the presence of mind not to switch to a commercial message.

1

I'll start by saying it's good to put this case to bed after seven years of being threatened by it. I'm Principal Investigator Martti Seppanen, and this is Cube One of the closing debriefs for Investigation 1832, Prudential Investigations and Security. The date is 17 April 2020, the time is 1320 hours, and the debrief officer is Carlos Katagawa, with company president Joe Keneely sitting in, which makes it old-timers' night.

Excuse me. I don't ordinarily ramble, but this debrief is Veritas-assisted.

We got involved with crucial evidence—information that led to the solution—months before the first of the crimes took place. That's happened to me before, which is why Joe calls me an evidence attractor. In an article he wrote on it for *The Journal of Forensic Psychology*, he even said I inspired the theory.

I'm not sure how seriously he takes the idea. Joe's an image maestro. His conservative suit—even the eyeglasses on his nose—are promotional; he's had his eyes reconditioned to 20/15. And his occasional provocative articles in symposium proceedings or journals are good for the company image.

Sorry. Back to the subject. On the evening of October 19, 2012, the LAPD got word that Tran Ngo, a wanted felon, had just gone into a porn theater near Hollywood and Bronson, so they sent a squad to pick him up. It turned out to be a mistaken identity, but there was a ruckus, and some of the customers ducked out the rear exits. And the police covering the rear let them pass, because none of them was a five-foot-three Oriental.

One of them had left a torn Life-Tex mask in the theater, and when the cleaning crew cleaned up afterward, they found it and turned it in. The theater manager turned it over to the LAPD, but the department could see no reason to keep it; Tran Ngo hadn't been in the theater. It was a weird find, though, and for whatever reason, they passed it on to us. The only information that came with it, and it seemed meaningless, was the circumstances surrounding it, and the name of the film: *In Hiding*.

Having the mask, Joe asked for and got a contingency contract for the Ngo Case. You seldom get any money on a contingency contract unless you come up with evidence that leads to at least an indictment. But it doesn't cost anything either, and Joe operates on intuition at least as much as I do.

A few weeks later, Ngo was arrested in Salt Lake, but Properties hates to throw anything away, so the mask went into a drawer in what we call "the limbo files."

I never imagined it would mean anything to me, let alone how much.

2

Two days after Elena Marquez had her psychotic break at the Academy Awards ceremony, her husband, Bo Haugen, took her to the well-known psychic healer, Olaf Sigurdsson.

Haugen's worth a lot of money, a lot of it earned, but his seed money was inherited. He's a low-profile Hollywood producer—actually San Fernando Valley—specializing in biographies and other historical series and miniseries. He's a very private man.

Elena Marquez's doctor had her doped to the gills, but Ole got beneath the drug level and regressed her to the ceremonies. She told him that crossing the stage, she'd been struck by a crushing head pain. Which was followed instantly by what she called an assault of "memories," of things she said she'd never even dreamed, but were as real as life and unimaginably terrible. Along with the feeling that someone or something was taking over her body.

That's when she'd passed out and gone into convulsions.

Interestingly, she had bruises, lesions, abrasions, burns, that so far as anyone knew, had never actually been inflicted on her. Somatic hysteria, her doctor called them, which amounts more or less to saying she'd imagined them so strongly, they'd appeared on her body. Her blood also contained enzymes which metabolize a class of aphrodisiacs, but not the aphrodisiacs themselves, which was a chemical anomaly the lab couldn't explain.

The intruding "memories" were of waking up naked in a place she'd never been before, having no idea how she'd gotten there. There'd been a dark-complexioned female nurse who spoke a little English, who'd given her a shot and then fed her. After that—

After that she'd been a sex slave to someone she described as an oil sheikh. To Elena Marquez, any wealthy Arab who wears robes is an oil sheikh. She was injected with an aphrodisiac before each of his visits, and to intensify his kicks and keep himself going, he had a Harem Smoke fumer. He abused her pretty badly, and after a week or so had brought in other men. One she thought of as a general—he'd arrived wearing a uniform loaded with medals. The others she thought of as sheikhs. She had internal injuries from the abuse she took. Between times the nurse wept with her, and treated her with what were probably antibiotics.

After a couple of weeks, the repeated drugging and abuse broke her sanity. She started hallucinating like a drunk drying out from a week-long binge, shaking so badly she couldn't feed herself, and what the nurse fed her, she vomited back out. She'd cry even under the aphrodisiac. Which annoyed the sheikh, who quit coming to see her, sending soldiers instead, several at a time. They were the ones who'd burned her with cigarettes. After several days of that, her memories of it suddenly stopped, and that second persona had "burst into her skull" in the middle of the awards ceremony, with a headache she wouldn't have believed possible.

And to top it off, she knew—*knew*—she'd died in that bedroom. Knew it without any doubt at all.

Though Ole could get her into a trance, then locate the traumatic incidents and get her descriptions of them, he couldn't defuse them until the sedative was out of her body. So he'd called in a music therapist; the music was to function in place of the drug. After a few days of music and detoxifying, he defused the whole sequence of traumas; it took just one evening and the following afternoon. I got to talk with her the day after that, and she seemed as poised and matter-of-fact as you could want. Ole didn't doubt at all that what she'd described had somehow really happened, but I wasn't so sure, even after I talked with her. I couldn't even think of an *unlikely* explanation.

Bo Haugen told me privately he'd have liked to believe it was all hallucination, but he acted on the assumption that it had somehow derived from a criminal act—perhaps before they'd met. Maybe after she'd finished an overseas film, and she'd suppressed the memories afterward.

I couldn't buy that, although I didn't say so to Haugen. I know Ole, and with him helping, she'd have dredged up the rest of the story if there was one. He's a master at fishing up buried memories, and without hypnosis.

At any rate, Haugen contracted with Prudential to find out what had happened and who was behind it. And because I'd solved "The Case of the Twice-killed Astronomer," and what my wife Tuuli and I thought of as "The Puppetmaster Case"—both of them damn tough—I got the assignment.

The first thing I did was create a time track for Marquez, going back to high school, and there was no unaccounted-for period long enough to accommodate the set of horrors she'd described. I told Haugen that, but he wanted me to stay with it, so Joe had Elena Marquez swear out a criminal complaint against a person or persons unknown, for her "covert drugging." That got me second-level access to the California State Data Center.

The only approach I could think of was to treat the "memories" as if they really were—as if those things had actually happened—and try to place the events geographically. Judging from the few words she'd learned, that Ole fished from her subconscious, the language there was

Arabic, probably the dialect spoken on the Arabian peninsula. And clearly the "sheikh" was someone important in government, perhaps a cabinet minister. Also it seemed to be one of the less secularized states, like Saudi Arabia, Ibadhan, or Yemen.

But we had no proof at all that any of it was real, and in whatever country it was, we'd probably have no legal standing anyway. I asked Haugen what good it would do him to find out who it was. He said it would be worth it just to know. Which may have been true, as far as it went, but I have no doubt he had thoughts of something more. It seemed to me, though, that there wasn't a chance in hell of having a murder contract carried out on some middle-eastern government minister.

I had Marquez work with a computer artist, Jamal Lodi, who turned out an iterative series of computer drawings of her captor. Then I turned to the web and checked the lifelike final result against pictures of wealthy or prominent Arabs. It was a close match with one of Rashid ibn Muhammed, the uncle, one-time regent for, and currently financial advisor of the Sultan of Ibadhan.

But Haugen also wanted to know how the crime had been committed, which promised to be a lot harder to learn. Impossible seemed more like it. Joe told him we'd go into fishing mode, and see what we found.

I used a computer program we called a "weasel," a tailored cyberbot that would search the web for anything that might correlate with things Marquez had told us and what we'd deduced from them. I also tried trolling, posting a request for information about beautiful women who'd suffered a recent psychotic break, another for information about anyone who'd been assaulted by a duplicate set of memories, and a third for women who'd hallucinated being a sex slave.

I hate trolling. It can bring a lot of useless replies, all of them requiring at least a little time.

3

For several days I got nothing worth more than a first look. Ironically, my first real lead was from Ole Sigurdsson, who'd just treated his gorgeous blond countrywoman, Ardis Halldórsdottir, the figure skater. Her experience was remarkably like Elena Marquez's, which of course she knew nothing about, *even including the same villain,* Rashid ibn Muhammed. The main differences were that her captivity had lasted only two days, until she'd kicked ibn Muhammed in the best possible place. His bodyguard had promptly shot her—killed her, she insisted—and she'd had her psychotic break in the privacy of the apartment she shared with her husband and skating partner, Peter Golovkin. What she'd done tickled hell out of me, but she provided no useful information except to validate Marquez's story. Neither Carlos nor I doubted now; somehow those things had actually happened.

The other lead was a lot different: I got a report of a woman who'd had what seemed to be hallucinations of being a sex slave. Nothing was said of any psychotic break. To talk to her, I was to call a certain number. It sounded fishy, but I called—and got a receptionist at a talent agency,

who connected me with one of the agents. He sounded
unfriendly, suspicious, and gay, but after asking a few
questions, he told me to meet him that evening at seven,
and gave me an address.

I said I'd be there, then called up the city directory.
The occupant wasn't listed, so I used my access to the Data
Center. It belonged to Misti Innocenza, Hollywood's most
popular porn queen. I suspected some kind of PR hoax.
Also I was chicken—I asked Carlos to go with me, and he
said sure. I assumed she'd be built, but I was surprised
how pretty she was, how sweetly innocent looking. Her real
name, it turned out, was Lindi Hall. A girl friend had told
her about my bulletin, and she'd had her agent follow up
on it. Her story somewhat resembled the others, but her
memories were of being held in what seemed to be a lodge,
and her captor was someone she'd recognized: the prominent TV evangelist, Buddy Ballenger.

For more than two days there'd been two of her—one
in a Simi Valley porn studio, or at home, or restaurants,
or with girl friends. While entirely unknown to that Misti,
another had awakened naked and handcuffed in an unfa-
miliar place. After injections, she'd spent two days and
nights on a big bed surrounded by mirrors, with Ballenger
and his bodyguard, whom Ballenger called "Billy." The two
men took turns, and with breaks for showers, naps, and
snacks, and injecting her repeatedly with aphrodisiacs, they'd
gone at her pretty much the whole time! Hard to believe;
Harem Smoke is notoriously hard on the heart. On the
other hand, the aphrodisiacs effective on women are hard
on the nervous system, and she was afraid they were killing her. So after the second day, she begged Ballenger to
let her go. He'd excused himself and left the bedroom, "for
just a minute," to "arrange transportation." Then the bodyguard had grabbed her and given her another injection, this
time with something that "burned like fire."

And that was the end of that persona. The original Misti
had just walked into her apartment when the godawful
headache hit her, and the torrent of memories "burst" into
her skull. *Burst*; the same word Elena Marquez had used.

But Innocenza didn't go psychotic. Kinky sex with strangers was no great shock for her, and behind that sweet innocent face was a hardbitten survivor, so after taking a handful of headache pills, brewing a pot of coffee, and burning herself pouring it, she'd sat up trying to sort things out on tablet paper. She failed, of course.

There were three things she was positive of: one, it had really happened; two, she'd died there, been killed; and three, her captor was Ballenger, "who didn't have guts enough to kill me himself." Also, through the bathroom window she'd seen a sandy beach about a hundred yards away, and pine trees with really long needles. And Ballenger had said something about the mainland. I remembered a vacation tour with my dad and mom; Innocenza could have been describing the Sea Islands off the Georgia coast, and Ballenger was from Georgia. Later, checking an atlas, I found Marcellus only a few miles inland.

Then she asked me if I knew someone she could hire to kill him. I told her I hoped she'd cool it long enough for me to get the evidence needed to pull him into court. Actually I didn't see a way in hell we'd ever get that kind of evidence, but there's always a chance.

And now I knew absolutely that somehow, someone had done something really evil to all three women. Someone a lot more dangerous than Buddy Ballenger, or even Rashid ibn Muhammed.

That night I told Tuuli what I'd learned, hoping she'd have a suggestion. After all, she was "the Psychic of the Stars." But this time she didn't.

4

I spent the next morning learning all I could about Buddy
Ballenger, the pride and embarrassment of Marcellus, Georgia. There was a lot, even leaving out the tabloid articles.
Examples: He'd lost a patrimony suit, been badly beaten
by an angry husband with a baseball bat, settled out of court
in an embezzlement case. . . . He was big, blond, and
apparently not very bright: a sort of caricature, more an
over-sexed jerk than a menace. Though judging from Misti
Innocenza's story, he could be dangerous. How a million
or more born-again Christians could be his dedicated
followers—his paying dedicated followers!—had to be a
major mystery and a major human commentary.

Tuuli had a two o'clock appointment to exorcise a ghost
in Beverly Hills, and the office wasn't far out of her way,
so we'd made a luncheon date. And arriving a few minutes early, she waited in my office while I finished reading some stuff I'd called up.

Andy Lopez, from Properties, looked in. "Martti," he
said, "any reason I should keep this? Joe wants me to cull
the limbo files." He held an object out for my inspection.

"What is it?" Tuuli asked. Which surprised me. Ordinarily she'd have said nothing while I was working.

"Hi Tuuli," Andy said. "It's a torn Life-Tex mask."

"Who is it of?"

"Probably no one in particular. No one any of us recognized."

She frowned. "Who was it made *for* then?"

I answered this time, embarrassed that I hadn't wondered myself. Given the expert fitting necessary, a Life-Tex mask was expensive. "We don't know that, either," I said.

"Find out," she told me.

"Find out? Honey, that case is closed, and finding out would take time."

"Try. It could be important."

"Could be? You mean like, 'might possibly be'? Or do you think it is?"

"I think it may be."

"Leave it here, Andy," I said. She was, after all, a celebrity psychic and sometime crime consultant who got sizeable fees from her clients. "After lunch I'll talk to Skip," I told her, "and see what he can do with it."

She drove us to Mr. Ethel's, on North La Cienega. It wasn't far, and the food is excellent, even if the waiters are a bit overdone. I asked for a corner booth near the kitchen door: The noise would obscure our conversation if anyone sat down in the adjacent booth, and for the same reason, probably no one would. After we got our menus, she started on the questions, as I'd expected.

"What theater?" she asked.

"You mean where the mask was found? One of the Pussycat Theaters. On Hollywood, near Bronson."

"What was the picture?"

She was fishing. When she senses something psychically and can't come up with it, she'll try to get some real-world information to help it surface. "I've heard," I told her, "but I don't recall; it didn't mean anything to me. It'll be in the file though."

Her eyes went unfocused—I notice things like that—and I kept my mouth shut to avoid disturbing her. Then the waiter came and took our orders, and we turned to other subjects. The mask didn't come up again until we'd finished our sandwiches.

"*In Hiding*," I said.

"What?"

"That's the name of the movie. *In Hiding*."

I hadn't realized it, but the waiter had just come out with our desserts, and overheard me. "You see that flick?" he asked.

I looked up. "No," I told him, "but I heard about it."

"Some show! I mean . . ." He looked at Tuuli then, embarrassed. "That Misti Innocenza is something else." He paused defensively. "She can act, too. Good enough, she could be in big-time flicks."

I decided I'd misjudged Mr. Ethel's waiters; this one anyway.

"I'm sure she could," Tuuli told him. He put down our sundaes and hurried away. "My next question," she said, "was who's the actress. And we've got the answer."

Misti Innocenza. Okay, but so what? Still, I felt a stir of excitement.

5

Life-Tex masks are carefully molded to the wearer's face, otherwise they're useless. This one had thickened the brow ridge, and given the face a broad, high-bridged nose and neat, reddish blond beard. So the wearer's hair was probably more or less blond. And the mask had a well-tanned complexion, which suggested the original didn't. For the camouflage effect.

At the lab I told Skip what I wanted, and left the mask with him. An hour later he buzzed me, and I went over. Using the computer, he'd developed a facsimile of the wearer's own face, and had tried three hair styles with it, printing off each of the versions.

I knew it at once, from my recent research.

"I've seen this guy," Skip said, "but I don't recall who he is. Someone on a magazine cover." He paused. "Or a tabloid."

I nodded. "Buddy Ballenger."

"That's it." Reaching, he touched a key on his intercom. "Fidela," he said, "could you come to the lab a minute? This is Skip." Fidela, who read the tabloids, confirmed the identification at once. When she'd left, Skip looked curiously at me. "What's this all about?"

I shook my head. It looked like Ballenger might have had a sexual fixation on Misti Innocenza, a fixation strong enough, he'd gone to a porn theater to watch her perform. He could have called up the flick at home, if he'd wanted to. Maybe he liked the vibes and smell of a porn theater. And the mask would keep anyone from recognizing him. But why would he take it off before ducking out when the police arrived?

I'd been thinking out loud, and Skip answered. Life-Tex masks aren't as convincing in reality as they seem on the screen. In extreme close shots—shots that show little more than the face—even Life-Tex masks don't look lifelike when the actor is talking. In films and holos this is dealt with by a computer process, but live that doesn't help.

So apparently Ballenger, fearing he'd be questioned, got rid of the mask. His face wasn't that well known, except to people who watched his show or read the tabloids, and hopefully any cop who might stop him wouldn't be one of them. Of course, the odds of his being questioned had been next to zero—the police were looking for a small wiry Asian, not a big blond Caucasian—but Ballenger hadn't known that. He'd panicked, and left his mask behind.

Interesting. But being horny over Misti Innocenza wouldn't mean a thing in court, any more than her story would. Not by themselves. What I needed to learn was how it was done.

6

Back in my office, I phoned Ole Sigurdsson. He was tied up that afternoon, but as a personal friend, I got an appointment for eight that evening. Tuuli went with me.

We were having an early April rain, unusually hard, with thunder and lightning. Ole's place is on top of a steep ridge between two canyons in Bel Air, and the goat-trail street that zigzagged up the side flowed like a shallow creek, between ivy-covered banks that glistened wetly in the streetlights.

From the front, his house looks small for Bel Air—one story high and not particularly wide—but that's the uphill side. Seen from downhill, it's the second floor. It contains a large room with bar for entertaining, along with a small kitchen and one and a half baths. And Ole's office—a kind of smallish sitting room actually, with a long sofa where he naps when he feels like it. He's in his eighties, and doesn't take as many clients as he used to. Downstairs are their living quarters, and Laura's offices. His wife is Laura Wayne Walker, a producer of theater and TV films and holos. She's a lot younger than Ole—maybe sixty-five—but they suit each other. Besides being compatible and highly competent, they have a lot of mutual admiration.

Tuuli was my in-house psychic, but Ole has a different

371

spectrum of talents, so I turn to him from time to time. What I wanted now was his viewpoint, which sometimes picks out things both Tuuli and I have missed.

I summarized the case for him, which didn't take long, then asked: "What actually happened, do you think? How did these assaults take place? Assuming it wasn't some kind of hypnosis."

He showed no sign of uncertainty. "They are real enough," he said. "Each of them lived two lives at vunce for a v'ile, as if they had parallel existences. Then something happened and vun of them died—and the memories of that self snapped back into the first vun."

"But *how*? How could something like that happen?"

He grunted. "That's your yob to find out. You're the detective. But these veren't no freaks of nature. Somevun *made* them happen, that's vun thing I'm sure of."

He had a small wood-burning brick stove, and had put on the same old-fashioned orange-red coffeepot I'd seen the first time I'd been there. It began to perk.

"Do you have any idea what kind of connection Ballenger might have with whoever—made these things happen?"

He shrugged. "I don't know. Maybe they both belong to a Misti Innocenza fan club on the Veb."

A fan club? I shuddered at the amount of work it would be to attack the case from that angle, though I might have to.

Ole got up and poured us coffee. He knew we took ours black, but he stirred cream and sugar into his until it had enough calories to feed the starving Sudanese. Then we sipped and talked some more. It was hard for me to accept parallel existences, even as part of quantum theory, and Ole had no more idea than I did how anyone could split a time line. Not at the level of particle integration that humans experience. But on the other hand, the breakthrough that produced the geogravitic power converter had given and continued to give rise to a whole spray of new developments, in both basic science and technology. A lot of us aren't as sure of what we know as people used to be.

Tuuli and I drove home without saying much. I didn't know whether the trip had been worthwhile or not.

7

I woke up in the morning with a decision, and when I got to the office, phoned Vic Merlin in Arizona. Vic and his wife were old friends of Ole's, that I got to know on the Puppetmaster Case. Vic is undoubtedly a higher powered psychic even than Ole. I gave him a rundown on what I was up against, then asked: "Can you think of any way someone could split a time line?"

Education, and decades spent away from rural west Texas, hadn't entirely erased his accent. "Not and transfer memories across like that," he said, then added what seemed like a total non sequitur. "But there's a guy named C.K.F. Linyetski in England, at the University of Birmingham, built an operating teleport a couple years ago. The only problem was, the block of iron he teleported arrived at the receiving plate as a little mound of fine dust—atoms of iron and assorted impurities in the same ratios as in the block."

I frowned. "What's the connection between that and splitting a time line?" I asked.

"I sure don't know; it just came to me." That definitely sounded like Vic. "I've got something else you might be interested in," he added.

❖   ❖   ❖

Vic's mainly a psychic researcher, but like Ole Sigurdsson, he's also a healer. He'd just treated an old friend named William Harford, who'd had a severe psychotic seizure and heart attack at his home in Los Alamos, New Mexico. When her husband's condition was upgraded to stable, Harford's wife had phoned Vic, and he'd flown to Los Alamos the next day. Vic had worked his way beneath the sedatives and Harford's severe confusion, and gotten a story that in important respects was like the others I'd heard. Harford worked for the government in weapons research—he did basic theoretical work in matrix physics—and his intrusive memories were of waking up in a clinic at a foreign laboratory, in India or Pakistan he thought. There he'd been grilled about his own research and related work. When he'd refused to cooperate, they'd tried drugs and psychological stress, and having a pre-existing heart condition, he'd had a coronary attack. And died. He was sure about that: as the duplicate Harford, he'd died.

And when the memories hit the original, he'd had a coronary of his own. But the "real" Harford didn't die.

It was an interesting report, but it didn't have the sort of information I needed. So I went to Gold's and worked out on the Nautilus equipment, then sat in the sauna and cooked out what remained of the tension. When I left, I knew what I was going to do next. I called Buddy Ballenger from a pay phone outside Morey's. I doubted he had a program he could trace the call with through our deadwall, but why take a chance?

A receptionist answered. "I need to speak with Reverend Ballenger personally," I told her.

Her sweetie-pie voice dripped Georgia honeysuckle. "Whom may I say is calling?"

"Mr. Smith." It wasn't a complete lie. In Finnish, a seppanen is a smith.

"And what may I tell him this concerns?"

"It concerns a young woman named Misti. And a Life-Tex mask in a Pussycat Theater. He'll know what I'm talking about."

She didn't answer, just put me on hold. The recorded music was of the McArdle family singing something about letting Jesus hold you in his loving arms. Love was foreign to the arms that had held Misti Innocenza. After a minute or so, Ballenger's appointments secretary came on the line, his voice challenging. I repeated what I'd told the receptionist, which got me Ballenger. I repeated myself again.

"I'm sorry," Ballenger said, "but I don't know anything about any Life-Tex mask, or anyone named Misti. If you're an attorney, I recommend you get in touch with my lawyer."

He didn't hang up though, which validated that he was our masked man. "Interesting," I said. "I have the mask. It was found in the Pussycat Theater on Hollywood Boulevard last October. The feature was *In Hiding*, starring Misti Innocenza. And I have a computer reconstruction of the face the mask was made for. Your face." I paused, then added, "Masks always pick up epidermal cells when they're worn; handy for DNA matches.

"But more important, I've spoken to Ms. Innocenza, and she knows you very well. Better than she wanted to."

There was a long lag before he answered. "That's impossible."

"You mean because she's dead? You're a religious man, reverend. You believe in souls. And some souls come back, looking for vengeance. If you're smart, you'll meet with me, and we'll talk about what it'll take to square things with her."

For about a minute, all I could hear was breathing. I think he hyperventilated. Finally he spoke again. "There's a restaurant at Marina del Rey, called Leon's, on Eton just west of the yacht club. We could meet there."

"What time?"

"I don't know your name."

"You don't need to. Not now, anyway. I'm six-one, 235 pounds, mean face, sandy hair. Thirty-two years old. You'll recognize me. What time?"

"Eight this evening," he said.

I told him fine, then hung up, walked to our building, and took the stairs to our floor, the ninth. It's a good leg/lung/heart workout, if you don't mind a damp tee shirt. I half expected Ballenger to unknowingly give me a lead that afternoon. If he did, I'd probably stand him up that evening. Let him sweat a little. He'd earned it.

8

I waited a bit, then used our case access to get into the Data Center's statewide phone records. It seemed to me Ballenger would have phoned someone after my call, asking for advice. At least. And sure as hell, immediately after we'd talked, he'd phoned someone named Charles A. Scheele.

The name meant nothing to me, but that was correctable. The California Data Center is Prudential's major information source, but its data are mostly in-state governmental and utilities records; stuff you don't find in libraries. Beyond that, virtually everything in paper libraries worldwide, along with an enormous amount of government and university information never otherwise published, has been scanned into the huge interlibrary public "Data Ocean." Some of it's restricted, requiring various authorizations and often cross-requirements for access, depending on the nature and degree of confidentiality. But a lot of what I found on Scheele was open—in newspapers for instance, and his high school and college yearbooks.

He was the son of a wealthy Bay Area corporate executive and his socialite wife, and like Ballenger, Scheele had grown up a caricature. In his case a caricature of a nerd. His IQ was 179, he'd gotten his BS in physics from Cal

Tech at age eighteen, *summa cum laude,* and at twenty his MS from Stanford in electronics. Two years later he'd completed most of his work toward a Ph.D. in physics at Stanford, when he was accused of injecting a coed with an illegal aphrodisiac, Take Me. The drug hadn't worked as intended. Instead, interacting with psychological factors, it had filled the young woman with rage and strength, and she'd clawed, punched, and kicked the snot out of him— then knocked him unconscious with a heavy vase, and called 911. While waiting for the police, she'd trashed Scheele's living room.

The police lab verified the injection, and Scheele, in the hospital with his injuries, was charged with attempted chemical rape. Meanwhile the local and university media had a ball with the story, making him a laughingstock. Taking advantage of Scheele's injuries and humiliation, his lawyer had gotten him off with a suspended sentence and two hundred hours of community service. Scheele was already wealthy by ordinary standards, from playing the stock market with money his father had given him, and he'd paid the coed an unknown sum to settle her civil suit out of court.

He'd dropped out of school then, and over the years since, had gotten or applied for seven major patents for industrial processes. Which presumably added considerably to his wealth, because he'd built a home on five acres in a very expensive, high-security development near Montecito. I knew the area from the Arthur Ashkenazi murder case.

I couldn't help wondering what Scheele might have invented and kept secret.

So I sent a weasel into the Web again, to learn who Scheele communicated with besides Ballenger. I was particularly interested in scientists and engineers, but anything was welcome. The Web, of course, has botphages circulating constantly, to destroy bots in restricted areas, but they'd ignore my weasel with its instantly verifiable forensic code. Someone like Scheele, though, would probably post cyberpickets to detect, report, and/or destroy bots interested in him, at the same time letting Scheele know someone was snooping him. Really sophisticated pickets could even trace their origins.

On the other hand, if a picket did intercept my weasel, I'd know where, in the convoluted "space-time" of the cybermatrix, it had happened. Which would give me a good idea of whether the picket was actually Scheele's.

9

Meanwhile Scheele seemed to be the man who somehow or other could split time lines to order. Or whatever had been done; I had a real problem with the concept of splitting time lines, and memories jumping from one to the other. If I was susceptible to headaches, this case would give me one.

I went to Carlos' office and told him what I'd learned. Then he called Joe, and I went over it again. We didn't have anything either the police or Haugen could go to court with, and none of us could see any prospects, but you never know. So Joe applied to the Justice Department for a contingency contract, on the basis that the Defense Department's William Harford might have been the victim of a criminal conspiracy.

The department's regional director for California, along with the head of the FBI's LA office, arrived the next morning to examine the evidence. We didn't show what we'd learned from Innocenza, which might prejudice them against us. Even as it was, they acted as if we were shrink cases, but two days later, Washington faxed Joe a contract. Prudential's reputation had come through again. There was nothing in it for us, of course, unless we came up with something that contributed to an arrest, indictment, or conviction.

10

Charles Scheele sat back in his chair and stared at the monitor. When his picket had intercepted the bogie, his beeper had alerted him, and he'd sent out a highly advanced bot of his own design, which he called "the snake." Through it he'd learned not only that he was being investigated, but by whom, and even who the agent was.

The name Martti Seppanen had been vaguely familiar, and a brief search in the Web told him the man was sharp, very sharp. And clearly Seppanen knew something, but how much could it be? Ballenger didn't know much. How many targets had Seppanen found, besides Innocenza? Only Innocenza could have identified the customer, unless Harwood . . . Harwood would explain the Justice Department's interest.

It seemed to Scheele he needed to find out just what Seppanen knew, and where he'd learned it, making no mistakes. Then do whatever he needed to do.

He felt pumped. He loved challenges, and this one was unlike any he'd dealt with before.

11

The next couple of days I tried every approach I could think of to get a lead on how someone might do what Scheele had seemingly done. I talked to half a dozen big-name theoretical physicists, including a couple with a reputation for being over the edge. Telling them only that my interest was part of a criminal investigation. I even visited Winifred Sproule at the Hypernumbers Institute.

No one had anything to suggest.

Next I phoned Ballenger, again identifying myself as Mr. Smith. He seemed unlikely to know much, but anything would help. And whether he knew anything or not, he'd probably call Scheele again, which might break something loose.

Ballenger sounded wary, but didn't complain about my standing him up. We agreed to meet at the same place—Leon's, at Marina del Rey—this time at 9:00 P.M. When I asked why so late, he said he'd be in Santa Monica doing a television interview from 7 till 7:30.

I went armed, of course. Ballenger might be more dangerous than he seemed, and according to Misti he had a bodyguard who probably served as all-purpose muscle. But a public place like a restaurant was a poor choice for a hit.

It was a miserable evening, with soggy air rolling in off the ocean. As I drove down Santa Monica Boulevard, it began to drizzle, and by the time I reached Marina del Rey, it was thick, if fine, blowing in off the Pacific. Late in the year for it, but in L.A. you take your rain when you get it. Through the murk, the argon sign marking Leon's glowed fuzzy blue, and as I ran from my car to the restaurant, I thought what this was going to do to the press in my suit.

Leon's had a nautical motif, the aisle ropes rough manila instead of velvet. Pictures of yachts and racing sloops were scattered over the varnished walls. There were only two couples in the room; given the weather, I wasn't surprised. The host who met me wore a jacket you might find on the steward of a third-rate cruise ship. His name tag said Adolphe.

"Good evening M'sieur," he said, "smoking or non-smoking?"

I hadn't heard enough Frenchmen to know if his accent was genuine. "I'm supposed to meet Reverend Buddy Ballenger," I told him. "He said he'd have reservations."

"Ah! M'sieur Ballenger! Of course. If you will follow me, please . . ." He turned away, and I tagged along down a short hall, where he showed me into a room maybe 15 by 20 feet in size, with a table that might seat six, set now for two. The floor was wide gray planks that looked like sand-smoothed driftwood, but the throw rug looked like a rice-straw mat from a dojo. On the walls were large pictures of nudes, eighteenth-century style, but showing more. The nudes were being carried off by large grinning satyrs, or over the shoulders of soldiers. One was disporting with a stallion. Along two walls were backless couches upholstered in velvet, too wide for comfortable sitting. I had no trouble at all understanding why the good reverend liked this place.

Adolphe gestured at a chair. "If you'd care to be seated, I expect Reverend Ballenger shortly. He phoned to say he would be a few minutes late." Then he left me with the menu.

This wasn't the situation I'd expected, so I rechecked my shoulder holster; its clip released easily as I drew. There was a side door that opened onto a dressing room with rods, hangers, and hooks. Connected with it were a shower room at one end and a toilet at the other. The shower room had wooden benches and four showerheads. Interesting restaurant.

I went back to the table and sat down. My chair was close to a window overlooking the marina, and through the thick drizzle, sloops and cabin cruisers were vaguely visible at their moorings. I wondered if anyone would be boating on a night like that. The menu was limited, featuring seafood and Mexican. Nothing was French but Adolphe, and I wasn't sure about him.

Ballenger arrived ten minutes later, led by Adolphe, who announced he'd be our waiter. Ballenger's suit was dry and neatly pressed, even the trouser legs, which raised my antennae right away. He asked if I'd eaten, and when I said it had been a few hours, he recommended the taco salad and tawny port. I took his advice.

Adolphe said it would be about five minutes, and missed by only two. Meanwhile Ballenger was in no hurry to talk business. Instead he told me how much he loved boating and the sea. I avoided asking if that included the Sea Islands. I could bring that up later, after we'd eaten.

Then Adolphe returned, put our salads and wine glasses in front of us, poured, and left again. The taco salad may or may not have been good, but the salsa was almost hot enough to numb your mouth, which may have been deliberate. After one bite, I turned to the wine, and hadn't much more than wet my upper lip when I realized two things, and put the glass down. First, my drink was doped. Adolphe had filled both glasses from the same bottle, so he must have put some powder in mine ahead of time. And that being true, Ballenger would have muscle standing by, probably with heat in a shoulder holster. Fortunately I'd barely tasted the wine.

"Watch out," I said. "That salsa is pure jalapeño." Then I picked up the glass again, pretended to drink, took

another bite of the salad and sat blankly for a moment.
"I believe," I said slowly, "that I had better go to the men's
room. I don't feel good."

"You don't look good," Ballenger said. "Let me get
someone to help you." He looked toward the door. "Billy!"
he called.

Billy. The name Misti had mentioned. The door opened.
"Yessir, reverend?"

"Help my guest to the men's room, will you Billy? He's
feelin' a little unsteady."

"Sure thing, reverend."

Billy was as big as Ballenger, and looked a lot more solid.
Unsteady as I felt, he could no doubt take me. "Here,"
he said. "Y'all look green around the gills."

I felt weak, but for someone who'd behaved like a patsy,
my wits seemed okay. I wondered if Good Old Billy was
really southern, or faking it. I'd heard that "y'all" was only
used for two or more people. He got a shoulder under my
left arm, with his right arm around me; I could have
walked, wobbled at least, but as he lifted, I let myself go
limp. "Thank you, Billy," I said, deliberately slurring.

"Reverend," he said, "this is a heavy dude. I'm gonna
need a hand with him."

"Set him back down on the chair then. Mr. Smith, just
rest your head on the table and we'll help you in a minute."

I did, cradling my head on an arm. After a few seconds
I opened one eye a slit. Ballenger was bent over, his head
lower than the tabletop, with Billy half crouched beside
him, his back to me. I switched wine glasses while Ballenger
pulled the throw rug back, and Billy raised a trapdoor in
the floor. The room was built over the water; with the
trapdoor open, I could hear small waves chuckling on
pilings. It didn't sound good at all.

Then they were back at the table. I lolled loosely while
they got me to the trapdoor and laid me beside it. One
of them fished out my wallet, and the Walther from my
shoulder holster. Billy went partway down the ladder,
grabbed my feet, and got me started after him, Ballenger
working from above, till they had me laid out on a little

dock, I guess you could call it—two planks side by side,
about the width of a wide bench. A rowboat was tied to it.

From there they dumped me into the boat, fortunately
in the bow. "Not now, Billy!" Ballenger said. "You know
I can't stand violence! Take him out to the *Simon Peter*
and do it on the fishin' deck; it gets blood on it all the
time anyway. But please, no more blood than need be. Just
hit him on the head." He paused. "You gonna need help
gettin' him loaded?"

"No sir, reverend. It's only 'bout four feet. He's a heavy
son of a bitch, but I got this length of rope . . ." He paused
as if doing something—maybe bending and holding a rope
up. "Everything's took care of. I'll tie it under his arms and
just hoist him in."

"You get that anchor like I told you?"

"Yessir. No need to fret. Like I said, I took care of
everything." Billy was starting to sound impatient.

The reverend sighed heavily. "I don't know why this had
to come up," he complained, as if to the Lord. Nothing
more was said then. After maybe ten seconds, I heard the
trapdoor thump quietly shut; Ballenger had taken his sensi-
tivities back into Leon's. I hoped the first thing he did was
take a big drink. Through slitted eyes I saw Billy crouch
and push off from the dock, then sit down with his back
to me, seat the oars, and start to row. I took a deep quiet
breath, exhaled, repeated it two or three times and took
stock of how I felt. Mentally I seemed okay, but physically
I felt out of sync.

There was a gaff beside me in the bottom, that I suspect was used as a small boathook. Along with the fact that
Billy thought I was helpless, it gave me a promising chance,
but I didn't have much time. When we got to the *Simon
Peter*, good old Billy would come up front with me to tie
the painter to a cleat; I needed to act while his back was
to me, meanwhile avoiding any movement he might feel.
Hopefully he wouldn't look back over his shoulder at the
wrong time, correcting course. Very carefully I turned on
my side, carefully drew up my legs, and carefully got the
little Beretta out of the holster by my left calf, all while

keeping my eyes on Billy. Holding the Beretta in my left hand, I carefully sat up and gripped the gaff with my right. He hadn't felt the movements at all.

Gathering myself, I got to my knees, and that movement he did feel. As he turned, I hit him *hard* with the gaff handle. He didn't make a sound, just fell backward. I pulled on him till his legs were off the rowing seat, then crawled over him and took his place. Hard as I'd hit him, I'd still rather have dragged him into the stern, where he'd be easier to watch. I wasn't up to it though, so I sat facing the bow and push-rowed. It was slow and awkward, but it kept Billy in front of me.

It occurred to me that Ballenger might not have drunk any more wine, might even be watching us through the window. Given all the city lights, the night was as dark as it gets in L.A., and thick with drizzle, but even so . . . With a gun, maybe my gun, could Adolphe serve as muscle? Instead of rowing back to Leon's, I tied to a wharf farther along the street. After rapping Billy again with the gaff handle, I frisked him and found my Walther, my wallet, and a Colt .32 he'd carried. The Colt and the gaff I threw in the marina. By then I was pretty bedraggled. Good Old Billy, though, would be soggy to the bone when he woke up. I hoped he got pneumonia.

Meanwhile the rowing had done me good; I was still a little unsteady, but had no real problem climbing onto the low wharf and up some steps to the sidewalk. It was abandoned, just me and the drizzle, but I had the Walther in my fist as I walked to the parking lot. My unmarked company car was still there. Powering up, I turned the heater on high to dry me out, and drove back to headquarters. I keyed open the garage beneath the building, and parked in the properly numbered space. Prudential had the security contract, and Ramon, the garage guard, had come over as I parked. "Bad night," he said, eyeing me as I climbed out. "Worse where you were, looks like. You need help?"

"Not now," I said, "but a while ago . . . Would you believe I got drugged and tossed in the bottom of a boat?"

His eyes were round. "Jesus!" he said. "Will I read about it in tomorrow's *Times*?"

"I hope not. I hope I didn't hit him that hard."

I really just wanted to get in my own car, which was parked outside in the rain, and drive home. But I made myself go to the elevator, key it, and go upstairs. There I summarized the evening into the computer, printed out a copy, and left it on Carlos' desk, along with my planned activities for the next day. I also checked something I should have checked sooner, and through the Data Center, learned that Leon's was owned by Robert Lee Ballenger. Buddy.

Then I went home. Tuuli was still up, and over a hot brandy I told her how my evening had gone. She knows how to comfort me after a tough day.

12

The next morning I slept late, then drove to the North Hollywood Shuttle Station and grabbed a flight to Santa Barbara. Frank Grady, from our office there, was waiting with the equipment I'd asked for. From there we drove to Montecito and out the Rhubarb Charley Road. Rhubarb Charley wouldn't recognize the area. His slab and tarpaper wickiup was torn down after he died in 1937, and the Rhubarb Canyon development is "vee double-X"—very expensive and very exclusive. And very secure, with a twelve-foot perimeter fence of expensive HardSteel mesh, electrified at the top. Except near the road, where it's reinforced concrete with stone facings. And like a lot of V-XX developments, it has a slim, HardSteel mast, with instruments that monitor floater and scooter overflights, recording the continuous identification signals, or the lack thereof.

Prudential had the security contract there, too, but the odds were that Scheele didn't know it. I didn't picture him interested in community affairs, and the Rhubarb Canyon Corporation required that our vehicles, equipment, and badges there all be marked "Rhubarb Canyon Security," not "Prudential." The car we were in had no markings at all, but the gate guards recognized Frank and waved us through.

Scheele's place had its own HardSteel fence—not that uncommon in the development. Signs and my instruments warned that the fence was electrified, and protected by alarm beams. Seen from the road, the large house was handsome, the external walls of sandstone slabs. Probably, I thought, overlying reinforced concrete.

What I'd hoped to find was radiation of unusual frequencies or intensities—something I could describe to engineers and physicists—and there wasn't a sign of anything like that. I said "hoped to find." I hadn't actually *expected* to, so I was surprised at how disappointed I felt. But I don't discourage as easily as I used to. I'd learned and relearned that a case can break when you wouldn't think there's a chance in the world.

With the fast and frequent shuttle flights, I was back at the North Hollywood Station before 1300 hours, and half an hour later, parked my car outside the office. I updated Carlos, and the only thing he could suggest was to keep groping till something broke. We could always cancel of course—tell Haugen it was hopeless. But it wasn't yet, and it wasn't what Haugen wanted to hear. It wasn't good PR, either. Giving up on cases buys bad word of mouth, and might get to be a habit.

My muse took over then, freewheeling. I could, I said, leak some hints into the Web, things that Scheele would pick up as worrisome but no one else would notice. The trick would be to make them convincing, which could be hard to do, knowing no more than I did. Or I might float Harford's name; I'd have to check with him. Or phone Scheele, tell him what had happened to Ballenger and good old Billy the night before, hinting they'd talked about him when they thought I was unconscious.

Carlos took it all in, then leaned back. "Martti," he said—speaking Spanish, something we often do for the practice, "I want you to be careful. Whatever he did to Harford and the women, he did without anyone knowing. Maybe he can do it to you, too."

Now there was a thought. "Maybe if he did," I answered, "I'd get a clue on how he did it."

"None of the others did."

"None of the others were looking for one, or had any idea what had happened to them. And maybe I can start wearing a transponder. How's that for an idea?"

It seemed to me that was the solution right there. With a transponder, all I needed was to get Scheele to do to me whatever it was he did to the others. I went down the hall and asked Skip if he could fit me with one. He said sure, but he and Sakata were both on a rush project for Torres. I told him the next morning would be fine.

I took compensatory time the rest of the afternoon, and went to Wu's for my first Choi Li Fut workout in more than a week. I don't go often enough to maintain the flexibility I should, but enough to keep me dangerous. Harve—that's Harvey Wu—had long since quit bawling me out about it, says I'm not a fighter at heart. He said maybe I should switch to Aikido, but I didn't feel like learning a new style from scratch.

Meanwhile, doing the forms relaxes me, a different relaxation than the deep tiredness I get from a Nautilus workout.

After an hour and a half, I went home and took a nap on the recliner, waking up when Tuuli came in. Talking Finnish for the practice, I told her about my discussion with Carlos, and that he was afraid Scheele would zap me like he'd done the others. She wasn't as worried as Carlos had been, but she pointed out that the memories might be ugly.

Then she said something else. "You know, it doesn't have to be two separate time lines. He may just duplicate people—make two of them. Like—what do they call them in plants?"

"Clones?"

"That's it. Maybe he makes clones. And when one of them dies, its soul snaps back into the other. That could explain the headache."

I opened my mouth to object, to ask how in the world anyone could do that without the original knowing. But the words died in my throat, because cloning sounded less extreme than splitting time lines in a way that memories could transfer back. Cloned! That had to be it. Or *could* be it. Maybe. Something had happened.

After we went to bed, I lay there thinking. Suppose Scheele did clone me in some undetectable way. It seemed to me I could handle it. And with a transponder, we'd have him by the short and curlies.

13

He'd been held up in traffic. An accident on Cahuenga Pass had blocked a lane on the southbound 101 Freeway, and he'd missed his first chance. Now, though, he stood behind his tripod, peering into the back of what looked like an ancient videocam, large and cumbersome. Briefly he'd pretended to shoot footage up and down Beverly Boulevard, occasionally panning on passersby, most of whom paid little or no attention. But he hadn't actually shot any of them, just pretended to.

What he was really interested in was across the street in Morey's Kosher Deli. Ferguson had gone over to check, and from the door had given him the high sign: Seppanen was inside eating breakfast.

One of the important parts of this work was to research your subject, learn his or her schedule, to the extent they had one. Another was to have a reliable assistant.

At last Ferguson came out, which meant that Seppanen had headed for the cash register. Scheele was so excited, he could taste it. The duplicator was ready, aimed and focused on the open door. With his right hand on the trigger and his left on the locking control, he stood in the mental posture of a leopard waiting to pounce.

Through the finder he could see someone moving toward the door. Seppanen stepped into the focus field, and in a single quick movement Scheele locked on him, framing him, clearing the field of everything else, then pressed the trigger switch. His target turned ninety degrees and started east down the sidewalk, the locked field holding on him. Scheele pressed the trigger twice more. I've got him! He rejoiced inwardly. I've got the sonofabitch! Three of him! It was all he could do not to dance on the sidewalk.

14

The rest of the story can be confusing, so I'll tell it from one viewpoint at a time, starting with one that woke up strapped to a gurney, in a small concrete cell with no window. I was naked, which meant I'd been stripped, because I knew from Harford's experience that clothes get cloned along with the wearer. Apparently they'd stripped me for the psychological effect: without clothes you feel more powerless, vulnerable.

Being strapped to a gurney does that pretty well by itself, in threatening situations.

I felt lousy: headache, queazy stomach, and an overall, unpleasant squirmy feeling. It seemed to me if someone let me loose, I wouldn't be able to stand up without help. Something held my head down, medical or duct tape I supposed; about all I could move was my eyes, and all I could see besides walls and ceiling was a small glass ball in a ceiling recess, that had to be part of a surveillance system.

I knew right away what had happened, and told myself I should have arranged for a transponder a day earlier. My jailers would have found it when they stripped me, but by then the company computer would have a fix on where I was.

The last thing I remembered before waking up was walking out of Morey's. What had happened must have happened on the sidewalk in front. No one had bumped me or spoken to me, but . . . There'd been a guy across the street with some kind of apparatus on a tripod, like a big old camera, aimed at Morey's. That had to be it.

But then how . . . The answer was unavoidable: I'd been transmitted! Like a radio beam! *Jesus,* I thought, *what am I? Some kind of holo?* That made no sense. A holo couldn't be raped, and a holo wouldn't have memories or feelings; it was nothing more than light.

But clone or holo, they'd duplicated me and transmitted the copy! Even though I didn't feel like a duplicate, that was more believable than splitting time, then looping memories from one time line to the other.

After spending maybe a minute on the question, I turned to something more meaningful: escape. I couldn't plan; didn't know enough about the situation. Presumably the original version of me wasn't out of action, and Scheele would know that. He'd cloned me to question me, find out what we knew and what we planned.

Or maybe to get even. I preferred not to look at that one, but there it was. Torture me in the worst way possible, then kill me-the-clone and visit those lovely memories on me-the-original. Ole could handle the situation, of course, or Vic or Tory or Bhiksu. Strip the pain and fear off, and the emotions, leaving just the unburdened memory. But even so, I'd be in for some God-awful hours or days, first here, then later.

I heard a door open, and a moment later a guy in a lab coat was looking down at me. He pressed a hypodermic against my chest and pulled the trigger. There was a hiss, a brief pause, then nothing.

Meanwhile the original me had gone from Morey's to the office without a notion that anything had happened. I checked the *L.A. Times* for anything about Ballenger, or anyone found unconscious in a rowboat in Marina del Rey. Nothing. Next I checked to see if Ballenger had phoned Scheele the last two days. He hadn't. So using my weasel, I checked for computer traffic between the two, and again came up with nothing. He'd probably used a pay phone.

There wasn't much I could do but wait, so I went to Carlos, who put me on the Pak Kyung So extortion case, helping Ernie Johnson. Routine digging that required patience and know-how, but no deep immersion—well suited to on-and-off work.

I hadn't left his office yet when the phone rang and Carlos picked it up. It was Tuuli. He poked the speakerphone switch so I could hear. She was telling him something was wrong with me, that I was in trouble.

"He looks okay to me," Carlos answered. "He's sitting about six feet away, looking fine."

"Then he's been cloned," she answered. "Somewhere there's another one of him, maybe more than one, on a table or—one of those wheeled tables. He's alive, but he can't move."

Carlos's lips puckered into an O, and his eyebrows raised halfway up his forehead. "Cloned," he said thoughtfully. It occurred to me I hadn't mentioned Tuuli's idea that Scheele cloned people instead of splitting time lines. "Do you know where he is?"

"I can guess," she told him.

So could I. So could Carlos. Was there really another me, or maybe more, at Scheele's place?

The upshot was that Carlos told her we'd get right on it, and buzzed Joe. Joe in turn got on the horn and called the Santa Barbara Sheriff's Department, asking them to get and serve a search warrant for the property of Charles Scheele, in the Rhubarb Canyon development. The object of the search was detective Martti Seppanen, who'd disappeared while investigating Scheele in connection with a claim by actress Misti Innocenza. She claimed she'd been kidnaped, and Scheele was suspected. There was also evidence that Scheele might be involved in a possible kidnaping and abuse of Elena Marquez—Mrs. Bo Haugen—and of William Harford, and the denial of their civil liberties. We were carrying out the Harford investigation on a contract with the U.S. Department of Justice.

Sheriff Nyberg wanted to know more about the evidence; the judge would ask. Rather than tell him he'd gotten the information from a psychic, Joe took refuge in the confidential status of the Harford case. He didn't mention that I was sitting across the room from him just then, either.

The whole damned situation felt like something from Alice's rabbit hole. It was Joe who said that, after he'd hung up.

Nyberg pulled it off; he got the search warrant. Judge Santos had always been sympathetic toward the problems of law enforcement. And Prudential's reputation must have helped, and mine; he mentioned my work on the Ashkenazi murder case. Anyway, less than two hours after Tuuli's call, two sheriff's department floaters lifted from their pads, loaded with officers that included a SWAT team. And Carlos, who'd caught a shuttle for Santa Barbara at the Larchmont Station.

Needless to say, I stayed in L.A. But from another point of view—a clonal point of view—I know what happened, beginning with the next time I woke up. I was still on the gurney, had been drifting in and out of dreams I don't remember, until finally I was fully awake. I wondered if I was wired, maybe to an EEG, because a couple of minutes later the same guy came in. Taking out a pair of heavy scissors, he cut the tape that held my head down. "Congratulations," he said, "you won the wake-up lottery. Time to go for your interview."

While he wheeled me down a corridor, I asked myself what I'd do if they took me off the gurney. They wouldn't, but if they did . . . I got a brief image of kicking the seeds out of everyone there, starting with Scheele, and if they shot me, what the hell? I'd be back at Prudential or wherever the real me was. But I knew they wouldn't let me loose.

The room I got wheeled into was an office. Two guys were there waiting. One was Scheele; I recognized him from his college yearbook. His hairline had receded a bit, and he wore a ponytail now—they were back in style— but he was Charles Scheele. And grinning like someone pleased at how clever he was. The other was the muscle. He didn't look like anyone I'd care to mess with, even if I was at my best. Good Old Billy wasn't in the same league.

"Mr. Seppanen!" Scheele said. "Welcome! I've looked you up. You're quite the Sherlock Holmes."

"And you're quite the Arne Haugen," I told him.

He laughed. "I'm having more fun than Arne Haugen had."

"Not with me, I hope."

He laughed again. "Preferably not. I do want information from you though."

"I suppose we clones are sort of disposable, eh? Question us, then kill us. Ash the remains and fertilize the garden with them."

"My my, Mr. Seppanen. May I call you Martti? You have a creative imagination. No, there are no bodies to dispose of. Not clonal bodies at any rate. If you were to die, you'd simultaneously dematerialize. As a matter of fact, you'd dematerialize after a bit anyway, though with someone of your mass, it might take six or seven weeks."

"What am I then? Some kind of holo?"

Still grinning, he shook his head. "No, you're quite material."

"But—then how would I dematerialize?"

"I haven't worked out the details yet; it's not that important. Basically though, it's part of the process. Have you heard of Linyetski's work on teleportation?"

"C.K.F. Linyetski at the University of Birmingham? The guy who teleported a block of iron, sort of?"

Scheele looked surprised, and mentally I thanked Vic Merlin for bringing it up. Actually I had remembered, from when it made the news, but I hadn't remembered the name. And I wanted to interest Scheele, keep him talking. What I learned, I'd take home with me.

"Correct," he said, "and I'd been working on the same principle. As others had: Schöndienst's work on matrix theory had made it seem distinctly possible. But the actuation?" He laughed again. "Theory is the first challenge, actuation the second. Teleportation seems to result in problems of stability. With Linyetski's work—which still has practical applications, you know—the instability is immediate. With my work it is delayed, the lag period being a function of mass. A second and happier discovery is that the original is not displaced. As I believe you know. Instead, a duplicate is created at the reception point. I must confess that both developments were entirely unexpected, the serendipitous results of incomplete theory. I'd intended only a simple teleport.

"And when dematerialization occurs, whether by, ah, termination or due to time, the duplicate—you for example—is not reduced to its constituent atoms and molecules, as with Linyetski's block of iron. You simply—disappear! And I have no idea what becomes of you. There aren't even gases given off; I've checked. What I would never have expected is what I have named 'the snapback effect,' with the clonal consciousness returning to the original. I learned of it only after, ah, delivering a number of clones to customers. Had I been aware of it sooner, I'd have done things a bit differently."

He peered curiously at me. "A penny for your thoughts, Mr. Seppanen."

"That's more than they're worth," I said. Actually I was wondering why he'd tell me all this. He must know I'd take it with me. But it wasn't something I wanted to point out.

"Perhaps you're wondering why I'm telling you all this," he said, then laughed at my expression. "Ha! Caught you, didn't I? But believe me, you won't tell anyone, because your original will die while driving home this evening!"

My guts shriveled.

"Yes, Mr. Clonal Seppanen, your original will die on his way home, with a little help from—your humble servant. Among other things, I've made myself quite the expert in explosives." He made a sweeping bow. "And your memories will have no one to home on. They will cease to exist, just as your clonal body will. But if you are sufficiently cooperative, your remaining weeks can be more than pleasant.

Would you like to spend some time with an attractive starlet clone? Or a porn queen like Miss Innocenza?" He laughed again. "The alternative is much less pleasant, I assure you. All you need do is answer my questions, all of them, accurately and completely. In an aura chamber and instrumented of course, so we can monitor your veracity.

"And do not imagine that silence is an option. If you'd like, I'll show you some of the implements Mr. Carver has at his disposal to ensure that." He gestured at the muscle.

Mr. Carver. I didn't like the name.

"Mr. Ferguson will perform the interrogation, and Mr. Carver will provide any necessary, ah, incentives. I prefer to be elsewhere."

Like Ballenger, I thought. "Why not just drug me?"

"Even the best truth drugs impair accuracy. Torture, or hopefully just the threat of torture, are preferable."

"What do you do if I die under torture?"

"That won't happen unless you have a cardiac condition. But if it should—" He smiled and pinched my cheek. "I have two more of you. Backups in storage, so to speak."

"You don't miss a bet, do you. And if I answer your questions, what happens to the other clones? Do you cut their throats?"

He chuckled. I wondered if he'd been watching mad scientist films from the 1920s. "Mr. Seppanen, we are not gauche here," he said, and turned. "Mr. Ferguson, do you have the, ah, quietus at hand?"

Ferguson put a hand in a lab coat pocket and came out with another hypodermic, a ring of orange tape on its cylinder.

"Put it on my desk, please," Scheele said, then turned back to me. "It is a quick poison. Struggles are unseemly. Now. I suppose you're willing to cooperate?"

"I guess I'd better. I don't care much for the alternative. But before you import any porn queens for me, how did you get a bomb in my car? I drove it to work this morning."

"Ah. I had a certain talented person kidnaped, replaced him with a clone, made other clones of him, each thinking

it's the original, and gave them jobs to do. I then disposed of the original. And I did not, I hasten to add,
use his ashes to fertilize the garden.

"But enough of that. We'll have time for your questions
when I've gotten mine answered." He looked at Ferguson.
"Mr. Ferguson, please inject Mr. Seppanen with the gamma-
Alprazolam." He smiled at me. "It allows us to remove your
restraints. The gurney doesn't fit in our aura chamber."

Ferguson took out another hypo, this one with blue tape,
and injected me. I didn't feel much effect. "It will take a
few seconds," Scheele added pleasantly. "Then you'll be able
to get off the gurney and walk unassisted. You'll simply be
weak and ill coordinated."

Ferguson released the strap across my knees, next the
one across my belly, then the separate straps that held my
arms. "Go ahead, Mr. Seppanen," Scheele said. "Sit up."

I did, slowly, testing my body. It didn't get a very high
grade. Abruptly we were interrupted by an English-accented
female voice from a speaker: "Mr. Scheele! There is a large
van on the front lawn, and armed officers are coming onto
the porch!"

Scheele's humor, poise, and jaw dropped like a rock, and
for a moment he simply stared. Over the intercom I could
hear door chimes, and pounding. Inside, someone with a
Hispanic accent was talking excitedly.

"Jorge says there are more in back!"

Scheele snapped out of it, and turned to Ferguson. "Get
rid of the others," he snapped. "They don't know anything."

"Yessir!" Ferguson answered, then turned and dashed
out. Forgetting the hypo he'd put on the desk, as if he
thought it was still in his pocket.

"What do you want to do with this one?" asked Carver.

I heard a muffled explosion over the intercom, as if
someone had blown the lock in the front door, probably
a heavy security door. That was followed by a scream, and
someone shouted an order to spread through the house and
search. Scheele stood with his face screwed in a tight frown,
pressured by haste, searching for a solution. Neither man
was paying any attention to me. I was about ten feet from

the orange-taped hypodermic, as close as Carver and closer than Scheele, but wobbly.

Deliberately I staggered and fell, in the direction of the desk. Carver scowled at me, then turned back to Scheele, whose mind seemed still frozen. Taking hold of the desk, I pulled myself back to my feet. "The vent!" Scheele said suddenly. "We'll knock him out and stuff him in the vent!" Still leaning on the desk, I moved a step nearer the hypodermic, and heard voices, sounding as if they were coming downstairs to the cellar.

"The vent?!" Carver half shouted it. His pistol turned toward me, boomed, and a blow in the chest knocked me against the desk. For a moment I blacked out, the black rose-tinted, and I realized I was on the floor. Someone screamed, Scheele I think. "There's no goddamn time for the vent!" Carver continued, yelling now, and fired again. The second shot hit me in the face, with less pain than I'd have thought, followed by spreading numbness. "I'd need a ladder, for chrissake, and a screwdriver to take the damned grille off."

Martti, I thought, *get ready. Here I come.* There was a shout in the corridor—"This way! This way!"—and thudding feet. Carver's pistol boomed again. . . .

15

The others had told about being hit by a crushing head-ache. Mine was different, short and sharp, leaving little more than its shadow. For a moment the memories con-fused me, but they weren't horrifying, and the confusion eased as they sorted themselves out. After half a minute I got on the intercom with Frank Brunette, our bomb expert, and we went outside to the public lot, where my car was parked. I felt—*weird* is the word—but it wasn't really troublesome, beyond interfering with my mental focus. After a five-minute preliminary check for booby traps, it took Frank maybe half a minute to find the bomb, a kind that doesn't require wiring to the electri-cal system. It had batteries, and a timer that actuated when someone sat in the driver's seat. The bomber must have had a master key for that year's model Mercury Solano, and access to the parking lot wasn't restricted. We went back in then, and Frank called the LAPD for a bomb squad. He could have disarmed it, but the law restricted bomb disposal to authorized government agencies, and anyway, no one in their right mind is eager to mess with something like that.

❖ ❖ ❖

Most of the rest I only know secondhand, but I'll review it. Carlos is retired now, but he's here from Hawaii for his debrief tomorrow. Joe, who's retired from day-to-day management, will debrief this evening. All of us were debriefed back in '13 by the feebs, but they didn't pass out copies. Too confidential.

Nyberg arrested all of Scheele's employees, including the household staff. My other two clones were taken into custody as evidence and material witnesses. The next day the feebs took them all from the county jail, apparently never to receive a public trial. The U.S. District Court had issued a confidential injunction to all of us peons at Prudential and the sheriff's department against anyone saying anything to anybody.

Meanwhile our security people at the Rhubarb Canyon Development had told us that immediately after the raid, a squad of feebs moved in by floater to guard the place, and that night a military floater had landed at the delivery dock behind the house, presumably to haul stuff away.

A week later, the company got an official statement from the Department of Justice, saying that the parties involved with the William Harford and Elena Marquez cases had been apprehended, as if we didn't know, and thanking Prudential for its "highly professional" services. It added that the case had national security implications, and no further information would be forthcoming. An accompanying document repeated the admonition not to mention this to anyone, under penalty of the Official Secrets Act, as amended 07/19/2006, except that we were authorized to show the statement to Haugen and Marquez as a basis for billing.

A few days afterward, the Justice Department, usually stingy and slow in dealing with private investigation firms, surprised Joe with a transfer of funds that qualified as generous—payment for information leading to solution of the Harford case.

My clones were never mentioned, but they were questioned exhaustively, without knowing each other existed.

And held, still separately, till on the forty-fifth day they jumped me only minutes apart. I'd been expecting them.

Meanwhile I seined the open Web for a few months until nothing more seemed likely to show up, watching for anything about certain people and certain places. Carefully of course, so it wouldn't draw attention. It brought me some interesting information. Any items that hadn't made the major media, I hand-carried to Joe and Carlos, but none of us said anything about any of it, even to each other. I didn't even say anything to Tuuli. Now, though, with recent developments, the records have been opened, some of them anyway, adding to what we already knew.

A week after his transfer to the federal high security prison near Bitter Springs, Nevada, Charles Scheele suicided. So the records say; I doubt it to beat hell. Two days later, his attorney, along with four other passengers, died aboard a transatlantic airliner, of salmonella poisoning, supposedly from eating tainted whitefish. Ferguson, Scheele's lab assistant, was reported killed that same week in a prison fight, a matter of homosexual jealousy. Carver, Scheele's muscleman, was "shot to death while assaulting a guard with a knife." Could be.

The day after Scheele's arrest, Buddy Ballenger was confidentially pulled in, questioned, and released, a no doubt very sobered reverend. Two days later he died in a traffic accident, along with an employee, William Bradley. The "accident" made the papers.

Within six weeks, Ibadhan's Minister of Finance died when his home was bombed; Shiite terrorists were blamed. That one came from UPA wire services. Three weeks after that, a massive explosion destroyed a weapons research installation in northern India, virtually wiping out its staff, and getting a lot of media attention. I could guess how it got detonated.

It took a year before I stopped worrying about something happening to me, and even then I wasn't totally sure. The government didn't want even a whiff of a hint that anything like a cloner existed, and I didn't blame them.

Then, last August, a news item hit the Web, papers, newsfaxes, and TV news channels: A physics professor at the University of Bologna, in Italy, had undertaken the maiden test on his newly invented teleport. He'd put a stone on the sending plate and closed the switch—and the stone still sat there, so he assumed it hadn't worked. Then his assistant in the other room shouted, "It works! It works!" The prof went in to see what the guy was shouting about— and there was a duplicate of the stone on the receiving plate. So he tried it with his watch, and got two watches, both showing precisely the same time.

He'd hurried to the Biology Department, borrowed a white mouse, and duplicated it too. Less than an hour later, while showing the two mice to his department chairman, one of them disappeared before their eyes. Then he'd checked his desk drawer, and the duplicate watch was gone.

By suppertime, the entire physics department, a bunch of other professors and grad students, a TV camera crew, and all of Italy had been treated to demonstrations. The cat was very thoroughly out of the bag, and by now, of course, the whole world knows about it. Which, along with the latest reform of federal security agencies, is why we got clearance to debrief ourselves on this, though the debrief is confidential.

Myself, I wish none of it had happened. The country— the world!—is having a hard time adjusting to the continuous major changes that shake their whole reality. Joe says we'll adjust, that most of us already are, and in the process we'll become a wiser species. I hope to hell he's right.

When it comes to the best
in science fiction and fantasy,
Baen Books has something for *everyone!*

IF YOU LIKE . . .
YOU SHOULD ALSO TRY . . .

Marion Zimmer Bradley .... Mercedes Lackey,
Holly Lisle

Anne McCaffrey .... Elizabeth Moon,
Mercedes Lackey

Mercedes Lackey .... Holly Lisle, Josepha Sherman,
Ellen Guon, Mark Shepherd

Andre Norton .... Mary Brown,
James H. Schmitz

David Drake .... David Weber, John Ringo,
Eric Flint

Larry Niven .... James P. Hogan,
Charles Sheffield

Robert A. Heinlein .... Jerry Pournelle,
Lois McMaster Bujold

Heinlein's "Juveniles" .... Eric Flint & Dave Freer,
Rats, Bats & Vats

Horatio Hornblower .... David Weber's
"Honor Harrington" series,
David Drake, "RCN" series

The Lord of the Rings .... Elizabeth Moon,
The Deed of Paksenarrion